I've travelled the world twice over,
Met the famous: saints and sinners,
Poets and artists, kings and queens,
Old stars and hopeful beginners,
I've been where no-one's been before,
Learned secrets from writers and cooks
All with one library ticket
To the wonderful world of books.

© JANICE JAMES.

RETURN OF CLAUDIA

In this the eighth and final book in the Claudia series, the author brings her memorable saga of a happy marriage to an end. Claudia and David are about to take a three month holiday in Europe. Their adventures crossing the Atlantic with fellow passengers make this humorous reading. After an extended visit to London meeting old and new friends, they visit France and the casinos. Then it is home once more to the United States, and the prospects of moving into a new house.

Books by Rose Franken in the
Ulverscroft Large Print Series:

ROSE FRANKEN

RETURN OF CLAUDIA

Complete and Unabridged

ULVERSCROFT
Leicester

First published in the United Kingdom in 1956 by
W. H. Allen.

First Large Print Edition
published August 1983

British Library CIP Data

Franken, Rose
    Return of Claudia.—Large print ed.
    (Ulverscroft large print series: romance)
    I. Title
    813'.52[F]   PS3511.R264

    ISBN 0-7089-1001-7

Published by
F. A. Thorpe (Publishing) Ltd.
Anstey, Leicestershire
Printed and Bound in Great Britain by
T. J. Press (Padstow) Ltd., Padstow, Cornwall

Love is
a time of enchantment:
in it all days are fair and all fields
green. Youth is blest by it,
old age made benign: the eyes of love see
roses blooming in December,
and sunshine through rain. Verily
is the time of true-love
a time of enchantment—and
Oh! how eager is woman
to be bewitched!

1

DAVID said that Matthew gave him a pain in the neck, only he didn't say neck. Claudia said how could he be so crude especially about his own child, but there was no denying that Matthew certainly possessed the art of irritating people. This morning, she had had to perform her usual function of peacemaker from the moment he burst into their room without knocking, and as speedily departed. "It's just that he's excited about going to Europe," she'd restrained David from dashing out of bed after him. "He'll calm down as soon as we're on the boat."

The boat, however, didn't meet with Matthew's approval. Possibly he expected sails. "This doesn't look like a boat," he kept accusing his mother in bitter disillusion.

Claudia was past answering him. She had a thousand and one things on her mind. David had told her to stand in the main lounge by the luggage while he straightened out some mix-up about the staterooms, and Bertha was

1

trying to keep the baby from squirming down from her arms, and there was no sign of Candy and John who'd said they wouldn't miss seeing them off for anything. "Keep an eye out for Candy and John." David had added to his instructions. "And whatever you do, don't take your eyes off my briefcase, it's full of all the red tape we'll be needing."

He didn't seem to realize that she had only two eyes, both aimed in the same direction, fortunately. "Let Michael walk, he's too heavy for you to carry," she threw out to Bertha from the back of her head.

"Better I don't with so many people rushing around, he will get pushed," Bertha demurred. "He is already upset, mein kleine engel."

"A little pushing won't hurt your kleine engel," Claudia told her. Michael had been almost as much of a devil all the morning as Matthew. They'd had to stay at a hotel in town overnight in order to be at the boat on time, and strange surroundings made him "ausgelassen", according to Bertha. Possibly by accident, but more likely not, he'd tipped a whole bowl of cereal over himself at breakfast, which meant unpacking a suitcase at the last minute to fish out clean clothes and a change of shoes. "Let him learn a lesson, let him go the way he is," David had ordained grandly, not caring whose nose he was cutting off to spite whose face. Travelling with bundles of children's impedimenta made you look like immigrants no matter how nice your luggage was, which theirs wasn't, and all they needed was an oatmeal-encrusted baby to complete the picture. Especially in a big suite on A deck, which they seemed to have been given by mistake.

A suite was the last thing they wanted, having taken pains to select from the ship's plans two minimum priced adjoining rooms on B deck, odd in shape, but entirely adequate for their needs. And then, when they came on board, they discovered that they'd been booked instead into some luxurious set-up on A deck with a fancy name on the door, instead of a plain number, and David had immediately gone down to the purser's desk to inform him of his error. "Insist on our original accommodation, tell them we have no intention of paying for a private drawing-room," Claudia had armed him with parting instructions. They were lucky, she felt, to have private beds for Bertha and the children, and upper and lower berths

3

for themselves, even though there was sure to be a big to-do about who should take the lower; Claudia rather liked the idea of climbing, but David being a gentleman, they'd probably both end in the upper one, which would be a tight squeeze, but an agreeable one.

"Matthew, stop pulling at me," she rasped. "Can't you see I'm busy watching. What is it?"

He stared mutinously around the marble foyer. "This ain't a boat," he insisted.

"You know perfectly well that it is," she reprimanded him coldly, "and kindly don't say 'ain't'." Out of a spare corner of one eye, she observed, with painful impartiality, that he was more than usually unattractive in his new going-away clothes. He was between sizes, so of course Bertha said to get size ten, as his old suits were size eight and fitted. In Bertha's book, it was throwing money away to buy anything for a growing boy that fitted. Like a fool Claudia had listened to her, so here he was, swimming in size ten, with his hat slipping loosely over a thrifty hair-cut, and one front tooth just growing like a blind yanked half-way down a window. Enviously, her gaze lingered on another boy standing

4

nearby; he was wearing his full quota of teeth, a miniscule cap perched on a shock of blond curls, and perky shorts above bare knees that emerged in moulded perfection from expensive English socks. Why couldn't Matthew look at least a little like that? But no. He had to insist on long trousers, so long that he appeared to be in a state of perpetual jumping, and he had to say "ain't" and drop his gs into the bargain, for which David was partly to blame, because he was such a stubborn believer in elementary schools. Not that they'd been able to afford a private school up to now, but even if they had, he would have argued that a private school wasn't a guarantee against a lot of worse habits than saying "ain't".

"I want to go on a real boat," Matthew's plaint kept up like a broken gramophone record.

She itched to administer a good sound slap to his behind, but in all fairness she hadn't expected this overwhelming opulence herself, for she hadn't been abroad since she was a child, younger even than Matthew, and all she had carried with her through the years was the sickening smell of rubber coming up at her in narrow passageways. Nor had she so much as seen the inside of an ocean liner since that time; the first World War, and then her personal war—which had taken David into the blistering hell of the South Pacific—had cut off Europe as a playground, and when the merry-go-round had finally started again, with Julia and Hartley practically commuting to Paris and London, there'd been no point in forever racing in from the farm to see them off. It always seemed more sensible for David to manage a lunch with Hartley downtown, and for Claudia to say good-bye to Julia over the telephone.

All at once, in the midst of the excitement of departure, she began to miss Julia and Hartley. One thing was certain: they'd have been down to the boat today, laden with presents. Julia had always had a special genius for presents, and in particular she'd had a sort of sixth sense about giving Claudia the very thing she didn't know she wanted until she got it—such as a dozen Georgian silver dinner plates to supplement the china set that had begun to show its age without benefit of antiquity. Or a new perambulator, with Julia anticipating that the old one had lasted from Bobby to Matthew and would be

on its last legs by the time Michael arrived. Usually, a sister-in-law was dutifully at-
entive rather than thoughtful, but Julia had
en both. Sometimes Claudia thought that it
in tacit apology for having looked down
atrician nose at David's falling in love
ce   an   unsophisticated   little   nobody,
he   y when he could have had his pick of
e a   uccessive   crops   of   debutantes.
ry,   In't been wildly enthusiastic about
the   modest taste in brides either,
been   David had been too pig-headed
sion,   on, and it would have served
m the   ad proved a dismal failure as
heart   t had been a pretty narrow
"Oh   the grace of God had she
again."   ugh these twelve years of
lization,   r. As a matter of fact,
she went   le it a couple of times,
e dreams   t except herself. Her
cling like   he staggering un-
d her lips   going down with
banish his   bad enough, but
ght. "I'm as   blocked the very
him.   nd plunged the
ars but the   and then only,
jerked away.   some hidden
time when she

would have leaned upon David in a need
beyond any need she had ever known, she
had, for once, to stand on her own feet, rather
than jeopardize the fragile building of his
returning health.

"Have you got a headache?"

Matthews's voice, troubled by her absen
from his universe, reached her from afar. S
forced a smile. "Don't be silly, I never hav
headache." His world had gone enough av
not only with his father's illness, but
inexplicable nothingness that had
Bobby. And then, to add to his conf
Julia and Hartley suddenly vanished fr
familiar pattern of his life. Claudia'
ached for the helplessness of childhoo
God, I wouldn't want to be young
There was an astonishment in the rea
because sometimes in her dreams
back to being a child, and they we
she cherished, and allowed to
cobwebs when she wakened.

In her pity, she bent and lai
against Matthew's cheek to
uncertainty and set his world ari
strong as a horse," she reassure

The assertion allayed his f
embrace embarrassed him. He

8

"I'm too old to be kissed," he scowled.

"I wasn't kissing you, don't flatter yourself."

"You were so." He rubbed at his face as if to obliterate the contaminated area. "You said we were going on a real boat," he reverted.

"Oh, shut up," she said.

His scowl faded to a sheepish smirk, as once more security enfolded him. He tugged at her hand. "Let's go," he said impatiently. "I want to see the Statue of Liberty. Why do we have to stand here so long?"

"Because."

"Because why?"

"We haven't got our right staterooms yet. See if you can see Candy and Uncle John anywhere."

"They're over there!"

"Where?"

He laughed uproariously. "I fooled you!"

"That's not at all funny. What are you chewing?"

"A rubber-band."

"Throw it away. That's all we need—to have you swallow it."

"I never swallow them," he said virtuously.

"There's always a first time. Take it out of your mouth at once."

He removed it untidily. "Is Uncle John a real uncle like Uncle Hartley?"

"Now don't begin asking idiotic questions. You know perfectly well he's not."

"Then why do I call him Uncle?"

"It's an old Spanish custom. Your father and I don't approve of the American custom of children calling grown-ups by their first names."

"I call Candy by her first name."

"That's different."

"Why?"

"Candy was hardly more than a little girl herself when you first knew her."

"Was she a little girl when she got married?"

"No, she was seventeen when Uncle John came along."

"Where did he come from?"

"You're playing with fire again," she warned him.

"What fire?" he asked, intrigued.

"Skip it. If you mean how did they meet: Uncle John was a young architect in Dad's office."

"Isn't he still in Dad's office?"

"Of course. Only he's Dad's partner now. Otherwise we wouldn't be able to take this trip if he weren't there to look after everything."

"He's building our house in the country too, isn't he?"

"Not building it. The house was built almost two hundred years ago. Uncle John's just supervising doing it over while we're away."

"Why can't we go back and live at the farm instead?"

"Ach now, Matthew, that is naughty," Bertha took over chidingly. "You know the farm was sold."

"But I liked the farm," he resisted imperiously. "Better than the house we had in the mountains, and better even than Aunt Julia's and Uncle Hartley's house in New York."

"I did too," Claudia agreed. "But those were only temporary."

"What's temporary?"

"Until we found another little place of our own. And it's going to be just as nice as the farm by the time we get finished with it."

"It hasn't got any cows."

"It will have, now that we were able to buy

11

the adjoining property and all those beautiful old barns."

"I guess we're millionaires all right, boy," he remarked with satisfaction.

She frowned her disapproval. "Where did you get such talk?"

"In school," he returned laconically. "What's a millionaire?"

"Somebody who has a lot of money, and nice people don't brag about it."

"Did we get a lot of money from Aunt Julia and Uncle Hartley?"

"I think the new little house is going to be even nicer than the farm," Bertha injected hastily.

"So do I," said Claudia. "I hate to miss all the fun of doing it over. I almost wish we weren't going away."

"You and Mr. David need a good holiday."

"You can do with a holiday, too."

Bertha looked gloomy at the prospect. "I will go crazy sitting with my hands in my lap for three months."

"Then go crazy," said Claudia. "It will be a pleasure to watch you.—Candy and John haven't come yet," she broke off, as David reappeared with a brace of porters. "I wonder what's keeping them."

If he heard, he wasn't listening. "Come along," he said, meaning business; "here, give me the briefcase. Matthew, hold on to your mother's hand or you'll get lost in this jam, and don't argue, do as you're told. Bertha, the porter will take that box, you don't have to carry it."

Against her will, Bertha surrendered a long, flat cardboard carton, tied unhandsomely with various knotted bits of string. "Be careful it should not come open," she cautioned the porter.

Claudia couldn't imagine what was so precious about it, but there wasn't time to ask. "Did you straighten out the staterooms?" she tagged along in David's wake.

"Yes," said David shortly. "We have the suite on A deck whether we like it or not."

"That's unforgivable. How could they possibly make a mistake like that?"

"Apparently they thought that we were the ones who made the mistake."

"What do you mean?"

"You'll see," he said, with a tight look round his mouth.

She saw. "But this must cost a fortune!" she exclaimed, aghast.

Bertha stood speechless in the middle of the

sumptuous drawing room, but Matthew's negation soared to heights of awed respect. "Is this a *boat*?" he reversed himself.

Nobody bothered to answer him. David opened a door to an adjoining room. "This is where you and the children hole in, Bertha. I hope you can make do with it."

Claudia watched Bertha's plump form dissolve into a vista of pale green carpet and coral satin beds. "Where do you and I hole in?" she asked grimly.

He opened another door on the opposite side of the drawing room, disclosing a symphony of the subtlest greys and yellows. "This is ridiculous," she said flatly. "We don't need anything like this, I refuse to take it."

"You've got it," said David.

"But why on earth didn't you insist on our original accommodations?"

"I did. What do you think I was doing? The other rooms are gone."

"Gone? That's inexcusable carelessness!"

"It wasn't carelessness, it was deliberate. This happens to be the suite that Hartley and Julia always travelled in so they booked us into it."

"But we're not Hartley and Julia," she

14

protested in mounting indignation, "so why should we be forced to pay hundreds of dollars more for something we don't even want?"

"If it makes you feel any better, we aren't paying any more for it. The boat isn't crowded at this time of year, the space was available, and I gather it isn't good policy to allow any branch of the Naughton family to travel at minimum rates on B deck."

"It doesn't make me feel better," she sputtered. "We don't have to accept any favours."

"That's the point," said David, not any more pleased about it than she was. "People who have to accept favours don't get any to accept."

Before she could say what she thought of such a perverse system, the porters appeared. "Just put everything down in the drawing room," David told them. "We'll sort it out later."

"Very good, sir."

They seemed happy with the tip, and withdrew. Claudia eyed the heterogeneous collection of luggage lugubriously. "It looks even worse against this background," she said, "though most of it is the children's. I've got everything of mine in one suitcase."

"I wouldn't boast about it," said David. "You should have bought yourself some decent clothes."

"There wasn't time. We decided in such a hurry, and besides, I've got enough old things for the boat, I'd rather buy what I need in London or Paris." A knock sounded on the door. "There's Candy and John. Come in!" she called out.

It wasn't Candy and John. It was a tall, lean, white-coated steward who introduced himself as "Orkins—sir," and "Mertie and Sands, sir, would be taking care of the ladies and the little ones, sir, if they could come in for a moment, madame."

Claudia caught the ball as "madame", and said, "Of course," whereupon two stewardesses appeared, and Claudia had the feeling that all three of them were averting their gaze from the middle of the floor. "We might as well start to get organized," David suggested robustly, and supervised the disposition of bundles and cases, with Bertha appearing in the nick of time to rescue her cardboard box.

"Would there be anything else, sir?"

"Not just now," said David.

The steward lingered on the threshold swallowing his large Adam's apple. "I'd like to say, sir, that Mertie and myself, sir, had the privilege of taking care of Mr. and Mrs. Hartley Naughton on many a crossing. We heard, later, sir, that they'd cancelled the boat this last trip in favour of the plane."

"Yes, they were in a hurry to get home." said David.

"It seems it must have been God's will," Mertie joined in sadly, "but it's hard to understand such a terrible needless accident."

"It is," Claudia said with effort.

"I hope it wasn't out of place to speak about it," said Mertie. "But it didn't seem right not to, under the circumstances. It gave us quite a turn when we saw the name of Naughton occupying this suite again."

"It gave us quite a turn, too," Claudia murmured.

"I said to Orkins, it was a blessing there were no children to leave orphaned."

As if on cue, Sands emerged from the green and coral bedroom, looking even more sepulchral, if possible, than Mertie. "The big one's very bright for his age," she offered

17

politely, "and the little one is as chubby as can be."

"That's what I call English diplomacy," Claudia remarked to David, as soon as they were alone. "You could tell she thought they were a couple of horrible little American monsters."

"Let's face it," said David. "They are."

"But it wouldn't stick out so much in our other rooms. Really, I could kill Julia and Hartley, excuse the pun. Having to live up to them isn't going to be easy sailing."

"Relax," said David.

They were both so busy relaxing that the sound of Candy's voice made them jump. "We knocked and you didn't hear us," she apologized breathlessly. "You'd think you were newlyweds, kissing like that! A fine goose chase you gave us. What's this all about?"

"We went down to B deck," John began to explain more lucidly, but Candy interrupted him. "The door was open, and a big fat man in shirt-sleeves and a beard was unpacking all over the place."

"That wasn't David," Claudia inserted mildly.

18

"I told John that it wasn't," Candy said, "but he insisted it couldn't be anybody else, because that was the room number David gave him."

Candy was improving, Claudia noted with satisfaction; she used to be quite literal. "Anyway, this is more like it," Candy concluded. "It's really lovely. The other place looked sort of bunky."

"The room the children would have had was much bigger, two portholes, and regular beds," Claudia stuck to their first choice. "But it seems that it would have been an embarrassment to the boat to have a Naughton sleeping in an upper berth, to say nothing of two."

"Well, make the best of a bad bargain. It's only five days." John consoled her.

"Five days is a long time to put up with all this," Claudia grumbled.

"It's a long time for the few measly clothes you've brought along," Candy amended. "And don't tell me you've enough sports things left over from the farm, and that twenty-year-old yellow for evening, or I'll scream."

"The yellow is not twenty years old,"

Claudia informed her stiffly. "I got it in the first year we were married."

"All right, my error—twelve years. And all of a thirty dollar dress to start with."

"It can ride along in the reflected glory of an eight-hundred dollar original model."

"Oh Lord, that ever-lasting legend of the pink net! Not that I ever believed it. I think it's just a good story to hand down to your grandchildren."

Claudia winced. "You can believe it. To this day I get absolutely sick at the thought of it."

"But you couldn't have been such an idiot as to think it was seven dollars and ninety-five cents when the saleswoman told you it was seven-ninety-five, especially in one of the swankiest shops in Hollywood of all places!"

"She could and she was and she did," David threw in from the other side of the room with a grin that almost cracked his face. "I think that's why she's had a blockage about buying clothes ever since."

"It wasn't as idiotic as it sounds," Claudia defended herself. "Nothing cost anything in Hollywood in those days, even though everything was on a palatial scale, even the markets. While David was busy at the

Architects Convention I used to wander around and simply drool. Spinach a penny a bunch, grapefruit ten cents a dozen, avocados three for a nickel, and giant chocolate malts with two blobs of ice-cream for a dime. If you don't believe it, ask Bertha. She still has the postcards I sent her."

"That doesn't pull the wool over my eyes. Two blobs of ice-cream and a bunch of spinach is another kettle of fish," Candy mixed her metaphors with a lavish hand.

"Now wait a minute, it isn't such another kettle of fish," Claudia argued heatedly. "Those were the days when you could buy all the little cotton or net dresses you wanted for about five dollars."

"They looked like five dollars, though."

"And the seven-ninety-five looked like seven-ninety-five. Pink with a big purple sash, and the layers of skirt not even hemmed! When I wore it that evening, David thought it looked a little cheap too—that is, before we found out it wasn't. And by that time it was too late to send it back."

"Tell me the truth, I mean really the truth. What did he do when he discovered how much it was?" Candy asked curiously.

"He laughed so hard he almost choked and

scared the wits out of me. Say, David, what are you ringing Orkins for?" she interrupted herself. "We've just got him out of our hair!"

"The name is 'awkins, my love."

"That's what I said. 'Orkins'."

"When you talk to him, put an H in, it'll improve international relations," David suggested blandly. "I'm ringing for some glasses. John and Candy brought a couple of bottles of champagne."

"We couldn't think of anything else to get you," Candy explained. "Steamer baskets seem so silly when you can get all the fruit and stuff you want on a boat."

"I'd have murdered you," Claudia said starkly.

"That's what I told John. Still and all, we didn't want to come 'empty-handed', as my mother-in-law would say, so we brought champagne."

In Claudia's opinion, champagne was highly over-rated, since, in many respects (such as bubbles), ginger ale answered the same purpose. Ginger ale, however, might not have had so fortuitous an effect upon Hawkins, for his long face brightened considerably at the suddenly festive atmosphere. Hartley and Julia had always had a lot of people trooping down to see them off, and champagne doubtless flowed like water, to quote John's mother again. "It was an inspiration," she thanked Candy fervently. "And also, I'm awfully glad John's so aristocratic looking and that you wore your new fur coat. You could see Hawkins was impressed with you.—Have they got on any further with the house, John, or didn't you have time to look in this morning?" she digressed wistfully.

"You only came into town yourselves late yesterday," John reminded her goodnaturedly, "but as a matter of fact we did call in on our way to the station. The panelling for the library finally came. It was just being unloaded when we got there."

"Did you look at it? How did it look?" David asked eagerly.

"Very fine," John said.

"I got a peep, too. It's beautiful: the wood has that lovely old patina like honey," Candy enlarged.

"Oh dear, I wish it had come before we left," said Claudia. "I can hardly wait to get home."

"Same here," David said.

"And they haven't even left yet!" Candy's

eyes filled. "I can hardly wait, either."

"How's the baby's cold?" Claudia changed the subject quickly.

"It's almost all gone." Candy blew her nose. "Today's Martha's day off, but with Mother Payne there, I don't have to hurry home. You have no idea what a comfort it is to have her live with us."

Claudia caught the swift gratitude in John's reach for Candy's hand. It wasn't easy for a man to divide his loyalties, and Candy, after much pain and blundering, had at last gained the maturity to realize it. She still looked like a child, though, with her taffy-coloured hair and healthy sunburn, as always, in her presence, Claudia felt the not unpleasant impact of her own thirty years. The more you had behind you, the less you had ahead of you—at least that's the way she hoped it was going to work out, although David said not to be too sure of it.

Nevertheless, the immediate future was certainly beginning to look rosy. Hawkins returned with the bottles of champagne in twin buckets of crushed ice, followed by Mertie, bearing silver platters of tiny frosted cakes and exquisite canapes, not, Claudia saw at a glance, compounded chiefly of sneaky

24

peanut butter and cheese-pastes, but chiefly of the blackest of caviar and the pinkest of smoked salmon.

It was uncanny the way Matthew always got wind of something going on. "You didn't tell me Candy and Uncle John came!" he materialized instantly in stormy protest.

"Pardon me," said Claudia.

"We only just got here," Candy soothed his ruffled feelings with a hug. He adored Candy, but he pulled away, his eyes glued to the plate of cakes.

"Hello," John said. "Remember me?"

Matthew favoured him with an assortment of teeth. "Yeah," he said. "Did you bring those?"

"Don't say 'yeah' and don't point," David reprimanded him.

"Sorry, we only brought the champagne," John apologized.

"I like the ice," said Matthew, scooping up a handful. "Can I have a cake?"

"*May* I have a cake, and put the ice back at once," Claudia commanded.

"It's gone," said Matthew, with a giant gulp. He wiped his hands on his new trousers. "Stop that!" David said. "Go back to your room and wash and dry your hands properly."

"They're dry," said Matthew.

"March." David's voice held an ominous stillness.

"You said I could see the Statue of Liberty."

"The boat hasn't sailed yet."

"Why can't I see it now?"

"I'd march if I were you," Claudia advised.

Matthew inched off. "Oh goddam," he threw back over his shoulder.

"He didn't pick that up in school," Claudia forestalled his father's yelp of rage.

"Be glad he's healthy," Candy offered.

"I am," said Claudia. "But there's no law that says he can't be a little more attractive and stay healthy, too."

"You can't be attractive while your teeth are coming in and going out at the same time," John told her. "Where'd he get that suit?"

"Bertha's selection. He'll be growing into it any year now."

"Poor child," said Candy. "Let's take Bertha a glass of champagne and some cakes."

"Let's," said Claudia.

26

David knew that the cakes weren't going to Bertha, who never touched sweets, but for a wonder he kept his mouth shut about it. To show she loved him for it, Claudia ruffled his hair in passing, which he hated. He ducked, and glowered at her. "Hey, quit it!" She ruffled it again because he looked the image of Matthew.

Bertha had already got to work on the bedroom. She had folded back the satin spreads and put white towels across the ornamental surfaces of tables and commodes. A favourite picture of Fritz that David had snapped one day on the farm and had had enlarged for her, shared prominence with her sewing basket and Michael's toys, replacing an impersonal perfection with an air of permanence and home.

"How'd you do everything so fast? I haven't even begun to unpack," Claudia said. "Here's some champagne. Where's your 'kleine engel'?"

Bertha beamed as if someone had given her a medal. "In the bathroom. Can you imagine such a good baby.—Thank you, but you shouldn't." She accepted the champagne with diffidence. "It is a shame to waste it on me."

"No more a shame than on me," said Claudia. "Drink it up. What's happened to Matthew?"

Bertha looked startled. "I thought he was with you in the other room."

"He was, but his father sent him back to wash his hands."

"I was attending to Michael, I did not see him come in again. He must be hiding somewhere to fool us." Bertha opened cupboards and peered into the luggage compartment stacked with empty suitcases and bundles deflated into neatly folded packets of heavy brown paper, spanned with cord. "That is funny. He is not here," she said slowly.

"No, but he's been here," Claudia discovered. There was an extra partitioned lavatory in the room, where a crumpled towel with damp smudges bore silent testimony of Matthew's fleeting presence.

"Maybe he went back through the corridor to David and John," Candy suggested.

"Maybe." Claudia peered into the drawing-room and then noiselessly closed the connecting door. "He didn't, but there's no use upsetting the peace, he couldn't have gone very far. Stick your head outside, Bertha."

28

"There is no sign of him in the hall," Bertha reported with increasing agitation. "If you will stay with the baby, I will look until I find him."

"I'd better look." Claudia's lips tightened less with worry than annoyance. "What's more, I shall personally administer a good whack to his behind for going off on his own like this."

"I'll go with you," Candy said.

The corridor was full of passengers and guests and baggage and flowers, all melting into the hubbub of sailing-time. Neither Hawkins nor Mertie was in evidence among the busy regiment of stewards and stewardesses, but eventually Claudia came upon Sands, snatching a quick cup of tea in the pantry.

"I'm sorry, madame." Sands wiped her lips a trifle guiltily. "I'll come directly. I didn't know you'd rung."

"I didn't ring. I'm looking for Matthew. He's supposed to be in his room and he isn't. Have you seen him?"

"No, madame, I haven't. Has he got lost?"

If, in Sands' voice, Claudia detected an inflection not wholly of concern, she both understood, and forgave. "Don't be an optimist, he's not lost permanently," she felt like saying. Instead she said, "He might be with Hawkins, only I can't find Hawkins, either."

"I expect he's in your bedroom, madame. Shall I enquire?"

"It'll be quicker if I run and see."

She met Candy hurrying from the far end of the corridor. "No luck. I even peeped into staterooms where the doors were open, he's such a little rubber-neck."

Peeping made Candy a rubber-neck, too, but Claudia refrained from mentioning it. "I finally traced Hawkins. He's in our bedroom. Come along. Matthew's probably pestering the poor man to death with questions."

Hawkins' opening words took her mind briefly but forcibly off the fact that the room was achingly empty of Matthew. "Mertie and I have unpacked the suitcases, madame, but your trunks haven't been brought in as yet. I'd better see what's holding them up."

Although she might be able, later on, to soften the blow that there weren't any trunks, there was nothing she could do to lessen the shock of his having been closely connected with the unpacking of her suitcase. She was the first to admit that she was not a gifted packer, but at the same time she had not bargained for a public exposé of her intimate possessions, which weren't very glamorous at best. For a fleeting moment of dismay, she recalled having swathed a bottle of hand lotion in an after-thought of toilet paper to keep it from leaking. Apparently the bottle had leaked a little anyway, for Mertie tonelessly volunteered the information that there was quite a bit of a sticky stain on the yellow dinner gown, and she had already given it to 'Awkins to give to the valet along with Mr. Naughton's suits to be pressed.

"It doesn't matter. It's a very old dress, don't bother about it, and don't bother about the trunks either," Claudia killed both birds neatly with the same verb, and went on to tell them of Matthew's disappearance. "I thought surely he'd be in here, and now I'm really getting nervous about him."

"They don't kidnap on boats," Candy read her thoughts, "and all the railings are much too high for him to fall overboard."

Hawkins ignored Candy's theories. He looked almost as upset as Bertha. "We'd better go on a search at once," he said, quite concerned. "Mertie, you see if he's gone on deck, while I see if he's been turned in at the purser's desk. The sooner we find him the better. It's no good having a child like that let loose."

"Let loose!" Candy echoed indignantly, as Hawkins vanished with Mertie on his heels.

"I didn't mind the 'let loose' as much as the 'like that'," said Claudia. "But in all justice we have to admit that Matthew is no walking advertisement to an exclusive suite on A deck."

"I know what you mean," Candy nodded.

"Let's go through the drawing-room in case he's come back for some cake."

"Where've you girls been?" David asked, as they drifted past.

"Looking round the boat," said Claudia nonchalantly.

Bertha was waiting for them on pins and needles. "You didn't find him," she saw from their faces.

"No, but Hawkins is sure to round him up. Is the baby still doing himself proud, or has he been lost too?"

"Ach, I was so worried about Matthew, I forgot all about the baby!" Bertha rushed off to the bathroom in an agony of remorse, and then there was a heavy silence.

Claudia tensed. "What's your kleine engel been up to?" she called out.

"Nothing! It is nothing!" Bertha called back with false assurance.

"I'll investigate," said Candy. "Sit down, you look a wreck. Really, I'm beginning to see that it's no holiday to take a holiday with children."

"It's no holiday without them, so you're licked either way. If Michael's fallen down the drain, don't tell me."

"He's all right," Candy brought back the cheering details. "He unwrapped a cake of soap to while away the time."

"What did he do with the soap to while away the time after he unwrapped it?" Claudia asked wearily. "Give it to me straight, I can take it."

"Well, from the way he's foaming at the mouth," Candy confessed, "he seems to have eaten most of it. Be grateful it was the soap," she added consolingly. "I'm reading a book on child psychology, and you'd be amazed what they can eat when they put their minds to it." She broke off at the sound of the warning gong. "That means visitors have to leave, and I simply can't bear to go until Matthew is found!"

Claudia rose to her feet. "I'd better not put off telling David any longer," she said whitely. "Maybe Matthew got mixed up, and went down the gangway again. It would be awful to leave him behind."

"If he's on the quayside, we'll take care of him," said Candy with relish. "I love the little brat, but he really does deserve a spanking for putting you through this. I wouldn't be surprised if he is here somewhere, enjoying all the commotion."

"That's the one thing he's not. He can't stand seeing me upset. I'm sure something must have happened for him to be gone all this time."

"It only seems a long time." Candy glanced at her watch. "We got here at about eleven and it's not twelve yet."

"It's long enough. I wish there hadn't been all that unnecessary publicity in the papers. I mean, not so much about the plane crash—that would be news even if Hartley and Julia hadn't been prominent. But whose business is it how much money we inherited?"

"Nobody's, but it leaks out anyway," said Candy. "And if you're thinking of ransom, that's absolutely ridiculous."

"It's easy to say that it's ridiculous."

Claudia bit her lips. "You don't believe such things can happen to yourself, or anyone you know, and then suddenly it does. Do you remember the little boy who disappeared a few months ago right in New York, on his way to school? The parents paid the fifty thousand the kidnappers asked, and still the police haven't found a trace of the child."

"You'd better tell David right away," Candy abruptly changed her tune. "Never mind if he gets mad!"

"Take one more look in the hall."

Candy took one more look, and returned, shaking her head mutely. Claudia walked into the drawing-room. John and David were standing up, and John had his hat and coat over his arm. "Well, I guess it's time to say good-bye to Bertha and the youngsters," he said, feeling worse about it than he let on.

It was as good an opening as any. "You can't," said Claudia. "Michael's just eaten a bar of soap, and Matthew's been missing for the last half hour."

The soap slid over David's head. "What do you mean, Matthew's been missing," he exploded, even angrier than Claudia had expected.

"He just washed his hands and left," she explained. "Hawkins is looking for him."

David's nostrils behaved in a way that boded no good for anyone, least of all himself. "Now please, don't lose your temper," she begged. "The important thing is, what do we do if Hawkins doesn't find him?"

David reacted exactly as he had with Michael spilling the cereal that morning. "We'll do nothing," he laid down the law with a large disregard of consequences. "We will simply let him stay lost until he gets a scare that he'll remember to the end of his days."

"What about the end of my days," Claudia began, and then the warning gong sounded for the second time.

"This is a hell of a way to begin a holiday." John showed more fatherly concern than David. "I hate to walk off and leave you like this."

"That's the way I feel," said Candy tearfully. "This is awful."

"Nonsense, he'll show up sooner or later," David insisted. "Run along."

There was nothing else for them to do. Candy gave Claudia a tense hug, and John gripped David's hand, hard, and said, "Send a wire to the office anyway, when you find him."

"Yes, please do," Candy implored. "I'll go back with John and wait until we hear."

"There's nothing to hear, he's all right," said David. "Take my word for it."

Candy threw her arms round him. "I almost believe you, David, you're a big comfort."

"He's a big bluff," said Claudia.

She experienced an engulfing emptiness after they had gone. David felt it, too, and for a long moment they were silent, sensing anew the strong cord of attunement that had emerged from the complicated fabric of the past. There was neither accident nor coincidence in the intricate weaving of human relationships. It meant more to have had John and Candy come down to see them off, than dozens of party-seeking acquaintances. Suddenly, out of nowhere, Claudia was sorry for all the times that she and David had not come down to see Julia and Hartley off.

"Thanks," she said, as wordlessly, David handed over his handkerchief.

"I guess I'd better take a look round for the little monster myself."

37

She managed a watery smile. "I wish you would. And I'll see if Michael's blown up into a soap bubble."

"You poor kid," said David.

The baby was asleep on the bed, a little washed-out, and sucking his thumb. "I could cut my both hands off that I did not stop the child," Bertha greeted Claudia.

"If you mean Matthew, how could you stop him when you didn't see him? Anyway, Mr. David knows about it now, and he's gone out to find him."

"Gott sei dank," said Bertha, who always lapsed into her native tongue in moments of stress.

"The baby seems awfully pale to me."

"He is all right. A little soap will not hurt him. Only let him have his thumb for this once."

"He's more than welcome to it as far as I'm concerned, but it's a good thing his father's not around." She felt a little dizzy, all at once, and realized why. "Bertha, we're moving!"

"Ach," said Bertha, as the dock slid slowly past the windows.

Claudia tried to control the screaming of

her nerves. "It's such a helpless feeling just to wait and do nothing! What if he went off the boat? Then what?"

"He would have no reason to go off the boat." Bertha's voice lacked conviction. Matthew didn't have a reason for a lot of things he did. "Mr. David will bring him back," she said. "I bet you twenty cents."

"I remember the first time you bet me twenty cents. I was hardly pregnant with Bobby, we'd only been married a few months. How could you have told?"

"Sometimes you do not know how you know. You are the same way, you also feel things in your bones."

"Yes, and it's a frightening way to be. Mr. David makes fun of it. He says if I counted out all the time I was wrong I'd be wrong more often than I'm right."

"He listens just the same to your feelings," Bertha remarked sagely. "But you have had enough to worry about in your life already. From now on everything will be only happiness for you, you will see."

"Thank you for nothing if this morning is an example of it."

"This morning could be just the last little bit for good measure."

"I hope you're right."

Michael stirred, and sighed in his sleep. "I am right," said Bertha. "Look, the baby has stopped sucking his thumb."

Claudia smiled faintly. "Big deal," she said. It was Matthew's latest and most favoured expression. He'd brought it home one day, with a passionate addiction to ketch-up. "Oh God, let him walk through that door, and he can pour all the ketch-up he wants on anything he wants to pour it on," Claudia offered in silent prayer.

The door opened. It was David. He gave himself away by saying, "We just passed the Statue of Liberty."

Claudia's lips went dry. "No sign of him yet?"

"I've been talking to the purser, and apparently it's nothing unusual to get lost on a ship this size. There's a couple of youngsters turned in on almost every trip."

"Then why wasn't Matthew?"

"He probably has been. There's more than one purser's desk, you know."

"No, I didn't know," she said, "but I'm relieved to hear it. If there's a separate purser for each deck, maybe he's been taken down to our original accommodations."

David cleared his throat. "I didn't exactly mean that there's a purser for each deck," he explained carefully, "but, anyway, Hawkins went there first thing. However," he added quickly, "there are a lot of other places he could be, and the whole boat's been told to be on the look-out for him, so cheer up."

"David, let's stop fooling ourselves." She tried to keep her voice steady. "No matter how many places he could be, Matthew's too old to be lost this long. He knows enough to give his name and it couldn't possibly take all this time to find out where he belongs."

"That is true." Bertha didn't even bother to try to keep her voice from shaking. "I have been thinking the same thing."

David didn't have an answer for that, so he got gruff to hide the fact that he was as worried as they were. "If you two women have any crazy idea that he's been kidnapped off the ship, you ought to have your heads examined." He lit a cigarette. "I'll go out for another look."

Claudia caught his arm. "Wait for me, I'll go with you. Anything's better than just sitting here doing nothing."

"You're getting worked up for no reason. What if he is missing for a few minutes?"

"It's more than a few minutes, it's almost an hour. Please let me go with you," she begged.

"It's cold on deck. Where's your coat? I'll get it for you."

"No, I'll get it. I threw it down somewhere in the drawing-room."

She looked high and low, but there was no trace of it. Funny how one could notice the trivial at a time like this; she noticed that the empty champagne bottles had been cleared away, the ash-trays cleaned and polished, and the sofa cushions plumped back in shape. "Who wants all this service?" she muttered, as she finally discovered the coat properly hung away in a cupboard in the foyer. She flung it across her shoulders, and started back to David. A light knock at the door caught her up short. She almost fell over herself in a headlong rush to open it, and there they were, standing hand in hand on the threshold, Hawkins so big and Matthew so small, with his poor little face blotched and swollen with tears.

"David! Bertha! Come quick! He's here!"

She was on her knees beside him, limp with gratitude. "Oh, thank you, Hawkins!" she

42

breathed. "Matthew, how could you do this to us? Where have you been?"

He couldn't talk. Unashamed, he clung to her, gulping his sobs and pressing his wet nose against her cheek.

"Stop that crying!" David's voice boomed out behind them. "Answer your mother. You knew you were disobedient. Why did you go off by yourself?"

For once in his life, Matthew had no defence: he could only gasp out disjointed words strung together on tiny sharp hiccoughs of terror. "I just wanted to see the Statue of Liberty, and a man took me away and wouldn't let me come back!"

"Mein Gott," Bertha whispered in horror.

"Matthew, don't add lying to your sins," David warned.

"He's telling the truth, sir," Hawkins interceded in a low voice. "That is, after a manner of speaking, he is."

"Go and wash your face and blow your nose, Matthew," David addressed him a little more kindly.

"Come, child." Bertha gathered him in her arms and, surprisingly, Matthew submitted to the indignity of being carried like a baby. He looked somehow so much littler than usual, that David bit back a scathing comment about big boys being able to walk by themselves. "What's all this about a man taking him away?" he asked Hawkins as soon as Matthew was out of earshot.

"Well, sir—" Hawkins looked distinctly uncomfortable. "The fact of the matter is, it was a case of mistaken identity, so to speak, sir. That is to say, Master Matthew went out to see the Statue of Liberty just as he told you, sir, and one of the deck stewards thought the little chap had gone off on his own, and took him straightaway to the purser's desk."

Claudia wheeled towards David in exasperation. "This boat seems to be making one mistake after another: you told me that the purser's desk was the first place Hawkins asked!"

"I also told you, remember, dear, that there was more than one purser," David calmed her down.

She'd have had to be blind not to see the grateful look in Hawkins' eyes. "I believe you've got the whole gist of what happened, sir. If anyone's to blame, it's the deck steward, who was in a bit of a muddle, I expect, what with the rush of passengers running here and there at sailing time. Not that it's an excuse, sir, for him to have jumped to conclusions; he should have made proper enquiries before he hustled the poor little chap down to second class."

David's lips twitched like a grin in the making. "So that's where you finally picked him up?" he said.

"No, sir, not exactly, sir." Hawkins' embarrassment flooded to his temples. "It seems, sir, when Master Matthew told his name, that the purser couldn't locate him, but begging your pardon, sir, again, sir, the name was located in third class, though not spelt the same way. No 'u' at all, sir, just plain 'Norton'. But it turned out to be a young couple, sir, married yesterday, with no children."

It was on the tip of Claudia's tongue to deplore the backwardness of the young couple, but all of a sudden she began to laugh, and she laughed so hard that the tears rolled down her cheeks. Hawkins concluded that she was having hysterics and felt terrible about it. "A bit of a sedative perhaps, sir," he suggested to David in a low voice.

"She'll be all right," said David, fishing out his handkerchief for the second time.

Claudia wiped her eyes. "I'm sorry," she excused herself weakly.

"There's no call for you to be sorry, ma'am," Hawkins told her earnestly. "You're the one that's due an apology, and you'll be having it soon, I can promise you. The deck steward is in for a rough time of it, never fear. I've got an idea, I have, that a wicked mistake like this could cost him his post."

"But I don't want that to happen," she protested. "This was one mistake that wasn't anybody's fault! I mean, what with Matthew's teeth and pants and everything," she rushed on inarticulately, "how can anybody blame anybody! David, do something about it, don't let that poor man lose his job!"

"He won't, I'll straighten it out," David said. He turned to Hawkins. "Thank you for finding the little brat."

"Thank *you*, sir. And I'd like to say, sir, that it's going to be a privilege to take care of you and Mrs. Naughton." He gave such a gigantic swallow that Claudia was almost certain she could see Bertha's bundles bobbing down over his Adam's apple, along with the yellow dress and no trunks, and even the original accommodation on B deck.

"Relax," she said to David, after he had come back from clearing the deck steward and sending a wire to Candy and John.

David got the point at once, which was another of the satisfying things about being married to him. He said, "The Lord works in mysterious ways, His miracles to perform. Let's go and unpack before lunch."

She gave him a withering look. "Don't be gauche," she said, "you've been unpacked."

2

CLAUDIA'S appetite, never bashful, bounced up as the excitement died down. "When is lunch? I'm starved," she announced.

David's eyebrow did its old trick of sliding up his forehead. "After all those canapes?"

"I had exactly one," she informed him wrathfully. "Before I had to go out looking for your son."

David denied ownership. "I want no part of him until he gets to be human."

"He's chastened, if that's any encouragement. There wasn't a word out of him when I broke the news that he was going to eat in the room with Bertha and the baby."

David looked very encouraged. "For the whole trip?"

"You're an optimist. Shall I wear my hat?"

"What for? You're not going off the boat."

"I'll wear it," she decided. "Then I won't have to use my hair until dinner. I washed it at the hotel this morning, and it hasn't settled down yet."

He waited, elaborately, while she tucked some intractable ends beneath a soft velvet beret. "And don't look so long-suffering," she told him tersely. "Precious little you ever have to wait around while I dress."

"Are you finished now by any chance?"

"I'm finished now by any chance—My gloves. Did you take them?"

He gave her a look.

"I don't need them anyway," she said hastily. "My nails always look their best after I wash my hair."

He yanked her away from the mirror, and planted a rough kiss on her lips which pleasantly disturbed her. "What's that all about?"

"Because you haven't changed since the day I married you."

It was strange that when he kissed her gently or when he kissed her roughly, the feeling she got was the same. "We'd better eat," she murmured.

"Is that all you ever think of?"

"Not quite all."

"Glad to hear it."

"I reckoned you might be. You haven't changed a lot, yourself. So it should be a very nice five days. The nights shouldn't be too bad either."

"Not too bad," he agreed. "Now come along."

"I have to say good-bye to the children first."

"Why?"

"Don't argue. That's where Matthew gets it from."

She opened the door to the drawing-room. Unobserved they stood watching on the threshold. It was a cosy sight. A round table, with a centre-piece of flowers had been set up in front of the fireplace. Bertha, who had finally managed to change from her non-committal travel clothes into one of her starched white uniforms, presided at the head of the table, with Michael in a high chair on one side, and Matthew on the other. Their separate experiences appeared have left them unusually docile, but from the strained look on Bertha's face, Claudia knew that she was itching to cut up the baby's chicken and drench his baked potato in globs of butter. Mertie and Sands, however, had taken over with a wholehearted solicitude undoubtedly engendered by Hawkins' change of attitude. At the moment, they were conferring with each other on the milk situation—"better to bring it to a boil," they decided, "after the third day out."

"Better we boil the second day," Bertha gave firm ultimatum. "My children are used to fresh milk every morning."

Sands placed a delicately golden breast of chicken in front of Matthew. "Right you are," she agreed at once, "best not to run any risk with the little ones."

Claudia could see Matthew writhe under the indignity of being linked with Michael, but all he said was, "Could I please have some ketch-up?"

Mertie looked blank. "Ketch-up, lovey?"

"That red stuff in a bottle."

Without further ado, Claudia pulled David back into the bedroom, and closed the door. "So he has ketch-up this once. I promise."

"Why promise him a thing like that!" said David, who wouldn't be caught dead with ketch-up except once in a blue moon—on beans.

"I didn't promise Matthew," she clarified, "I promised God that if only He let Matthew get found, he—Matthew, not God—could pour all the ketch-up he wanted over anything he wanted to pour it over, and in

51

view of future favours I don't think it's good policy to go back on my word."

David couldn't think of a sufficiently withering reply. "I thought you were so hell-bent to say good-bye to your little cherubs," he barked at her.

"I changed my mind when I saw them. Why ask for trouble? Let sleeping dogs lie, I always say."

"Every so often you surprise me by showing a glimmering of intelligence," he commended her grudgingly.

"Every so often I surprise myself," she said.

Hawkins had already consulted them about their deck and dining reservations. "We want our deck chairs separate from the children's," David had stipulated.

Claudia thought he was being a little crass about it, but Hawkins saw nothing unnatural in his attitude. "Yes, sir. That's quite the usual procedure, sir, when one travels with a governess."

Throughout Bertha's many years of devoted service, she had been variously labelled housekeeper, cook, nurse, laundress and even cleaning-woman, but no one had ever mistaken her for a "governess". She wasn't going to be any too pleased about it, either; she'd met too many of them in the park.

"And in the matter of dining, sir," Hawkins went on, "do you wish the children to be served in the suite with the governess, sir?"

"Definitely," said David.

"Once in a while Matthew could eat with us," Claudia interjected.

Hawkins looked doubtful. "If you're at the Captain's table, madam, I wouldn't let the little chap count on it."

David said, "We are not at the Captain's table."

"In that case, sir," Hawkins received the information without a change of expression, "I expect you won't be very happy in the main dining-room."

Claudia bridled. Why wouldn't they be, and where else were they supposed to eat? David didn't bridle, but at least he told Hawkins by all means to reserve a table in the main dining-room. Then he added, rather cravenly, she thought, "I think Mrs. Naughton might enjoy it."

Hawkins continued to remain inscrutable.

"Very well, sir," he said, "you can always change to the café."

The very word "café" sounded unimportant, if not second-rate, making it obvious at this point that they had somehow back-slid in Hawkin's estimation—possibly because they hadn't been invited to sit at the Captain's table. As the implication seemed to escape David, however, she didn't say anything about it. "Watch it, you're getting supersensitive in your rich old age," she warned herself.

She managed to push the incident to the back of her mind until they went to lunch. "We'd better take the elevator," said David.

She was vaguely aware of a long swoop downward which left her rather shaken, but she forgot about it when she stepped out into a small foyer and glimpsed, through vast double doors, the far reaches of the most magnificent room she had ever seen. So this was were Hawkins had inferred that they would feel out of place! She could feel her lips getting a running-stitch round them— like a spinster with a grudge. "Well!" she vouchsafed on a snort.

"What's the matter?" asked David, with a hide as thick as an elephant's.

"Nothing. If you don't know, never mind."

"It is pretty overpowering," he remarked dubiously. "And it looks as if we'll have to wait before we get our table. Would you like to change your mind and go up to the café?"

"I would not."

"You don't have to bite my head off," he said. "Good. We won't have to wait after all, the dining steward seems to be heading our way."

The dining steward looked like Hawkins cut in half and dressed up. "Mr. and Mrs. Naughton? It's a pleasure to have you aboard. Right this way, please."

They followed his immaculate black back, with Claudia forcing her gaze away from the magnetic pull of the long buffet board. "I think you might be more comfortable at this end of the room." The steward's voice was low and liquid. "Naturally, if you prefer another table, or choose to dine with friends, it can always be arranged."

There wasn't much chance of that, as they didn't know a soul on board. "This table will do nicely," David said. The dining steward bowed. "Thank you very much, sir." He flowed backward, and a waiter flowed forward, producing a mammoth menu which he presented to Claudia. "Thank you, madame." He placed another menu in front of David. "Thank you, sir."

"You're welcome," Claudia replied silently, and decided that she'd better ignore his gratitude, particularly since the waiter continued to thank them for everything he did. A change of plates elicited a light "Thank you!" A serving of butter brought forth a gentle "Thank you". A retrieving of her napkin from the floor moved him to a devout "Thank you, madame!"

"You're a napkin dropper," David reproved her.

"He makes me nervous. I wish he'd stop thanking us," Claudia muttered.

"You'll get used to it. What would you like to eat?"

"Everything!" she enthused. "And to think it's only lunch! What on earth more could be on the dinner menu?"

She didn't have the chance to find out, because half-way through a trout and fresh asparagus Hollandaise, some super-salesman in striped trousers ruined her pleasure by inveigling them into signing up for a very special turtle soup, a brace of very special grouse, and a special soufflé as a sweet.

"Now I haven't anything to look forward to," she gritted her teeth in complaint to David. "Why can't we choose from the dinner menu when the time comes? A soufflé's only an exploded omelette, and I don't even like turtle soup and grouse."

"You've never eaten grouse."

"I don't want to. It's one of those English birds. Very gamey like bad chicken. We don't always have to order special dishes, do we?"

"If you don't mind breaking his heart, we don't."

"I'd rather break his than mine," she said. "I'm going to read the menu anyway tonight to see what I missed."

"You do that," David indulged her.

If anyone had prophesied that a dinner menu would be the last thing she'd want to look at that evening, she wouldn't have believed it for an instant. She'd never felt better in her life as she finished up lunch with a delectable dessert, and then companionably accepted one of David's biscuits, indecently heaped with a superbly runny Brie cheese. "God bless your appetite," he said.

"I wouldn't enjoy being married to a woman who picked," she observed complacently. "Would you enjoy sitting opposite someone who was always saying that she wasn't hungry, or this or that didn't agree with her?"

"I haven't the vaguest notion what it would be like," said David. "Would you care for some more of my cheese?"

"Coax me."

Eventually she leaned back in her chair, and cast appraising eyes about the vast room. "It's after two, and people are still coming in."

"Only country bumpkins like you rush in the minute the doors open."

She let that one pass. "Look over there. It looks like someone's not satisfied with the table they've been given."

"He wouldn't be," said David.

The gentleman who wasn't satisfied was obese and wore a beard. His wife looked like his twin: she was fat and wore a little of a beard, too. Eventually, they settled for a table within ear-shot, and then seemed only reasonably content. "I think," Claudia moved her lips, "from what Candy said, they're the ones who have our accommodations on B deck."

"Speak up," David adjured her, "I can't hear what you say?"

"If I speak up, *they'll* hear what I say."

"Not a chance, they're talking too loudly themselves."

"They look and act horrid enough to be celebrities of some sort. What's your guess?"

"My guess is, he's in ladies' underwear," said David.

"With that beard?"

"He doesn't necessarily use his beard."

"It's silly to wear a beard and not use it for anything."

"I think the wine's gone to your head."

"I think so too," she agreed amiably. "Are we going to drink wine at every meal?"

"Every meal but breakfast."

The sommelier had ears in the back of his head. He refilled Claudia's glass. "Oh dear," she murmured. "It's such a beautiful pale red, I can't resist."

"I thought you'd like the colour. That's why I ordered it instead of a Moselle, which would have been better with trout."

"Is that why the wine steward looked grieved?"

"Yes. They wound easily."

The wine steward hovered, his large

bouquet of keys inert against his ample front. "Excellent," David congratulated him. "Madame is very fond of a Rosé d'Anjou."

The sommelier proffered the wine card with an inward shrug and no joy. "For dinner, monsieur, you are having grouse?" he enquired distantly.

"They must have an underground," Claudia marvelled.

David ignored the wine card. "A Musigny '47, if you have any left."

"That did it," thought Claudia, watching the wine steward become a new man, his keys clanking happily. "A Musigny '47, monsieur? We have an exceptionally fine '47, sir. You have made a splendid choice, sir, if I may say so."

"If I may say so, I say so too," Claudia added her compliments. "I love the way you call me 'madame'." She drained her glass. "Madame wouldn't mind a little more."

"Madame has had enough," David said firmly. "I didn't know I was married to a little drunky."

She giggled. "I didn't know it, either. I'm glad I wore a hat, everybody's wearing hats. They look like dish pans upside down. It's the newest style, and I think it's simply hideous."

David looked around. "You seem to have the distinction of being the only beret."

"I have. I am. I've always liked berets, they're comfortable and they never go out of fashion."

"They don't?"

"Of course not, why should they? It's a little warm in here. Can't we go, if you're through with your coffee?"

Instantly a bevy of waiters sprang to pull out their chairs. "Thank you, madame. Thank you, sir."

Claudia caused a major traffic jam by going back for a final sip of water. "So thirsty," she explained apologetically. She dropped her purse. One of the waiters reclaimed it, and presented it with a bow. "Thank you, madame."

"Thank *you*," she said.

Passing the buffet board, she turned her gaze away. "I'm a little dizzy from the wine," she said to David. "It's really very hot in here, isn't it?"

"I didn't think so. Shall we walk upstairs or take the elevator?"

"The elevator might make me even more dizzy."

They walked. "The boat's moving," she said.

"I hope so."

"You know what I mean. It's moving sideways."

"This ship always did have a roll."

"Is that good?"

"I don't mind it."

"Oh, neither do I, I think it's fun," she said gaily, she hoped. "Oh look, there are beautiful shops on this deck!"

"The same as on Bond Street," said David.

She peered into a show window. "Look at that sweater for only seven dollars and sixty cents."

"Seven pounds, six shillings," he corrected her.

"Oh. I haven't caught the hang of a shilling yet. But pence is a little 'd' isn't it?—David, movies! At five o'clock every afternoon, and nine at night! We're going to have trouble with Matthew."

"For a change," said David dryly.

"It's television you don't approve of for children," she reminded him. "My legs are tired. Is there still another flight of steps?"

"There is, if you want to go on deck."

"I do. I'd like to see our chairs."

"Do you expect them to have bells on or something?"

"I'd like to see which ones we have, anyway."

The air was beautifully cold, and almost smelled of salt. The deck steward seemed to recognize David, and hurried towards them. Without his uniform, he wouldn't have been at all handsome, but he had a nice squarish face, and there was no nonsense about him. "I'm sorry about what happened this morning with the little fellow, Mrs. Naughton," he apologized. "Mr. Naughton was very kind to speak to the chief purser the way he did, and I appreciate it, I do indeed, ma'am."

"He shouldn't have been on deck by himself in the first place," said Claudia.

"I don't think he'll do it again, ma'am. He just passed by a few minutes ago, and he was holding on to the governess's hand for dear life. Would you like to rest in your chairs now?"

"I could do with a walk," said David.

"Oh, let's try out the chairs," said Claudia.

"Then we can wait for Bertha and the children to walk past again."

"I'll humour you this once," said David. "But I don't intend to spend all my time in a deck chair."

"What do you intend to do?" She felt quite coquettish from the wine.

"I'd like to see the boat. The engine room, in particular."

"Oh."

"Oh, what?"

"Just oh. Under which circumstances, I'd like to see the kitchens."

"Done. I'll set it up for tomorrow."

"We'll be having busy days, what with the shops and movies, and everything."

He looked at her beneficently. "Having a nice time?"

"Wonderful!"

Their deck chairs, replete with soft pads, already bore their names. "I've reserved chairs on the sun deck as well, sir," the steward said, as he expertly tucked a blanket round Claudia's legs. Then he started on David, who waved the blanket away. "Don't be so manly," said Claudia, "it's sheer heaven." She looked round to see if other men were averse to tucking, but the row of

64

chairs was empty, this first afternoon, except for a middle-aged woman who lay, swathed like a mummy, her eyes closed and her face tense with the dedication of absorbing air and rest. "A professional relaxer," Claudia commented.

David didn't hear her. His eyes were glued to a distant point at the far end of the deck. "Look!" he commanded.

She looked, but all she saw were a couple of children, accompanied by a nurse in a voluminous dark blue cape, with a long matching veil floating out behind her. A reminiscent smile tugged at her lips. "I remember when those English uniforms were all the rage. Julia gave one to Bertha for Christmas, years and years ago, and she was so proud of it. She had her picture taken in it on the street next to a pony, with Matthew in his perambulator. I was mighty proud of it, too: it made me feel as if I played bridge in the afternoons."

"How mighty proud does it make you feel now?" David asked in such an odd voice that she stared at him, and then stared back at the approaching apparition. "It can't be!" she gave out on a bleat.

"It is," said David. "But where on earth has she hidden it all this time?"

"Probably," said Claudia, "on a top shelf way to the back, in a big flat cardboard box tied with pieces of string knotted together."

David kept his face straight with difficulty. "What are you going to tell her?"

"I'm going to tell her she looks stunning," said Claudia firmly.

It could have been Bertha's ancient blue serge uniform stirring up all sorts of old associations, but whatever it was, Claudia had a most unsettling sensation as they wandered back to their rooms to bathe and dress for dinner; it was as if the wide corridors grew slowly narrower, with a vague unpleasant smell of rubber seeming to come up at her like a ghostly vapour. She had to battle an absurd idea that the floor went soft beneath her feet. "Hurry up," she said to David, who had paused to light a cigarette.

"Don't tell me you're hungry again."

A faint shudder passed through her. "It's not necessary to serve tea after such a big lunch," she observed a trifle petulantly.

"The English think it's necessary, but it

66

wasn't exactly necessary for you to take any," he remarked.

"I didn't want to hurt the deck steward's feelings after he went to the trouble to wheel the wagon right up to my chair."

It was an endless walk to their suites. When they got there David was impelled by a sudden rush of paternalism to look in on his sons. "What's got into you? You just saw them a little while ago," Claudia told him tersely, and headed towards their own bedroom.

Her yellow dress had been returned from its visit to the valet. By the combined magic of cleaning fluid and steam iron, it would have looked like new if it hadn't been so old. Apparently Mertie deemed it proper to wear this evening, because it was swinging from a hanger outside the cupboard door, rubbing shoulders with David's dark blue suit. One didn't "dress" the first night out, but the yellow could have passed for not dressing, as it had puffed sleeves and was of an in-between length that could pinch-hit either way. Nevertheless, Claudia wished it weren't quite so yellow; and that it would stop swinging. She sat down in the nearest chair, and closed her eyes, so that she couldn't see the swinging. However, she could hear the creaking that made the swinging. Little squeaky creaks and gusty drawn-out creaks. It sounded as if the boat was coming apart at the seams, and they were barely out of sight of land. It was nerve-wracking to say the least, even though she wasn't one to mind noise. David had minded the city traffic and horn-tooting last night, but she'd slept through it like a log. For some reason, though, this stealthy creaking was unbearable.

"What's the matter? Have you got a head-ache?"

She opened her eyes, and saw David watching her with Matthew's frown of apprehension. "Of course not," she said automatically.

He kept on studying her. "You look like a piece of cheese," he stated flatly.

He couldn't have chosen a more unpleasant word, either aesthetically or factually. "I think the cheese at lunch must have disagreed with me," she admitted, closing her eyes once more.

David's voice came at her like an accusing finger pointed in monosyllables. "You, my dear girl, are seasick."

If he had struck her she could not have been more affronted. She tried to focus a cold stare upon his blurring face. "I won't even answer anything as stupid as that." She rose unsteadily and turned her back on him. The bed got in her way, fortunately. "That's right, lie down for a while," he added insult to injury. "I told you this boat had a roll, you'll get used to it."

He gave her an encouraging pat, forgetful of all the times that they had gone sailing with Candy and John. Had she ever been sea-sick, no matter how rough? No. Had she ever been ill in a plane? No. On the other hand, anyone could eat something that disagreed with them. "Leave me alone. Just leave me alone," she repulsed him.

He gave her another pat. "I'll take a bath. Call me, if you want anything."

She wanted to tell him not to be so high and mighty, but it was more expedient not to open her mouth. A few minutes later she heard him whistling above the rush of water in the tub. She had never thought that the day would come when she would envy his radiant well-being.

"Mother?"

"Go away, Matthew," she said hoarsely, without opening her eyes.

"Have you got a headache?"

"Yes. Go away."

"But you said you never had a headache," he reminded her accusingly.

"Well I've got one now, I don't want to talk. Please get out."

She felt, rather than heard him back away from her; she knew that he needed her usual assurance that she was strong as a horse, but what was to be gained from deceiving him? It was far more likely that he would be motherless by nightfall, poor child. Nobody could feel like this and live.

"Ach—" That was Bertha. "I thought Matthew was making it up, but I see he wasn't. Come, I will help you to get undressed."

"I don't want to move."

"You will be more comfortable. It is a shame it should happen so soon, but I think you will get used to it. There was another lady on deck who was seasick already also."

"I am not seasick!" Claudia managed to gasp out.

"You are not?"

"Of course I'm not."

Bertha was more dubious than apprehensive. "If you are sure you are not, what do you think it can be to make you feel so bad?"

She felt reckless with misery. "It could be a stoppage of some sort, where everything wants to go backward. Or maybe just the flu," she added more conservatively.

Bertha's broad palm rested on Claudia's damp forehead. "You have no fever," she offered doubtfully. "But it is better you go to bed anyway. Come, let me help you get undressed."

Gratefully Claudia submitted to Bertha's knowing ministrations. "This was supposed to be a holiday for you, and look how it's started," she bemoaned. "You haven't had a minute to sit down all day."

"The children are fine now, that is one good thing," said Bertha. "And tomorrow you will be fine, too."

"Impossible. I'll never be fine again."

David emerged from the bathroom with nothing but a towel around his middle, and Bertha fled before she could bet another twenty cents. "You'd think she'd get used to it after all these years. Say, you're not in bed, are you?" he broke off incredulously.

His tardy solicitude mollified her slightly. "You didn't believe me when I told you how awful I feel."

"I believed you," he said. "But I didn't

71

think you'd go to bed just because you were a little seasick."

"How many times must I tell you I am *not* seasick. It's probably the flu. All right, I haven't any fever," she beat him to it testily, "but people have been known to die without fever."

"You only feel as if you want to die. I tell you what. We'll take a walk around the deck before dinner, a little air will settle you."

She didn't want any air and she certainly didn't want any dinner, and after he got that through his head, he seemed to be worried for the first time, and felt her head again. "I'd better not leave you."

"You've got a date with a turtle and a grouse."

"So I have. I'll have them brought in here on a tray and keep you company."

"You will not!" she gulped. "Eat in the dining room!"

"I'll hurry back," he promised.

She couldn't have dozed off—she never slept in the afternoons—but it was as if time dissolved in misery, because the next thing she heard was Mertie's voice, full of sympathy. "Mr. Naughton told me on his way to dinner you were feeling bad. Could I get you a cup of hot tea, or a bit of clear broth?"

Claudia made a limp gesture of refusal.

"There's a new pill," Mertie continued in her rhythmic monotone. "They say it's the best of all these seasick remedies. I wonder if you have it?"

"I'm not seasick, and I haven't got any pills at all," Claudia said quite loudly.

"Oh," said Mertie. She felt Claudia's forehead. "You're in a cold sweat, and that's a fact. You'd better have the doctor take a look at you, in case it's your appendix."

Claudia moved her lips but it took too much strength to explain that her appendix had vanished long since in a ruptured blaze of glory, but there were plenty of other kindred organs such as liver, kidneys, heart (on a long shot), spleen or gall-bladder that could well be at the bottom of this inexplicable on-slaught of dis-ease. "Doctor to-morrow maybe," she got out weakly.

"In the meantime, I'll put a hot water bottle at your feet, that's always a real comfort."

A wave of warm affection swept over Claudia. Beneath her remote English exterior, Mertie was an understanding and compassionate human being. And then her next words showed her up to be a snake in the grass. "While I'm about it," she said, "I might as well get you a couple of those pills. We're not supposed to give out medicine, but I'm fairly positive you're just seasick, and in that case the sooner you have them, the better you'll feel. Take one at once and the second one in three hours."

"Thank you, but I don't need them," Claudia replied with hauteur.

"Well, I'll leave them anyway. And if you should want to get up for anything at all," Mertie added delicately, "you'd better not try it alone, just ring for me."

"I have no intention of getting up, thank you."

"You can't tell," said Mertie.

Eventually Claudia found herself alone with the power of suggestion. She fought against it and lost. With a vestige of remaining pride, she refrained from ringing for Mertie, but when she finally reached the bathroom, she regretted her decision. She couldn't get out fast enough, the room became a suffocating enclosure of wild creaking and lashing towels. Bathed in a cold blanket of perspiration, she navigated the weaving floor and gained the safety of the bed once more. The two little tablets that Mertie had left winked at her from the night table. She winked back at them, and suddenly they weren't there. Why should they be? Everything movable on the table had slid a little with the tipping of the boat, the tablets could easily have rolled off, and been lost under a piece of furniture. Too late, she remembered Mertie's instructions to take one every three hours. Oh well, an overdose couldn't make her feel any worse than she felt now. She switched off the bed-light, and pulled the covers up to her chin. The hot water bottle really was a comfort, supplying a pleasant island of warmth against her chilled limbs. The fresh air blew in from the window and felt good against her face. The creaking of the boat grew less . . . and less . . .

It didn't seem possible that she could have slept so soundly. "I don't believe it!" she said flatly, when David told her it was after midnight, and felt injured when he proved it to her. "How could you have left me alone all this time?" she reproached him.

He sat down on the edge of the bed and took her hand. "I didn't. I came back twice to see how you were, and you were snoring away, dead to the world, so I tiptoed out again."

"I don't snore," she said. "What have you been doing all by yourself? And how was the grouse?" (Amazing that she could say the word without her inside turning upside down.) Silently, she mouthed the word "cheese", and all it did was make her look as if she was smiling. She felt as good as new.

"You're feeling better," David discovered at the same moment.

"I feel fine!" she exulted and sat up in bed and punched the pillows against her back. "It was just a touch of ptomaine."

"Nonsense. How could you have got ptomaine? We both ate the same things at lunch."

"It could have been the oysters last night at the hotel."

"They didn't upset me."

"That's because you had clams."

He was almost convinced. "As long as you weren't seasick," he said, "I forgive you."

She decided to let actions speak louder than words. "You didn't tell me how the grouse was."

"Excellent. The dining steward sent you

his deepest regrets. He said it was too bad that madame wasn't a good sailor."

"And you let him think so?" she demanded in outrage.

"Well, it sort of looked like an open and shut case, if you know what I mean. Incidentally, I bumped into the Woodburns. They have the suite next door."

"Who are the Woodburns?"

"We met them at Julia and Hartley's one night at dinner."

"Weren't they supposed to be very influential? He was the head of some soft drink or other?"

"No, those were somebody else. The Woodburns had just come back from a trip round the world on their private yacht. A nice elderly couple."

"Oh yes, I remember. Elderly, but youthful. And so frightfully well bred that they said thoid for third."

"The same. They asked us to join them at lunch tomorrow, and I said we would if you were feeling better."

"Oh dear," she thought, "cheating shows, now I'll have to get some more pills to be on the safe side." Aloud, she said, casually, "I'm sure it would please the dining-steward to see us at a table with friends. Important friends with private yachts."

"He won't see us. The Woodburns eat in the café, they wouldn't be caught dead in the main dining-room."

"Oh," said Claudia in a small voice.

"What's the matter?"

"Nothing. Not a thing," she evaded quickly.

She lay awake, long after David's breathing came to her, light and steady, above the sporadic creaking. Why had she let him think that she had known all along that the café was for snobs, instead of the other way round? It wasn't lying exactly, but it wasn't completely honest either. Any more than it was completely honest to have told him about taking the seasick pills, because the truth of the matter was, if she hadn't been seasick, they wouldn't have cured her. "I'll confess about the café before the trip is over," she decided, "but I'm going to tell him about the pills the first thing in the morning," which wasn't too frightfully honest at that, since it was highly probable that she'd need a whole bottle of them to get her through the trip, and he'd be bound to find out sooner or later that he was married to a woman with a squeamish stomach and clay feet. "I'm certainly not as nice underneath as I seem to be on the surface," she reflected sombrely. "I still have quite a lot of work to do with myself." It wasn't anything large, but it was those little odds and ends that could creep up and undermine a marriage before you knew what was happening. Like the first couple of ants in a kitchen. If you didn't get after them right away, they'd multiply like mad, and be into everything. That was another of the reasons, she thought, as the two pills wafted her off again on pleasantly disjointed clouds, that it was so wonderful suddenly to have enough money to do over the little hip roof house from top to bottom. By the time they finished the remodelling they'd not only have cows in the barns, but there wouldn't be a wasp left in the attic, or a termite in the cellar, or a single tiny ant crawling out of a crack looking for mischief . . .

In the morning, she remembered having a lovely dream about the library panelling. She told David about it the moment she opened her eyes. He was immediately interested. "Was it nice?" he wanted to know.

"Beautiful. The wood was the colour of honey, exactly as Candy described it."

"Why didn't you wake me up to see it?"

She giggled. "Why didn't you open the door and walk in? It's your house as much as mine."

"So it is. Then why stand on ceremony? Shall I visit you, or would you like to visit me?"

"What time is it?" she asked doubtfully.

"Half-past seven."

"Is it safe?"

"Safe how?"

"Matthew. He's sure to be bouncing in any minute."

In answer, David prudently locked both doors en route to her bed. "How do you feel?" he asked as an afterthought.

"Fit as a fiddle."

He eyed her appraisingly, leaning on one elbow. "You look as fit as a fiddle."

"I wonder what a fiddle's got not to be fit about anyway?"

"Wonder later."

What with the library panelling and one thing and another, she'd forgotten all about confessing to the pills. "Anyway," she murmured, "I guess there aren't any ants in this marriage."

He thought she said pants, and as it made quite some sense, he let it go at that, and so did she.

3

POSSIBLY David was right in his contention that seasickness was largely a state of mind, because there were so many things to do before getting up, including breakfast, that she didn't have time to think of herself, and consequently she continued to feel fine, even after orange juice and pancakes and a huge pot of coffee. To begin with, Hawkins deposited a large stack of reading matter on each of their night-tables, a quick scrutiny of which disclosed an impressively engraved passenger list, a complete programme of the day's activities, a puzzle involving the names of flowers, an ocean newspaper, and an invitation to join the Captain for cocktails that evening.

"Life was never like this at home," said Claudia. "Lunch with the Woodburns, there's a movie this afternoon we've been waiting to see, a cocktail party before dinner, and horse races after. Which leaves no time for the concert in the lounge, ha, ha.—What flower of three syllables involves a letter of the alphabet, an exclamation and a part of the body?"

"Peony," said David, immersed in yesterday's stock quotations.

"P-oh-knee. Of course. I have the hang of it now. Row-die-den-drum. . . . Few-sure. . . . Pan-see. . . . Daffy-dill. . . . Two-lip. . . . John-quill. . . ."

"Could you do your puzzle to yourself, please?"

"I've lost interest, it's too easy."

"There'll be a stickler stuck in somewhere."

"How do you know?"

"There always is."

"I've just come to it. I can't think of any flower with six syllables. Can you?"

"Sure," he said promptly. "Minxiorinbunda."

"You're making it up. Oh, well, I'll put it aside and take another whack at it later. What a long passenger list, and what a lot of titles! Do you see us? Look."

"Read us to me," he humoured her.

"*Mr. David Naughton*. And under that, Mrs. Naughton, without the 'David', which is rather abrupt, but I suppose they have to leave something to the imagination. And under that, Master Matthew Naughton, Master Michael Naughton, and Governess. We're quite a crowd—" her voice trailed off. She was thinking, "Bobby's name would have made us complete."

David reached across the space between the beds. How did he always know what she was thinking? "He'd have loved this trip, wouldn't he?" she said softly.

"Yes."

"Eleven. We wouldn't have had to treat him like a baby, the way we do Matthew."

"No."

"I love you, David."

"I love you too, darling."

The names on the passenger list blurred before her vision. "Mr. Woodburn's first name is only Henry," she said, clearing her throat. "You'd think it would be something much more impressive, travelling with a manservant, plus a personal maid for his wife. I call that a needless extravagance—couldn't one do for both?"

"We'll ask them at lunch."

"What time is it?"

"Five past ten."

"No! Already? And we're still in bed?"

"It's only five past nine, our time. We're gaining an hour each day."

"I forgot it's five hours later in London than New York. Coming back, though, we'll lose an hour, and that'll get us home faster."

"I thought you were enjoying yourself so much?"

"I am."

"Are you sure you feel all right this morning?"

"Fine." ("I'll let you know how fine after I get up," she amended silently.)

"It's a little rough this morning," he mentioned helpfully.

"But I love it rough," she insisted, with a false smile.

"I'm going to make a confession," he said bluntly.

She felt the colour mount warmly to her cheeks. The confession was on the other foot, if he only knew it.

"When you turned pea-green last night," David continued, "I was deeply disappointed in you. If you were the type to get seasick, I'd have never married you."

"I know just what you mean, I wouldn't have married me either. I think I'll take my bath this evening," she quickly changed the

85

subject, "as long as I have to wash my neck low down anyway, for the pink net. Not every cloud has a silver lining. It's a good thing I didn't wear my yellow last night, now I can wear it tomorrow night."

"You've got problems."

"I have. I had no idea we were going to be so social. Even wearing my suit again at the end, I'm one night short of a dress."

"That should be interesting," said David.

"Maybe I'm not completely over the ptomaine," she tried him out tentatively. "Having to stay in bed one more night would solve everything."

"It certainly would, because I'd break your neck."

"Now I know exactly where I stand," she thought unhappily. "This is no time for honesty."

She was about to slip into her robe and slippers and go in search of Mertie, and more pills, when there was a discreet knock on the door. She hopped back into bed with alacrity.

"Well, if it isn't our governess with her two little charges," said David, who seemed to be feeling unusually full of good-will and jocosity. "Good morning, Master Matthew!"

Matthew's mouth slithered around self-consciously as he tried not to grin. He tugged at Bertha's arm. "Come on, let's go."

"One minute until I talk to Mama," said Bertha, looking like some strange order of nun in her flowing veil. "My both children are fine," she reported. "They sleep all night, and ate big breakfasts, and did everything, and now we go on deck until lunch-time."

"I'm glad about 'everything'," Claudia murmured.

"Hurry up, Bertha," Matthew yanked at her impatiently.

"What's the big rush?" David wanted to know.

"I want to play ping-pong, and throw rings."

"But if any grown-ups want to use the games," Claudia instructed, "mind your manners and stay right away."

"That is why we are starting early," Bertha explained, "nobody will be there." Obviously, she had neglected to set her clock forward, and Claudia smiled to think what a comedown it would be for her to discover that she wasn't the first on deck the way she'd always been the first in the park.

"They have a whole new world to discover," David said, after they had gone.

"A whole new world right in the middle of thousands of miles of sun and air and ocean."

"Would you like to be a child again?" Claudia asked him curiously.

"At very wide-spaced moments, and this is one of those moments." He leaped out of bed. "I'll go up and join them. I promised Matthew he could use his binoculars. Maybe we can sight another boat, or a school of porpoises."

"Bless you. Real playmates," Claudia spoofed. "Stop! Don't!" she warded him off. "I mean it, I think it's wonderful what the sea-air has done for your fatherhood already! Go ahead, I'll wait in bed till you're out—"

He was dressed in no time. "Where'll I meet you?" he remembered to ask at the door.

"I'll be in the deck chair. It'll be the safest," she added, with a vestige of honesty.

She thought how ambidextrous he was— terribly attractive both in sports clothes and black tie. The middle thirties, she reflected, were more becoming to a man than to a woman, especially if he kept his figure, as David did. She'd kept her figure, too, though it was nothing to brag about in this day and age of burgeoning bosoms. Conservatively speaking, she was neat but not gaudy. At least she could get away without wearing a bra and still look as if she wore one, which David said was much more desirable than vice versa. She didn't need to put on a completely new face every day, either: it was a shame to waste the virgin expanse of the vanity-table with a lone jar of cleansing cream and a box of powder. All of which introspection was nothing but a cowardly evasion of braving the bathroom. Gingerly, she explored the possible effects of a perpendicular position. So far so good. "Maybe I'd better make hay and get my bath behind me," she decided. She might not feel up to it later on, and besides, it would look better for Mertie to find a proper number of used towels.

The panel above the bath had as many knobs as a soda-fountain. After first turning on the shower by accident and getting her hair sopping wet, she selected a judicious mixture of hot and cold salt water. It gushed in as if the ocean wanted her to know that her slightest wish was its command, so she said to it, "If you really want to oblige, just don't play so rough, please."

Apparently it was the nature of oceans to play rough indoors. The water dashed up against one end of the bath in green waves, and then went spanking off to the other end. She didn't wait to sit down: she got in and out like Matthew washing his face. Yesterday, it had seemed to be gilding the lily to have bells in the bathroom, today she understood why they were there.

"You rang, Mrs. Naughton?" Mertie gave one look at Claudia's face. "Come, let me pat you dry and help you back to bed."

Claudia swallowed more than her pride. "I can manage, if you'd just get me a few more of those pills you gave me last night, Mertie."

"I'd love to," Mertie complied, as she got busy with a towel, "except that I gave the last of them to another lady not ten minutes ago. It seems she had plenty of them in a little white envelope, but her maid tossed the envelope by mistake into some empty flower-boxes."

There couldn't be too many personal maids floating around. "Mrs. Woodburn?" Claudia queried feebly.

Mertie dropped the towel in her surprise. "How did you guess?"

"We're having lunch with the Woodburns."

Mertie was so beguiled by the social implications that she failed to register the complete lack of logic in the explanation. "Since you're friends," she said, "I could easily ask for a few of the pills back."

"No, don't," said Claudia. By some subtle and not wholly admirable magic, Mrs. Woodburn's inadequacy seemed suddenly to make her feel a lot better. "I don't need any, really."

Mertie looked doubtful. "I wouldn't be too sure, there's a bit of weather coming up, according to last reports."

"But weather doesn't bother me. I told you I never get seasick," Claudia insisted. "It's those bad oysters I had the night before we sailed, and this is just the tail end of them."

"Oh," said Mertie, blankly, like a person discovering she'd been going round in a circle.

"In fact, I'm not going back to bed, after all. I'm going up on deck."

Mertie continued to have doubts. "I hope you can make it," she said.

"I hope so too," said Claudia.

She managed to get dressed, but half-way along the corridor, she almost turned back, afraid to face the ignominy of becoming ill in public. However, she didn't want to face

Mertie, either, so she staggered on, feeling as if she were climbing sideways uphill.

Once on deck, the fresh air cleared her head and put some bones back into her knees. The steward caught sight of her, and hastened to unfold the blanket and arrange the pillows. "Good morning to you," he said cheerily. "Mr. Naughton said to tell you he's up on the sun-deck, in case you want to join him."

"Not just yet," said Claudia. Swathed like a cocoon, she lay back and saw the ocean slowly rise above the railing of the deck and then dip slowly out of sight again. Quickly, she reached for the book that David had left on his chair. Reading wasn't a smart idea, either. She settled on watching the parade of people, tramping past as if they were going somewhere. Some were walking arm in arm, others were alone. When the boat tipped, they tipped, laughing, as if it were a game.

The professional relaxer suddenly emerged into the outdoors, with an unbecoming scarf over her head. She plopped into her chair and closed her eyes while the steward wrapped her up. "I'll have lunch on deck," she told him thinly. "Dry toast and tea and celery."

"Yes, madame. At what time?"

"What time is it now?"

"Just short of noon, madame."

"I didn't have any breakfast," she said plaintively. "I might feel better if I ate something."

"Thank you, madame. I'll see it's brought up at once."

The woman opened her eyes eventually, and turned her head in Claudia's direction. "I suppose you're one of those people who don't mind rough weather," she said quite nastily.

"I don't like it when it's too smooth," Claudia admitted with becoming modesty.

"The last trip, I never left my bed the entire crossing."

"That's too bad," said Claudia.

"I've always been a very poor sailor," the woman said, with a hint of pride.

"She's not a professional relaxer," Claudia changed her opinion. "She makes a profession of being seasick, and I'd rather not be around." She unscrambled her feet from the blanket. "I think I'll go and look for my husband," she excused herself.

She started off, and with every step she gained assurance and spring. She was like a vampire, absorbing strength from the weakness of her fellow-beings—first Mrs.

Woodburn, and then her pallid neighbour in the deck chair. She didn't know how it worked, but it did; she felt fine by contrast. David was undoubtedly right: seasickness was a state of mind.

She came to a steep narrow flight of outside steps leading up to the sun-deck. She hesitated. Her head was clear, but not that clear, and her stomach was barely learning to hold its own against the insinuating motion of the boat. Stairs would only be asking for trouble. She walked on.

Without warning, the motion suddenly changed, and she began lurching against the rail, trying to look as if it were fun. "By Jove, but it's getting choppy out there," someone called to someone else, and she couldn't have agreed more. She was wishing she wasn't so far from her home-chair, when she came in sight of Bertha's long blue veil floating out on the breeze as she pushed Michael in his folding perambulator. She quickened her pace until she caught up with them. Bertha was manifestly pleased to see her up and about, and adjured Michael to say "hello, mother".

"Hello," said Claudia. "Where's Matthew?"

Bertha gestured towards a pair of deck

chairs set back in a protected enclosure. "He has made friends with a nice lady, I was just going to tell him it is time to get ready to eat."

"He oughtn't to make a pest of himself," Claudia demurred.

"She likes him," said Bertha simply. "She says she likes to hear him talk."

"She must be crazy," said Claudia. "You stay here while I see what it's all about."

The pair of them were so engrossed in a game of tick-tack-toe that they did not look up at her approach. At first glance, Claudia judged Matthew's new-found companion to be a mature, sensible person, who didn't fancy herself romping around on a child's intellectual plane. There were such grown-ups, of course, but they were mostly a little fey, like women who went in for cats, referring to them as "interesting people" or "delightful individuals". David, no less than she, loved animals to the point of even loving skunks, but they weren't quaint about it. It was just short of being quaint for a complete stranger to be playing tick-tack-toe with Matthew. "I hope," Claudia offered politely, "that my son isn't being a nuisance."

Matthew was annoyed at the interruption.

95

"Oh, mother, do you have to talk? I was just winning!"

"I'm sorry, but Bertha's waiting for you. It's time for lunch."

"Never mind, we'll have another go at it tomorrow." The woman put aside the pad and pencils, and gave him a friendly pat. "Be a good fellow and hurry along."

"Okay." Matthew departed reluctantly. The woman waited until he was out of earshot before she turned to Claudia. "I assure you, he hasn't been a bit of a nuisance. You see, I've never played tick-tack-toe before, and Matthew tells me that, with a little practice, I shall be quite good at it." She had an extremely nice smile, in spite of not awfully good dental work, and her hands, Claudia noticed, before she slipped them back into cotton gloves, were large and nicely bony. She was, on the whole, one of those pleasantly unremarkable women, who, were she an American, Claudia would have readily identified as the ideal schoolmistress, or the kind of indispensable, non-youthful secretary that was David's so far unrealized dream.

"I've just been a month in New York visiting my daughter and my grandson, who is Matthew's age exactly," the woman mentioned quietly, as if in answer to Claudia's unspoken questioning. "Christopher's teeth are in the same state, and they both seem to use the same expressions when they talk."

Belatedly, Claudia returned her smile. "I knew there must be some kind of bond between you, because Matthew doesn't take to strangers as a rule. And I'm not just saying it, I really mean it. You see, we had two Great Danes—" She heard herself, and stopped short. She couldn't abide people who bored other people with personal reminiscences.

"Great Danes are quite wonderful," Matthew's friend encouraged her to go on, "though not too bright."

"No, and because they're so huge, very few people realize that they're big sissies."

The woman nodded in agreement. "Actually, they think they're lap dogs."

"That's what I meant," said Claudia. "Ours didn't care whose lap it was, and everyone was always so flattered that it became a standing joke for us to say that they hardly ever took to strangers." She stopped herself again. What possessed her to keep on chattering? "I went a long way round to make my point," she faltered, "but, anyway, don't let Matthew be a nuisance."

"I shan't."

The conversation seemed to have come to an end. "Good-bye," said Claudia, after a moment.

"Good-bye," the woman returned.

Claudia felt as if she ought to say something else, but there wasn't anything else to say.

David was waiting in his chair for her. "Well, where've you been?"

"Walking. Where've you been?"

"Looking for you."

"You didn't kill yourself."

"I went to see if you were still in bed."

"Why should I be in bed?"

"You shouldn't," he took for granted.

She directed his eyes towards their supine neighbour. Her frugal tray, with a remaining stalk of celery, was on the vacant chair beside her. Her eyes were closed, waiting for her tea to disagree with her. "How would you like to be married to *that*, mister?"

"I wouldn't."

"You had a mighty narrow escape," she informed him silently.

He glanced at his watch. "It's one o'clock. If we're to meet the Woodburns at one-thirty for cocktails, we'd better get washed."

She knew one last moment of panic as the walls of the bathroom closed in on her, and the towels swung out at her. She made short work of it, and sought the comparative airiness of the drawing-room, where the children were having lunch, with Bertha in sole and triumphant attendance.

"Do I have to eat in here every day?" Matthew demanded.

"My heart aches for you," said Claudia. Firmly, she removed the bottle of ketch-up from the table. He let out a wail of protest. "But I have to have some over my spinach!"

"That's what you think," said Claudia brutally.

"I had it yesterday."

"Yesterday was different."

"Why?"

"Because."

"Mamma is right," Bertha said. "It is terrible to put that stuff on nice meat and vegetables."

There was a little too much talk of food. Quickly, Claudia went back to the bedroom. David had changed to a conservative flannel jacket. She regarded him in dismay. "Oh dear, I suppose I should change, too."

"You don't have to. What for, you look fine," he said without so much as glancing at her.

"Let's face it. I don't. Everybody seems to be wearing knitted things. Maybe I should buy one of those sweaters out in the lobby. With mink round the collar."

"Go ahead and do it."

"Some have pearls instead of mink."

"Get pearls, then."

"I don't like them. A sweater's a sweater, and should know its place. Shall I wear my hat?"

"Do we have to go through that again?"

"I forgot to tell you. Matthew found a friend. They were playing tick-tack-toe."

"That's good. I noticed quite a few children on board."

"This is not children, it's a middle-aged English woman. In a beret."

"She sounds screwy."

"Because she wears a beret?" Claudia took umbrage.

"In general."

"I know. But she's not, really."

"She must be. How can an Englishwoman swallow Matthew?"

"She has an American grandchild, who probably drops his gs, and uses ketch-up, too."

"Watch it, anyway."

"We don't have to. She's just a nice quiet person, who wears cotton gloves, and sensible oxfords. I was telling her about Bluff and Bluster."

A shadow crossed David's face. "Dogs ought to have longer lives," he said.

"Yes."

They fell silent. "Come on, let's go," he said at length. "Half the afternoon shot to hell with lunch," he added dourly. "I wish I hadn't let us in for it."

"So do I," said Claudia devoutly. "Do we have time for another turn round the deck?"

"We'd only have to come right back again. We're meeting them for cocktails next door. Anyway, since when are you so fond of walking?"

She wasn't. But he had such an unsullied opinion of her at this moment, that she thought it best not to mention the word "air". "Oh, I just thought a little exercise might sharpen our appetites," she said.

The boat gave her a shove. She slid across the floor. "You don't need anything to sharpen yours," he told her, as he caught her deftly and gave her a kiss. She was glad to know that her face had told no tales.

It was somewhat of a shock to discover that Mrs. Woodburn's face told no tales either. She had changed not at all since their last meeting; she still looked like a bright little grey-haired apple, and her welcoming handshake was as hardy as could be. "My dear, I was so glad to learn" (only she said loin), "that you and your husband were on board, but I'm sorry you were ill last night. Are you feeling better?"

Claudia gave David a mental kick under a table that wasn't there. Did he have to go around advertising the state of her health? She met Mrs. Woodburn's seasoned blue eyes without flinching. "It was just a touch of ptomaine," she said. "But how are you feeling, Mrs. Woodburn?"

"I?" Mrs. Woodburn laughed lightly, and in her cheery reply there wasn't the faintest hint of the pills that she had literally robbed Claudia of that morning. "I'm an old veteran of the seas, child. Nothing ever bothers me."

"Oh," said Claudia, gulping down her

amazement that anyone so well-born could be such a liar. And then Mr. Woodburn, knife-lean, and finely edged, the way David would probably be in his sixties, put his arm round his wife and said proudly, "This is a great little sailor. Three trips round the world on a small yacht without missing a single meal is something of a record."

"It certainly is," said Claudia in a small voice. Her own private struggle to preserve David's respect for a mere five days on a big ocean liner was as nothing compared with the endless vigilance and fortitude attending Mrs. Woodburn's monumental deception. "Poor thing," she thought compassionately, and wondered whether husbands were worth all the sacrifice and anguish.

"I wonder what's keeping Linda," Mrs. Woodburn had already changed the subject. "My niece, Mrs. Harwell," she explained. "I asked Lady Gresham to join us for lunch too, but she stays very much by herself since Lord Gresham's death. Henry, don't you think you ought to telephone Linda's room, and see if anything's wrong?"

"She'll be along," Mr. Woodburn said easily, "but there's no need to wait for our cocktails. What will you have, my dear?"

Claudia shook her head. "Nothing, thank you."

"A little sherry," Mrs. Woodburn suggested, all solicitude. "It won't upset you, it's very soothing."

"You should know," Claudia returned silently. Aloud she said, "I'd rather just have the canapes."

She selected a tidy assortment of the most indigestible variety, aware that she was scoring a minor victory in this undeclared battle of wits between herself and her hostess. "Only please don't go round making trouble down there," she exhorted a succulent disc of truffle and goose-liver. "They're delicious," she enticed Mrs. Woodburn. "Aren't you having any?"

Mrs. Woodburn got out of it deftly. "I always watch my calories on board ship," she said.

"But you don't have to worry about gaining weight, you're tiny!" (I'd hate me, but she deserves it.)

"That's the trouble, my bones are small," Mrs. Woodburn adroitly held her position, "which means that I have to be doubly careful. My husband would divorce me if I turned into one of those tubby old ladies, wouldn't you, Henry?"

"What was that, dear? I was talking to David, I didn't hear what you said."

Her aplomb tottered a little; it was one of those longish, involved sentences that would only peter out with repetition. "Not of any importance, really, dear," she said hastily, and began a fresh conversation entirely. "Are you planning to do much travelling on the Continent, Mrs. Naughton?"

"No," said Claudia. "We'll be in London for a week, and then we'll go straight to Switzerland and stay there until the end of March."

"How sensible. The mountain air will do the children so much good," said Mrs. Woodburn tactfully, as if she didn't know that it was David who was the one to be done good to. "And after Switzerland, Paris?"

"Yes, but not for long, we return early in April."

"But Spring is so lovely in Paris!"

"It's lovely at home, too."

"You're quite right. New York is at its best during April and May."

"We don't live in New York," Claudia told her. "We were lucky, we found an old house with beautiful meadow land just outside Greenwich."

"Ah yes, I seem to recall Julia saying that you'd rented a little farm up there near your husband's partner."

"We bought it," said Claudia. "We're in the middle of remodelling it, which is another reason we don't want to stay abroad too long."

"Oh, I see," said Mrs. Woodburn, in a voice that showed clearly that she didn't see at all. Her impeccable breeding, however, did not permit her to ask what disposition had been made of Julia's and Hartley's beautiful town house, but Claudia thought that, since they both had difficult husbands to live up to, she might as well soften, and explain that Julia had willed the house to an elderly cousin. "Julia and her wonderful flair for presents," Claudia had rejoiced to David. "Her last and best was not burdening us with a five-storey mansion to run."

"She must have known," David had agreed, equally touched, "how we'd have hated to live in it, and hated even more to sell it."

They'd meant it, but Claudia wondered if it might not sound like sour grapes to Mrs.

Woodburn, who seemed to be able to run houses with one hand and her eyes shut. "They're going to spend February and March at their villa in the South of France," David had mentioned last night, and Claudia remembered Julia and Hartley visiting the Woodburns at their summer home in Rhode Island, and she also had a vague memory that they had flown out to the Woodburn ranch in Wyoming, where Hartley had broken his ankle. All of which tended to reduce the problem of a single New York house to a mere nothing, but anyway, there wasn't time to explain about Julia's leaving it to her cousin, because Linda Harwell came in at that moment and Mrs. Woodburn got busy with introductions.

"Aunt Emily told me you were on board, how nice to meet you."

Claudia was susceptible to voices, and Mrs. Harwell had a low, rich one, and looked exactly as one would imagine a niece of Mrs. Woodburn's to look, almost too patrician, if anything. She was tall, nearly as tall as David, and her figure—the word came unbidden into Claudia's mind—was willowy. At first glance, she seemed as plain as Matthew's tick-tack-toe acquaintance, with her hair drawn straight back and twisted into a knot at the nape of her neck. On second glance, however, she was far from plain. Her clear, pale skin and unpretentious hair-do spelled the ultimate in careful grooming, and her simple grey wool dress, though not notably fashionable, carried the same mark of restrained and expensive tailoring that had always distinguished Julia's wardrobe. Claudia battled an instinctive distrust of such composed perfection, and put it down to sheer, unadulterated envy.

"I hope," Mrs. Harwell was apologizing, "that I haven't held everyone up. Greg wasn't very quick with his spinach."

"That sounds familiar," Claudia said.

Mrs. Harwell turned to her with a smile. "My aunt told me that you had a little boy too. We must arrange for them to meet. Greg needs companionship of his own age."

"So does Matthew."

"I wish I hadn't promised to take him to the movies this afternoon, as a special treat, but perhaps tomorrow we could bring them together."

"Yes, do work out something," Mrs. Woodburn urged. "What will you have to drink, Linda?"

"I don't think I'd better have anything, Aunt Emily. The motion of the boat seemed to have upset my equilibrium this morning."

"Why, Linda, how unusual for you to be seasick!" Mrs. Woodburn said, quite eagerly.

"Isn't it? I even had to ask my stewardess for some dramamine tablets."

"And do they really help?" Mrs. Woodburn enquired, as if butter wouldn't melt in her mouth.

"They certainly helped me," Linda said. She turned again to Claudia. "Are you one of those indestructible people like my aunt who feels that mal-de-mer is an ignominious declaration of weakness?"

Claudia flashed a message to her hostess: "I'm ready for a truce; if you confess to the pills, I will." But Mrs. Woodburn showed no desire to play ball. "I think it's high time we thought about luncheon. That is, if our two invalids feel up to it?" she added playfully.

"Then there's another one of me!" Linda laughed. Her eyes sought David's. "Oh, but not you, surely?"

"No, I'm afraid I belong to the enemy faction. But Claudia had a touch of ptomaine last night from some oysters she'd eaten." He put his arm round her with so much love and trust, that she felt abased for having tricked him into believing the oyster story. Why couldn't she have been as simple and natural as Linda Harwell about the whole thing, pills included? It wasn't as if it were necessary to make a production of it, like her neighbour in the deck chair, nor go to the other extreme and emulate the machinations of Mrs. Woodburn, who was unfortunate enough to be tied up to a yacht-happy husband. But there was no reason to lie to David, except for the one small drawback that she'd never hear the end of it for as long as she lived. "I don't care, I'm going to tell him anyway," she resolved anew. "I'm going to tell him I'm sorry to destroy his illusions, but the oysters had nothing to do with it, I was just plain god-awful seasick, whether he likes it or not."

Now was not the time, of course, to bare one's soul in front of strangers. She'd always found that there was no place quite as suitable as bed for things like that.

Her decision made, she felt surprisingly light-hearted; even the risk of lunching in public ceased to fill her with trepidation, and actually, the café turned out to be easier on one's stomach than the main dining-room. It was small and intimate, and opened up on to the top deck, with the riotous sun-flecked ocean seeming to pour in through the wide windows. "It's so much pleasanter," Mrs. Woodburn murmured elliptically, meaning that nobody who was anybody ate downstairs with the masses.

According to an inconspicuous notation on the menu, there was an extra charge for service in the café, although there apparently wasn't any difference in the food. You could get a big blob of caviar in the main dining-room.

"I envy you," Linda Harwell said, as she watched Claudia add a generous portion of chopped onion to the blob, but Mrs. Woodburn was content to stand with half a grapefruit, and said that she had got out of the habit of eating luncheon during the war. Claudia wondered what the war had to do with it, but she had to take her hat off to Mrs. Woodburn—bringing in the war, willy nilly, was a masterly stroke.

"There's Bill Hendricks coming in," Mr. Woodburn said. "He seems to be alone. Should we ask him to join us, Emily?"

"By all means. I'm sure the Naughtons must know him."

"I know who he is," said David, which was more than Claudia knew.

Mr. Hendricks joined them with a delighted little fling of his arms. He said he'd just had a swim and a massage, and felt tip-top. Superficially, he looked and smelled tip-top, exuding the nice, clean fragrance of cologne. Yet something kept him from being really handsome: it was hard to know what it was. Maybe it was because the flesh round his jaw and under his chin was nowhere nearly as firm as David's.

He took possession of his chair and Claudia's hand at the same time. "Lovely, lovely," he announced, in beaming approval, and then turned to Mrs. Harwell on his left. "Linda. My dream girl."

"Order your luncheon," said Linda brusquely.

"Consommé and an omelette fines herbes," he said, without bothering with the menu. His hand covered Claudia's again. "Now tell me, you young and lovely creature, where have you been all my life?"

It was difficult to eat with one hand, and, besides, she was awkward at small talk, especially silly small-talk. "Nowhere," she said, with an uncomfortable feeling that her smirk was a little like Matthew's.

You would have thought that she had said something excruciatingly witty. "Oh, come now," she wanted to shut him up, "I'm not so young, and I'm certainly not lovely, so don't be an ass."

"Who is that Bill Hendricks, anyway, besides having polo ponies?" she asked David when they were walking back to their room after lunch.

"The second rate son of a first rate man. His father was President of Cosmopolitan Steel."

"Isn't it funny how often that happens? And the other way round, too. What about Mrs. Harwell?"

"What about her?"

"Why is she travelling without her husband?"

"It's more convenient. He's dead."

"Oh dear."

"What's the matter?"

"I didn't want to feel sorry for her, I thought maybe she was divorced, but I didn't know she was a widow. Long?"

"About a year. There was quite some notoriety about it. He was pretty high up in

Washington, and got into some sort of mess, and blew his brains out."

"How awful! How can a woman ever really get over a thing like that?"

"From what the Woodburns told me, she hasn't. That's why she's going to spend the rest of the winter with them in the South of France."

"Is she Mr. or Mrs.' niece?"

"Mrs."

"Not English."

"Apparently not."

"She sounds English. And really terribly attractive. But I don't grudge it to her now. It's even worse than being a widow from natural causes like kidney trouble or pneumonia."

"Or T.B.," David said.

Although it was a shock to hear him come out with it like that, it was a good sign because they hadn't, either of them, been able to bring his illness into the open and talk about it easily and normally. Pride had kept him silent, but with her it had been fear, always fear. Even yesterday, she had walked on the boat, stalked by a nag of terror that he might have a "flare-up" while they were away. Suddenly, now, the fear lost its power

114

over her. He was alive and well, and her heart sent up a prayer of thanks. "Oh, David, I'm so lucky," she breathed, "and after all the things that have happened to us, I never thought I'd be able to say it and really mean it."

David's voice was husky. "We both needed this trip. It's going to be a hell of a fine holiday," he answered obliquely.

They had reached their suite. "I guess the children have had their nap and are up on deck, there's no one here," said Claudia.

"That's mighty obliging of them," said David.

"I don't think the movie can be anything we'd enjoy, especially if Mrs. Harwell's taking her little boy to see it as a 'special treat'."

He had to have his wits about him to catch up with her on that one, but it turned out that he was far ahead of her.

Afterwards, she thought it might be the auspicious moment to get her confession about being seasick over and done with, but it seemed a pity to spoil the tag end of such a lovely afternoon. It was bad enough to have to get up and get dressed for the Captain's cocktail party.

It was a small world on board ship, because the first people they bumped into at the party were Linda Harwell and Mr. Hendricks, and the last guests to arrive were the Woodburns, and they all greeted each other like old friends. In fact, Mrs. Woodburn buried the hatchet right off the bat. "You look so much better than at luncheon, my dear," she said. "And very charming, too."

"I feel much better and very charming," Claudia dimpled, though she didn't have a dimple to her name. She drained the last of an over-sized glass of tomato juice that Bill Hendricks had managed to get for her, instead of a cocktail, and realized suddenly that small-talk no longer presented a hurdle; she could hold her own with the silliest of it, without feeling clumsy and embarrassed.

She felt the touch of lips against her cheek. "Oh, it's only you," she said in disappointment. "Bill, please!" (It was first names, now, without a second thought.)

"Did I tell you before that you look enchanting?" he whispered in her ear.

"I'd rather look like Linda," she said. Linda was more than ever willowy in a severe black satin sheath.

"Linda's striking," he agreed, "but not

116

enchanting. You're enchanting. How did you like your 'tomato juice'?"

"Very much. It had a lot of Worcestershire sauce in it. What's so funny?"

"You," he said. "I adore you. Would you like another tomato juice with a lot of Worcestershire sauce in it?"

"Yes, I think I would. It saves explaining that you don't drink if you have a glass in your hand."

"I could eat you up, you're so cute!"

"Don't be a silly ass," she said.

It wasn't until she had finished the second tomato juice that she discovered that it had a lot of vodka in it, too. Or rather, it was David who happened to discover it. Something that Bill said that really wasn't so funny struck her as being inordinately funny, and David left Linda's side to find out why she was laughing so hard. "Two Bloody Marys," Bill Hendricks told him with a grin. "Man-sized."

David frowned. "Claudia doesn't happen to drink."

Bill's grin vanished as his jaw dropped. "You're kidding," he said flatly.

"No he's not, I don't drink," Claudia chirped, but she could have been talking to the wind for all the attention they paid. Bill

Hendricks just kept on staring at David and finally he said, "You mean when she asked for tomato juice, she asked for tomato juice?"

"I mean just that," said David.

Bill threw back his head and roared, but David seemed to have lost his sense of humour. "Come along, Claudia." He took her arm. "If you want to go to the horse-races, we'd better not have dinner too late."

"Horse-races!" Bill said. "You don't want to go to those toy horse-races."

"I don't, particularly, but Claudia might find it amusing."

"Oh now wait a moment, darling, if you don't want to go, we won't go," Claudia said virtuously, "and I know you don't like that big noisy dining-room, so we won't eat there, either. Besides, Bill's already asked us for dinner. Everybody we know will be there, the Woodburns, and Linda, and Lady Gresham—we almost know her because she was supposed to have lunch with us—and who else, did you say, Bill?"

"The Nicholsons and Barry Conwell.—And I just want to express my humble opinion, Mr. Naughton dear, that a couple of drinks didn't do your little bride one tiny bit of harm."

"Who said it did?" Claudia demanded belligerently. "I feel simply wonderful!"

"A little too wonderful," said David grimly.

She felt terribly hurt. "Don't you want me to have a good time?"

"Certainly he does," Bill said. He clapped David on the back. "Don't you, old chap?"

If there was one thing David hated it was to be clapped on the back. "Look, dear," Claudia jumped in hastily, "those are the Nicholsons over there. Talking to the Captain in green. I mean Mrs. Nicholson is in green, and she thinks you're very handsome. And you know who Barry Conwell is, but which one is Lady Gresham?"

Bill Hendricks looked round the crowded room. "I guess she hasn't come yet," he said, "but I'll go and see."

"Claudia, we're not barging in on his dinner-party at the last minute," David said in a voice that brooked no argument. "Now come along."

"I think you're being stuffy," she told him, drawing herself up to her full height. "Very stuffy indeed. And we're not barging in. Bill says we're part of their crowd, we belong, and that from now on, we don't ever have to be alone again."

"Very well, if that's what you want."

She was close to tears; all her feelings seemed to be going to extremes. "It isn't what I want, darling, it's what he *said*!"

Linda Harwell drifted over towards them. "Bill just told me that you were dining with us. How very nice. I was rather dreading the evening up to now."

"So was I," said David.

Claudia bestowed a dazzling smile at him for giving in so sweetly, and then she stopped smiling as, rather mistily, she tried to analyze a simple statement that wasn't as simple as it sounded. She wondered what he meant by it.

She didn't have time to wonder long, because amid much affectionate leave-taking, the party began to break up, only to reassemble, in large part, at various tables in the café. The room was lovely at night, and gay with intimacy, except for one or two isolated couples who were trying to look very interested in each other, and very disinterested in the exchange of chatter and laughter going on all round them. "David and I would be all by ourselves like that, if it weren't for the Woodburns," Claudia thought. She felt unexpectedly tender towards the Woodburns; in fact she loved everybody all at once, even Mrs. Nicholson, whom she didn't care for at all, and Barry Conwell, whom she actively disliked because he was so cocksure of himself, and looked muddy round the ears. Mrs. Nicholson, who turned out to be none other than "the *Nicholson*" that David had bought fifty shares from on the stock market last year which paid for Matthew's tonsils by splitting three for one whatever that meant, would have high-hatted anyone as uncouth as Barry Conwell if he didn't happen to be America's proud contribution to the world of letters. For several years, he had been the critics' darling who could do no wrong, but his current novel, audaciously soaring above the mundane shackles of punctuation in every last one of its six hundred pages, had established him among the literary immortals. David had skimmed through the book, and dismissed it as pretentious and young, but Claudia hadn't been able to read beyond the first chapter, and a little of the end, which was supposed to be highly censorable. She had found it merely irritating because it was plain dirty without

121

reason to be. She felt somewhat the same way about Mr. Conwell himself, but maybe she was wrong, because Mrs. Nicholson certainly seemed to be crazy about him, the way she hung on every word he uttered, with her eyes focused on his rather thick and unattractive lips. Not that Mrs. Nicholson was any too attractive herself. Her face was so thin and sharp that one didn't expect her busts to be so big that her low-cut green satin gown had a hard time of it. Linda Harwell's gown was low-cut, too, but her busts behaved like gentlemen, and although she was deep in conversation with David, her eyes were decently focused on the slab of pâté that started off the six-course dinner Bill Hendricks had ordered in advance. "How is it?" he asked Claudia anxiously.

"You sound as if you'd slaved over a hot stove all day," she told him. "It's very good." Truthfully, she didn't think it could compare with caviar, but it turned out that he had caviar up his sleeve, too, mixed through the baked potatoes, which she considered sacrilegious. Besides, so much rich, salty food made her intolerably thirsty, and she couldn't seem to make any headway in getting a glass of water. There was a whole regiment of assorted goblets at her place, but they all got filled up with white wine, red wine and, in due course, champagne. The champagne had the virtue of at least looking like water and being icy cold, but, in the long run, it didn't serve the same purpose as water and the more she drank of it, the more frustrated and depressed she became. She caught David's eye, or rather he caught hers, and out of a clear sky, he shook his head at her and frowned, which depressed her even more, because she couldn't imagine what she'd done to displease him. She leaned across the table and asked him in a perfectly nice way what he was frowning about, but he deliberately ignored her and began talking to Linda Harwell.

She was hurt to the quick, but she wasn't going to let him see how hurt she was. She turned back to Bill. "Where is Lady Gresham?" she asked, in sudden sprightly interest. "I still don't see her, and I think it's such a pretty name, don't you?"

"The Lady or the Gresham?"

"You mean the Lady or the Tiger," she amended, as a story that had been compulsory reading in high-school popped into her head.

Bill Hendricks blinked. "I didn't know about the tiger. I guess neither of them must have come," he concluded.

"They didn't come for lunch either," Claudia recalled.

"I can't speak for the tiger, because I never met him," Bill said, "but ever since her husband died, Lady Gresham never goes anywhere. And I think that's very sad."

"I think so too," said Claudia. "And I think it's sad that I can't have a glass of very cold ice-water."

He was contrite and tender. "Are you thirsty, baby?"

"I'm dying," she told him starkly.

"Waiter!"

The nearest waiter pranced through the air. "Yes, sir!"

"Mrs. Naughton's champagne glass is empty."

"I'm sorry, sir. Thank you, sir."

"Oh dear," said Claudia, "I wanted water."

"I never heard of the stuff," Bill said. "It sounds absolutely poisonous."

Claudia started to protest but she was so thirsty that she was ready to drink anything, and by this time she didn't mind the bubbles so much.

Finally the dessert was borne in, a miniature fairyland of spun sugar, reposing on an immense silver platter. "How poifectly beautiful!" Mrs. Woodburn said. Claudia noticed, however, that she helped herself to an infinitesimal portion. Not that she missed much. When it came right down to it, it was only vanilla ice cream fancied up with macaroons, "All front and no back," Claudia commented, severely.

"You're adorable," said Bill Hendricks. "Let's dance a while, and then we'll take a stroll round the deck. Shall we?"

"I haven't danced for years, I don't know any of the new steps."

"I'll teach you," he said.

For once, she had no inhibitions. She thought it would be wonderful to dance, until the waiter pulled back her chair, and in standing up, she somehow lost her balance. Then, out of the blue, she felt David's arm round her like a vice. She wanted to be flippant and say, "Fancy meeting you here," but her lips felt as thick as Barry Conwell's and the floor suddenly dissolved beneath her feet.

"Oh, David, get me out of here," she gasped in panic. "I'm sea-sick!"

His grip around her waist tightened, quite ungently. "You're not sea-sick," he ground out between his teeth. "You drank too much, you crazy little fool."

Nobody heard him, or thought it in any way unusual that they should return to their suite before joining the others on the dance floor. "Be sure you bring her back, David!" Bill Hendricks called after them.

"Tell Bill I can't dance, I'm seasick," she moaned, after David had helped her to get to bed. "And please, David, ask Mertie to get some of those pills from the doctor—"

"You don't need any pills," he informed her tersely. "You're no more seasick than I am."

This was the most confusing thing that had ever happened to her. Here she was, baring her soul at last, and he didn't believe her. "Oh David, you have to face it even if it destroys your respect for me," she entreated. "You married a woman who gets seasick!"

"I married a real little drunky, that's what I have to face," he corrected. "Two Bloody Marys and five glasses of champagne! Didn't you see me warning you across the table?"

"Yes, but I thought you were frowning at me!" She felt quite relieved and happy now that she knew he hadn't been angry with her, and she also felt deeply righteous because she had confessed about the pills. All at once she loved the whole world again. "You don't have to go to bed, darling," she told him magnanimously. "Go back and dance with Mrs. Nicholson."

"Thank you. You're so kind."

"But, Baby, you might enjoy it. She might split three for one again."

"Sleep it off," he advised her shortly. "I don't understand a word you're saying and neither do you."

"I do so," she denied indignantly. She started to repeat it, but her tongue got in the way. "Dance with Linda," she said, which was much simpler.

He understood that, all right. He said. 'Now you've got something." The room was dark, and not being able to see his face, she couldn't tell whether he was being funny or serious.

In the morning, she found out, although it dawned on her by slow degrees. At first, she couldn't even think straight because as soon as she opened her eyes, there was an explosion of thunder inside her brain, and then she discovered that it was only Matthew tip-toeing into the room. "Has mother got another headache?" he whispered.

"Matthew, stop shouting!" she wailed.

He was too surprised to stand up for himself. "Your mother has a hang-over," David explained kindly.

"That's a fine thing to tell a child. I'm just seasick, Matthew, and I don't want to talk, so please get out and ask Bertha not to come in with the baby. I can't stand all this tramping around."

"I'll see you later, son."

"All of a sudden, 'son'," Claudia mumbled.

"Come back to the room at eleven o'clock," David went on, oblivious, "and you'll meet a little boy your own age."

"I don't want to. What's his name?"

"Gregory."

Matthew's distrust flamed to interest. "Gregory Mandelbaum?"

"Who's Gregory Mandelbaum?" David demanded sourly.

"He's in my class in school."

"This isn't that Gregory."

"I have to play tick-tack-toe."

"March," said David. "And see that you're back here at eleven. Sharp."

Claudia gathered the separate parts of herself together, and sat up, holding her head in order to keep it aloft. "Just when did you work out this arrangement with Linda Harwell to bring your two sons together?" she asked with difficulty.

"Last night when we were dancing," said David cheerfully. "Are you ready to ring for breakfast?"

Claudia bit her lips to keep them from trembling. "I don't want any breakfast," she said.

4

MERTIE couldn't understand her aversion to food after yesterday's huge breakfast. "Mrs. Naughton thinks she's seasick," David again took it upon himself to explain, and this time with even more unction.

"But the ocean is as smooth as a lake today," Mertie expostulated. "Might it be the ptomaine after all, not out of her system yet?"

"I forgot about the ptomaine," Claudia pounced on the suggestion feebly. "That's what it is. Thank you, Mertie."

"You've confused the poor creature," David remarked after Mertie left the room. "I bet she's saying to 'Awkins, 'I'd swear it was a clear case of the morning after, except she was in bed at ten o'clock last night, and I know for a fact she doesn't touch a drop of liquor'."

"I'm not amused, and you're not a talented mimic. Will you stop joggling me? What are you doing?"

"Trying to get you to sit up to drink this."

"My head doesn't want to sit up. Drink what?"

"Black coffee."

"I hate it black."

"This isn't for enjoyment."

She swallowed the bitter liquid under protest. "I don't like it but it seems to like me," she said, after a thoughtful interval.

"Have another cup."

"No thanks."

A little later, she said, "I think I'll take you up on that other cup if you still have it around."

"I still have it around."

"Could I borrow a piece of toast to go with it?"

"Shall I lend you some bacon too?"

"Well, if you insist. Is that today's puzzle?"

"Yes, do you want it? It's the names of rivers."

"No thanks. I only know the Hudson and the Mississippi intimately."

"That's what I thought. Here's a couple of invitations. Mr. and Mrs. Merrick Bliss request the pleasure of our company at dinner at nine o'clock." He opened the second envelope. "Cocktails with the Nicholsons at seven-thirty in their suite."

"I'm not mad about the Nicholsons, and we don't even know the other people, although the name sounds familiar."

"He was Ambassador to Russia. Also friends of Julia's and Hartley's. I met them last night."

"Oh really? Why didn't you tell me all the interesting things you'd done last night?"

"You were still sleeping it off when I got in."

She tried to keep light about it. "In twelve years we've been married you never once went out without me, and this is twice in a row."

"See that you stay on your feet, and I'll be glad to take you with me this evening."

She ignored that one. "Who else did you dance with?"

"Nobody."

"Just Linda Harwell, the whole time?"

"Only part of the time. We went to the ship's auction after a while."

She had a passion for auctions, and he knew it. "How could you let me miss it?" she reproached him, meaning, "how could you go with anyone else?"

"They have one every night."

"They do?" She was mollified, but also amazed. "What do they auction off?"

"Mileage."

"Say it again."

"Mileage."

"That's what I thought you said."

"It's a pool," he enlarged, a little too patiently. "You bid on the number of miles the ship makes in twenty-four hours."

"And they call that an auction?"

"Did you expect furniture?"

She did, rather, but she didn't say so. "Does Linda Harwell dance well?"

"Very."

"And how did you manage to manage with the new steps?"

"I managed to manage."

She couldn't let it alone. "How about the rhumba?"

"It's not hard to catch on to with a good partner."

"Mrs. Harwell seems to be good in everything." She swallowed heavily; if she said any more, she would be downright nasty. What was this intangible something that kept them from coming close to one another? And to think she'd had visions of cosily sharing an

133

upper berth! At this rate, they were hardly sharing a room. For all she knew, he might have tip-toed in at dawn this morning. "I'm jealous," she thought with chagrin, and it wasn't even a first-rate jealousy, it was just a petty mean streak of hurt feelings hiding under spite; and spite, in her opinion, was one of the most inferior of female emotions.

"Look, David, I'm sorry I got drunk last night," she apologized like a man. "It won't happen again."

He laughed out loud, his sense of humour, thank goodness, back to normal. Then he sprang out of bed, and her heart lifted like a balloon as he bent over her. "That's a nice girl," he said, with a tweak to her nose, and off he sprinted. A minute or so later, she heard the water gushing into the tub, accompanied by a lot of silly whistling. She called him names she didn't even know she knew, and felt good and nasty and didn't care.

What remained of the black coffee had grown horribly luke-warm. She gulped it down anyway, for its medicinal effect, because this was not the auspicious moment to mope in bed. She had left it up in the air with Bill

Hendricks about some deck tennis if it was a nice day, and it was a nice day. The sun mightn't be shining on her private world, but it was shining on the ocean, flecking it up so that it looked like an exaggeration painted on a coloured postcard. So why shouldn't she enjoy herself? Let David spend his morning making a fool of himself by bringing together two children, one of whom obviously didn't want to be brought together. Such a rush of fatherhood was so foreign to his nature that she could only conclude that he was motivated, subconsciously or otherwise, by a desire to see more of Linda Harwell.

Judging by the continued but sporadic activity of his vocal cords, he was through with his bath, and using his razor. Claudia felt torn. He always gave the bath a considerate swish round, with the air of rolling out a red carpet for her, and it had become a pleasant ritual to start the day, her bathing, and him shaving. But not this morning, thank you. Much as she disliked using anybody else's bathroom, especially the children's, she gathered up an armful of clothes, and yanked her one pair of slacks off its hanger. She was sorry now that she hadn't listened to Candy.

"Don't take along those old slacks," Candy had advised.

"Why not? I'll probably not need them, and if I should, they still fit."

"The new ones taper in the leg, and you're going to need at least one more pair for deck tennis."

"We won't be playing deck tennis."

"It's not as strenuous as it sounds," said Candy who knew that David wasn't supposed to go in yet for heavy exercise. "Oh well," Claudia had shrugged, "it's best not to take any chances, I can live without deck tennis."

So she hadn't bought any new slacks that tapered, and here she was, about to play deck tennis with another man, while David was whistling his head off about another woman. "This is the beginning of the end," she thought, tearfully, going back to see if there was just a little more black coffee. There wasn't. Everything seemed to be against her. Even the ocean gave her a shove into the sofa as she made her way to the children's bathroom.

Bertha's quarters were immaculately tidy as usual, with the beds stripped to the bone. She had made them herself the first day but as it had screwed up the daily change of linen, she now contented herself with a violent airing of the blankets and pillows. The bathroom, however, was her undisputed kingdom. Every available horizontal fixture was festooned with wet-wash. Claudia ducked beneath a brace of slow-dripping pyjamas, and accomplished a nerve-wracking bath, punctuated by icy drops down her spine. She disengaged the last clean Turkish towel from under a row of moist socks and handkerchiefs, and dried herself gingerly with its clammy surface. She'd neglected to bring her toothbrush and comb, but at least the fundamentals were behind her.

It was significant that when she returned to the bedroom, David didn't notice that she'd been away. He was prancing into his trousers, and after he'd zipped himself up, and strung his belt round his middle, he said, "Better get dressed, it's almost eleven o'clock. Linda will be here any minute."

Claudia froze. "I am dressed," she informed him icily. "All but my teeth."

Before he could answer, she slammed the bathroom door in his face and locked it. They never locked doors, but even the loud click of the latch failed to elicit a reaction from him. "I bet that little brat doesn't show up!" he

137

shouted through to her. "I'm going out to look for him!"

Experience should have taught him that looking for Matthew was like looking for a needle in a haystack. There was no sign of him, or David either, when Mertie announced that Mrs. Harwell was waiting in the drawing-room with Master Gregory. "Tell her I'll be right in," said Claudia, and muttered inwardly, "I hope Master Gregory is fat and sissy," which were the two things that David admitted that he was glad Matthew wasn't.

So much for wishful thinking. Gloom thickened upon her when she discovered that Linda Harwell's son was none other than the handsome little boy she had caught sight of on the dock before the boat sailed. "Greg, this is Mrs. Naughton, Matthew's mother," Linda introduced him, as if he were a grown-up.

"How do you do," he acknowledged in a polite little pipe of a voice.

"How do you do," Claudia accepted his small, clean hand, noting the firm grip of it. Matthew's hand was still at the slithering stage, and usually damp from something or other. "This is no sissy," Claudia concluded morosely. On the contrary, his carriage was erect, his gaze straightforward, and his body solidly compounded of bone and muscle; and as if that wasn't enough of a windfall for one child, he boasted his mother's best features, and presumably his father's thick blond hair. When David finally appeared, all but dragging Matthew by the arm, the contrast was painful. Hastily, Claudia piloted him away from the immediate neighbourhood of Mrs. Harwell's faultless beige slack-suit. "This is Greg, Matthew."

"How do you do," Greg said.

"Hello," Matthew responded laconically, after which spirited exchange, there ensued the prolonged silence of mutual evaluation.

"Bertha's waiting for you both by the ping-pong table," David suggested at length.

Matthew found his tongue, and used it obnoxiously. "I'm a good ping-pong player," he swaggered. "Boy, am I good! I can beat anybody, I bet. I bet I'm the best player on this whole boat. Can you play ping-pong?"

Greg nodded. "Quite well," he said conservatively.

"Okay, let's go." In his haste to depart, Matthew knocked over a chair, and Claudia disliked him intensely. "He's certainly a hoodlum next to Greg," she surrendered unequivocally.

"You can be proud of that youngster," David added his congratulations.

"He's better than he was," Linda acknowledged. "There's room for improvement, though, and being with Matthew is just what he needs."

This was carrying modesty and politeness to an extreme, Claudia thought resentfully, and David echoed her sentiments. "I think it's the other way round," he said. "I hope a little of Greg rubs off on Matthew."

He got his wish. Quite a bit of Greg rubbed off, for by the end of the afternoon, Matthew had developed a thriving stutter. It was one of the few bad habits he hadn't acquired, and if it hadn't been sad, it would have been funny. "Linda thought I knew about it," David explained apologetically while they were dressing that evening, "but the youngster doesn't talk very much when he's with grown-ups, so I didn't really catch on when she said he was better than he was."

"Which only goes to show that all is not gold that glitters," Claudia observed, overcoming a very natural impulse to crow.

"Linda's done a good job anyway," David

went on, "and against considerable odds. What with this business with the father, the boy must have had a hell of a childhood."

"All children have a hell of a childhood one way or another, so suppose you start making a few allowances for Matthew and his mother?"

"I'll start right away," he obliged.

She gave him a push. "Please. This poor old yellow won't stand any rough treatment, I doubt if it'll last through dinner."

"That's fine, it's done its duty, buy another one tomorrow. I noticed something with a lot of glittery stuff in one of the show-windows."

"That's sequins and they're terribly expensive. I happened to price the dress when I was buying a pair of slacks before I went up on deck this morning. Or didn't you notice that I had new slacks?" she added bitingly.

He thought about it. "I don't think I saw them," he didn't lie.

"Maybe you're right," she forgave him. "I changed back to a dress before lunch. Anyway, they cost more than I expected they would, so I'm certainly not going to buy a new evening dress to wear for one night on the boat, which is all it amounts to."

"Oh go ahead, treat yourself. We can afford
it. Didn't I tell you I won the pool?"

"No, you didn't. How much?"

"Ninety pounds."

"But that's a fortune in dollars!" she
exclaimed incredulously. "Just think what it
would have meant to us when we really
needed it for doctor's bills and everything!"

"I wouldn't have won it," said David
"because I wouldn't have had the money to
place the bet in the first place."

"It's funny," she said.

"What is?"

"Money's like a magnet, the more you
have, the more you get. And the less you
enjoy it," she added soberly. "Ninety pounds
all of a sudden wasn't important enough for
you to remember to tell me about, and if I do
buy the sequin dress tomorrow, it won't be as
much fun as finding something a quarter of
the price at a sale."

"Pretend it's a quarter of the price at a
sale."

She shook her head. "It wouldn't work
The magic's gone."

"You poor thing."

"I am, a little," she said. "And so are you.'

He tied his tie in silence. "You have a

point," he conceded at length. "On the other hand, would you honestly like to go back to scrimping and trying to make ends meet?"

"No, I wouldn't," she admitted. "There's too much that's nice about having money. For instance, it's going to be wonderful to be able to give Mertie this yellow dress in the morning for her daughter, who's eighteen and mature for her age."

"That's nice."

"Not that Mertie's hankering for it. She's richer than we are. All the money in the world wouldn't buy us a daughter. Now."

His arms were gentle, and all at once, after so many years, she could talk about it. "I heard her cry. Just that one tiny little cry when I was coming out of the ether. And then when I found I couldn't ever have another, I felt I'd let you down terribly."

"Look. I'm not so badly off. I've got a couple of pretty damned fine sons."

"Well!" she exploded, "it's high time you finally admitted it!"

They were right back to where they'd started, just as if there were an automatic safety-valve that invariably went off in time to keep them from getting maudlin about the past. "Don't go having ideas that they're perfect," he said. "Michael's rotten spoiled, if you ask me."

"Nobody asked you."

"And getting back to Matthew," he ignored her, "Greg mightn't be the ideal answer under the circumstances, but I still insist that it's an unhealthy and abnormal state of affairs for him to be hanging around some crack-pot of a middle-aged woman."

"He isn't thinking of marrying her," Claudia remarked pleasantly, "he just likes to play tick-tack-toe with her."

He fought a grin. "I don't think that's funny."

"I do," she said.

"And apropos of that ninety pounds," he remembered suddenly, "I didn't tell you about it because I couldn't find you to tell. You were playing deck tennis with Hendricks."

"Any objections?"

"I wouldn't say yes, and I wouldn't say no."

"That makes us square," she said. "Don't let's ever get to the stage when we don't care enough to care."

"That's pretty fancy double-talk. But I agree. Don't let's."

144

"You're always k-kissing," Matthew remarked from the doorway in disgust. "I knocked but you didn't hear me."

Claudia hastily forestalled another K. "All right. Ketch-up this one last time on your scrambled eggs, and that's all."

He pressed his luck. "C-can't I even have it tomorrow for supper?"

"Out!" David ended the discussion.

"I wish," said Claudia, after the interruption, "that we hadn't got talked into dinner with the Blisses. We could have eaten downstairs in the main dining-room just by ourselves."

"We'll do it tomorrow night," he promised.

"I'd love to. Then we can see all the people we saw the first day, like the big fat man with the beard who has our rooms on B deck. And, incidentally, Matthew's girl friend has a room on B deck. I saw her coming out of it when I went to the beauty parlour this afternoon to have my hair done. How does it look?"

"Her room on B deck?"

"Answer me!"

"What did you have done to it?"

"Washed and set, and red polish on my

nails, to dress up the yellow. Does it help?"

"Shall I be perfectly frank about it?" he asked owlishly.

"Don't. I'll do as much sitting as I can so as not to disgrace you. It's not so bad from the waist up."

When they reached the cocktail lounge for the interminable stretch of drinks before dinner, Mrs. Nicholson's sharp eyes immediately raked the poor little yellow to pieces. "My dear," she exclaimed with hypocritical fervour, "the gown you wore last night was definitely Hollywood, but this one actually screams Paris."

There were two words that Claudia never used simply because she didn't like the sound of them. One was "stinker" and the other was "bitch", but both of them together didn't do justice to the way she felt about Mrs. Nicholson at this moment. She might be David's pet stock on the stock market but underneath she was nothing but an ugly cat of a woman, and suddenly Claudia felt an impulse to stand up for the yellow as it had stood up for her throughout the years. "It's probably the oldest living dress on record," she acknowledged with what she hoped passed for quiet dignity.

It certainly passed for something, because Mrs. Bliss, who was dowdy with diamonds but gentle as a sofa cushion, nodded sagaciously and said, "It's my contention that a good gown is like an aristocrat, it never loses what it has. And what this little frock has—" she paused to gather the right words—"well, I'd call it a naive sophistication, if you know what I mean."

"I know exactly what you mean!" Mrs. Nicholson said, "and it's what I said to begin with; the dress absolutely screams Paris."

"She meant it," Claudia thought blankly.

The bar steward was waiting for her order. "Ginger ale," she told him, still in a daze. Bill Hendricks started to change it to tomato-juice (with a broad wink), and respectfully didn't, and then Claudia knew that, thanks to Julia's and Hartley's money, she could even afford to be peculiar.

She took only a sip of the ginger ale. Firstly, she wasn't thirsty, and secondly, it was a dull drink. Very dull. It seemed forever before somebody or other got hungry and discovered that it was late enough to dine.

Late as it was, however, the café seemed unusually crowded and noisy. The large round table awaiting their party was the only unoccupied space, and Claudia heard Mrs. Nicholson say to Mrs. Woodburn, "Isn't this the limit? It invariably happens towards the end of every crossing."

"Still, it's so pleasant up here for the first few days, I suppose one oughtn't to complain," Mrs. Woodburn returned.

Claudia didn't have any idea what they were talking about, until, to her surprise, she saw the fat man with the beard sitting with his fat wife at a small table against the wall. They smiled and waved, and Claudia smiled back. "Friends of yours?" Bill Hendricks murmured slyly.

As they weren't, really, there was no need to defend them, but just the same, his attitude of superiority was insufferable. "Surely you know who they are?" she served him right.

"Unfortunately, yes. Locusts from the main dining-room."

"No, the name isn't 'Locust', they happen to be the Count and Countess Cazzoni."

He gave her a quick look and apparently decided she wasn't smart enough to try to fool him. "Don't be taken in by them. I never heard of a Count Cazzoni."

"I didn't either," she retorted silently.

"Besides, they aren't even on the passenger list."

"They're too important, they're travelling incognito, but don't tell anyone I told you."

He still didn't believe it, but nevertheless, she could see him riffling through the social pages of his mind to make sure. "Oh good, we're back to caviar!" she announced sunnily, and hoped that Mrs. Bliss was sufficiently unimaginative to follow up with a plain old-fashioned noodle soup.

On the contrary. The caviar preceded a cold beet soup with sour cream, and immediately the cat was out of the bag. "A Russian dinner," Mrs. Nicholson exclaimed. "Oh you cute trick, you!"

"Even to cheese blintzes for dessert!" Mrs. Bliss's two small chins trembled happily. "I thought it would be such a fun thing to do for a change!"

Claudia didn't dare catch David's eye. That particular expression always put his teeth on edge, and as for herself, she wished she hadn't counted on the noodle soup, and had accepted a second helping of caviar from the friendly little waiter who had come to know her weakness. The Russians could keep their beet soup and cheese blintzes, but it was a crying shame that they had caviar tied hand and foot. In her opinion it was the one invention to their indisputable credit.

It was her first evening of dancing, and she wasn't as bad as she thought she was going to be. She'd have preferred to try herself out with David, but Bill Hendricks pulled her on to the floor without asking any questions. She had limited herself to a glass and a half of champagne at dinner, which was just enough to make her feel pleasantly relaxed and unselfconscious. A little less, and she'd have been too stiff; a little more, and she'd have been too limber. "You're like a feather," Bill murmured. "Sorry. My fault," he gallantly assumed the blame for falling out of step. He said, "David and Linda make a lovely couple, don't they?"

"Yes," said Claudia. "I was just watching them." She felt as heavy as lead all at once, and the calves of her legs tightened into an ache. She longed for the music to come to an end, but when it did, it started up again, and before she could do anything about it, Mr. Nicholson had clasped her to his stiff white shirt-front. He held her so close, in a purely avuncular way, that she was sure she humped out in the rear, for the simple reason that two things could not occupy the same place at the same time. The awkward position made her more than ever aware of Linda's slim grace melting into David's masculine embrace. David might not have taken dancing lessons to catch up on the new steps, but he looked like a beautiful dancer, because he kept his shoulders so straight and still. It was more than could be said for Mr. Nicholson, who fell just short of being an arm-pumper. She hoped she wouldn't have to make the rounds with either Mr. Woodburn or Mr. Bliss. As an Ambassador, Mr. Bliss had probably had to learn to be a ball-room dancer, and though he was proficient, he was nevertheless a little fancy round the feet. Mr. Woodburn, on the other hand, wasn't at all fancy. He and Mrs. Woodburn looked as if they were just enjoying a leisurely walk round the floor, impervious to everything but themselves.

Luckily, the Chief Purser claimed the next dance. He didn't connect her with Matthew, so she didn't bother to refresh his memory. He was surprisingly young, without his desk in front of him, and British as an actor in a rosy, uniformed way, and everything about him was professional, from the easy glide of his limbs to the engaging smile that lit up his handsome face like the fake glow of an electric wood-burning fireplace. Claudia concluded that it was part of his job to warm up in the evening, and charm the women into feeling and looking their best.

"Why couldn't you have cut in when I was dancing with Mr. Nicholson?" she demanded of David resentfully.

"Guess?" he said, and started whirling her round the floor like a maniac. By the skin of her teeth she kept her balance and her dignity. "Where's Linda?"

"She went back to her room to look at Greg."

"Oh, I see."

"See what?"

"That's why you interrupted my dance with the purser, you had a little free time on your hands."

"Guess again."

"You're making a spectacle of us. And kindly don't squeeze me so tight."

"Who has a better right?"

"I don't like it."

"You lie."

"If you want the truth, I don't trust it. I think it's just left-overs from Linda."

He slowed down and held her decently. "You're on the right track," he said gravely. "But it's not the left-overs. It's the whole works."

Her heart went dead inside her. "Wasn't it always the whole works?"

"Yes."

"But you mean it could be that it doesn't keep on being?" she asked with effort.

"It's been known to happen."

"It's not fair," she said finally. "You have no competition. Bill Hendricks is hardly a man, but Linda's really a woman, all the way up and down."

"It's still the whole works, darling. If there's any unfairness, it's the other way round. I've got my competition ahead of me."

"I wouldn't worry about the purser, exactly," she told him tremulously.

They hardly knew when the music stopped. "It's just midnight," he said. "The moon's out, we'd have time for a stroll round the deck."

"Not before the auction, I don't think. Everybody seems to be going into the smoking room."

153

"I forgot about the auction. Did you want to go?"

"If it were antiques instead of mileage, maybe. But I thought you wanted to go."

"I won't push my luck. I won last night."

"Could we slip away without being noticed?"

"The Woodburns are married too, and they seem to get away with it. I saw them last night, and the night before that. Standing by the rail. Holding hands in broad moonlight."

She couldn't rise to his teasing.

"You were with Linda when you saw them."

"Yes."

"Do you think Mr. Woodburn's happy?" she asked after a moment.

"A good sight happier than anybody else in this crowd. Not counting me."

"Basically, I guess Mrs. Woodburn and I are a lot alike," she said thoughtfully.

"That's an odd comparison if ever I heard one."

"No it isn't, we're both just a little bit not on the level, but I don't suppose any woman in love really is. Shall we go?"

"On deck?"

"It's too windy."

"To the auction?"

"It's too stuffy."

"Let's," he said.

She tried to forget. She couldn't, quite. David said, "I think we need more air." He rose and opened the port-holes wide. Then he came back to her, and touched his lips to hers, and climbed into his own bed.

After a time, she said, "Did anybody ever say that marriage was easy?"

"Nobody that's ever made a go of it."

"When things are the hardest," she brought out gropingly, "that's when it's not hard at all. I mean, grief, and illness and loss keep happening, and hold you together. That is, if they don't knock you apart."

The silence ached. "Do you think I'm talking double talk again?" she asked timidly. "Or are you asleep?"

"I wasn't asleep. And I don't think you're talking double-talk."

Miraculously, their hands touched across the space between the beds.

"With the rough years behind us, we might have a little tough sledding over the easy years. But I think we'll make it," he said softly.

"I think so, too."

She felt shaken as if something tremendous had happened to them again, and she knew that he felt the same way. It was as if they had grown together and been cut in half, and were becoming whole again. And that was the trick in it, to be able to stay together, with nothing to bind you.

"Dear—"

"Yes, David?"

"We've made good mileage tonight. And on a sea that wasn't as smooth as it looked."

It was at once a confession and a pledge. She lay awake long after his breathing told her he was sleeping. She needed to be awake by herself. It was strange how a moment of such profound and disturbing illumination could have been born out of a tangle of trivialities. In some short-given wisdom and humility, she knew that it was a moment not to question, or to trade with.

In the morning, they were back to trivialities.

5

FOR once, there were no invitations on the breakfast tray. "What a relief," said Claudia. "We're dated up this evening, anyway."

David refolded the custom-blanks that had been added to the usual morning reading matter. "Sorry to break the news, but it looks like it's up to us, now," he said.

"You mean we're supposed to give a dinner-party, too?"

"Make a stab at it, at least."

"When?"

"That's the trouble, tonight's our only chance."

"But we'd planned to eat in the main dining-room by ourselves, don't you remember?"

"Sure, I remember."

"Then why not tomorrow evening?"

"A dinner-party on the last day is impractical. Everybody's busy packing and filling out forms."

157

"Oh dear. All of a sudden the time went so fast towards the end."

"It always does."

"We haven't even made our tour over the boat, and now it's too late."

"No it isn't, I can set it up for this afternoon. Linda said she wanted to go along, if we didn't mind."

"Oh." Somehow, after last night, she hadn't expected Linda to pop up again. "I suppose she'd have also liked to go slumming with us in the main dining-room. If we didn't mind."

It was a fair-sized barb, but he was so thick-skinned that it bounced right back into her lap. "That's a brilliant idea," he said. "We could give the whole blasted dinner-party in the main dining-room."

"Oh, what a fun evening!" she exclaimed.

He dipped a teaspoon into the glass of water on his tray, and aimed it deftly. She picked up a cereal spoon. Matthew came in. "You never let me have a water-fight," he accused them.

"Little mother was having a fun-time," David explained. He added sternly, "You didn't knock again."

Matthew recognized a break when he saw

one. He stood his ground and grinned.

"Grin some more," said Claudia. "I want to see your teeth."

Matthew obliged. David shuddered. "That's enough for this early in the morning, you can close up now. How's your girl-friend?"

Matthew looked blank.

"Witty Daddy means the lady you play tick-tack-toe with."

"She gave me her pencil, it writes b-black and red."

"Were you hinting for her to give it to you?" Claudia reproached him.

"Not much," said David. "See that you give it back. You know better than to accept presents from strangers."

Matthew decided on retreat. "I have to g-go now. I have to meet Greg for p-ping-pong."

The faint echo of his stutter lingered on the air. David glowered. "I didn't say anything, dear," Claudia murmured. "Were you really in earnest about tonight?"

David was not a mood-holder. "I'm no more enthused," he said, "than you are, but reciprocation is one of the unwritten laws of an ocean voyage."

"Yes, and it's a bore. Somebody buys

somebody a drink and nobody stops until everybody's been paid back. Which is another idea. Couldn't we give a cocktail party instead of dinner? We don't pay for the food anyway, so it wouldn't be a case of being cheap about it."

"I thought of that, but Linda's planned one for this evening."

"Oh. It's nice of you to remember to tell me. Or perhaps I wasn't invited?"

"Well, now that you bring it up, Linda did say she'd rather you didn't come."

"It wouldn't surprise me.—Isn't it too late to ask people for tonight?" she suggested hopefully.

"On the contrary. They're probably waiting for us to make the next move."

"Then I guess we'd better start in phoning right away."

"No hurry. They're all asleep at this hour, except Linda."

"You're pretty familiar with her habits."

"She says she has to get up early on account of Greg."

"David, will you stop being so damned reasonable!" she burst out irritably. "Can't you see I'm being nasty?"

"What have you got to be nasty about?"

"There you go again. You make me feel like a shrew. Nothing. I'm a fool. Do we have to have Barry Conwell or Helen Nicholson?"

"We do not."

"That's the one bright spot so far." She shoved the telephone towards him. "You might as well start with Linda as long as you're so sure she's up."

"You call her," he said. "I have to find my cigarette lighter." He got out of bed, and began rummaging through the pockets of his trousers; then he went to look for it in the drawing-room, leaving her no alternative but to pick up the receiver and ask to be connected with Mrs. Harwell.

So instantly did Linda answer, that she might have been glued to the telephone, expecting it to ring, but she said that she'd just that moment walked in, having safely deposited Gregory at the ping-pong table. "I'm so grateful," she went on. "Greg is a different boy since he's met Matthew."

"So is Matthew," Claudia felt like saying.

"And thank you, too, for letting me barge in on your tour round the ship. I've always wanted to see the kitchens, but I never had the initiative to do anything about it."

"I'm glad you'll be along because David's

more interested in the engine rooms, so we'll be two against one."

"You're very sweet to make me feel welcome."

"You should know how sweet I'm not," Claudia retorted inwardly, and was about to get on to the business of the dinner, when Linda said, "Oh, before I forget, will you tell David that he left his cigarette-lighter, I have it for him."

There were any number of places that he could have left it, but Linda volunteered no further details. Claudia had to swallow and wet her lips before she could make her voice come naturally. "I'll tell him; he's just been looking for it." It was a temptation, all of a sudden, not to mention the dinner, to call the whole thing off, and hold David to their original plan of dining alone. But apparently being alone didn't mean very much to him, or he wouldn't have suggested the party in the first place. Whether he admitted it, or was even aware of it, the dinner was one of the few remaining excuses whereby he and Linda could be together without being too conspicuous about it. Under the circumstances, it took all her will-power to extend the invitation.

Linda, however, did not appear to notice any lack of cordiality. She not only accepted with a low laugh of delight (so that's what a low laugh sounds like), but simply adored the perfectly priceless switch of eating in the main dining-room. "What a terribly fun idea!" she exclaimed.

This was the last straw. For the infinitesimal splitting of a second, Claudia felt sicker than when she was seasick to think that Linda was already sharing David's intimate little idiosyncrasies. And then she realized that Linda hadn't explored that far, she really meant that it was a "terribly fun-idea", which, in turn, undoubtedly proved that David hadn't yet glimpsed the tiny soft spots that peppered the underneath coating of Linda's lovely exterior. With nine-hundred-and-ninety men out of a thousand, soft spots wouldn't matter, but David was funny in a lot of little ways that took a lot of knowing.

When he stomped back into the room a minute or so later, Claudia was lying on her pillows with her hands clasped in serenity across her stomach. "You look like a new-born corpse," he said in a vile humour. "Why the Mona Lisa smile?"

"Was I smiling? It must be my natural sweetness shining through."

He grunted. "What did she say?"

"Linda?"

"Yes, Linda."

"About the dinner tonight?"

"You're asking for trouble," he warned her as if she were Matthew.

"She said—" Claudia decided to withhold the embellishments of the acceptance. Why hurry matters? Sooner or later Linda was bound to cook her own goose all by herself. "She said she would like very much to come. Did you find your lighter, dear?"

"No, dammit."

"I didn't think you did, because she also said to tell you that she'd found it."

His eyes lit up, dispelling all the darkness from his face. When they were first married, he'd had a favourite pipe-scraper that made him look like that. "So that's where I left it!" he exclaimed in immense relief.

It would have been easy to ask him, then and there, and once and for all, where "where" was. But it didn't matter now. Poor Linda. She couldn't possibly have discovered in a few short days the baffling contradictions in David that had taken a wife twelve long years to learn. It was so silly how he could forgive many of the major shortcomings of the female sex, but he couldn't condone little things like red toenails sticking out of sandals, or baby-talk, or a passion for concocting creamy mixes to dip potato chips into, or squeamishness with animals. Linda wasn't guilty of the first offence, nor the last, but she was getting mighty close to the danger mark with her "fun-idea". Particularly since David's interest in the fun-idea soon fizzled out into a healthy indifference. "You'd better go down and fix up a menu with the dining-steward," he said, blithely washing his hands of further responsibility.

Claudia baulked. "I will not. It was your suggestion, not mine. Besides, I can't think of anything we haven't already had except hash."

"I like hash, hash is fine," he said.

"At the beginning of a trip, but not at the end. I'll compromise, we'll go together."

"Oh, to hell with it," he said.

"You can't say to hell with it, after everybody's accepted."

"What's the matter with everybody reading

the regular menu and ordering what they want for a change?"

"It would take forever with so many people. Also if you give one of these silly dinners, you're supposed to do the thinking in advance. Like Bill Hendricks and the Blisses."

"I'll ask the chief steward to come up here, and we'll let him do the thinking."

"My hero," Claudia said.

The chief steward, whose name was Bixby, appeared like a genie out of a lamp. Automatically, and in a purely perfunctory performance of duty, he whipped out a small pad and started to write down the list of guests. With each successive name, his enthusiasm became more manifest. Evidently, he hadn't expected such a bonanza, and Claudia could see him literally throw his whole heart and soul into the dinner right on the spot. "First, if I may jot down the seating arrangements."

"Husbands and wives next to each other," said Claudia promptly.

"We're not all husbands and wives," David reminded her.

"Very true," she agreed. "Mr. Hendricks

next to Mrs. Harwell, Bixby, and Mr. Naughton at her left."

"Thank you." Bixby jotted and bowed. "And at your left, Mrs. Naughton?"

It was such an exciting toss-up between Mr. Woodburn, Mr. Bliss and Mr. Nicholson that she couldn't decide which to choose. "Surprise me," she purred.

Bixby's dedication was such that the sacrilege of levity passed completely over his head. This was his great moment. For four days, he implied, with and without tact, he had been throwing pearls to swine, who invariably clung to the unimaginative caviar, trout, Chateaubriand, and Baked Alaska.

"I can't help it, I still like caviar," Claudia confessed with a blush.

"In that case," he made the best of it, "allow me to suggest the *Caviare Exquise*, served with heart of palm, and garnished with a small rose-sprig of pimento and peppers . . ."

"Splendid, Bixby, we'll leave the entire menu in your hands," David interrupted, and would have been off like a shot if Bixby hadn't been too quick for him. "Thank you, sir, but I would like your approval, sir, of dishes that are a bit out of the ordinary. For example, a very delicate bisque of she-crab—"

Claudia could have sworn that he said "she-crab", and it not only turned out that he really had said it, but that David had known she-crabs intimately from his earlier architectural jaunts to Charleston. His interest revived. "I must say I didn't expect to run into a she-crab on an English boat," he commented.

"Yes, sir, it is a bit unusual, sir," Bixby conceded, "but the fact is we always made a point of getting some for Lord Gresham, sir; bisque of she-crab and Dolphin Steak as well. You see, sir, he had occasion to go South whenever he came to America and those were prime favourites with him."

"I didn't know dolphin was procurable in the general market. Your Lord Gresham was evidently quite an epicure."

"He was, sir, but never objectionally so, if you know what I mean. And as for the Dolphin Steak, we always managed to get a small quantity of it from a private source, knowing his fondness for it, and Lady Gresham's also. A sort of courtesy, sir, without their asking for it. But now that Lady Gresham is travelling alone, she's scarcely eaten a morsel of anything, so there's no reason why you and your guests shouldn't enjoy what we have on hand. And I might say," he added deferentially, "that very few passengers indeed, sir, would appreciate the delicacy of Dolphin Steak—or bisque of she-crab either, for that matter."

For all Bixby's compliments and enthusiasm, the completed menu made Claudia feel slightly ill, what with eating a dead man's food, followed by a crown of baby lamb, so young that it was practically unborn. Even the heart of palm had a macabre sound to it. She settled, without demur, on a mandarin ice for dessert, though she preferred something with chocolate, and David selected the wines with a dispatch that elicited Bixby's respectful and unqualified approbation. "I believe I have it down correctly, sir—Vodka with the caviar, to be followed by a white Burgundy for the Dolphin, preferably a Chassagne-Montrachet; then a Romanée-Conti '47—an excellent Burgundy if I may say so, sir—and a Piper Heidsiek—We'll do our very best, sir."

"I'm sure you will." Unobtrusively, a folded note found its way into Bixby's palm. "Thank you, sir. Thank you very much, sir."

Claudia waited until his spidery body had bowed itself through the door. "David, you never told me you knew all those rare wines and high-toned fish!" she expostulated.

"You never asked me," he returned. "Now come on, we've wasted enough time on food, let's get up on deck."

"You get up on deck, I'm going to buy the sequin dress to live up to those she-crabs. We really ought to thank Lady Gresham. I wonder what she's like? Everybody keeps inviting her but she never accepts. She's either terribly grief-stricken or a dreadful snob."

"Maybe she's just intelligent," said David. "How about four o'clock for going round the boat?"

"Remember, we want to see that French movie this afternoon."

"We'll be back by five. Linda wants to see it, too."

"Oh," said Claudia.

"You don't mind, do you?"

"Not if you don't mind my tagging along wherever you go," she returned sweetly.

"Don't be an idiot."

"Don't you be."

"Look. She's a niece of the Woodburns,"

he rationalized. "She's had a rough time of it, and she seems to be at a loose end."

Claudia couldn't see why David should have elected himself to be the one to tie up Linda Harwell's loose ends, but on second thoughts, the answer was obvious. Apparently he found it very pleasant and congenial work. She decided, in a sudden fit of pique and self-pity, that they could go to the movies without her. She'd promised to play ping-pong with Matthew, and five o'clock was as good a time as any.

Five o'clock, however, turned out to be the only free hour that Alphonse could give her. She hadn't reckoned on another visit to the Beauty Salon, but once she began with the sequin gown, she was into it up to her ears, both literally and figuratively. It clung to her with seal-like perfection, it didn't need a bit of alteration, and yet something was wrong. "The dress is beautiful, but I'm not," she summed it up abjectly. "It doesn't seem to go with me."

The woman who was in charge of the informal little shop was remote yet efficient, chewing her words into an effortless monotone. "It's difficult to judge this particular gown without the correct accessories,

171

accessories are so important, you know."

"Even allowing for sports shoes, though—" Claudia felt unnecessarily loud-mouthed as she tip-toed up on imaginary high-heels—"it just isn't my style."

"Actually, I don't agree, madame. If I brought the gown to your suite where you could try it on with your evening slippers, and the proper hair-do and earrings, you'd see that it's quite the perfect outfit for you."

Claudia shook her head. "Thanks just the same, but this is the way I always wear my hair, and I don't own any earrings."

"May I?" The woman's face remained an enamelled mask, but the tell-tale looseness of her knees as she walked across the room to a small jewellery counter, hinted of weary glands and aging bones. It was hard to be a saleswoman, Claudia thought with compassion. Reluctantly, she submitted to having her hair scrunched back between a parentheses of tortoiseshell combs, and dangling earrings screwed against the lobes of her ears. "I had a shampoo and set yesterday," she protested feebly.

"With Alphonse?"

"No, just one of the girls."

"Alphonse has his special clients. Mrs.

Hartley Naughton always regarded him most highly. I expect, if he knew who you were, he'd do his best to fit you in."

"I expect he would," Claudia murmured. She might as well get used to the fact that travelling with the name of Naughton on this trip was like being given some sort of an extra passport to new worlds. The trouble was that passports carried obligations, which was part of the reason why she ended up with a pair of long gold earrings, and cut short her tour of the boat in order to keep an appointment with Alphonse. Luckily, she never took long under the drier, so she was sure there'd be time to play at least a little ping-pong with Matthew before dinner.

She was an optimist. The drier was the least of it. David was already at the stage of perfecting the bow of his black tie when she dashed into the bedroom. "Do you realize it's seven-thirty," he began, and stopped dead as he caught sight of her in the mirror. "For God's sake, what have you done to yourself!" he exploded in unflattering horror.

"This is only half of me, don't judge yet," she besought him. She began peeling off her slip-over sweater, contorting it free of her

lacquered hair-do. "And please don't look a
me until I say so," she emerged breathlessly

"It will be a pleasure," he rejoined drily
He turned on his heel and left the room.

"Where are you going!"

"To say goodnight to the children."

"That's good. Stay long enough for me t
get dressed. And tell Matthew I'm sorr·
about the ping-pong, I'll be in later t·
explain—"

When he came back he said that they wer·
asleep, and would she please hurry up, wh·
was she always late?

"I'm not always late." She walked back
wards to him. "Here. Zip me up."

He huffed and puffed. "It's too tight."

"It's supposed to be tight."

"The zipper won't make it."

"It's *got* to make it. Ouch, that was me you
caught!"

"Stand still."

"I am. I'm just putting on my earrings to
save time."

"*Earrings!* What for?"

"To go with my hair. And my hair goes
with the gown." She swept round. "Now you
can look. How do you like it?"

"I don't," he said flatly. "What's all that black mess around your eyes?"

"It's not black, it's three skilfully blended shades of green, brown and blue. Alphonse in the beauty salon did a professional make-up job on me, he gave me a completely new mouth."

"I'm not blind. It's big enough for two of you. You'd better wipe most of it off, you look like a clown."

"I expected this reaction," she said coolly. 'I'd have been surprised if you thought I was as stunning as I am. And now, if you'll excuse me, I'll look in on Matthew and the baby."

"I told you they were asleep."

"I'll take a peep at them, anyhow."

He blocked her way. "You haven't got time."

"I'm sorry but I must. I haven't seen them since lunch."

"You don't must, they're all right," he said, steering her out the door to the corridor. 'You'd only wake them up and frighten them. Incidentally," he added with a grimace, "am I supposed to kiss that face?"

"You most certainly are not. Alphonse says if I want it to last, I shouldn't even wash it before I go to bed."

"That's just ducky," said David grimly.

His carrying on like that built her up for a fine anti-climax. Judging by his reaction, she expected to cause a real sensation at Linda's cocktail party, but not a soul noticed her changed appearance; she simply faded, quite innocuously, into the general blur of glittering gowns, big mouths, mascaraed eyes and enamelled complexions. Mrs. Woodburn alone was conspicuous for the small grey bun at the back of her head, and the candid splash of sea-freckles highlighting her elderly skin. She said, "I didn't see you at the movies, my dear."

"Yes, we missed you," said Linda, who had to go and be wearing pure white and practically no make-up, "and we were sorry you missed the picture, it was completely delightful."

Mrs. Nicholson shrugged. "I didn't think too much of it." She eyed the sequin gown. "So you're the one who bought it. I tried it on but it was just a little snug across the bust."

"I'll bet it was," Bill Hendricks slipped an arm round Claudia's waist. "That's the understatement of all time."

"Bill, that's not nice," Linda chided.

"Oh I don't mind. That is, if you don't," Mrs. Nicholson added with a small laugh.

"Linda doesn't," Bill answered for her. "It's a fair exchange." His arm tightened a little, pressing the cold beads against Claudia's flesh. Linda said reproachfully, "You're being very naughty, Bill."

"Look who's talking." Mrs. Nicholson laughed again as she snaked an elusive olive out of her empty cocktail glass. Claudia felt humiliated. It was all very oblique and sly, but the implication was unmistakable, and with sufficient reason. After the first ten minutes of their tour round the boat, there was little doubt how Linda Harwell felt about David. And as for David, the way she'd spoken his name and looked at him was enough to lull any man into a state of suspended mental functioning.

He probably wouldn't have batted an eyelash this morning if he'd heard Linda say that this evening was a "fun-idea". In fact, he didn't seem to object to anything about her, from earrings, to open-toed sandals. On Linda, everything looked beautiful.

"Come on, Claudia honey, change your

mind, and have a Bloody Mary, it'll cheer you up," Bill urged.

"I don't need any cheering up, but I'd like one anyway."

"That's my girl."

She felt like telling him that it wasn't a gesture of courage, it merely gave her something to do while everyone else was drinking. Would they never stop? She glanced down at Bill's dangling wrist to see how late it was. It was a quarter to ten. For no less than the third time, she removed his arm from her waist, and rose to her feet, thereby succeeding, at long last, in catching David's attention. She made her point succinctly. "Shall we eat?"

It was not the most polished means of putting an end to somebody else's cocktail party, but it worked. There was a general exodus to the elevator, which was too small to accommodate the entire party, so the men walked down the several flights of stairs to D deck, with Linda deciding at the last moment not to be lazy, and to walk, too.

"This is really a lark," Mrs. Bliss confided, as she made herself as flat as possible against the wall. "I'm embarrassed to say that I've never even seen the dining salon on this ship."

"Neither have I, and I'm not embarrassed about it," Mrs. Nicholson retorted. She had eaten off some of her lipstick with the canapes, and the frugal lavender of her natural mouth showed through in a peevish bowknot. Her evening was jaundiced by the absence of Barry Conwell, and after three double martinis, she was beginning not to care who knew it.

"It's a poifectly lovely room," Mrs. Woodburn adhered gently to the original topic, "if only it wasn't so far down."

It really was far down, and doubtless Mrs. Woodburn had fortified herself with a brace of seasick pills. Claudia wished that she had had the sense to do the same. The smell of rubber was much more noticeable on the lower decks. She closed her eyes as the cage swooped to a dizzying halt, only to open them with a small yelp of pain as Mrs. Nicholson's heel dug into her instep.

"Sorry. Was that your foot?"

"Yes, it was, you damn stupid clumsy imbecile of a woman," Claudia seethed behind a wooden smile.

Bixby, with an escort of lesser stewards,

awaited them at the threshold. Not that they needed to be shown to their table, the lit candles and a giant centre-piece of fruit and flowers were enough of a beacon. Nevertheless, Bixby led the way, blowing an invisible trumpet, and causing the curious stares of earlier diners to follow them across the room. Claudia wondered if David felt as uncomfortable as she did for having authored this show. His back was towards her, and ahead of her, so she couldn't see his face. "In season, this must be a really ghastly tourist nest," Bill Hendricks murmured at her side, "though it's not too bad when it's half empty."

"I hate snobs," Claudia returned shortly.

"But I'm enjoying it!" he insisted. "I think it's a cute idea."

"Well, I'll tell you what I think," Claudia snapped back at him. "I think a pedestal is a pretty shaky thing to get up and down on, you can break your neck on it."

"You can break your neck on a soap-box, too," he said.

It was the first intelligent remark he had made, and she was about to tell him so, when she caught sight of Matthew's friend sitting alone at a small table against the wall. Their eyes met, and the woman beckoned with a slight but unmistakable nod of her head. Claudia paused, undecided whether to heed or ignore this ill-timed exploitation of what was hardly an acquaintanceship. The poor thing must be trying to impress her fellow-diners. And what a snide little thought *that* was for anyone who preached so glibly of pedestals and snobs!

"Excuse me a minute," she said to Bill. "We'll finish the argument later. Tell David everyone should sit down, not to wait for me."

Before he knew what she was talking about, she was on her way to the far side of the room. Strange, she thought, everyone looked different in the evening, but Matthew's friend looked just the same as she had looked on deck—a little thinner, in an ageless grey dinner gown, yet essentially untouched by the magic of shaded lights and soft music.

"Good evening," Claudia said politely, and after an instant's hesitation, accepted the chair that the waiter swiftly placed for her. It was so hard to eat all by oneself. She remembered the long months her mother had lived alone in New York. "I never see anything but one poor little lamb chop and a few eggs in Mamma's ice-box," she used to tell David. It had made her heart ache for all the lonely women in the world, and she felt sad now, for the aloneness of a stranger whom she scarcely knew.

"I'm sorry to have called you away from your friends." The rather bony, reddish hands, guiltless of jewellery except for an old-fashioned gold band, rested quietly on the white cloth, and were somehow appealing and not unbeautiful. "It doesn't matter, I wish you could join us," Claudia said impulsively.

"Thank you," the woman declined with a faint sense of withdrawal, "I merely wanted to find out what the doctor had to say about Matthew this evening."

"The doctor?" Panic brought Claudia to her feet again. "I didn't know anything was wrong with him, I haven't seen him since lunch!" It was a shameful admission, even though there was an explanation. "Please tell me—" she faltered.

"I didn't realize that you didn't know, or I shouldn't have spoken of it. Don't be upset, I'm quite sure it's not serious. His foot caught in one of the deck chairs this afternoon, and he fell and struck his head against the metal hinge—"

Claudia didn't wait to hear any more. Only a few moments had passed, her guests were still in the process of finding their place cards and no one would miss her. The elevator was in use. She rushed up the stairs. It was a longer climb to A deck than she had realized. Would it never end?

Mertie and Sands and Hawkins had gone off duty. The young night steward was in the pantry, filling thermos jugs with fresh water, and yawning largely as he did so. He hadn't expected anyone to pass at that hour and when he saw Claudia, he quickly closed his mouth with an air of slapping his own wrist. "Good evening, madame."

"Good evening."

David had said, "Don't let me forget to leave a tip for the night-steward and the waiter we had the first day"—David always bent backwards when it came to tipping, he'd even remembered the steward who supplied Matthew with ping-pong balls and rackets. . . .

Her thoughts swung back to Matthew, and the old recurring fear gripped her heart as she pushed open the door of the drawing room, familiar as home after five short days. The impact of opulence no longer startled her senses. She had grown accustomed to it. The room was dim, now, with only a single lamp casting its glow upon Bertha, who sat in a straight chair, with her mending basket on her lap. She was doing something or other to one of the knees of Matthew's trousers, turning it this way and that with a frown of indecision.

"Bertha! Why didn't anyone tell me, how is he?"

Bertha pulled her sewing-spectacles from her ears, and down her nose. "Ach! I did not recognize you!" she exclaimed. "I thought it was somebody else! But you look very stylish," she amended hastily. "And Matthew is all right, he is fine. He is asleep, so I did not want to have the light in the bedroom." She searched Claudia's face. "Mr. David said he did not want you to know until tomorrow, but I said you would be sure to find out anyway."

"Not from him I didn't," said Claudia bitterly. "I was a fool, though, not to know something was wrong when he hustled me off without letting me say good-night to the children. He had no right to keep it from me."

"But it is not dangerous, Gott sei dank. Mr. Naughton was here with the doctor at six o'clock, and there is surely no concussion, and tomorrow Matthew will be as good as new. So Mr. Naughton said it was no sense to worry you."

"I'm his mother and it's my place to worry. You should have called me the minute it happened, Bertha. Really."

"It would have been foolish, in the middle of having your hair washed. Besides, the nice lady that likes Matthew so much, helped me carry him to the doctor's office, and then she took care of the baby for me while I put Matthew to bed. I am telling you because maybe you will want to thank her."

"I have, and I'd also like to send her a little something before we land. Remind me to get her name from you in the morning."

"I do not know her name, I never asked."

"Matthew must know it."

"He makes fun and calls her Mrs. Tick Tacktoe."

"That's a help."

"Anyway, you go back to your party, or Mr. David will be angry."

"Let him be angry. I want to see Matthew first."

"But he is asleep."

"I'll be careful not to wake him."

"Mrs. Naughton, what is the use, if you cannot speak to him?"

"I just want to look at him. I'll feel easier." She stiffened distrustfully. "Is there any reason you don't want me to go in?"

"Surely not. It is only that he has a bandage round his head, so do not be upset when you see it."

It was hard not to be. It seemed a very large bandage, and the whiteness of it lent him a kind of unearthly beauty. Claudia's heart tightened. "Whatever meanness is in him is mostly our fault," she thought humbly.

She stood watching the shallow rise and fall of his breathing, and gently touched her lips to his. His eyes flickered open, and for a long moment, she could discern not the faintest glimmer of recognition in his unblinking stare. Fear raced through her anew. Perhaps it was a concussion, doctors weren't God, especially ships' doctors. "Matthew," she whispered, "don't you know me, it's mother!"

He spoke. He said, "Boy. Do you look crazy."

She could have burst out crying with relief.

"Why, you little brat," she retorted in a shaky voice, "how do you think *you* look in that bandage?"

She saw the silly teeth slipping every which way through the grin that tugged at his lips. Thankfulness welled up in her. He was homely again, and fresh. And almost asleep. She tip-toed out.

Bertha was hovering anxiously at the door. Claudia patted her shoulder. "You don't have to worry," she said. "He's fine."

Back in the dining-room, she headed straight towards Matthew's friend. "I want to thank you for all you've done. I saw him, and the doctor said he'd be up and around again tomorrow."

"Splendid," the woman said. "But, please, don't let me detain you. I'm afraid I've already made you quite late for your dinner-party."

It was at once an acknowledgment and a dismissal. Claudia hesitated, irresolute. She wished that she could clear herself, make known, somehow, that a senseless and un-precedented coincidence of circumstances had conspired against her. "I don't blame you for thinking I'm one of those giddy society

187

mothers, especially in this get-up," she wanted to say, "but won't you believe that I'm not." She couldn't bring the words to her lips, explaining one's position was demeaning. Still, for some strange reason, she would have liked not to appear less than she was in this woman's eyes. "I'm sorry," she said lamely. "And thank you again." She held out her hand impulsively, and Matthew's friend smiled, a lovely and unexpected smile, whose business it was to light the eyes and warm the face, and never mind whether the teeth were straight or crooked, or overlapping. "I think I know why Matthew's such a fine little fellow," she said. "It does show up, you know."

Whatever she meant, it was good. "I'm glad I didn't explain," Claudia thought, as she hurried back to her table. "I didn't have to."

With one accord, the men rose, David a shade less quick on his feet than the others. She glowered at him across the expanse of white damask, adding his lack of chivalry to her grievances. She would not easily forgive him for keeping her in ignorance of Matthew's fall, and by the look of him he had

the audacity to be annoyed with her for finding out.

Bill Hendricks interrupted the private
exchange of marital hostilities. "So this is
where Lady Gresham has been hiding out,"
he said. "I didn't realize you were on such
intimate terms with her."

It took a moment to catch on. Bill had a
sharper wit than she had given him credit for.
First, his rather astute remark about the soap
box, and now a neat return on her jibe about
Count and Countess Cazzoni. Not that
Matthew's friend could, or should be,
bracketed with the bearded fat man and his
fat wife, but dinner conversation didn't seem
to require either continuity or intelligence.
The main thing was just to keep on gabbling
on about anything at all. "Actually," Claudia
returned with forced levity, "I was speaking
o her about my son. They're the ones who
are intimate."

Bill shook his head as if to clear it. "I give
up," he said. "Anyway, I understand that
we're indirectly beholden to Lady Gresham
for this superb menu."

"Only the fish," Claudia qualified. She had
missed out on the caviar, but she was just in
time for the bisque, which everyone was

going into ecstasies over. It was sheer mes
merism. He-crab or she-crab, it wasn't much
different from any ordinary cream-soup.

The Dolphin, however, was very tasty
according to Mrs. Bliss. Claudia had always
associated the expression with the sort o
person who dotted "I's" with little circles
and leaned towards writing paper with
coloured pictures on top. Possibly Mrs. Bliss
under the relaxing influence of "such lovely
white wine," had slipped painlessly into tha
cosy period of her life that predated her hus
band's ambassadorship. She must have been
someone nice to know in those days, Claudia
reflected, warm, and human, like Bertha. I
was interesting the way a little drinking could
make people into what they were, whereas
too much could make them into what they
were careful never to let themselves be.

She had seen a woman no older than hersel
carried out of the café the previous evening
her mind paralyzed beyond the point o
vigilance. "How poifectly revolting," Mrs
Woodburn had pronounced, but Mrs
Nicholson had argued, rather pugnaciously
that she had known Cora Vanderlip before
she ever touched the stuff, "and believe you

190

me," said Mrs. Nicholson, who was apt to become a shade blatant with her third or fourth cocktail, "the way that husband of hers is carrying on, I, for one, don't blame her."

"Cora Vanderlip," Mrs. Woodburn had stood solidly upon her customary glass of sherry, "was born vulgar. And not because her mother happened to run a boarding-house. I had a great respect for Cora's mother."

"Now did you really, dear? However did I get the impression that it was Henry who was such a close friend of Cora's mother?"

It was never easy to negate the poisonous sweetness of Mrs. Nicholson's insinuations, but Mrs. Woodburn had turned an unruffled smile in her husband's direction. "A very close friend. In fact, it was Henry who introduced me to Cora's mother many years ago. Cora was in her early teens and some-what of a problem even then, as I recall."

Later, Claudia had asked David what he thought Mrs. Woodburn would be like if she ever got a few Bloody Marys into her by mis-take. "Just more of the same," he'd said.

She hadn't realized until this evening that she had propounded the rudiments of an interesting theory. At least it seemed that way, for with the re-filling of the wine glasses and a second passing of the Dolphin, everyone began to act like an intensified version of himself. The men, with the exception of Mr. Woodburn and David, welcomed another serving with a gusty appreciation of good eating, while Mrs. Bliss did so with a guilty conscience. "I know I oughtn't to, but I just can't resist," she said.

"You're a big fat slob," Mrs. Nicholson told her, "the damn stuff is loaded with calories. Watch how I do it." She waved the waiter away, and he ended up at Linda's side, a pair of sizable serving spoons poised between the two middle fingers of his right hand. Claudia tried to study out how he managed to fulcrum the implements without the aid of his other hand, but inasmuch as David was incessantly decrying her lack of mechanical ability, she decided that she might as well not bother to learn. By her husband's standards she couldn't even use a can opener properly, which was enough to give any woman a manual trauma.

She was fascinated, anyway, and watched the waiter lift, with dexterity, a neat segment of Dolphin towards Linda's plate, only to have her stop him mid-air with a little shriek. "Oh don't, I shouldn't!" she cried.

The waiter was confused and so was the Dolphin. It slithered, like a live thing, back on to the platter. Linda regarded it ruefully. "Oh, dear," she wailed, "It was so heavenly, I'm almost tempted to change my mind."

"Well, for God's sake, go ahead and stop holding up the show," Mrs. Nicholson barked.

The seductive curve of Linda's lips puckered into a childish moué. "Oh, don't be such an old meany," she said plaintively, "just because you happen to be running over with strength of character, don't expect everybody else to be. David, shall I, or shall I not?"

"If you want it, take it."

"You're an old meany, too," she pouted.

Bill Hendricks rescued Claudia's napkin and returned it to her lap. "I've never seen Linda high before," he chuckled. "I watched her upstairs, she kept on ordering drinks so that everybody else would keep on ordering."

"Poor thing," said Claudia. She meant it, for although Linda might not know it, she was slowly but surely coquetting her way into the realm of still another of David's pet abominations. How they used to squabble in the early years of their marriage because Claudia could never decide what to order in a restaurant, and saw nothing amiss in each selecting something different, and sharing. To this day, in fact, she harboured a secret resentment to his persistent aversion to a perfectly reasonable scheme.

"I'll take some more if you'll take half," Linda was piping away, like a little girl wanting to be coaxed, and practically out on her ear at that point.

In answer, David beckoned the waiter. "I'll help Mrs. Harwell," he said shortly. He picked up one of the spoons, scooped a sizable chunk, and deposited it on Linda's plate.

She uttered a squeal of protest. "Oh David, you bad boy, I wanted an ittie bittie *bittsie* piece!"

Claudia averted her eyes. She hated to watch even a worm suffer, and she had no love for worms. Linda wasn't suffering yet, but it wouldn't be long now. Nor would Linda ever know what had happened, or why, or when. "Such an ittie bittie *bittsie* dolphin," Claudia brooded happily, "to cook such a great big goose."

She could feel rather than see David glaring at her across the table. She straightened her face in a hurry. This was not the time to be sporting a Mona Lisa smile.

6

IT was one thing to have Linda's frailties come as a shock to him, but why, Claudia asked herself resentfully, should he keep on behaving as if she were to blame? There was a limit to even a wife's tolerance, and David reached that limit when she managed to slip over to his side as they were leaving the dining-room, and said, offering him plenty of lee-way to re-establish friendly relations, "What was the idea of giving me those looks across the table?"

"We'll talk about it later," he rejoined coldly.

Talk about it later, and sit through the remainder of the evening with his high-and-mighty disfavour hanging over her head? They'd talk about it right now, since she was the one, and not he, who had cause to be angry. "I'll never forgive you for not telling me about Matthew," she took the offensive.

He shrugged. "I knew you'd snoop around until you found out."

"All the more reason not to have kept it from me!"

"Lower your voice, you're making a spectacle of yourself. Matthew is perfectly all right."

"Perfectly all right, with his head cut open!"

"Maybe he'll learn to look where he's going now."

"You're just plain heartless when it comes to your own son! And don't tell me he's my son!"

"Hurry up, you two love-birds," Mrs. Nicholson called out from the elevator. "There's room for both of you."

"I'll walk," David elected tersely.

"Take my blessing with you," Claudia muttered. She stepped into the cage, a careful smile frozen to her face. The door slid closed. "A poifectly lovely dinner," Mrs. Woodburn congratulated her. "But if you'll excuse me, Henry and I won't join you in the lounge, we're going to toin in early."

"I think I'll turn in early too," said Claudia, "Matthew's had a little fall—"

"David told me, but I didn't think you knew," Linda broke in sympathetically.

197

"Anyway, Aunt Emily saw him, and said he seemed quite chipper."

"Did you?" Claudia asked Mrs, Woodburn. (I'm only the child's mother).

"Yes, I'm sure he'll be fine by to-morrow," Mrs. Woodburn assured her.

"I don't trust any injury to the head," Mrs. Bliss put in a firm two-cents worth.

"Oh pooh, kids fall down all the time." Mrs. Nicholson seemed bored with the whole episode. She yawned widely. "Excuse me. Sleepy. Thank heaven mine's married, now his wife can worry about him."

Claudia hadn't thought of Mrs. Nicholson as having any children, much less a grown son, presumably as old if not older than Barry Conwell. It was certainly an involved little bunch of people—Mrs. Bliss had told her confidentially that Bill Hendrick's wife had killed herself with a hunting gun less than a year ago, although it had been hushed up as an accident.

"It was an accident, all right," Mrs. Nicholson had added drily. "An accident that she was pregnant and everyone knew that it couldn't possibly have been poor Bill." Claudia had meant to ask David why it couldn't possibly have been Bill, but she hadn't got around to it. They hadn't had much time to themselves on this trip, and the once they had planned to be alone this evening had come to nothing. If they weren't careful, they'd end up being as involved as the rest of them, including Mr. Woodburn and Cora Vanderlip's mother, which must have been quite a story in its day. It was a toss-up whether it was less complicated if you got into trouble because you had the money to do it with, or got into trouble because you hadn't. One thing was certain: she and David had never been in a mess like this when they had the farm; they were too busy counting every penny to buy fertilizer for the land and feed for the animals. Now they were so busy keeping busy that they didn't have time to attend to their own back yard, which was beginning to sprout all kinds of alien emotions and misunderstandings. Tonight, for example, she'd go to bed, and he'd come in late, and she'd be too proud to let him know she was awake, and in the morning the hurt that resided between them would be so elusive, that it would seem not to be there. That was probably the reason married people went from separate beds to separate rooms, and blamed it on snoring, or having to read with the light on. In that way, they never really had to get down to rock bottom, because they didn't see enough of each other to make it worth the effort.

"Good evening, madame."

"Good evening," she said, wishing that stewards, especially night stewards, would take it for granted.

He was just coming out of the drawing-room, having placed the usual handsome basket of fruit upon the coffee table. She'd promised herself to sample one of the persimmons before the trip was over, but that was another thing she hadn't got round to. They always finished dinner too late, and ate too much. Even the children didn't give the festive arrangement a second look after the first excitement wore off. Bertha had begun by putting away an occasional apple for a rainy day, but it soon became evident that there weren't any rainy days, and besides it made the room smell. There was always a definite little smell in the children's room anyway. It wasn't objectionable, it was good, but David said he liked the way a barn smelt better.

Claudia listened at the closed door, attuned to the emanations of sound and silence. They were all asleep: she could hear the faint rumble of Bertha's breathing, the stillness of Michael's small body, the infinitesimal grunt of Matthew, busy in his dreams. Satisfied, she turned away, and saw David watching her from the threshold of their bedroom. He must have taken the stairs at a pretty fast clip to be here almost as quickly as she was. Maybe he had come to his senses and was ready to let bygones be bygones—whatever they were. "They all seem to be asleep, so everything must be all right," she said again, willing to meet him half way.

He bit her head off for her pains. "What did you expect? I told you there was nothing to get hysterical about."

It was infuriating to be called hysterical when you were perfectly calm, and yet she could see that his ill-temper stemmed mainly from his cigarette lighter; he stood there trying to work it, and muttering something about it being shot to hell and what the devil had she done with it.

"Nothing," Claudia pleaded, innocent. "I didn't touch it."

"You know damn well I don't mean you!" he flared at her.

Of course she knew it, but she wouldn't

have been human if she hadn't goaded him into saying it. At the same time, and quite inconsistently, she was a little disappointed that he was behaving so tritely, blaming his wife because another woman had let him down. It was the way most men might react, but not David. She waited, with a kind of clinical curiosity, for what he was going to say next. He said, with no lessening of ill-humour, "Are you going to stand there all night and listen to see if he's breathing?" He flung the lighter down on the table, and lit his cigarette with a match. "From the first day out that little brat has been a pain in the neck," he said, and again he didn't say neck. Claudia's anger flamed up. "Please don't take it out on an innocent child!" she adjured him sharply.

"Just what do you mean by that little remark?"

"You know what I mean, and stop wiggling your nostrils at me like that, you look silly."

His nostrils stopped wiggling, and turned a waxy white, which meant real trouble. "I know how you feel," she said contritely, "and I'm sorry."

"The thing that gets me is that it was bad taste to begin with," he burst out, as if she had inadvertently released the full force of his seething resentment. "Such lousy bad taste."

The word "lousy" sat oddly on his lips. He was past master at first-rate bad language, but he seldom went in for the mediocre. "I think you're being a little harsh," she defended Linda out of pure justice. "It was only because of hospitality that she had a little too much to drink."

He turned on her. "What the hell are you talking about!"

"What the hell do you think I'm talking about," she retorted smartly. "How many people do you know gave a cocktail party tonight!"

"If you mean Linda, her actions have no bearing whatsoever on your own behaviour."

"My behaviour?"

"Yes, your behaviour! I couldn't believe my eyes when I saw you fawning over Lady Gresham like a cheap little social climber!"

She was too surprised to be angry. "You're out of your mind, I never even met Lady Gresham!"

"Exactly. So you had to go and use that damned fish to wangle an introduction. And I repeat that it was lousy bad taste!"

Now that she knew what was upsetting him

(or what he thought was upsetting him), she got so boiling mad to think that he'd think her capable of that kind of—well, there was no other word for it—"lousy bad taste", that she couldn't talk straight enough to tell him what she thought of him for thinking it. And where did he ever get such an idea in the first place? It was so unlike him to jump to any such ridiculous conclusion. Or could it be, it suddenly made sense, that he'd had one ear cocked in her direction at the table, and had overheard Bill Hendrick's paying her back for Count Cazzoni? Which in turn could very easily account for the way he'd kept glaring at her from the moment she sat down.

"I see nothing funny about it," he said stiffly.

"I do," she hiccoughed between giggles. "It serves you jolly right for eavesdropping, old chap."

"That, dear girl, is your department, not mine."

"You're hitting below the belt. I haven't been a listener since we had a party-line telephone on the farm, and that was years ago!"

"Don't try to change the subject. If there's any reasonable explanation of your performance this evening, I'd like to hear it."

"I'm not in the habit of explaining my position." She left him standing there, and walked into the bedroom. She didn't want him to see that all at once she realized how wonderful it was that he was so much more disappointed in her than in Linda. The lesser impact of another woman's defections might not be the yardstick for measuring love in most marriages, but it was a good enough yardstick for two people who felt the same way about little things being more significant than big things.

She was aware that he had followed her into the room, and she busied herself at the dressing-table, unscrewing her earrings. Through the mirror, she saw him rummage through a drawer for his tobacco pouch. He found it. "I'm going out for a breath of fresh air," he informed her tersely. "Don't wait up for me."

She barely caught him by the coat-tails. 'Oh, come back here, you idiot! That wasn't Lady Gresham I was talking to, it was Matthew's girl-friend. She happened to be on deck when he fell down, and she couldn't have been nicer, Bertha said. You don't believe me!" she broke off, aghast.

"Did you expect me to believe you?" he asked quite reasonably.

"This is ridiculous!" she sputtered. "Ask Bill Hendricks!"

"I don't have to ask Bill Hendricks." He took her hand. "Suppose we sit down quietly and talk this over."

"You don't think I'm lying, you think I'm crazy!"

"Well," he admitted reluctantly, "just an ittsie bittsie bit."

She regarded him gloomily. "Those are the damned things that make me love you in spite of everything. Come on to bed, and I'll see that you meet her in the morning."

"Who?"

"Matthew's girl-friend."

"What's her name?"

"I don't know, but I saw her coming out of her stateroom, so I can ask her stewardess."

"I'll save you the trouble. It's Lady Isabel Gresham."

"But I told you it wasn't!"

"And I'm telling you it is. Linda introduced me to her at the movies this afternoon."

Claudia stared at him. "I don't believe it," she denied flatly. "You're crazy."

"Touché."

She went back to the dressing table bench and sat down. "I could wring Bill Hendrick's neck for fooling me, he told me it was Lady Gresham."

"So you did know it!"

"Of course I didn't, I thought he was making it up!—I still do. I think you're in cahoots with each other."

"Ask Linda."

"Oh, all right, touché to you, too," she gave in. "I just don't understand it, though. Lady Gresham, on B deck, with cotton gloves, and plain as anything."

"You don't know English nobility," David told her, with an air of authority, not unmixed with respect.

She eyed him scathingly. "Oh, so now she's nobility, but before she was some middle-aged crack-pot who didn't have anything better to do than play tick-tack-toe with Matthew!"

"That's the one angle of it that *I* don't understand," he admitted.

"Naturally you don't," she said coldly. "You have always underestimated my son. And I think you owe me an apology all round."

"I might consider it, if you wipe that face off."

"But I'd never get it back on again, let me keep it until we land."

"Off."

"Now?"

"Now"

"All of it?"

"All of it," he said firmly.

She left a little of the mouth and eyes, partly for local colour, and partly because she ran out of cleansing tissue. Her hair presented an additional problem. Antoine had cautioned her to sleep in a net, and to lie as quietly as possible in order to preserve the contour. "Antoine told me that some of his clients even sit up all night," she debated aloud.

"They probably haven't got anything better to do," said David.

"Probably not," Claudia agreed. "Would you mind if I listened to see if Matthew's all right, first?"

"I not only wouldn't mind, I'll listen with you."

He couldn't have been more engaging in every conceivable way, and at last she was absolutely certain that the ghost of Linda was forever laid. "This is almost as nice as an upper berth," she murmured, as she fell asleep.

She slept fitfully, perhaps because they weren't as young as they used to be, perhaps because of worrying about Matthew in the back of her mind. Mrs. Bliss was right in saying not to trust a head injury, maybe he'd wake up in the morning with some unforeseen complication.

He seemed, however, more than normal when he awoke. In fact, Claudia secretly considered him obnoxious, the way he played up his bandage for all it was worth. It had slipped down across his cheek during the night, but he wouldn't let Bertha adjust it. "It'll bleed again!" he fended her off.

"Ach no, there is nothing to bleed now, be a good boy and let Bertha straight it, you cannot eat your breakfast with one eye."

"I can see," he insisted, tipping the cream jug over in his haste to elude her.

"Leave him alone if he thinks he looks pretty, and likes to eat with one eye," Claudia said shortly, and left the scene before she lost her temper.

"How is he?" David called out from the bathroom.

"His old sweet self. Can I come in?"

"No!"

"Tell me when, then. And hurry, I want to be dressed when the doctor gets here."

By the time the doctor arrived, the bandage was practically a noose. "Look here, old chap, that's not doing us very much good, is it?" he said, and snipped it in two and tossed it into the waste-basket, applying in its place a very undramatic patch of adhesive tape.

Matthew was affronted. "Is that all?"

"That is all," the doctor confirmed cheerily. "You're in extraordinarily good shape."

Matthew tested the advantage of being in extraordinarily good shape. "Okay, then I can play ping-pong," he announced.

"Oh, I shouldn't try it today, old man. Tomorrow perhaps."

"How can I play tomorrow," Matthew caught him up, "when I won't even be on the boat tomorrow."

"Right you are, but I expect you'll want to be feeling fit when you get to London, won't you?"

"What's fit?" he demanded suspiciously.

"Matthew, you're being purposely stupid," Claudia reprimanded him. "Should he stay in bed, Doctor?"

"I don't think it's necessary, no. But I shouldn't advise going on deck until after luncheon, and then only if the sun comes out."

Matthew said something under his breath. The doctor looked startled. "Never mind, the baby will not go out either this morning," Bertha jumped in quickly. "We will all have a nice time indoors."

"Oh, shoot," said Matthew.

Claudia followed the doctor to the door. "My husband will be sorry to have missed you, he's filling out some forms, but please tell me the truth if you feel there's any danger of a concussion."

"I should say none whatsoever at this point. Unavoidably of course, he'll carry a slight scar on his temple."

"If I know Matthew," said Claudia, "it won't be slight, and he'll love every minute of it."

"Bright little chap," said the doctor, politely.

It was a rushed and disjointed day for everyone, especially for Bertha, with both children on her hands, and packing besides. Sands offered to help, but no, Bertha had to do everything herself. "I'm no megalomaniac like you," said Claudia, "I'm going to let Mertie do mine."

Bertha was a genius at packing, but Mertie was an artist. She folded everything with such exquisite precision that even an old sweater breathed importance from its cocoon of pristine tissue paper that appeared in limitless plenty out of nowhere. Claudia blushed to remember the bottle of hand lotion wrapped in toilet paper. That first day on board seemed a lifetime ago. How embarrassed she had been to find Hawkins and Mertie unpacking the motley collection of suitcases, with their noses in the air. Now Mertie was packing the same suitcases with the same things, but her nose wasn't in the air any longer. She folded the old pink net into an impeccable oblong. "The new gown is handsome," she said, "but not as fine as this, nor that little yellow gown either. I'll never get over you giving it to my daughter straight off your own back so to speak."

Claudia had been tempted to take the yellow back and give Mertie's daughter the new one instead, but now her hands were tied. She was lucky the sequin gown was the only casualty of the trip, except for Matthew's bump on the head. David had got off pretty well, too. Judging from last night, his bump with Linda had left no scar at all.

"There," said Mertie, with satisfaction, "that's one suitcase out of the way. I'd better leave the others for after, and help Sands with the children's lunch."

"It can't be that late!"

"It is, or fairly close to it."

She thought, regretfully, how she had planned for Matthew to have lunch with them in the dining-room at least once or twice during the trip, but somehow they'd got themselves tied up with the café crowd day after day.

"Mertie, could you manage two extra?" she suddenly asked.

"It would be nothing at all," said Mertie. "I'll have a menu brought in straightaway."

Claudia gave a slight shudder. She knew the long, elaborate menu by heart, and she was appalled by the monotony of variety: there wasn't a single thing that could possibly tempt her. "Don't bother with one," she said. "What are the children having?"

"I believe, madame, that it's filet mignon, vegetables and a sweet of some sort."

She shuddered again. "Could we order something special, do you think?"

"Certainly. Anything you wish. I'll speak to the chief dining steward."

"Tell him two ham sandwiches, on rye bread, and not to cut the crusts off, and three bottles of beer. Not warmish, though. Cold. Very cold."

"I'd hardly call that a very 'special' lunch," said Mertie, "in fact I'd hardly call it more than a tea-time snack. Wouldn't you care for a bit of broth, and a sweet as well?"

"Not even a sweet," said Claudia. "Maybe a pot of coffee, though."

"And you'll all have it together in the drawing-room?" Mertie asked delicately.

"All five of us," said Claudia.

She wondered what was keeping David so long. She went in search of him, and found him at the purser's desk, along with a lot of other passengers, all asking endless questions about customs and currency and when the boat was due to land at Cherbourg. "Good," he said, when he saw her. "I was just going to look for you. Here, sign your name."

She signed. "We're having lunch with the children in the room."

"Sign again." He gave her another paper, and pointed to a blank line. "Why?"

"Because.—How soon will you be through with all this red tape?"

"I'm through now. It's messy to eat in the room with a bunch of kids."

"It's not a bunch, it's only two."

"It'll seem like a bunch."

"Too bad about you. You didn't make any other plans, I hope?"

"It was hard to get out of, but I didn't."

"Who?"

"Linda and Bill Hendricks."

"Oh. Would you rather?"

"I would if I'd known what I know now."

"You'll have to live through it."

When he saw the ham sandwiches and the beer, he said to Matthew in a stern voice, "Your mother's a wonderful woman, my lad, and don't you ever forget it." He felt one of the bottles of beer. "A remarkable woman," he amended. "Your glass, Bertha."

"Ach, thank you. It is better than champagne."

"Much," said Claudia. "Stop leaning on the mustard, David."

"Hold your horses."

The baby threw his spoon up in the air. He laughed inordinately, baring his teeth like little kernels of new corn.

"Quit showing off!" Matthew commanded him imperiously.

"Mr. Big-mouth himself," said David.

"Yah, yah, yah!" Matthew shouted.

"Look. The three of you. Behave yourselves," said Claudia. "Do you want Mertie and Sands and Hawkins to think you're nothing but a lot of wild Americans? Not a peep out of you when they come back with your dessert."

"Peep," said David.

"Peep peep," Matthew topped him.

The baby looked thoughtful. Bertha hastily took his mind off with a spoonful of spinach which he hated. She turned to Matthew. "Did you give Mamma the nice letter you wrote to Aunt Candy and Uncle John to mail with hers to-night?"

Claudia put the remainder of her sandwich back on her plate. Suddenly she didn't feel like eating any more of it. "No, he didn't give it to me," she said in a strained voice. "But it isn't too late to go with mine." She couldn't believe it of herself. Not once, in all these five days, had she thought to write to Candy. "I won't be able to wait until we get your first letter from the boat," Candy had said tearfully in parting. "Make it a long one, and be sure to put it into the mail-bag at Cherbourg, we'll get it faster than from Southampton."

"I will," Claudia had promised. "I will. I'll write a little every day—"

But she hadn't written a word, except for the cable to relieve their minds about Matthew. "Matthew safe and scared. Stop. Mislaid in third class. Stop. Details follow."

"What's the matter," said David, "aren't you going to finish your sandwich?"

She looked at him reproachfully. How could he have forgotten too? "I've had enough, I'm not hungry any more. Do you want the other half?"

"No thanks. You, Bertha."

Bertha was full of conflict.

"I will save it for later," she weakened. "It is a shame to waste such a good sandwich. Nice rye bread and mustard. Like home."

Like home. Five days, and she hadn't once thought of home, and the honey-coloured panelling for the library, and the way the new silos would marry to the old barns, and the ancient sweetness of the little hip-roof house. . .

"Oh David, we ought to be ashamed, not writing to Candy and John the whole trip," she said, as soon as they were alone.

"Speak for yourself, I've written John twice."

"You have? I didn't see you. When?"

"On deck, the second day out, and I got off a letter in the writing-room this morning. I had a couple of ideas on the Kipp Memorial project," he added a little sheepishly.

"But that's downright sneaky. You're not supposed to be having ideas, you're supposed to be loafing!"

"You can't turn your mind off like a faucet."

"I thought that was what an ocean voyage was supposed to do. It did it for me. I didn't even remember to write Candy."

"Well, you see it works this way, the more mind you have the harder it is to turn off."

"Don't try to pass it off as a joke. John told you to forget the office for three months."

"'John told me'," he repeated with a short laugh. "Now let me tell you something, my girl. If we land that Kipp contract, it'll be the biggest thing that ever happened to us.

Furthermore—and get this through your head—I'm not taking orders from anybody any longer, no matter whether I've been on my back in the Adirondacks for a year, or whether I'm sitting on my rear in the Alps, or anything else."

"Especially the 'anything else', which, knowing you, I gather means having a little money, to put it conservatively."

"You gather correctly."

She sighed. "'Once an architect always an architect.' I don't believe you've really tuned out of the office this whole trip."

"Oh, I wouldn't say that. There have been moments."

"What kind of moments, may I ask?"

"Good, bad, and indifferent."

"And which moment was I?"

"Remind me to tell you some day. Gott sei dank we don't have to dress tonight. Has Bertha got a needle and thread?"

"Does a duck swim? Don't be silly. What do you want it for?"

"A button's loose on this shirt."

"I have enough needle and thread for one button. Are there decent pens in the writing room or are they thin and squeaky?"

"Thin and squeaky. Here, I'll lend you

mine, but see that you return it. And you'd better hurry, the mail bag for Cherbourg closes at six."

"I will. Talking of Bertha, did I tell you I told her who Lady Gresham was this morning?"

"Wouldn't it be a little more accurate to say you told her who Matthew's girl friend was? What did she say when you told her?"

"She said she was a very nice lady *anyway*. I don't think Bertha's ever been over-enthusiastic about the English. How do you think she'll like coming back on a French boat?"

"I'll give you three guesses."

"Well, I suppose it's the same as with you—once a German always a German. It's a good thing we're spending most of our time in nice old neutral Switzerland."

"Nothing about spending most-of-our-time-in-Switzerland is a good thing," David returned sourly. "And don't tell me we're racing over there for the children's sake."

"But we are. Paris is horrid now—"

"Don't be blasphemous, Paris is never horrid."

"Weather-wise it is. And London is no place to be in February."

"What's wrong with it? Wait'll you see the red cheeks the English kids have. Rain and fog agree with them."

"But you're not an English kid," she almost gave herself away. "I think I'll write my letter to Candy down here and keep you company," she wisely changed the subject. "What are you doing, anyway, addressing all those envelopes?"

"Easier to distribute the tips in the morning."

"You said to remind you about the night-steward and the waiter we had the first day."

"I have them down."

"And don't forget the men in the elevator—particularly the lame one, Bertha says he's so sweet with the perambulator."

"He lost his leg at Dunkirk," said David, which meant that he hadn't forgotten him.

She thought that possibly they might be making a little too much of a production of tipping, what with all the envelopes and lists, but at cocktails that evening, she discovered that everybody made a production of tipping. As a matter of fact, it was Mrs. Nicholson's chief topic of conversation, and it seemed that she had got the whole thing down to a science. "You ought to publish a handbook,"

Linda remarked, with considerable acid in her tone. Bill Hendricks put his arm round her. "Linda, my pet, you've acted real edgy all day," he said, and Mrs. Woodburn agreed, a little anxiously, that she had noticed Linda wasn't quite herself.

"Please, I'm perfectly all right," Linda insisted. "I always find the last night of anything a little depressing."

Bill Hendricks gave his usual unsubtle wink. "Cheer up, sweet, you'll still have a week of London. By the way," he turned to David, "we all missed you and Claudia at lunch, old boy. The Blisses said they saw you going down to the main dining-room with Lady Gresham."

"Oh no, I didn't, Bill," Mrs. Bliss contradicted quickly. "You misunderstood me. I just said I *imagined* they might be lunching with Lady Gresham."

"We had lunch with the children," David explained tersely, and Linda, poor thing, really did look more cheerful about everything.

"How much are you giving your steward and stewardess, David?" Mrs. Nicholson shot at him across the table.

Claudia was afraid he was going to say

"None of your business," but he replied, a little too civilly for comfort, "I haven't decided."

"Well, don't go overboard, and spoil them for the rest of us. Three pounds each is more than sufficient. Jacques is different. There's no set rule about head waiters. Personally we always give him five pounds the first day, and then we're sure of a decent table and decent service."

"I see," said David, who had apportioned Jacques two pounds, and Mertie and Hawkins six pounds each. He didn't say anything else, except, "I see," so Claudia filled in an awkward silence by asking what was proper to give the men on the elevator. Mrs. Nicholson shrugged. "Frankly," she said, "I don't bother with a regular tip for any of them." She shook herself more securely into her sable jacket. "Good heavens, one must draw the line somewhere on a big boat like this."

"I see," Claudia echoed David. Only she didn't see. She began to feel as depressed as Linda, but for different reasons.

Fortunately, no one wanted to sit around after dinner: it was as if the trip were already over. Without regret, Claudia said goodbye to the Nicholsons, who had suddenly changed their plans and were getting off at Cherbourg early the next morning. Barry Conwell was getting off at Cherbourg, too. He didn't bother to say goodbye to anyone. "That's fine with me," said David, as they walked back to their suite.

"Fine with me too," said Claudia.

While they were at dinner, Hawkins had piled all the luggage in the drawing-room. The only thing that was missing was the flat box that had held Bertha's dark blue cape and flowing veil—she was wearing it off the boat. Contemplatively, Claudia took stock of the conglomeration. "I don't seem to mind it so much now. Why?"

"The rich can afford to be shabby," David returned, curtly. He picked up the stack of neatly labelled envelopes from the table. "What do you want to do about these?" he asked her.

There was no point in pretending that she didn't know what he meant. She didn't have to be a mathematician to figure out that David's tips came to easily twice as much as they should have—according to Mrs. Nicholson. "Whatever you say, dear," she replied.

"It's not too late to take out a pound or so here and there," he said.

Her heart turned a little sick inside her. They were acting just like rich people. She supposed it was bound to happen, but just the same she wished that money hadn't become quite that important. It was important, of course, when you didn't have enough of it, and had to stay awake at nights worrying about making ends meet, but when you had so much more than enough, what was the point of letting it become so much more important than when you didn't have any?

"Whatever you say, dear," she repeated, and went into the bedroom as he sat down at the table and began to rummage through the envelopes. She didn't want to see him "take out a pound or so here and there." True, she'd never been one to be frightfully generous in a taxi-cab—that is, she'd always hated to see the meter drop a nickel at the very last instant—but this was different. Watching David "take out a pound or two here and there" would be like seeing something die a little. It was probably inconsistent and silly, since she'd never been above scolding him for being over generous, but, on the other hand, she couldn't bear the thought

225

of being married to a stingy tipper. "I counted my chickens too soon," she thought. "The sequin dress isn't the only casualty of this trip."

The lights were out before David brought up the subject again. "I might as well confess something," his voice came gruffly from his bed. "And call me any names you want, but that damn Nicholson dame with all her millions made me see red, so I changed a couple of tips."

"I know," Claudia said. "I saw you. Which ones did you take a pound or two out of?"

"Jacques," he said with grim satisfaction. "He'll have the shock of his life when he opens his envelope. But that lazy devil gets enough and without doing a damn thing to earn it."

"Any more?" Claudia asked in a small voice.

"Any more what?"

"Did you take out of?"

"Not exactly."

"How, not exactly?"

"Well, if you must know, I added a pound here and there."

She could hardly speak for the way her sick

heart got up on its hind legs. "The elevator boy who lost his leg at Dunkirk?"

"He was one," David admitted. "And I thought Sands deserved a little more than Mertie, for putting up with Matthew."

"Don't say any more," Claudia broke in. "I think you're extravagant, foolish, spiteful and wonderful." She jumped out of bed. "Move over."

It seemed that they'd scarcely fallen asleep when a great noise of silence wakened them. "The boat's stopped!" Claudia exclaimed. "What's happened?"

"We're at Cherbourg." David was already on his way to the window. She caught up with him, and they stood looking out into the still, grey mist of morning towards the shadowy coast of France. Claudia slipped her cold hand into his warm one. "I didn't know I'd be this thrilled," she said.

"I'd divorce you if you weren't."

"Yes, but watch that I don't get to be a bore about it. After all, millions of all kinds of people go to Europe all the time, so it's nothing new to anybody."

"It's new to us."

"Only to me, not to you. You studied abroad for a year."

"That was before we were married," he said. "Now it'll be new all over again."

It wasn't often that he was so sweet so early in the morning. She hoped that Switzerland would have the same effect on him.

Getting off the boat later at Southampton was more full of red tape than getting on. David said, taking his brief case with him, "Wait here in the lounge until I come back for you, and don't you dare," he warned Matthew sternly, "budge away from your mother's side."

"Thanks," said Claudia dryly. Impossible as it might seem, Matthew had outdone himself all the morning. "I'm glad to get off this old boat," he kept proclaiming raucously, and kicked Hawkins in the shins and called Mertie a bad name, which had elicited from Bertha a severe, but not too pained rebuke. Bertha, for all her wonderful traits, was not above a possessive streak when it came to the children, therefore Claudia tactfully refrained from advancing the theory that Matthew was, in truth, so devastated at the thought of leaving the boat, that he tried to hide his feelings by pretending the opposite. As always, and in spite of her annoyance with him, she felt that strange identification with the subtle woes of childhood. Poor Matthew. He had found a whole new world on shipboard, only to have to relinquish it.

"Why do we got to stand around here so long?"

"Not 'got' and don't shout, and stop pulling at that adhesive tape."

"It hurts my head."

"It doesn't."

"Anyhow, it itches," he compromised.

"That shows it's healing."

"What does healing mean?"

"Getting better," Bertha pinch-hitted. "Stand quiet and be a good boy like Gregory."

"I want to go—"

"You don't," Claudia interrupted firmly.

"Just only over there," he whined. "I got to see something."

"You know what your father said," she began and broke off as Mrs. Bliss, looking like at least two different people in a high peacock green turban, and leopard coat, bustled up and exclaimed with an air of discovery, "Oh there you are, my dear! This is always such a dreadfully boring business of waiting around at the last minute, isn't it?"

She darted a glance of startled approval a Bertha, who stood out in her flowing veil lik a monument of decayed aristocracy.

"Say hello, Michael," Bertha beamed fatuously. Michael didn't say hello, but Mrs Bliss rose to the bait just the same. "What darling baby!" she enthused. "And *thi* handsome fellow! Why, you're just as good a: new after that nasty fall, aren't you, sweet heart?"

"This is little Gregory Harwell," Claudi interceded hastily. "Linda asked us to keep an eye on him while she went to the purser': desk." She was ignominiously glad tha Matthew, contrary to his father's instruc tions, was at the moment busily engaged ir not minding his own business. As luck woulc have it, however, he suddenly had enough o: watching how an old gentleman's hearing-aic worked, and ambled back to them. The smal patch on his forehead left little room fo doubt. Mrs. Bliss blinked, and then provec that she was every inch the diplomat's wife by giving no hint that Matthew had crossed her vision. She said, *sotto voce*, "Claudia, tel! me, have you heard the latest gossip?"

"About us?" Claudia asked with forced lightness. (Linda had hot-footed it after

David with her landing card not ten minutes ago.)

"Heavens, you silly girl, of course not!" Mrs. Bliss laughed unconvincingly, and lured Claudia to a discreet distance. "First off, they say Cora Vanderlip tried to slash her wrists last night—an ambulance is meeting her at the dock—"

Claudia was shocked. It was such a painful messy way of doing it, second only to window-jumping. "How dreadful! I hope she'll be all right."

Mrs. Bliss shrugged. "She will. Suicide is a sort of hobby with her, she tries it all the time, mostly with sleeping pills, but she always manages to yell for help before it's too late."

Claudia felt uncomfortable. She wasn't a gossiper by nature, but when Mrs. Bliss divulged her second morsel of scandal, it was difficult to resist a ghoulish interest. "You mean that's why he suddenly changed his plans and got off at Cherbourg?"

"Absolutely. And of course Helen Nicholson has no idea that he's in a jam with the government, and makes a perfect spectacle of herself tagging along after him! Why, Barry Conwell is young enough to be her son! And really, there's bound to be a lot of publicity, because sooner or later they'll catch up with him, and he'll have go back to the States, and there'll be hearings on television and that sort of thing, particularly since he's got all those prizes and everything. Not that I ever liked his last book he wrote—"

"I thought I heard you say you did," Claudia murmured.

"To be truthful, I'm not what you'd call a great reader, so I only read the naughty parts," Mrs. Bliss admitted with a small giggle. "My husband says 'violence is in vogue these days', which I think is quite well put, don't you?"

"Very," Claudia acknowledged politely.

Mrs. Bliss edged up closer. "Apart from what's come to light of his past record, every word of that novel," she enunciated, not opening her lips in order to achieve a combined emphasis and secrecy, "is screamingly communistic. Between the lines, of course. It's all for the *little* man."

If, by the "*little* man," Mrs. Bliss meant gardeners and garbage collectors, and carpenters and plumbers (before their wages went up and their hours down), Claudia had an abiding affection for them.

"Here comes that attractive husband of yours," Mrs. Bliss was off on another tack.

"All set, let's get started," said David, piloting Linda through untidily moving groups.

"Come along, Greg, Aunt Emily and Uncle Henry are waiting for us." Linda took Greg's hand, and said good-bye. Mrs. Bliss said it was only "au revoir", they'd be seeing each other in London, and rushed away to find Mr. Bliss. Bertha picked the baby up in her arms. Matthew said slowly, "G-good riddance to this old b-boat."

The trip was over. It was like a small lifetime, Claudia thought. What a lot could happen—or not happen—in a world at sea.

7

DAVID had arranged for a car to meet them at the boat. It turned out to be a very imposing limousine with walnut fittings and silver clothes-brushes, and not much trunk room. "How did we get more luggage than when we started?" he wanted to know.

"We didn't," said Claudia, "it only seems like more every time we pack."

At last everything was fitted in like a jigsaw puzzle, except for the baby's teddy-bear and folding perambulator which sat up on the front seat next to the uniformed chauffeur. "I don't think, from the look of his back, that he likes it," Claudia mentioned behind the glass partition.

"I'm sure he doesn't," said David.

"I like it, though. Just think of the nuisance of taking a train and piling into taxis."

"I thought of it," said David succinctly. "Matthew, stop breathing all over the window."

234

"I have to look out," said Matthew. "Is this London?"

"Ach no," said Bertha. "We do not get to London for a long time yet."

Soon the docks and the busy streets of Southampton were behind them, and the countryside began to open up ahead. "'Winchester,' 'Basingstoke,' 'Staines,'" Claudia read the signs aloud in awe. "Listen to me, I'm starting to be a tourist and a bore the minute we land."

"Oh go on, have yourself a thrill," said David generously.

"It is not cold like I expected," Bertha marvelled. "The fields look green, and already daffodils are beginning to come up."

The glow on David's face darkened. "And we have to go high-tailing it off to Switzerland," he muttered.

"You've been so sweet up to now, please don't get nasty," Claudia implored him. "Imagine all that nice white snow on the Alps." She was imagining it herself, and not enjoying the prospect; they had had enough of snow and mountains last winter. But who would have thought that England would turn out to be warm and balmy in the middle of February? You could go down to Palm Beach and run into a lot worse. Not that they'd ever had the money to follow the sun: in fact they'd congratulated themselves for staying at home whenever they heard about blizzards in Texas, or floods in Florida, or smog in California.

"Maybe it's just showing off for today."

"What is?"

"The sun. We'll probably have a pea-soup fog with hailstones tomorrow."

"Nonsense!" said David, and it was plain that he was going to stick up for the weather no matter what it did. She had a premonition then and there that they'd never end up in Switzerland.

They reached the outskirts of London well before noon, and with an unwonted absence of incident. The baby slept soundly in Bertha's arms, and Matthew's nose remained pressed against the window staring after the bicycles that whizzed past. "We're lucky we have children who don't get car-sick," Claudia said.

"We're entitled to one break," David replied.

He was unfair: they weren't that bad, but she didn't want to miss anything by arguing the point. Her nose was pressed as closely against the window as Matthew's. Secretly, she was a little disappointed; they could have been passing through sections of the Bronx or Brooklyn for, with the exception of the advertisements (she knew what Bovril was, but not Hovis), the streets were less quaint than dingy. "The approach to any big city is grubby," David read her thoughts.

"Even Paris?"

He hedged. It killed him to say anything against France. "I haven't been there for fifteen years."

"Twelve and a half," she corrected him. "You were only back a few months when I met you. Full of dreams. You wanted to build a great cathedral some day."

He was silent. She shouldn't have brought it up. "Dreams don't die, they just change a little," she offered timidly. "They have to, when things happen. Big things, like marriage and war."

"Thank you, my little back-seat philosopher."

"Well, it's true."

"I'm not complaining."

"I wouldn't mind if you were. I minded that far-away look that came into your eyes all of a sudden."

"You and your imagination."

"Try to fool me."

"Fat chance," he admitted sheepishly. "Anyway, if you catch that look again, just give me a swift kick."

"Why should I? I'm glad to discover you're not so damned grown-up."

"There's a dirty dig in that."

"No, there isn't. I really mean I'm glad. It makes me feel better about my own lapses."

"You haven't got too many of them. Any more."

She felt that funny little warm glow whenever he paid her one of his rare and wonderful compliments. Rare, she supposed, because there wasn't much that he could compliment her on, since she wasn't beautiful, or brilliant, or even stylish. Not to be overmodest, however, she was good company morning, noon, or night, which was more than could be said for a lot of wives.

"We're coming into Piccadilly," he announced.

She sat on the edge of her seat, but Matthew's interest lagged, now that the fascinating stream of bicycles had given way to a dense tangle of cars and buses. He yawned and moved his arms restlessly, poking his father in the ribs. Claudia pinioned him with dispatch. "You've been very good, don't spoil it, we're almost there."

"How many more minutes?"

"Two and three quarters," David said, not even feeling the poke, he was so excited. "The Palace is over there behind the trees—"

"The only thing I remember about London is Madame Tussaud's," said Claudia.

"Shame on you. Don't you even remember the Changing of the Guard?"

"I was only five years old!" she said indignantly.

"Ach, the horses and the big red hats!" Bertha exclaimed. "Look quick, Matthew!"

"*Dumbkopf*," David followed up congenially, "you're looking out of the wrong window. Here. Squeeze over to this side."

Claudia winced. "That was my toe, if you don't mind."

"We don't mind," said David. "Do we, son?"

Whenever he said "son" like that, it was a sign that he was getting mellow round the edges. He had all but melted into a jelly of possessive reminiscence by the time they drew up in front of the hotel where he had cabled for accommodation the moment their plans were finally set. "It's hard to get rooms there, and if they don't know you, it's almost impossible," he'd explained.

"Why waste time then?" Claudia had asked, reasonably enough. "There must be other hotels that aren't so fussy."

"They'll remember me," he'd assured her smugly.

"After so many years?"

"Certainly. I stayed there three months."

That was when she'd begun to have doubts. "It couldn't have been a very expensive place to stay. Was it?"

"Oh, so now you want only the expensive places," he'd taunted.

"You know perfectly well what I mean. It may have been fine for a bachelor, but how is it going to be for children?"

"A lot healthier than hotels teeming with rich tourists. This is still unspoiled, the Americans haven't discovered it yet."

Her doubts crystallized into definite misgivings as soon as they stepped into the draughty old-fashioned foyer, heavy with rose-wood balustrades and velour portières. David was right in one thing, though—it wasn't teeming with rich tourists. It wasn't teeming at all, except for a group of women who looked and talked like Lady Gresham, and a rather shrivelled little man, sitting in a chair reading the *Times*. She suddenly understood why Helen Nicholson had bluntly delivered herself of the opinion that nobody in his right senses would deliberately choose to stay at such an old flea-box.

"Very good, sir. Will that be all, sir?" the chauffeur murmured, washing his hands of them and the teddy-bear in one fell swoop.

David quickly checked the mountain of suitcases and bundles to see if anything had been left in the car, and said that that would be all.

"Thank you, sir. Thank you very much, sir. I believe the governess has the small parcel, sir," he added delicately.

"Yah, I have," said Bertha, who had prepared for the baby not to last over two hours. "Ach, listen! They speak German behind the desk!" she discovered happily.

"That's something new since my time," said David, slightly crestfallen, but Claudia was glad that Bertha felt at home, and the luggage looked at home too, sprawling over the shabby oriental carpet.

"I'll fetch it upstairs later, sir," the porter said. "It's not going to fit in the lift with us."

It was a tight fit to fit in the lift even without the luggage. The small open cage clanged its ropes and hiccupped its way to the third floor, executing a brief shimmy of indecision before it finally quivered to a stop. "The children will use the stairs hereafter," Claudia made mental note, and bet herself twenty cents that Bertha had arrived at the same decision.

The corridor smelled of fresh paint. It was surprisingly long and involved with many twists and turnings, further complicated by mattresses and odd pieces of furniture stacked against the walls. The porter hopped along ahead of them, and flung open a door at the farthest end, cheerfully waving them into an outstandingly unspacious room, with a tiny night-table crammed in between a pair of brass beds, and the brass beds crammed in between wall and door. The rest of the furniture consisted of an out-dated chiffonier, two side chairs, and an overpowering wardrobe, which, for all its massiveness, Claudia knew with absolute certainty would be an inch too narrow to hold clothes hangers without angling them sideways.

"The other room has a fireplace," the porter announced, as he opened a connecting door, "though it is a bit smaller, I'd say."

"I'd say too," said Claudia. "Matthew will have to sleep in the sitting-room."

"There isn't any sitting-room, madame, just the two bedrooms and a bath."

She swallowed. "Only one bath?"

"I hate this!" Matthew announced in a loud voice. "This is stinky!"

"Hush," said Bertha, also swallowing, but valiant. "That is not nice to say."

David was too proud to swallow, but he cleared his throat. "I'm afraid this accommodation will be a little cramped. "Will you call the desk and say that we'd like a larger suite? And with two baths."

"No use, sir. I know for a fact that we've been turning away some of our oldest clients, sir. The fact is we're doing some decorating and that's why we're a bit short at the moment."

"There's nothing to be lost by asking," said David, a little sharply.

"As you wish, sir."

The conversation over the telephone was brief. The porter hung up the receiver. "Nothing at present, sir, though I happen to know that there might be a chance of a suite for next week."

"Next week we'll be in Switzerland," said Claudia shortly. It didn't hurt to nail it down for David's benefit, and besides, she was ready to turn round and walk out, not only because of the impossible accommodation, but because this antiquated little hotel was independent to the point of indifference.

David cleared his throat again, this time in abject surrender. "Dear, if you're going to feel cramped—wait a moment," he stopped the porter on his way out, "don't bring up our suitcases—"

"But we can't go traipsing around at this point," Claudia broke in impatiently. "The children had a long ride, it's past their lunch time."

"We don't have to traipse," said David. "I'll telephone the hotel where the Woodburns are staying. Mrs. Woodburn said she'd alert the manager, she didn't think we'd be comfortable here."

"Well, this is a fine time to say so!"

"Now wait a minute, be reasonable. This would have been perfectly all right, if we could have had two baths—"

"—*and* a sitting-room, *and* decent closet space, *and* a little sun and heat . . ."

244

"What are you talking about, it's like Spring out—"

"Out. Not in," she qualified coldly. "It's unspeakably bleak and dreary with these soggy net curtains keeping out all the light. However, it's getting late, so let's stop shilly-shallying and have the luggage sent up." She turned on her heel and left him in the middle of a gape. She found Bertha, buttoning up the children in a long, narrow bathroom that was adequate without charm. There were no ingratiating touches, merely the basic necessities. "Bertha, do you think you can squeeze by in that little room with an extra cot in it?"

"Aber sure!" Bertha's optimism was doubtless coloured by the lingering echo of her native tongue. "After lunch, while the children are resting, I will unpack and put everything away, and you will see it will be all right. Leave the keys for your suitcases also."

"You're a glutton for punishment."

"But this is very nice. It is only that we are spoiled by so much fancifulness on the boat."

"I never thought of that," said Claudia. It was true, too.

If they'd kept their original accommodation

on B deck, these rooms might have indeed seemed "very nice". Funny. She could have sworn that she had remained completely immune to the kiss of luxury, but apparently a person could change without knowing it. It was something to think about. Also, it was an excellent reason to put up with a few inconveniences without complaining. (A much worthier reason than running away from smoke because you were afraid of fire. The Woodburns being the smoke, and Linda the fire.)

"Bertha always rises to challenge," she reported back to David quite cheerfully, "so we'll give her a chance to exercise her megalomania."

He had no idea what had occasioned this abrupt turnabout (he was too undevious to link it up with Linda), but he wasn't in a mood to look a gift horse in the mouth. "Good," he said, with relief. "Let's wash and go down and have a cocktail."

"The children are still in the bathroom. Anyway, I have to wait to see if they can have lunch brought up to the room."

Give him a finger, he took a hand. "Of course they can. This hotel has first rate service."

"What makes you so sure?" she enquired acidly.

To prove his point, he rang for the maid. She came at once, with an air of having been hurrying from a long distance—a little mosquito of a woman in a fulsome white apron and a Cockney accent. She was only "the relief", she explained, but she'd see to it that a menu was sent up straightaway. "And would there be anything else, madame?"

"Some hangers," said David, who'd got his first glimpse of the inside of the wardrobe. There were three wire ones, and one wooden one which bore the name of another hotel. "Every cloud has a silver lining," Claudia remarked sweetly. "I'd hate to think what we'd do if I had a lot of clothes."

David was conveniently deaf. "What are those brats doing in there, anyway? They'll have to learn not to take all day."

"That goes for you too, mister," she reminded him. "It's going to be catch as catch can."

"In other words, the early bird catches the worm."

"Or, after a manner of speaking, All is not gold that glitters."

There was a knock on the door.

It was the mountain of luggage.

"Oi," said David.

Ignominiously, they left the field to Bertha, lunch and all. "I could do with a drink, myself," Claudia said.

Things looked a little more heartening downstairs. She caught a glimpse of a pleasant dining-room, and David recognized the old mahogany hat-rack outside the bar, and the old barmaid recognized David, which did wonders for his drooping ego. There was a joyous reunion between the two of them. Claudia watched and listened with motherly tolerance while David retasted his youth along with a double Scotch, and grew expansive beyond his wont, enquiring for this one and that one, and how about the red-haired Professor—what-was-his-name—?

"Archie Gibbons! Dropped in last week, he did. Lives in Oxford now. Had a stroke, poor lamb, but still as bright as a cricket on his good days—"

The porter peered round the dim room, and then hurried to their table. "Telephone, Mrs. Naughton."

Claudia pushed back her chair. "Who is it?" David asked her inanely.

"How should I know?" she retorted, although she had a suspicion that it was Linda, or maybe Bertha, snowed under with suitcases and calling for help.

"This way, madame. I'll show you where the booth is."

"Thank you."

She slid into the small enclosure, fastidiously leaving the door ajar because of the leftover smell of a cigar. "Hello?"

"Claudia! Is that you?"

At first she thought it was Bill Hendricks simply because she didn't know any other man in London who would call her by her first name like that. And then she recognized the voice out of the long, far past. "Jerry! We had no idea you were home. We thought you were in Africa!"

"I was, but I finished my assignment sooner than I expected and got back yesterday, and found Candy's letter, saying you were coming over. What luck we didn't miss each other! Tell me, how is David?"

"Fine, Jerry. His old self, really."

"Oh God, that's good to hear. And you? I don't have to ask, you sound like your old self, too."

"I am."

Jerry said, so simply that it might have been a compliment from David, "I always thought you were a wonderful pair of people. Tell me about the boys. Candy said you were bringing them along with Bertha. How is Bertha and has she ever forgiven me?"

Claudia laughed. "It seems like another lifetime, doesn't it? I don't think you ever saw the baby, did you?" (Bobby had been his favourite, and the only one of the children he had known well.)

"I believe you're right," Jerry said. "It's over two years since I was in the States.—And Candy and John are well and happy?"

"Oh fine—But tell me about you, Jerry. We were very excited about your last book, and David says you've done a beautiful job on the African report. He read a long excerpt of it in one of the papers—"

"I respect David's judgment," Jerry dismissed his accomplishments unaffectedly. "But look here, we could go on talking forever, and you're probably at lunch. Is it too soon to pop in on you this afternoon?"

"I should say not. I can't wait to see you. David either when he knows you're back in London. The only trouble is," she remembered dubiously, "I don't know where we can put you to sit—"

Jerry laughed. "I know. There are only one or two decent suites in the whole place, but it's about the only really English hotel left in London. I'm glad you got in. It's rather difficult if they don't know you—"

"David stayed here before we were married," Claudia said, with a hint of complacency. (What a difference a point of view could make!)

"Ah, then that explains it," said Jerry. "Look here, I'll tell you what. You and David come over and have tea with me."

"That would be much better," she agreed.

"Will you be able to make it about five?"

"As well as at any other time. How do we get there?"

"Just tell the taxi-driver you want to get to the Albany."

"I hope I remember. The Albany. Is it a hotel?"

"No, it's just flats. David knows."

She was discovering by slow degrees that David wasn't as naive as she'd thought. She returned to him in a chastened frame of mind, and was glad to find he was alone. The room had taken on a flurry of activity while

251

she was in the phone booth, which had put an end to his reminiscing with the barmaid. He looked up and pulled out her chair—a decided improvement, she noted. He always made the gesture, of course, but she'd usually been content to take the will for the deed and stop him before he got half-way to his feet.

"You look very pleased with yourself. Who was it?"

"Guess."

"Male or female?" he asked cautiously.

"Male."

"I thought we'd got rid of him for a while."

"Who?"

"Don't be coy, you know who," he said dourly.

"So you're still jealous of Bill Hendricks!"

"I'm not jealous. I think he's a big bore."

"Oh, not a big one, just an ittie bittie one," she conceded. "Only it didn't happen to be Bill. It was Jerry."

His face brightened. "Jerry Seymour?"

"How many other Jerrys do we know? He'd just got Candy's letter. Isn't it nice he came back before we left?"

"Very. When do we see him?"

"This afternoon. At his place. There's not room to sit and talk upstairs. Around five, I said. That gives us a chance to rest," she added tactfully.

"In that bedlam?" He signed the bill. "Come on, let's get lunch behind us, and we'll have time to go to Westminster Abbey first."

"You sound like one of those tourists you don't like."

"I'm an architect. Remember?"

"I'm remembering we had an awfully early breakfast," she switched to safer ground.

The menu was large in size, but small in choice as far as she was concerned. The Specialité du Jour was Jugged Hare, which David pounced on with disgusting delight. "How can you?" she reproached him. "Such innocent little creatures!"

"You eat chicken and lamb, don't you?" he embarked on one of their old farm arguments.

She was going to order cold salmon, because of the cucumber, but he could say that it was an innocent fish, so she changed it to an omelette, which was dull, but uncontroversial.

"Since when do you like omelettes?"

"I don't, I'll make it up with dessert."

The jugged hare arrived, decently concealed in a casserole of heavy black sauce. Her

stomach untwisted. For all she knew it migh
have been served with its ears on, like a roas
pig with an apple in its mouth. David sniffed
the aroma, rolled his eyes like an idiot, and
told the waiter to bring an extra plate fo
madame. She almost choked with exaspera
tion. The irony of it! After all these years o
refusing to share in a restaurant, he had to
start with a rabbit! "Leave madame out o
this," she said frigidly.

"I just want you to taste it."

"You're making a spectacle of yourself.'
(How often he had said those words to her.
On the other hand, this might establish a
valuable precedent for their whole future
She lifted a frugal morsel of the stuff to he
lips, while he awaited her verdict with
fatuous anticipation. "How is it?"

If she hadn't known what it was, i
wouldn't have been any worse than a third
rate pot-roast. She started to say so, and ther
didn't have the heart to spoil his pleasure
She couldn't bear women who held fortl
about men being like little boys, but at this
moment, he was certainly managing to look
and act like one. She could only hope that i
was a temporary aberration, and wouldn'
keep up for the entire trip. "It's delicious,'

she said, and was rewarded by the spon-
taneous pressure of his knee beneath the long
tablecloth. She felt no shame. She hadn't
been a wife for twelve years without learning
a little something about marriage. Certainly it
had to be built on honesty and trust (even a
white lie like not being seasick was definitely
on the shady shade) but, on the other hand,
an occasional dash of gentle deception was all
to the good—

"Would you care for a sweet, madame?"

That was putting it mildly. The dessert
wagon passing by every so often was the only
thing that had kept her chin up during the
omelette. From a distance, the trays seemed
to be full of all sorts of delectable things, but
when the waiter rolled it up to her, it turned
out to be mostly large glass bowls of stewed
fruits, with the nerve to include prunes, and
small dishes of a pale custardy concoction
aptly described as trifle.

"How about some ice-cream?" David read
her disappointment.

She brightened. "What kind?"

He grinned. "You sound like Matthew."

The pot calling the kettle black. "I'll have
some cheese," she said with dignity. "Brie."

"I'm afraid we haven't any Brie today,

madame. But I can recommend the Stilton with port wine. Or the Rocquefort."

She wasn't crazy about any cheese with black specks.

"I'll have the Stilton," David broke the gloomy silence. "Dear, try the trifle. You might like it."

She tried it. He looked anxious. "How is it?"

The moment had come for their marriage to stand or fall. "It's terrible," she said.

When they went upstairs after lunch, she found Bertha knee-deep in suitcases, but apparently undaunted by the horrific task ahead of her. One room was piled high with all the things she had unpacked, and in the other room, the children were piled on one bed, fast asleep. It would have been sheer catastrophe if Matthew, particularly, was to regain consciousness, so Claudia lingered only long enough to give ear to Bertha's importunate whisper please not to try to help her, it was better if she could be left alone to work out where to put everything.

"I get your point," said Claudia, and told her that Mr. Jerry had just returned from Africa, so they'd get out of her way by going over to his apartment for tea. Bertha was delighted on both scores, for she had grown very fond of Jerry over the years. "Have a good time and do not hurry back." she said.

"We're to have a good time and not hurry back," Claudia reported to David, who had retired to the bathroom in cowardly escape. He gave no indication of having heard her. His eyes were riveted on the cosy array of toothbrushes in the old-fashioned holder. She took his hand and pumped it. "Well, hello there, if it isn't Goldilocks and the five brushes!"

He ignored her levity. Mentally he was picturing Matthew's well-known disregard of whose was which, and the prospect was appalling. "Anything but sharing tooth-brushes," he backed down.

She wondered how he was going to take to the nightly festoons of dripping pyjamas and underwear, but for the immediate present he was chiefly concerned with the more intimate hazards of the situation. "And how, may I ask," he went on with gathering significance, "are we going to keep our towels separate from that little brat?"

"Your guess is as good as mine," said

Claudia amiably. "There's certainly no space in our bedroom to hang them."

"I think," he reached an abrupt conclusion, "that I ought to phone Mrs. Woodburn."

"We're staying right here," Claudia interrupted with finality.

"But I want you to be comfortable."

"You mean you want to be under the same roof as Linda."

"I've been trying to manipulate it without rousing your suspicions," he admitted morosely, "but you thwart me at every turn."

"Seriously," Claudia said, "it isn't worth the bother of moving for such a short stay, so you'll just have to stop finding fault with unimportant trifles like not having your own private towel."

"Look, I was considering your comfort, not mine," he made a right-about-face. "I'm perfectly happy here, I think it's a first-rate hotel."

"Well, I don't!" she also right-about-faced. "I think it's exactly what Helen Nicholson said it was, and I loathe jugged hare, and what's more, the attitude of the management is arrogantly anti-American! And stop shouting or you'll wake the children."

"Vixen!" he said.

"David, don't! Let me go!"

"Why?"

"Because. We promised Bertha to get out of her way."

"No rest for the wicked. Come on, let's go to Westminster Abbey. There's another green tooth-brush here besides mine!"

"Calm down, they're not the same size, one is the baby's. Do you think Bertha will be hurt if we remove ours from the family circle? She might think we're being snooty instead of sanitary."

"Maybe we'd better be on the safe side, and invest in a couple of new ones to hide in our closet."

"What a fun idea! Sort of like leading a double life."

"I'll be grateful," said David wryly, "if we can just go on leading our old ones."

There was a light knock on the door. Claudia opened it. Bertha stood on the threshold, with Michael half-drowsing in her arms.

"The baby woke up," she apologized, "but I think he will go to sleep again."

"It's all yours," said David. "We were just leaving."

On the way out, he stopped at the desk. "I'd like to see the manager."

The clerk, who was tall, gaunt, and young, but withal quite unattractive, eventually glanced up from whatever he was doing, and said that Mr. Lindt had just gone out.

"Then I'll talk to the assistant manager," David said, in a tone that meant business.

After a moment or two of indecision, the clerk vanished behind a wooden partition, only to reappear with the information that Miss Bachman was also unfortunately engaged elsewhere. "Perhaps I can help you, sir," he offered bloodlessly.

"I think not. Please tell the manager that I wish to talk to him when I return."

"I will give him the message. Your name, sir?"

Something in the way David's nostrils wiggled must have warned the young man that he had reached the limit. He gave a small deprecatory laugh. "But of course. Now I recall. You signed in at noon today. Rooms 42 and 43. The reservation was made from the States. Mr. Naughton, I believe, sir?"

It was a purely rhetorical question, requiring no answer. "Swine," David muttered under his breath, as he turned away.

"I'm too thoroughbred to say 'I told you so,'" Claudia murmured.

"It's new management," he alibied.

"Odd for it to be German."

"Austrian or Swiss, more likely. They seem to have taken over the hotel business in America, too."

The doorman, however, was as English as Hawkins. "Have you your own car, sir?"

"We're walking," said David.

"We're not, are we?" Claudia protested. "We've been up since dawn. I'm pretty tired," she added diplomatically.

"A block or two won't kill you."

She wasn't in the least tired, and the air felt good. Her gaze fastened longingly on a small antique shop across the street. David caught her from tripping over a sudden curb. "Look where you're going. That's a good idea about a car. I'll see about renting one tomorrow."

"What's the matter with cabs? There seem to be a lot of them around," she hinted broadly.

"I thought you wanted to buy toothbrushes?"

"We can do it on the way back."

"What's the rush? Westminster Abbey won't run away."

"If you're sure it won't, can't we let it go until tomorrow, and just drive around to get the feel of the city until it's time to go to Jerry's?"

"Very subtle, but if you're doing it for my sake—"

"I'm not," she broke in. "I haven't got my land legs yet."

"Nonsense. Nobody gets land-legs any more."

"I happen to have two of them," she retorted smartly.

He put one of those long-suffering looks on his face, and hailed a taxi. She climbed in. "It's a darling little taxi," she gushed. "So high up and short-coupled, and patent leatherish. And look at the meter. Shillings and pence. Isn't that quaint?"

"I'm in no mood for any more of your monkey-shines," he warned her.

"All of a sudden I'm not either," she subsided soberly. "I'm just trying to hide how excited I am inside. I have to pinch myself to realize I'm really in London."

He smiled unwillingly, for the clerk still rankled, and sat forward to talk to the driver, who was much more elderly than New York taxi drivers, and gave the impression of wearing a high fur cap, which of course he wasn't. "We'd like to be at the Albany at four-thirty—" David began, but the old man didn't wait to hear any more. "Right, sir. With any luck at all as regards the traffic, I'd say we could cover a fair bit in an hour. Begin at Bond Street we will—all the ladies want to see the shops in Bond Street first." He squared himself up on his tall seat, as if he were flapping the reins of a pair of horses, spat generously out of the window, and they were off. Claudia leaned back against the worn seat. "Bond Street," she echoed softly, "and Piccadilly and Big Ben—" Her hand sought David's. "I wish Matthew were a little older. He won't remember much of this trip."

"He'll remember the damnedest things," said David. "Like the Wax Works."

"I know. Strange how the mind has a life of its own."

"He'll get a kick out of the starlings in Trafalgar Square, though."

"Bobby would have, even more. He loved anything that was alive."

"Including caterpillars."

"Yes."

They were silent until suddenly, turning her head to peer at the great stone lions in Trafalgar Square, she said, "Aren't they supposed to roar?"

David slipped his arm round her and pressed her close. "Yes, darling, but not at you."

"Oh," she said. "Do I show it as much as that?"

"As much as that," he told her.

It was wonderful how he could remember his way round the unpredictable winding streets, as if it were only yesterday that he had been in London. They made a game of it, David calling the shots before the driver made the turns. "See if you can find Bloomsbury from here," said Claudia.

"Who do you know in Bloomsbury?" he humoured her.

"It epitomizes all the English novels I ever read. Bloomsbury, Chelsea and Harley Street."

"In a little while," he said, "we'll be passing the British Museum. We'll go through it tomorrow."

"I thought we were going to the Tower of London tomorrow, and the Abbey."

"If you're so hell bent to leave in a week, we'd better get the museums in, too."

"How many are there besides this one?" she asked apprehensively.

"The Victoria and Albert, and a couple of smaller ones."

"Ouch. My feet are falling off already. When do I buy sweaters and linens?"

"You don't," he said callously.

"But I need presents!" she wailed.

"Buy them when you get home. They're just as good, if not better."

"You don't understand. It's not the same."

"If you think I'm going to spend the few days we've got here stewing around in shops, you're mistaken."

"I thought you wanted some fishing tackle—"

"That's different."

"Pipes are different, too, I suppose," she accused him bitterly. She looked out of the window. "Now where are we going?"

"To Jerry's. It's twenty to five. I'm glad you can see the Albany. It's the oldest apartment house in London, and some of the great names of England have lived there. And are living there now."

"Well, bully for Jerry," she said. "It's a long cry from that tumbledown little red cottage he was renting the summer we first met him."

"The summer you picked him up and foisted yourself on him," David amended starkly.

"I did not foist myself. He happened to be passing by on a deserted road and I merely asked him to fix a flat tyre for me. Which he refused to do. And for which I will never forgive him."

"I seem to recall," David jogged her memory, "that the one night I had to go out of town and leave you alone, I came back to find you having dinner with him in his little red cottage, all dressed up in a hand-me-down *négligé* of Julia's."

"I was leading him on. He thought I was some poor little farmer's wife with psychic powers, because I knew all about the book he was writing. I did, too. We were on the same party line, I listened in, whenever his phone would ring, don't you remember?"

"Vividly," he assured her dryly.

Her voice choked up. "What a lifetime ago

it all seems. Mamma spent the summer with us, and Matthew hadn't been born yet, and Candy and Elizabeth hadn't begun to be a part of us. Or a part of Jerry."

"Keep this up," David said, "and you'll be quivering like a bowl of jelly when we get there."

"You're right. Isn't this New Bond street, again? I recognize the auction galleries."

"Unrecognize them."

"You're not going to let me have any fun."

"You'll have fun in Switzerland," he said meanly.

The taxi slowed to a crawl in a tangle of late afternoon activity—buses, cars, people rushing home. The lights had come on, and there was a fog, which made them blurry around the edges, like one of those modern paintings. "We're almost there," said David. "It will be quicker if we get out and don't try to buck this traffic."

He paid the driver, and the driver thanked him, and then they both thanked the driver for a lovely ride. "Do you mind walking half a block?" David asked belatedly.

"No, it'll feel good after sitting so long."

"Cold?"

She shook her head. "I love the mist," she

said generously. "It feels so nice against your face."

"It does, doesn't it?" He tucked her arm into his companionably. "Happy?"

"Yes," she said. Her heart was too full to say any more. It was more than happiness that filled her. It seemed as if they had never been so deeply together.

She was sorry when the walk came to an end. Her feelings were sweetly confused with the richness of new experience and sensation, and only vaguely was she aware of vistas of grey stone arches, dark with age. The doorman seemed far off at the opposite entrance. "It's down this way" said David, as if he knew. Later, Claudia couldn't remember whether there were fountains, but if there weren't it seemed as if there were.

"This is it," said David, and before they had reached the top of the short stone steps, the door opened, and Jerry was there, waiting for them.

"Claudia!" He held out his arms to her, and it seemed so natural and simple for her to go to him. He held her against him for a long moment, and then held her away from him to look at her, and she said, "Oh, Jerry!" and their lips met, and David stood watching and smiling, because he could feel what they were feeling. "This is great," he said simply.

"To think I might have missed you," Jerry said, his hand on David's shoulder. "I hadn't intended to be back until next week, you know, and, according to Candy, you'd have been gone by then. David, you're looking well. I'm satisfied with you."

"I'm glad," said Claudia tremulously. "It means a lot to hear you say it."

"I'm satisfied with both of you," he said. He led them indoors, into a small foyer, with an old-fashioned hat rack, like the one outside the bar in the hotel. He took their coats and hung them up. There was a mahogany mirror, but the glass was dim and wavy with age, so it didn't do her much good. "There's a better mirror in the drawing-room," Jerry smiled. "But you don't need a mirror, you haven't changed. I was afraid you might have, but you're just the same. David, too."

"You've changed," said Claudia.

"I needed to," he said.

"You've put on weight," said David, but not in criticism.

"And I like it," said Claudia. "You were too thin when we first knew you. It made you seem supercilious."

"I was," said Jerry. "A supercilious ass. I can't imagine how you tolerated me."

"As I remember," said David, "we didn't."

"I think," said Claudia slowly, "that you didn't really belong in America." She looked round the room, not large, not beautiful, but there were things in it that were beautiful, like the worn fabric on the settee, and an oversized gate-leg table full of a clutter of books and magazines and pipes. "You belong here," she said, finally.

"This was my father's flat," said Jerry. "I haven't done very much to it. Elizabeth said that it felt like home to her, strangely. She said she would have wanted to live here, if it weren't for Candy."

"I know," said Claudia. "She told us that when she wrote to us. There was time for only one letter, but it was such a happy one. I kept it for a long while, and then I gave it to Candy when I thought she was ready for it. It was hard for her to believe that her mother could have known that kind of happiness again. But she believes it now."

"I think she does," said Jerry. "All her hatred and bitterness towards me has gone."

"Candy had a tough time of it," said

David. "Largely of her own making, but pretty tough."

"John's going to Korea right after the baby was born wasn't of her own making," Claudia protested.

"I went to New Guinea and left you with three children," said David.

"I was older and I didn't have other problems. In fact, I never had a mother-in-law at all."

"I did," said David, "and it was pretty wonderful."

Claudia felt her throat tighten. "Mamma was different. She adored you and you adored her. But John's mother wasn't an easy nut to crack, and you know it."

"I rather felt," Jerry injected, "that Candy didn't try to crack it. She let it crack her."

"It almost did," said Claudia. "Last summer was pretty ghastly."

"I love the kid," said David, "but she should have had her tail kicked."

Claudia smiled faintly. "I did."

"She worships you," Jerry told her. "I can't tolerate people who are do-gooders, but you accomplished a miracle with Candy."

"She accomplished it for herself," said

271

Claudia. "She decided that if I had lived through things, she could too."

"You've lived through a lot worse things than Candy will ever have to live through, I hope." Jerry's eyes were candid and appraising. "You've grown into a lot of woman, Claudia. And yet you *haven't* really changed. David, it's true, isn't it? She hasn't."

"It's true," said David. He grinned. "She's hell to live with, but it would be hell to live without her."

"It's so nice to have you talk about me like this," said Claudia demurely. "Please go on."

"Brazen," said David. "Pay no further attention to her, Jerry. I want to hear about Africa."

"There'll be plenty of time for that. Tea, Claudia? Or a cocktail?"

"Tea," said Claudia.

"David?"

"I'll have tea too," said David, though he wouldn't be caught dead with a cup of tea at home. Neither would she, for that matter.

A telephone rang in the next room. "Is that your bedroom?" she asked curiously.

"No, I work in there. I'll show you round

after tea." Jerry stirred the fire. "Are either of you cold?"

"Not a bit," said Claudia. "Just awfully chilly."

"You'll get used to our English heating." He added more coal. She stood before the blaze, enjoying the quick, shallow warmth. "There's so much I want to hear about," he said. "Tell me about the children. And the house—you're only a mile or so away, Candy says.—Tell me, is it anything like the farm? But it can't be. There'll never be another farm like that one . . ."

"It's going to be even nicer in a way," said David. "It's nearer New York, less than an hour to the office."

"That means a lot," Jerry agreed. "Is it an old house?"

"Yes. It's a hip-roof. And unspoiled. A farm hand lived in it, fortunately, and when we found it it was in its original condition—"

"Except for a dreadful porch tacked on," Claudia said, "and the most outrageous kitchen—that's why nobody bought it, I suppose. It needed too much done to it. We could never have afforded it either. It seems as if it were Julia and Hartley's last and most wonderful gift to us."

"That's another thing that hasn't changed you," said Jerry elliptically. "Either of you. But then, it shouldn't have. You were always the two richest people I ever knew."

"We were," said David, "even though there were times after the war when we didn't know how we were going to make ends meet."

Jerry nodded. "I remember. Architects were fairly expendable in those days, weren't they?"

"Almost completely," said David.

"Good God, what exciting things are happening now, though! I saw a film recently, of Park Avenue in the middle fifties. Incredible. And the Kip Memorial sounds immensely exciting. I'm keeping my fingers crossed for you."

"How did you hear about it?" David asked quickly.

"Candy mentioned it in her letter. She seemed certain that you and John would land the contract."

"Candy should keep her mouth shut," David growled. He was as superstitious as any silly female, but he'd never let on that he was.

A maid entered with the tea. She looked

274

like a maid, because of her starched apron. She had white hair and wrinkled pink cheeks. Jerry took the heavy tray from her. "Matilda, these are my very good friends from America. Matilda's like your Bertha, Claudia. She's been in our family for years. I can't think what I'd do without her."

"You've taken beautiful care of him," Claudia smiled. "He's put on weight in all the right places."

"Thank you very much, ma'am. I was glad to see him walk in this morning safe and sound, I can tell you, ma'am. I didn't have an easy minute while he was in that jungle." She lowered her voice. "That was Lady Gresham on the telephone, sir. Would you please to call her when you're free."

"I will. Lemon, Claudia?"

"No, milk, please. And two sugars."

"Lemon," said David. "No sugar."

"He's too manly for sugar," said Claudia. "That wouldn't be our Lady Gresham, would it? On the phone, I mean?"

"Why, yes! Isabel docked this morning also. This is very nice—that you know each other—"

"We don't really know each other," Claudia explained hastily. "Actually, we met through Matthew. Matthew seemed to be the only person on the boat she talked to."

"Isabel never was very gregarious, and she's less so since her husband died. She's quite a wonderful person."

"You seem to know her well," said David.

"Very. I did a great deal of work with Lord Gresham."

"There's the doorbell," Matilda said. "Are you expecting anyone else, sir."

"Yes, bring two more cups, Matilda, please, after you open the door. Mr. and Mrs. Dobson said they might drop in. I want you to meet Ann Dobson," he said. "She's your sort, you'll both like her."

"My pet!"

Claudia didn't think much of Ann Dobson. She was fat and homely, with buck teeth and a blond fringe. She flung herself at Jerry and kissed him noisily. "Jerry, you miserable wretch, I didn't know you'd got back until the doorman just told me. Angel, you look marvellous, so tanned. No tea, thanks—I'm late. My publisher's due at six—darling, when shall I be seeing you? Drop in tomorrow for cocktails—"

"This is Mrs. Naughton, Mr. Naughton—"

Jerry inserted firmly. "They just arrived from America today."

"What fun! Jerry must bring you up to my flat one day, I'm on the floor above—And now I must dash. Good-bye, my sweet—" She stood on her pudgy toes, clasped Jerry's face between her pudgy hands, said, "Bless you!" and was gone, leaving the air heavy with a perfume that wasn't all perfume. It was hard to think of something nice to say about Mrs. Dobson, whom contrary to Jerry's assertion, wasn't their sort at all.

"That was a quick visit," David filled the gap.

Jerry laughed. "Maggie's always like that."

"I thought you said her name was Ann."

"Good Lord, no. That was Margaret Remington."

Claudia gulped on a watercress sandwich. "Not Margaret *Remington*—"

"Didn't David tell you? These flats crawl with writers."

"She's so—so *fat*," Claudia stammered, "and the 'Wild Nymph' was such a gay, delicate story—I've always loved her books."

"She's a magnificent novelist," Jerry agreed. "No," he reverted, "Ann doesn't write, she's editor of one of the magazines her husband publishes.—Now tell me, before they come, what are your plans, and how can I best make you happy, and how long, actually, will you be here?"

"Just a week," said Claudia.

"That's too short," Jerry said. "Far too short."

"We're going to Switzerland," David explained grimly, and was about to go on feeling very sorry for himself, when Mrs. Dobson arrived. She was exactly their sort. At least, Claudia liked her at once. She liked everything about her, the freckled face and forthright blue eyes and pleasant smile, and unaffected voice. She wasn't full of chatter, and didn't ask them any questions about anything. She poured herself some tea, told Jerry she had missed him hideously, and that Pete would be along any moment. "We have tickets for the new Bickley play. It opened last night to a good press. I have to cover it for the magazine, but Pete suddenly sprang a board meeting. You wouldn't want to go with me, your first evening home, would you?"

"I would have loved to," he said. "But Claudia and David won't be in London very long, so I'd like to spend as much time with them as they'll let me."

"Then why don't we all go?" Mrs. Dobson suggested. "We can easily get two more seats."

"Wonderful idea, Annie. How about it, you two?"

Claudia hesitated. "I thought maybe we ought to go to bed early."

"The theatre in London starts at seven-thirty," said David. "You know you'd like to go."

"I would, but is it all right to walk off and leave the children in a strange hotel?"

"With Bertha there?" Jerry scoffed. He turned to David. "She's the same old worrier, isn't she?"

"Yep," said David cheerfully.

"Well, we've overridden all your objections," Mrs. Dobson smiled.

David returned her smile. "Fine. If we're not barging in—"

"You're not barging in," Mrs. Dobson said.

"And make no mistake, Ann wouldn't be past telling you if you were," Jerry added. "We'll pick you up at seven-fifteen. You haven't too much time."

They were held up at the door for a few minutes because Mr. Dobson arrived.

Claudia had expected him to be a little more dashing, but he seemed very nice in a rather middle-aged, sandy sort of way. "I'm glad Mrs. Dobson is safely married," Claudia remarked, as they hurried to find a cab.

"Why?" David asked.

"Because I liked her. She's someone I could be jealous of in earnest. We forgot to buy toothbrushes. Oh well, it's only little boy spit."

"You don't object, do you?" David enquired, "if I feel mine before I use it?"

She giggled. "And if it's wet, where will that leave you?"

"It'll leave Matthew with a red behind," said David.

Having seen Jerry's flat, the foyer of the hotel didn't seem as stuffy and antiquated as it had at first. "I think it's just that it's English," Claudia decided.

David, too, must have readjusted his attitude, because he forgot all about seeing the manager, until the manager saw him and hurried out from behind the desk to apologize quite obsequiously for the unsatisfactory accommodation. He was a supremely neat little package of a man, and reminded Claudia of an inch-worm. "I regret," he said, with a small click of his heels, "that we cannot offer you at the present time a larger suite, but I have arranged for the nurse and children to have access to a bath that adjoins one of the rooms that we are remodelling. I trust that it will be at least a slight contribution to your comfort."

"It will," David accepted with alacrity, but Claudia had visions of Matthew and Michael shivering in their pyjamas down draughty halls, "How far away is the bathroom?" she enquired prudently.

"It is almost directly across the hall, madame. And anything further that we can do to make your stay pleasant," he concluded with another quick click of his heels, "will be our privilege."

"Hangers," said Claudia.

This time he bowed instead of clicked. "Miss Bachman, my assistant, has already attended to the matter. If you need additional ones, you have only to ask." He pressed the bell of the lift before he left them. "May I?"

"Oily," Claudia commented. "I wonder what brought about this sudden passionate desire to make us comfortable. You don't think they could have possibly found out who we were?"

"What else?" said David. "They recognized me in the bar right away, didn't they?"

"Oh," she said. She'd meant was it the same story as on the boat?

The lift descended and disgorged some black ties and dinner gowns. Why hadn't she thought to ask Mrs. Dobson about dressing?

"From now on," David reverted with an almost nauseating smugness, as they stepped out on to their floor, "you'll see that we'll be getting a little service around here."

He was obviously expecting her to say he was wonderful or something of the sort, his ego like a hungry puppy waiting to be fed. Oh well, why not give in to him a little? To be fair about it, it was necessary to his morale to feel that he had got the extra bathroom and the hangers strictly on his own and not because of Julia and Hartley, who, incidentally, had probably never set foot inside this hotel. She glanced at him out of the corner of her eye. He looked so justified, it was pathetic, and yet she'd be damned if she'd tell him he was wonderful. She said, instead, and with a sincerity and fervour,

"It's certainly a blessing we didn't buy the toothbrushes," and moved ahead of him, to peer under a large napkin covering a huge tray that was sitting on the floor.

"What on earth are you doing?" he hissed in her ear.

"Nothing. I just want to see what the children had for dinner and if they ate it."

"Put that napkin back, you idiot, we're two doors further on!"

"Sorry, my mistake," she said meekly.

"Toothbrushes," he muttered, as he yanked her to her feet.

The corridor was deserted. She lifted her lips contritely. "Oh, darling, you're so wonderful," she murmured.

"Why?" he demanded distrustfully.

"I don't know, you just are."

He gave her a brisk shove—she had given him too little and too late. "Come on, get a move on," he said.

"Did you notice the black ties in the elevator? I hope Bertha's unpacked your dinner jacket."

"Whether she has or not, I'm not wearing it. We haven't got time to change."

"I suppose not, we'll even have to rush through dinner."

"We haven't got time for dinner," he informed her flatly.

"Theatre on an empty stomach?"

"Your stomach isn't so empty, you just had tea."

"It'll groan, and I'll be embarrassed. Shh. Tip-toe, in case the children are asleep."

"I will not tip-toe in my own room. Hey, what's happened here?" he broke off.

It didn't take an architect to figure it out—everything was not only as neat as a pin, but the beds had changed places with the wardrobe, thus allowing enough space for two night tables. "And we have an armchair!" Claudia discovered. "Nothing of beauty, but it looks comfortable enough."

David plopped into it. "You bet it's comfortable. Try it."

"Let me go, I've sat in chairs before. There's no sign of Bertha and the children. I'll have to find where their bathroom is. Bertha must have worked her head off—their room is as immaculate as ours," she threw back over her shoulder.

"We've got more hangers than we know what to do with!" David announced smugly. "Didn't I tell you we'd be getting service around here?"

"You told me," she muttered under her breath. "Now shut up about it."

"What?"

"Nothing."

It wasn't difficult to find the bathroom. A door across the hall was ajar and Claudia walked through a dismantled room, guided by the shrill piping of the baby's screeches, and Matthew's lordly injections of superiority. "I like cold water, I'm not a sissy. Throw some more on my chest, Bertha, I like it!"

"Shh, not so loud," Bertha cautioned. She was on her knees beside the bath, washing both of them at once. "You're a better man than I am," Claudia remarked from the threshold. "Bertha, after all you've done today, why didn't you let them skip a bath for once?"

Bertha blew a damp strand of hair from her eyes. "Ach, they will sleep better if they are clean. Is it not lovely that we have our own bathroom? This way, everybody can take their time. Mr. David does not want to be hurried when he shaves. It was the only thing I did not like here. One bathroom."

"We didn't like it any more than you did," Claudia assured her.

"Say hello to Mamma, Michael," Bertha reminded him. "Ach, do not throw water at Mamma, that is naughty."

"We took a walk. I want a bicycle," Matthew shouted.

"Jah, I had them downstairs for a little while," Bertha said. "Such nice people. There is a little dining-room where we can have our meals. Is it all right the way the beds in your rooms are?" she digressed anxiously.

"All right? It's absolutely sublime. The extra night table too. How did it happen?"

"Miss Bachman came up to the room, and I showed her how it was not so comfortable for us."

"She brought the hangers," Matthew announced loudly. "Her nephew went to school with Bertha in Germany."

"Ach, not with me, foolish boy. With my cousin's son," she explained to Claudia. "They were together in Heidelberg. Is it not a funny thing that we should happen to find it out while we were talking."

"Very funny," Claudia agreed. "Very, very funny," she amended, as she began to put two and two together. She should have guessed it the moment Mr. Lindt had sprinted out at them from behind his desk.

There could be no doubt of it. Bertha's fine Teutonic hand was at the bottom of the extra bathroom and the abundance of hangers, personally supervised and delivered by Miss Bachman. Swiss, German or Austrian, they spoke the same language. Poor David! What a dreadful setback this was going to be to his reviving ego.

"The manager is also very nice," Bertha was saying. "He told me the children can always have chicken whether it is on the menu or not. We have only to ask. It is so gemütlich, this little hotel. I like it very much."

"Bertha, I commend your good taste," David said from the doorway. "Stop splashing, you brats. Go talk to Linda, will you, Claudia? She's on the phone."

Claudia wanted to ask him why he didn't talk to Linda himself, but there was a more important issue at stake. She tried to catch Bertha's attention. "Yes, and I want you to realize, Bertha, that we're pretty lucky, we really are—" she said quite loudly.

Bertha's attention was caught. "Jah, I know. The hotel is all full up, the manager told me."

"Exactly. And if it weren't for the fact that

287

Mr. David had stayed here for *three whole months twelve years ago*, we couldn't have even got in, much less have this extra bathroom and special food for the children and everything else—"

"Special food for the children?" David beamed.

"Yah," said Bertha. "They are so nice to us. I could not imagine why they would be so nice, but now I know why."

"Yes. Now you know," said Claudia. She blew a kiss behind David's back as she hurried away to see what Linda wanted. Bertha was well skilled in the art of marriage, for she and Fritz had spent over half a happy lifetime together, and she'd learned that little things were often as important as big things, and sometimes more important. It was not the first time that she had turned conspirator to a gentle deception.

8

CLAUDIA wouldn't have blamed Linda if she had hung up; but she hadn't. "I'm sorry to keep you waiting, I was across the hall."

"David told me." A note of wistfulness crept into Linda's voice. "He said you'd given up any idea of changing over to our hotel."

"It's such a nuisance to move around with the children," Claudia explained. She wondered why Linda hadn't been satisfied to talk to David, and let it go at that. She glanced nervously at her watch. It was almost seven o'clock: she'd barely have time to wash her face and comb her hair, much less change from top to bottom if she wanted to wear the sequin dress. Eventually, however, Linda came to the point. "David said I should ask you about taking Matthew to the Zoo tomorrow morning, with Greg."

"Matthew would love it," said Claudia. "The only thing is, we'd sort of hate to miss it ourselves."

"Come along!" Linda pounced on the suggestion with such alacrity that the idea must have been at the back of her mind. "The more the merrier. And afterwards we can come back here for lunch. Aunt Emily wanted me to ask you, even if you didn't go to the Zoo."

Claudia was dismayed, What had she let herself in for? David would simply murder her if she tied up the whole day with an aimless programme of trivialities. And if she got out of it, it would be a sort of a shabby trick. Linda had probably suggested the jaunt in the first place, because she was counting on David's passionate addiction to elephants and seals, and she'd end up with Matthew instead, and Matthew would end up with a stutter. The best thing to do was to put everybody's cards on the table.

"Linda, you don't want to be burdened with Matthew," she said, "and our time is so short that we just can't fritter it away looking at animals that we can see at home."

"David more or less told me the same thing," Linda admitted, "but he said to ask you about Matthew. And I think you're right. We've got zoos at home, so I won't bother to take Greg, either. Aunt Emily's maid is staying on a few days before flying to the Riviera to get the villa in running order, so I might as well let her look after Greg while she's here."

"I think you'd be silly not to," said Claudia.

"As a matter of fact, she's staying with him this evening. I'm going to the ballet with Bill Hendricks. Any chance of you and David joining us? It's a little late to ask. I called before, but there was no answer in the room."

"We were out, and Bertha was downstairs with the children, very likely. I'm terribly sorry, we're just about to leave for the theatre."

"Then I won't keep you," Linda took the hint. "But before I ring off, Aunt Emily said in case you couldn't make it for lunch tomorrow, what about dinner?"

Lucky Linda to have Aunt Emily as a smoke screen, because one thing was clear: Linda didn't want to let David slip out of her life. Not that there was anything of the siren in her; on the contrary, she was rather painfully reticent and certainly imbued with a becoming sense of propriety towards another woman's husband. Yet David seemed to have filled a great loneliness, and Claudia suddenly felt so sorry for her that she vowed she would never again ridicule the infantile streak that popped up in Linda now and again. "We haven't a thing planned for tomorrow evening," she said.

"Wonderful," said Linda.

"Fine," said Claudia.

"What's fine?" David was at her side, distrustful and glowering. "And hurry up, it's time to start."

"I can't dress?"

"You cannot. Why did you talk so long?"

"Talk so long!" The unmitigated nerve of him! "I'd like to know why I had to act as a go-between, why were you too bashful to tell Linda yourself that we'd love to go to the Zoo, and have lunch afterwards with her and the Woodburns?"

"*What!*" he gave out a bleat of horror.

"But isn't that what you wanted?"

"I wanted you to get us out of it!" he roared.

"Well now, how would I know that?" she asked reasonably enough.

She let him fume about it until they were ready to leave. "You don't deserve it but I did get you out of it. However, we'll have to have dinner with them."

"Why?" he said flatly. "We had five days of them on the boat."

"That's the reason. You can't drop people like hot potatoes. Especially Linda. She might not know it, but she's terribly in love with you."

"You're talking through your hat. Ten to one she's going to marry Bill Hendricks."

"Ten to one she is, but she'd rather marry you." She was more than half serious about it, but she felt so safe in saying it. Divorce, separation, intrigue, could happen to anyone else in the world but not to herself and David. They were inviolate and secure in the specialness of the love they bore each other. She had wakened early this morning to the sense of it, as they had stood hand in hand, looking out towards the coast of France. She had felt it this afternoon, and she had walked into Jerry's arms, wearing the aura of it like a mantle. And now, once more, their marriage seemed to strengthen and blossom against the arid emptiness of Linda's widowhood. Yes, she could afford to be generous.

"I wish we didn't have to go to the theatre," she said.

"So do I," said David. "Not that I'm tired," he added quickly, "if that's what was in your mind."

"It wasn't," she said.

Jerry was just getting out of the taxi when they came downstairs. "We didn't have time to dress," Claudia explained breathlessly.

"We didn't dress either," Jerry said. "David, you sit at the back with the girls, I'll take the bucket seat."

Mrs. Dobson moved over to make room. "This is nice," she said, in her pleasant voice. She smelled clean and fresh, though Claudia noted that she was in the same blue suit and white blouse that she had worn in the afternoon. It was always an effective combination. Claudia often wished that she was more of a tailored suit person. Linda wore suits, too, but they weren't severe: they were more on the expensive dressmaker type.

"Before I forget," Jerry said, "I have a message for you from Isabel—Lady Gresham. She'd like you to join us for lunch tomorrow at the House of Lords."

"The House of Lords!" Claudia echoed incredulously.

"I'd like it very much," said David. "I've

never been through Parliament. But I'd like to know why Lady Gresham should ask us."

Jerry's voice smiled. "Well, it would appear that any friend of Matthew's is a friend of hers. At any rate, we were lunching there anyway. I'm meeting her at her husband's office to go through some of his papers with her. She did all of his editing and typing. That's why his death is doubly hard for her—they were so close in every way."

"I don't feel sorry for her," Mrs. Dobson said.

Claudia was taken aback. How could anyone, much less a nice person like Mrs. Dobson, not feel sorry for someone who had lost her husband? She was interested enough to want to ask Jerry about it, but the drive to the theatre was a short one, and they were soon caught up in the milling crowds in the small foyer. "This is one of the oldest theatres in London," Jerry told her.

Oldness seemed to be a virtue in England. She supposed that she ought to say that it was full of atmosphere, but it was difficult to indulge in small talk, especially with Jerry. She said, merely, "It seems strange to go downstairs into the orchestra."

"Our seats aren't together, so you and I will pair off, shall we?"

Normally she would have preferred to sit with David, but it was pleasant and oddly stirring to be with Jerry after all these years. It made her feel as if she were young again.

"What are you smiling at?" he asked.

"I'm remembering our first meeting."

"I'm remembering our second. You led me a pretty dance."

"You deserved it."

"I don't doubt it. What a pompous fool I must have appeared—and been—in those days."

"But you were a gentleman. David told me it was just my dumb luck that you weren't a cad."

"What a fruity, Victorian word. It doesn't sound like David."

"Maybe he didn't say cad, exactly."

"Bounder?"

"No, I'm sure it wasn't bounder. Because you weren't, really."

"I might have been, if David hadn't put in an appearance when he did."

"I'd like to think so. As a point of pride," she added quickly.

"Make no mistake about it, you were very

desirable in your sublime lack of significance."

He helped her off with her coat, and picked up her purse which had slithered to the floor. They settled back in their seats. David and Mrs. Dobson were sitting in the row in front, a little to the side. Apparently, Mrs. Dobson wasn't a purse dropper; she was taking out a pair of spectacles, which she put on to read her programme. Claudia was glad that she didn't have to wear them. Linda needed glasses when she read a programme or a menu, but she used a lorgnette, which gave the impression of being ornamental rather than necessary. Mrs. Dobson's glasses were sizable, horn-rimmed ones, designed to function. She still looked attractive, though not romantic, which was all to the good. Impartially, Claudia's gaze lingered on David. "I could fall in love with him all over again," she thought. She glanced at Jerry's profile. He had always been handsome, but now he possessed a solidity and a distinction that she had not remembered him to have had in the early days. Elizabeth must have recognized the potential of all that he would grow to be, Claudia reflected, otherwise she would never have married him, for she hadn't

297

intended to marry again. She had worn her widowhood with beauty and dignity, and an ineffable acceptance.

"It's a first-rate cast." Jerry folded his programme and put it away. "This is wonderful," he said simply. "I'm very happy." He placed his hand over hers for an instant, and it felt like David's hand, warm and comforting. "To think," she said softly, "that less than a week ago, we were spending the night in a hotel in New York; it's as if we've lived a whole new lifetime in a few short days."

"It isn't how long, it's how much," Jerry said. "All of eternity was in those two short months with Elizabeth."

"It was like that with Bobby, too."

Again his hand found hers, and their shoulders touched and she was conscious of his closeness with a strange new awareness, and all during the first act, she was aware of him beside her, in the darkened house. She had never felt that way about anyone except David.

They had planned to change places during the interval, but there were the coffee trays to complicate matters—coffee trays passed over everybody's laps, with a great rattle of cups and silverware.

"Your eyes are popping out. Would you like some?" Jerry asked her.

He took her indecision for an answer. "We'll join you in the foyer later," he gestured to David.

She wasn't as hungry as she had thought; or perhaps the bread and butter sandwiches were rather crumbly and dry; or perhaps it was a custom so alien to the theatre as she knew it, that she could not overcome a certain self-consciousness. It was one thing to wheedle David into buying her a slab of chocolate at a movie and sneakily try to open it without rustling the paper, but eating and drinking with the lights full on, was something else. "Your lovely appetite," Jerry smiled, as she turned her attention to a melting square of ice-cream on the tray. The spoon wavered a little as she carried it to her lips. "Oh, slob!" she berated herself.

He gave her his fresh white handkerchief.

"No, I'll use the napkin—" She rubbed at the spot. "Does it show?"

"Only if you look at it," said Jerry. She giggled. It was an English version of David's kind of humour. The girl gathered up the trays. David and Mrs. Dobson paused at the end of the aisle as they went back to their seats. "What's so funny?" David wanted to know.

The funniness would have gone out of it if she tried to explain, and, anyway, the theatre began to darken for the second act. "We forgot to change seats," she whispered to Jerry.

"David looks quite happy. Annie's good company," he said.

"Annie." It carried a special fondness, different from calling Margaret Remington "Maggie". "I meant to ask you," Claudia remembered suddenly, "why doesn't Mrs. Dobson like Lady Gresham?"

"But she does. And Annie is one of the very few people to whom Isabel feels really close. Why would you think otherwise?"

"Because when you were talking of Lady Gresham being so alone after her husband's death, Mrs. Dobson said she didn't feel sorry for her, and she said it with such—bite."

Jerry was silent, as if searching for the right words. "Actually, it was hurt, rather than bite," he said finally. "I think Annie was trying to say that death can be a less bitter and desolate bereavement than another kind of separation. You see, Pete wants a divorce."

"*He* wants it? But Jerry, I should think she'd be a wonderful person to be married to!"

"She is. And they've been happy, and compatible, and very much in love. Then, out of the blue, a couple of months ago, Pete lost his head over someone else, and there you have it."

"Oh," Claudia said again. After a moment she said, "I never would have thought it, seeing them together."

"That's because Ann has set the keynote for their behaviour. Left to himself, Pete would be rather hysterical and explanatory about it. I doubt that Ann will even mention it, and I shouldn't have either, if you hadn't noticed that little crack in the very solid front that she presents to the world."

"I'm sorry I brought it up. And I'm sorry about the divorce."

"You're a nice person."

The only excuse for letting him think that she was a nice person, was the curtain going up on the second act. It wasn't a very good play, so she didn't miss anything by not concentrating on it. She had said to David, "I'm glad Mrs. Dobson is married because I like her so much." She wasn't serious about it, or at least she hadn't thought that she was serious about it.

She needed to go to the cloakroom during the last interval to wash her hands from the sticky ice-cream spoon, and Mrs. Dobson went with her. "You really meant you only wanted to wash your hands," she discovered. "You must be a joy to go on long car drives with."

"I am," said Claudia modestly.

"I am, too."

They looked at each other and smiled. "I like your husband," Mrs. Dobson said.

"So do I. Should I try some more water on this spot?"

"I'd leave it alone."

"I would if we weren't going to a restaurant—"

"Hold your hand over it, nobody'll see."

"Don't I look awfully amazed, and full of palpitation?"

Mrs. Dobson studied her. "More like a garden club lady who's just done a beautiful flower arrangement."

Claudia laughed. "I know what you mean. Do you have those over here, too?"

"Not quite like the American dowager. I

can say it with impunity, because I'm not English myself."

"You're not?"

"I was born in San Francisco. But I've been over here for ten years. Ever since I was married."

"That explains a lot."

"What, for example?"

"Your voice, for one thing. Not your accent, but your voice."

"I trust you mean it kindly."

"Oh, I do!"

"I'm sorry I shan't see more of you and your husband," Mrs. Dobson said abruptly.

"Oh, then David told you were going to Switzerland next week? I'm glad he's resigning himself to it."

"No, he didn't mention it. But I'm leaving next week for the South of France."

"Oh."

"Why do you say 'oh' like that?"

"I suppose because—" She floundered a little. "Friends of ours are going to the Riviera for the season, and you didn't seem the same sort that they are."

"I'm not going because I want to. I have to go. Last winter we bought a little villa outside of Nice. I'm going to try to let it. Or sell it.

And this is the time to do it. Though I detest crowds. Pete and I planned never to use the place during the height of the season."

"We don't like crowds either," said Claudia lamely. She wanted to say, "I know why you want to sell the place, it must be heartbreaking for you." But Mrs. Dobson changed the subject. "Jerry told me that he'd met Elizabeth through you and David."

"Yes. She was Roger Rillion's cousin—he was David's senior partner; he died about five years ago—"

"I knew Roger," Mrs. Dobson said.

Claudia felt suddenly too discursive. "Did you know Elizabeth?"

"I wish I had. Pete and I were in India when Jerry brought her here. By the time we returned—it was over."

"She knew," said Claudia simply. "Looking back on it, David and I both feel that she knew when she married Jerry that it wouldn't be for long. But it was long enough to have made him into a quite different and wonderful person. She was older than he, you know."

Mrs. Dobson nodded. "Jerry needed someone who was older. He doesn't now though.

She must have been a rather great woman, in a wise and gentle way."

"She was. You remind me a little of her."

"Why, thank you. I'm truly touched. But I'm afraid I'm neither wise nor—gentle.—Shall we go? Jerry hates to be kept waiting."

"David, too."

The foyer was emptying, people were going back into the theatre. "Shall we change seats?" Mrs. Dobson asked Claudia.

"I left my coat and gloves—"

"Then that settles it," said Jerry. "We stay as we are."

The last act was short and unsatisfactory. They all agreed about it, discussing it at the table in the restaurant. Claudia, who had once been stage struck, was more explicit in her criticism than the others. "You have a good mind," Mrs. Dobson said.

"You seem surprised," said Claudia.

"I am, a little. But I mean it as a compliment. It's so easy to wear one's brains on one's sleeve."

The waiter hovered for the order. David decided on oysters and scrambled eggs and mushrooms, and Jerry and Mrs. Dobson applauded his choice and followed suit. "I had an omelette for lunch," Claudia demurred.

"Here we go again," said David with a long sigh.

"I'll start with the oysters, anyway—"

"You won't like them," said David.

"But I love them!"

"English oysters are coppery," said Jerry. "Try the scampi, they do them well here."

"'Scampi'. It has a lovely sound." She peered at the menu. "Where are they?"

David rolled his eyes. "She has to see it in black and white."

"Under fish," Mrs. Dobson steered her straight.

"Oh. Fish. What kind?"

"They're like shrimps," said Jerry.

"I'll have them. And some cucumber," she remembered being cheated out of it at lunch.

It was a wonderful evening, so much more warmly intimate than their evenings on the boat with Linda and Bill Hendricks. David broke down and accepted a scampi or two, and she had some of his mushrooms, and one of Mrs. Dobson's oysters, which she wouldn't admit she didn't like, though the taste of it was worse than coppery.

"What can I give you," Jerry asked.

"Eggs, no," she declined. "What else did you have in mind?"

David and Mrs. Dobson laughed, but Jerry pondered the problem gravely before he answered her. "Nothing that you haven't got," he said.

It was past midnight when they tiptoed into their room, careful not to waken the children. The boot was on the other foot, though. The sporadic rhythm of Bertha's snoring sawed through their nerves as they tried to go to sleep; moving the beds meant that her head would have touched theirs if it hadn't been for the thin wall between them. "This is awful," Claudia whispered, and added apprehensively, "Will we always have to whisper?"

"Depending," David said.

"What'll we do?"

"Nothing."

"Nothing?"

"How can we? We don't want to hurt her feelings."

"Oh."

"What do you mean, 'oh'?"

"You're right."

"About what?"

"Hurting Bertha's feelings."

"Oh," said David.

"Well, good-night."

"Good-night, darling.—It was a nice evening, wasn't it?"

"Shh.—Very. But an awfully long day, with all that red tape getting off the boat. Aren't you tired?"

"I feel fine. What was that?"

"Just me, knocking on wood."

"About what?"

"Your feeling fine. I wonder if Lady Gresham really asked us for lunch tomorrow on account of Matthew?"

"Sure," said David. "It pays to know the right people."

"Of course Jerry might have had something to do with it," she conceded. "Was he always so attractive?"

"You ought to know. You were in love with him."

She rose idiotically to his bait. "I was not! I've never so much as looked at another man but you! And if I did, it was only because he turned my head, and anyway, it was so long ago—"

"You're protesting too much," he observed mildly.

It was a suggestion that bore sober contemplation. "Maybe," she admitted at length. "It was a funny thing, in the theatre. I was never conscious of anybody else's coat sleeve next to me except yours."

"I'll break his neck."

"He didn't do anything. I think it was just the past sweeping over me, and making me feel young again."

"It had better be that's all it was."

"David—"

"Yes?"

"Don't lie to me," she said with difficulty. "You're only pretending to be jealous. And that's worse than being. Or not being."

He took so long to answer that it was as if he had not heard her. Then he said, "That wouldn't make much sense to anyone else."

"I know it." She almost wished that it hadn't made sense to him, either. She made an effort to dispel the tenuous abstractions that bedevilled her. "You'll have to let me off Westminster Abbey tomorrow morning, ice-cream is the worst thing."

"Say it again, I'm lost."

"The spot on my jacket. I can't make it budge. I shall have to have it cleaned. Mrs. Dobson gave me the name of the place where she bought the suit she had on, ready-made. I'll have nothing to wear for lunch if I don't go shopping."

"You'd cause quite a sensation in the House of Lords. Incidentally, Annie said she'd try to join us."

"Annie?"

"What?"

"I didn't say anything."

"It must have been Bertha, gulping a snore."

He got the gulp on the nose, but it hadn't been Bertha. She said, "We'd better go to sleep. It's late."

"What's your hurry? It's only seven o'clock at home."

"I wonder what Candy and John are doing."

"Wondering what we're doing—Listen. She stopped."

"It's even more upsetting, you begin to worry if she's still breathing. Is your mattress comfortable?"

"Pretty. Is yours?"

"Pretty. Mrs. Dobson is going to the South of France next week."

"I know," said David.

She felt an uncontrollable hurt. Why

hadn't he said so? She remembered how fully they had discussed Linda the first time they'd met her—her husband's suicide had been common knowledge, David had said, but from what Jerry had mentioned, Mrs. Dobson's divorce wasn't common knowledge, so David evidently didn't intend to betray "Annie's" confidence, even to his wife. It was all very vague, nothing to really put one's finger on, but again, a subtle unrest invaded her. What was happening to them? Now that the confining crises of living had finally lightened sufficiently to permit them to circulate in the open, so to speak, they'd certainly begun to circulate with a vengeance. If they didn't watch out for the danger signals, she brooded drowsily, the sheer centrifugal force of new interests might whirl them apart . . .

When she opened her eyes, a thin grey light was showing through the net curtains on the narrow windows. There were street noises outside; London street noises, muted and early. David was still asleep, but in the next room, she could sense rather than hear that the children were awake, with Bertha cautioning them to be quiet. She closed her eyes again, trying to recapture the dream she had had. She hadn't dreamed for a long while, not dreams that she could remember. In the beginning, she had dreamed of Bobby almost every night, always the same dream, that he was alive and close by her, and it had been difficult to drag herself back to reality and emptiness. She had dreamed, last night, too, a warm, lingering dream of love, that still cradled her like tender arms. It could only have been David who had held her to him in the dream, and yet she remembered being confused because it had seemed to be Jerry. . .

"Mother! Are you asleep?"

How hard it was to come awake again. She registered hazily that Matthew had his coat on. "Don't disturb Daddy," she whispered.

"Daddy's up, he's taking a bath!"

She leaned on her elbow. David's bed was empty. Bertha, in her flowing veil, stood in the doorway, with Michael. "You can't be going out already, what time is it!" Claudia expostulated.

"Nine o'clock." Bertha beamed. "It is good you slept late, for once."

Sleep, as Bertha viewed it, meant physical respite, and not a retreat into forbidden ecstasies of the spirit. "I'm ashamed,"

Claudia said with honesty. "I should have been up and doing an hour ago. Where are you three off to? How's the weather?"

"Mr. Lindt told us the directions to walk to the park. Maybe it rains later, so better we go early while it is nice."

Matthew pulled at her arm. "Hurry up!"

"Not so fast, the park will not run away. Tell Mamma good-bye first."

"Good-bye," said Matthew.

"Good-bye," said Claudia. "We'll see you before we go to lunch." She wanted to tell him about Mrs. Tick-tack-toe, but he was already out of the door. Once more, he had a new world to explore, only to relinquish it after a few short days. She began to feel sorry that she had been so adamant about Switzerland. Jerry had said, last night, "You're right about the climate, I daresay, but I wish Switzerland was nearer."

David came bounding in with a towel wrapped round his middle. "Well, lazy, what about ordering breakfast? We have to hurry up." He sounded like Matthew.

"You were going to let me off Westminster Abbey," she reminded him.

"You could meet me there after you've finished shopping."

"I can't tell you how long I'll be. You'd better go by yourself." She was sorry about it, but she wasn't heartbroken. She wasn't a born sightseer, which was something David hadn't discovered as yet. She was positive that she was going to develop two feet in one shoe at the very sight of a museum or cathedral, so Parliament would be quite enough to tackle for one day. She'd have to wheedle a quick refresher course on English government before lunch. It was trickier to keep the Conservative Party and the Labour Party straight than the Republicans and the Democrats. Republicans made no bones about anything; Claudia had noticed it, especially on the boat. Helen Nicholson would get downright objectionable in her sweeping denouncements. It was rather shocking on the whole, because, after all, Presidents, past as well as current, were entitled to some degree of respect, no matter how hard you were hit in your stocks. She was glad that David had consistently refused to be drawn into the violent discussions. His convictions were deep-seated, but he didn't go round airing them all over the place. He had convictions about English politics, too, and maybe he'd be co-operative and lend her one or two of them in the taxi on the way over, just in case she needed to keep her head above water. David knew that she was an ignoramus, but she certainly wouldn't want to disgrace Jerry. If it hadn't been for that unsightly spot on her suit, she could at least have had Westminster Abbey under her belt before lunch. It was a good thing that David was Cathedral-minded. He'd sort of be eating-for-two conversationally.

A cab brought her painlessly to the address that Mrs. Dobson had given her, and she bought a tweed suit, a cashmere coat and a mannish sports hat. Miraculously, nothing needed alteration, so she walked out in her new clothes, feeling very British. The prices seemed much cheaper than in America, until she reckoned it out in dollars on her way back to the hotel, and it came to pretty much the same. Even though she didn't have to worry about spending money on clothes any longer, she apparently couldn't shake off the habit, after so many years of biding her time for the after-season sales and nursing her old beaver coat winter after winter.

She ran into Bertha and the children coming out of the lift on their way to the dining-room. "Pardon me," she stopped them, "haven't I met you before?"

"Ach!" Bertha recognized her belatedly, "It's your mamma!"

Matthew covered his chagrin with a scowl. "Every minute she has a new dress on," he disapproved raucously.

"Be quiet, you horrid little American," Claudia hissed.

"It is wonderful material, and very good on you," Bertha made quick atonement. 'Maybe you will come with us and see the nice little room where we eat."

"Is Mr. David upstairs?"

"Just the minute before we went down he came in."

"We saw the Changing of the Guard!" Matthew clamoured for attention. "Boy, you should have seen those horses!"

"Horsies!" Michael echoed shrilly.

People in the foyer turned, and one or two, who were children lovers, or horse lovers, more likely, smiled indulgently. "Come along, I'll sit with you while you eat," Claudia decided quickly.

Luckily, there was no one else in the small room behind the main dining-hall. "I want to go back this afternoon!" Matthew persisted.

"Bertha says they change the guards twice a day! What's that?" he digressed accusingly.

"A nice mutton chop," said Bertha, cutting it up in little pieces.

"What's mutton?" he demanded in mounting distrust.

"An elderly lamb," said Claudia, "and be grateful it's not jugged hare. Eat."

He shivered largely as he encountered an infinitesimal shred of fat, but when he came up against his first brussels sprout, his body contorted in revulsion. "It's cabbage!" he protested on a bleat of horror.

"Oh, no, it isn't, it's worse," Claudia placated him.

He was taken off his guard, and swallowed it down. "The desserts in England are lovely," she went on with enthusiasm. "There's something called trifle that you'll just love."

Bertha nodded in elaborate accord. "We had it yesterday already. It is delicious."

"It was custard," Matthew recalled bitterly, and shuddered again.

"They will get used to the food," Bertha murmured. "Already they are used to the weather. All morning long they were out even

317

when it began to rain, and see how nice and rosy they are."

"I saw," said Claudia. "Didn't you notice me touch the backs of their necks to see if it was fever?"

"Michael's not swallowing, he's holding everything in his cheeks," Matthew remarked.

"Ach," said Bertha, who had slipped up on that one. "Do not upset him, or he will choke."

It was Claudia's turn to shudder. She was a coward when it came to anything getting stuck in anybody's throat, her own included. "I must go now," she said, "be good, my pets, and bless you."

"That's crazy talk!" Matthew threw after her.

"Isn't it?" she agreed.

David greeted her with the announcement that he had been waiting for over an hour. It was the kind of lie she expected and rather liked. She circled slowly. "How do I look?"

"Nice," he said, which was the equivalent of another man's rave.

"I'll be imported material when I get back to America. Did you miss me at Westminster Abbey?"

"I didn't go."

"You didn't go! Why not? What did you do all morning?"

"I found a two-ounce fishing rod," he confessed sheepishly. "It's a beauty. I bought one for John, too."

"Kiss me."

"Why?" he asked cautiously.

"Never mind why."

"Hey!" He held her away from him. "What's this all about?"

"Don't you like it?"

"Sure I like it."

"Hey!" she gasped.

It was as if they had been away from each other for a couple of days, instead of a couple of hours. "I dreamt about you last night," she murmured. It must have been David, she concluded in relief.

"We'd better get started," he said finally.

"We'd better," she agreed. "Is that a letter from Candy on the bureau?"

"One from John, too."

"Already?" she sighed, blissfully. "The children's red cheeks, your clay feet, and now mail from home."

"You're making less and less sense. How would you like a seven-star bull?"

"Dearly. Whom have you got in mind?"

"Hussy. Take a look at this folder that John forwarded."

She took a look. "Oh dear, I always wanted to go to a cattle auction, but we'll just miss it, won't we?"

"Not necessarily. We could change our passage to a week earlier. It's worth it, best blood lines in the country, and a seven-star bull is nothing to turn your back on."

"I should think not!"

He smothered a grin. "Shopping certainly seems to agree with you."

She nodded. "I always did have a passion for a two-inch fishing rod!"

"Two-ounce," he corrected stiffly.

"Sorry. Say, isn't air mail marvellous! I wouldn't be surprised if they've received our letters from the boat already, would you?"

"Extremely surprised, since we've hardly been here a day."

"It doesn't seem possible. What's happened to time, anyway? Maybe there isn't any. In dreams, you live a whole lifetime in a moment, so why not in real life?" She settled herself to decipher Candy's letter. Candy belonged to the more recent era of square, round, handwriting, deceptively clear at first

320

glance, but not so clear when it came to reading it. Handwriting always intrigued her. Jerry had a handsome hand: she remembered his letter when Bobby died—it was a little like David's writing in its straight, forceful simplicity. She couldn't completely accept a man who emerged in a spidery slant, or with an immature non-conformity . . . Why were her thoughts wandering? She brought her mind back to Candy's determined newsiness, which all the same revealed how deeply she was missing them. Vile weather, freezing cold and sleet, but the work was progressing on the little hip-roof house, she'd passed it this morning, to see how everything was. Both she and John had been so relieved to get the wire about Matthew—even John's mother had laughed, and Mrs. Payne didn't have that kind of sense of humour, as a rule . . . Elsie Miller—she'd been standing on her porch when Candy had driven past—sent her love. (I must buy Elsie a present, Claudia reminded herself.) Elsie had proved an awfully good friend, though the "Elserob" sign in front of her cottage down the road was an atrocity. Robert was Elsie's husband, needless to say. But his brother was in the local police force, which was fine in case of emergency.

"Leave John's letter until you come home, it's mostly business," David suggested.

"Nothing new about the library? Or the grounds? Candy was vague."

"How could there be? Panelling is slow work. And they won't be moving in the heavy machinery for dredging the river until the frost is out of the ground. Which won't be soon."

"I hope not. I want to be back to watch it."

"So do I. They have to be careful about the banks of the river. I don't want too much of the brush disturbed, or we won't have any wild ducks or birds."

"I should say they have to be careful. Elsie Miller promised to look in every so often with corn for them."

"They've probably been scared away by the workmen, but they'll be back in the spring."

"And so will we." The telephone rang. "That must be Linda about tonight."

"Can't we get out of it?"

"No!"

It wasn't Linda: it was a message from Mrs. Dobson's secretary—Mrs. Dobson was just leaving her office. "I forgot to tell you," David explained hastily, "Annie's managed to join us for lunch, she's going to call for us in her car."

"Oh. You didn't tell me you'd talked to her."

"I didn't talk to her. Jerry called a few minutes before you came home. He said she passes the hotel on the way from her office so she might as well pick us up."

"How nice," said Claudia. "I didn't know she had a car."

"We ought to buy one over here," said David, "use it and take it home with us. I've always wanted a good English car. What do you think?"

She was cagey about it. "Will you let me drive your good English car?"

"I will not," he said, and meant it. That was one of the most exasperating things about him—his opinion of women drivers.

Mrs. Dobson's car was in such good taste that it was almost in bad taste. It looked as if it had just walked out of a bandbox: pale, pale grey, upholstered in soft, morocco leather, with square cut, feather-edged lines. It was a relief from the brilliant colours and fantastic shapes of the American cars, and David promptly fell in love with it, in the same way he'd fallen in love with his two-ounce fishing rod. "Damn it, but the English know how to do these things," he said. Of course, the car didn't run by itself and do everything but the laundry, like American cars. On the contrary, it had four gears, that worked from a heavy short leather-topped little stick on the floor, but David seemed to like that inconvenience as well as everything else. In the middle of the street in front of the hotel, he lifted up the bonnet, and peered at the engine. "What a honey," he said.

"It's the same as the Rolls engine, only smaller," Mrs. Dobson said, who didn't seem to mind him peering at her car. He closed the bonnet. "Do you know how many thousand miles this car has done?" he asked Claudia.

Claudia said she didn't, adding to herself why in heaven's name should she?

"A hundred and ten," he announced proudly, as if he were responsible for it, "and it's good for another hundred and ten."

"You must drive quite a lot," Claudia said politely to Mrs. Dobson.

"Actually no. Pete and I have put about thirty on it, that's all. The car was fourteen years old when we bought it, you see."

"I thought it was new!" Claudia's amazement was not perfunctory.

Mrs. Dobson laughed. "'Not on a publisher's and editor's salary. When this car was made, twenty years ago, it cost four thousand pounds. We paid nineteen hundred for it."

"I wish I could find one like it," said David enviously.

"We could look around," Mrs. Dobson suggested.

"It'd take time," said David gloomily.

"It would," Mrs. Dobson agreed, "unless we were very lucky. We got this one by luck—a dealer had just taken it in part exchange for a new one. They've come down a lot in price, and have all the modern gadgets, but they're not the same great cars as they made twenty years ago."

"Not by a long shot they're not."

"Do you want to drive it?" Mrs. Dobson hesitated before she climbed behind the wheel.

"I'd like to, but I'm not sure enough of your traffic rules yet."

"Any time you want to borrow it, please

do. I'm not taking it with me to the Riviera, and Pete will be in New York."

"Thanks. But we won't be here, either. Next week at this time, we'll be staring at an Alp for no good reason."

"I'm the villain," Claudia acknowledged. "But how was I to guess that the weather would be so nice here?"

"I know," Mrs. Dobson smiled. "The only way for you to get back in David's good graces is to pray for sleet and fog. We've had plenty of it up to a few days ago. There's not room for three in front. Do you two want to climb in the back seat?"

"Let David sit with you," said Claudia generously. "He can pretend he's driving."

He didn't have to accept with such alacrity. He settled himself in, and promptly leaned forward to study the dashboard. It seemed to be a very complicated one, with two of everything. The shifting was also complicated, but Mrs. Dobson slid noiselessly and competently from one gear to another, and David told her she drove like a man, which made Claudia want to pick up the whole car, and throw it at him.

Mrs. Dobson turned briefly, so that Claudia saw her profile, with its firm chin and nicely upturned nose. It was the sort of plain, open face that was built to wear, like the car David was so crazy about, and it, too, wouldn't look much different after twenty years. You wouldn't be able to notice when her hair turned a little lighter into grey, or more lines came round her mouth or eyes, to add to those already there, lines of laughter and trouble and work. Mrs. Dobson's face, thought Claudia was young, but it didn't have that unfurnished look that many women's faces had. Mrs. Dobson had moved into her face, bag and baggage. You could keep on looking at it, and not get bored with it. You couldn't help getting a little bored with Linda's face, for example, after the third or fourth look, in spite of the fact that she was a mother and a widow. Linda seemed always to be busy looking like a madonna. There was nothing of the madonna in Mrs. Dobson's face. She was smiling now as she glanced at David. "I presume that I may take it as a compliment, that I handle a car like a man?"

"You may," Claudia answered tersely. "He wouldn't say it to me, even if I did."

"Of course not," Mrs. Dobson smiled again. "You're his wife."

Claudia pondered it. "That could mean any number of things."

"I didn't intend to be abstruse," Mrs. Dobson said quickly, "I suppose I meant, chiefly, in your case at least, that David doesn't have to pay you compliments."

David was apparently listening more than he let on. His eyebrows slid up his forehead. "On her driving I couldn't," he said.

She began to sputter. He was so manifestly unfair. Had she ever so much as got a ticket for speeding, or going through a red light or anything else? But he'd probably never forget the garage door for as long as he lived, and of course, whenever he did let her take the wheel, he'd make her so nervous just sitting next to her, she couldn't even park decently especially if she had to go in backwards between other cars. Doubtless, Mrs. Dobson could go in backwards every time on the first shot.

Jerry was waiting at the main entrance for them. "Isabel's meeting us in the dining-room," he said. "We'll have lunch directly and then I can show you round afterwards." He drew Claudia to him in greeting, and kissed her so easily and naturally that she was abashed at the tumbling of her senses. Had it

328

been David in the dream, after all? It was so hard to tell; and they did smell alike, a tangy tobacco smell, mixed with the clean spice of shaving lotion. She was acutely conscious that he did not release her hand as they moved along the stupendously imposing hall. It seemed wrong to be so aware, because Jerry appeared to be feeling nothing at all, except the simple pleasure at being together. "I'm glad you're not the sort of people who gush and rave," Mrs. Dobson was saying.

"I know what you mean," said David. "I'm stirred up inside, though."

"So am I," said Claudia honestly.

"Wait until you see the view of the Thames from the upper floor. Not being English born, I don't have to be as reticent as Jerry."

"I'm not reticent," said Jerry. "I'm very happy. And when one is very happy, it's difficult to talk. Besides, Claudia and David aren't tourists, you know. I don't think they're even going to buy a postcard of the Houses of Parliament. '*We were here today and it was thrilling.*'"

"You over-estimate me," said David. "I had every intention of sending one to my secretary, and saying just that."

"And me, to Elsie Miller—she's a

neighbour. But now you've made me self-conscious," said Claudia.

"Don't pay any attention to Jerry, you go right ahead," Mrs. Dobson said. "I sent postcards like mad when I first came here to live. And I bet Jerry sent dozens of the Empire State Building and the Statue of Liberty."

"Of course I did. Why not?"

They laughed, and it was strange that four people, and one a total stranger until last night, could be so in tune. It was like being with John and Candy. It had been so different, Claudia reflected, with Linda and Bill Hendricks. In all their close association on the boat, they had never really come to know each other, nor felt completely happy or relaxed in each other's company. The touch of Bill's hand upon her own had been an intrusion upon her private being, and she could see, now, that Linda's near-infatuation had been irksome to David.

It was even more strange that the presence of Lady Gresham did not dissipate the easy cameraderie between them. She looked and acted exactly the same as she had on the boat, but she no longer seemed alien and a little unreal. "We were the ones who were the aliens," Claudia decided, and no wonder

Lady Gresham had put a barricade round herself. There were no barriers, now. She kissed Mrs. Dobson affectionately, and they clung together for that extra instant of good friends meeting after a separation. "It's good to see you both again," she said to Claudia and David, with her warm, firm handshake.

"It's good of you to have asked us," said David, who found his tongue more easily than Claudia.

Claudia felt that maybe she ought to say something of the sort too, but Lady Gresham smiled her nice, toothy smile and said, at once, "Our table is ready."

It was an airy, simple dining-room, that filled up gradually with men mostly, ranging from middle-age to old, and all of them very dignified. There didn't seem to be a menu, at least none that Claudia could see. "I'll have the tomato cocktail and the sole," Mrs. Dobson said automatically, and Claudia took the same, and Lady Gresham said, "Broth and a very small omelette, thank you," and David and Jerry followed suit. When dessert came, it was pudding, which Claudia wasn't sure was rice or bread, but it didn't matter as it was most unextraordinary in both cases, and that didn't matter either. She was glad that they had had the experience of the hotel, and Jerry's apartment, or it would all have seemed a little odd whereas now she felt, and she was sure that David felt, that this was not only the proper, but the aristocratic way to live. She could understand why Lady Gresham had felt a little aloof from the flagrant opulence of ocean travel. Obviously, everything was done for the benefit of the Americans. Still, it must have been a nice change for some of the English, too. Lord Gresham had probably enjoyed his periodic fling with the little she-crabs and the Dolphin steaks.

Having lunch in the middle of the English Government, so to speak, the conversation might well have plunged straight off the deep end into world affairs, but no sooner had Jerry bent to retrieve Claudia's napkin from the floor, than he asked, still upside down, "Is there any particular rush for you to get to Switzerland?"

Obviously, he didn't realize that he was stirring up more trouble for her than if he had embarked on a discussion of nuclear physics and the Suez Canal combined; she tried to catch his eye, but it was difficult under the circumstances. It wouldn't have done any good, anyway, because David didn't even wait for Jerry's head to appear above the table again before he was smouldering with his grievance. "If we never get to Switzerland, it's all right with me."

Jerry laid the napkin across Claudia's lap. "I have to be in Paris next week, why not join me? It's an easy stop-over for you, and if the weather turns miserable, we could cheer Annie up for a few days while she sells her house, and then you could make connections to Switzerland from Nice. How about it?"

"Please do! It's a beautiful idea." Mrs. Dobson turned to David. "Do it for Jerry's sake, if not for mine. He needs a holiday. I happen to know that the African jaunt was a lot tougher than he admits."

"Never mind you and Jerry. I'd jolly well like to do it for my own sake," said David, becoming very British all at once. "Give in, Claudia, admit that this Switzerland ruse you cooked up is a wash-out."

Because she wanted the trip to Paris, at this point, as much as he did, she felt that she ought to make one last stand for the plan she had indeed "cooked up" in a secret con-ference with the specialist who had first

diagnosed David's condition. Though no
mandatory, Dr. Morrison had told her, a
winter in clear mountain air would certainly
be more beneficial to David than the
uncertain climate of England or France. "I'l
pretend it's for the children's sake," she had
decided then and there, and Dr. Morrison
who had sized up more than the spot in
David's apex, had gone along with her on it

Now, for the last time, she tried to put it on
Matthew and Michael. "David, be practical
I don't want to hibernate in Switzerland any
more than you do, but it's no vacation to
travel around with a couple of hoodlums.'
She appealed to Lady Gresham. "You know
I'm right, don't you?"

Lady Gresham smiled. "I know what you
mean," she amended. "I happen only to have
seen Matthew's fall, but Bertha gave me a
lurid account of his getting lost, and the
baby's splurge with the soap."

"And all inside five days."

"That's because they were restless," David
had the nerve to say. "Moving around will
take up their slack."

"What about Bertha's slack? She's
supposed to be getting a little relaxation ou
of this trip, too, and it's not any fun to keep

on packing and unpacking and getting settled in a new place every few days."

"Not with perambulators and teddy bears, it's not," David was the one to give in. "The next time we go away, we'll leave the brats home."

"Then why not leave them where they are?" Mrs. Dobson suggested. "You'll be a great deal nearer them on the Continent than if they were in America. You could always fly back in case of any emergency."

Jerry brightened up. "Annie has something here!"

"Except that they'd go crazy staying in that little hotel room for any length of time, and so would the hotel," said Claudia.

"Reluctant as I am to admit it," David said, "Claudia's right."

"She may be right about leaving the youngsters in the hotel," said Jerry, "but hold on a minute, I have the perfect solution!"

"Drown them," David offered amiably.

"Shame on you," said Lady Gresham.

"It happens every day in America," he teased, quite as if he had known her for years. "However, we can always keep it at the back of our minds, in case Jerry's 'perfect' solution doesn't work out."

"Oh hush, I'm waiting to hear what it is," said Claudia, "though I can tell you in advance that it won't work. Wherever we leave them, suppose Bertha broke her leg o got sick?"

"Stop borrowing trouble," David adjured her.

"It happened last summer," she insisted stubbornly. "You seem to forget that she fell down the cellar steps and landed in the hospital for six weeks. And wouldn't that be a pretty state of affairs if she was all alone with the children in a strange country?"

"My solution takes care of all that," said Jerry smugly. "Let them stay with Isabel."

Claudia thought, of course, that he was fooling, and so did David. "I'm sure that Lady Gresham is very grateful to you for the suggestion," he said with broad irony.

"I am, rather," Lady Gresham told him. "It would be like having Christopher back."

"You're joking!" Claudia exclaimed. "You couldn't possibly mean it!"

"But of course she means it!" Mrs. Dobson broke in. "Jerry, it's an absolutely inspired idea."

"Certainly it is. Only I suspect that Claudia and David don't think so, because they don't know the set-up. You see," he explained to them, "Isabel has an enchanting house near Kensington Park, with a completely separate self-contained flat over the garage that her daughter and son-in-law used before they went to America to live."

"After they left," Lady Gresham added, "I had one very unfortunate experience in letting it, and I haven't tried again."

"You'd be in for another unfortunate experience," said David, and it was clear that he still wasn't taking the idea seriously. And yet, to Claudia it suddenly made sense, for looking back on it, the small state-room on B deck and the impeccable shabbiness of Lady Gresham's modest wardrobe could well have spelled expediency rather than eccentricity.

"Isabel rattles around all by herself in that empty house," Jerry dispelled any notion that she was surrounded by a staff of servants. "She never bothers to cook a proper meal for herself."

"Nonsense!" Lady Gresham interrupted. "The less one eats at my age, the better. Besides, eating is rather tiresome when you're alone."

"That's why you shouldn't be alone," said Jerry.

"Many women are," Lady Gresham replied quietly. "And remember, too, that it's my own choice that I'm not willing to sell the house and move into a small flat. I expect I'll come to it, but I'm going to be soft with myself for a bit longer."

"Soft with yourself. We should all be as soft with ourselves as you are," Mrs. Dobson said.

"You're doing all right," Jerry told her obliquely. "Now let's get back to Bertha and the children. How about it?"

"Please," Lady Gresham stopped him. "You're pushing Mr. and Mrs. Naughton into a most awkward position, merely because you feel it would be for my good to have the flat occupied."

"It's the other way round," Claudia protested. "It would be entirely for our good, and I think it's the greatest presumption even to suggest it!"

"So do I," said David.

"You mustn't feel that way," Lady Gresham said. "I grew very fond of Matthew and the baby, and Bertha, and Jerry's quite right in one respect—they'd be near enough to allow you to leave them with a feeling of ease, and yet they would be living on their own. Besides," she ended with unemotional simplicity, "any additional money, no matter for how brief a time, would be very welcome to me at this particular moment."

Claudia felt a rising respect for Lady Gresham. As a rule, she didn't like people who made a fetish of being poor any more than she liked people who made a production of being rich, but Lady Gresham was merely accepting a lack of money as a not very important circumstance in her life. Maybe it was the English in her, or maybe it was just being an aristocrat in any language or nationality. If David hadn't changed his opinion of her by this time he deserved to have his tail kicked. In any event, it was up to him to make the decision about Switzerland for, personally, she was ready to accept Lady Gresham's offer without any reservation whatsoever, and it went without saying that Bertha would jump at the chance to keep herself busy with a little housekeeping. Besides, Bertha liked Lady Gresham, title and all, but David could be a stickler in his preconceived ideas about people. He might still feel that the children ought not to be exposed to a "middle-aged crackpot of a woman". She glanced at him out of the corner of her eye, for the silence was becoming uncomfortable. "Dear?" she prodded him tentatively.

"I'm prejudiced," he finally came out with it. "I think it's not only a wonderful break for the boys, but for us, too."

Jerry and Mrs. Dobson said "Hurray", or something of the sort, and Lady Gresham said, "Thank you, David," and the way she said it made Claudia wonder whether she'd noticed that he had mentioned the boys first, and themselves afterwards. She concluded that Lady Gresham probably had noticed it. It took an aristocrat to recognize one.

9

ARISTOCRAT, indeed. She regretted having thought so kindly of him. Couldn't he have been content to give Parliament a lick and a promise after lunch, and go over to see the apartment with her? But no, not David. He had a one-track mind (though he always accused her of having one) and he not only made her trudge through the House of Lords from top to bottom (on the theory that they might never have the opportunity again), but he blithely assumed that she shared his intention to listen to a debate scheduled for three o'clock in the House of Commons. By this time, Lady Gresham had departed to keep an appointment with her lawyer, Mrs. Dobson had returned to her office, and Jerry was manfully carrying on the obligations of host. He also had the key to the apartment, and said that he would take them over there whenever David was ready to go. "He's ready to go now, this minute," Claudia firmly put her foot down on the debate. "I want to see the place in daylight, at least."

"You're right," David acknowledged a little too readily. "Let's do it in the morning."

"We will do no such thing. It's nice enough of Jerry to ruin his afternoon for us."

"As a matter of fact, I do happen to be tied up in the forenoon tomorrow," Jerry backed her up. "Besides, it is going to take a bit of doing to establish Bertha and the children in new surroundings, so you ought to decide on the apartment as quickly as possible."

"We've decided," said David blandly. "Why waste the time looking at it? If it was good enough for Lady Gresham's daughter, it's good enough for our two brats."

"Don't be so gallant," Claudia told him impatiently. "Lady Gresham wouldn't hear of our renting it sight unseen. You know perfectly well how finicky Bertha is about a stove and ice box."

"Now what possible use would I be to you," he interrupted with a great show of logic, "when it comes to kitchen stuff?"

"None whatsoever." She addressed herself to Jerry. "He poses as one of those manly men who can't even boil an egg straight, so

342

let him listen to the debate, and we'll go without him."

David grinned. "You took the words right out of my mouth," he said. "I'll meet you back at the hotel in time to dress for the Woodburns."

"Why so late?"

"I want to do a little car shopping if Annie can get away from the office early enough."

"That's a splendid idea," said Jerry, and Claudia wondered whether he meant the car, or the fact that they were free to go off and look at the apartment by themselves.

"This is a nuisance for you," she said contritely, as they emerged into what remained of the thin afternoon sun. "Out-of-town visitors can disrupt your whole routine, they're a pest."

He smiled down at her. "Some are." He hailed a taxi and gave the driver instructions.

"Especially visitors who are distant relatives," Claudia pursued the subject. "Not that we have any, or close ones either. You and Candy and John seem to be all the family we have left."

"Thank you for including me."

"I never did before," she said with candour. "You were just someone who

343

wandered in and out of our lives, without meaning very much one way or another, until yesterday David and I both suddenly realized how important you are to us."

"That's because you're strange here, and I happen to be your one familiar tie with home."

"That's true, but I think it goes deeper than that."

"I know that it goes deeper with me," he said. "Annie told me after we'd left you and David last night, that I'd taken off five years in a single evening."

"Make it two years or you'll be younger than I am by the time we get to Paris."

He took her hand in his. "You're not young," he said gravely. "You have youth, and you'll always have youth, but you were born old."

"It's odd for you to say that."

"Why?"

"Because David told me the same thing before we were married. I was just eighteen, with the shape of a blue-fish, and Mamma said I was too much of a child to know my own mind and Hartley went even further than that, but David wouldn't listen to reason—"

"He listened," Jerry said. "The way Elizabeth listened."

"I remember all the horrid gossip," said Claudia softly. "Everyone said it was sheer infatuation on her part, and you were only after her money. We're lucky that the two people we loved took a chance with us. It's a lot to live up to."

"I hadn't thought of it like that. But you're quite right, it's a lot to live up to and we can't let them down." He seemed aware for the first time that he was holding her hand. He carried it to his lips for an instant, and then gave it back to her. Her heart stirred. How often Bill Hendricks had kissed her hand on the boat. The courtly, meaningless gesture was second-nature to him. But this was different. Or was it? When Jerry spoke again, his voice confused her with its matter-of-factness. "We're going out of our way a little, because I want you to see the parts of Kensington that are still unspoiled. Don't miss this little section we're coming to now."

"Oh how lovely! Peter Pan is sure to be lurking around here somewhere, excuse the whimsy. No, but really, it's so much better for the children, than living in the hotel in the middle of crowds and traffic."

345

"You'll find crowds and traffic here, too. Not quite the same as Mayfair, however. Kensington's become like areas of New York that have passed their vogue."

"I see what you mean," she said as they circled back into a broad motley thoroughfare that reminded her of New York's upper West side. "Doesn't Lady Gresham mind what's happened to the neighbourhood?"

"I rather imagine that she'd prefer that it hadn't changed, but when you come to know Isabel better, you'll find that she's quite impervious to conditions that would bother most of us."

"I wish I had more imperviousness to insignificant things."

"I always thought you did."

"Then something's happened to it. Take tonight, for instance. I have nothing to wear that everybody hasn't seen before. Can you imagine Lady Gresham caring what she wore?"

"Actually no, but it's rather nice for you to care."

"Stop making allowances for me. I can't imagine even Mrs. Dobson caring."

"That's different. You carry your foibles more gracefully than Ann.—By the way, why are you so formal with her?" he digressed curiously. "I notice you keep calling her 'Mrs. Dobson'."

"I don't know. I wonder about it myself. Especially since David called her 'Annie' right away. Maybe that's why I didn't," she admitted. "Not that it makes any sense, I mean, I like her tremendously, I just don't know," she finished lamely. "It's hard for me to call people by their first names until I know them. It's hard for David too, as a rule. I'm beginning to notice that we don't unbend easily."

"You've been by yourselves a great deal."

"And that's bad, isn't it?"

He shook his head. "No. It's just that most of us can't afford to be."

She thought about it. "That's frightening," she said at length. "And yet it isn't good to live in an isolated world. People are important. But it's also important to be able to take them or leave them, and that isn't so easy I suppose, when you have a lot of money. Or anyway, enough to do everything everybody else does. Which is something we never had before."

"You didn't need a lot of money. At the risk of repeating myself, and sounding pretentious, you were rich without it."

"I hope it doesn't work both ways with us," she said, half serious.

"From all present indications, it won't," he assured her.—"We just passed some shops where Bertha can market."

"Then we must be almost there?"

"We are there." The taxi made a left turn and slowed down. "That's near enough, you can stop here, driver."

She swallowed her disappointment. She hadn't expected such a prosaic little street, devoid of charm, and dwarfed by a modern apartment building looming up on the farther corner. Peter Pan wouldn't be caught dead here.

"Come along," Jerry paid off the taxi, and piloted her towards a cobbled driveway that lay hidden behind a pair of short stone columns, grey-black with age. A small house, of faded brick, sat well back, remote as an island in its tree-shaded courtyard. "I forgive you," Claudia said.

"You forgive me? For what?"

"For saying at lunch that Lady Gresham had an enchanting house in Kensington. It didn't sound like you. I thought you were

348

being flowery. You weren't, though. Enchanting is the only word for it."

He was nonplussed for a moment. "Look here, you wouldn't hold a little thing like that against me? What if I were guilty of something truly unforgivable?"

"I wouldn't mind as much."

He continued to regard her quizzically. "I do believe you wouldn't."

"It's silly, isn't it? But I'm that way with David, and he's that way with me."

"In which case, I feel honoured."

"You should. I don't even feel like that about Candy and John, I expect them not to be perfect. I'm talking in riddles. How do we get up to the apartment?"

"The entrance is down the path behind the garage. You're not talking in riddles, your contempts are subtle, vigorous, and disconcerting.—Watch out for that step."

"I see it.—Oh, there's a garden back here, too, the hyacinths look just about ready to bud! Bertha loves to weed, the simpleton."

"Aren't you taking a lot for granted with Bertha? She might not like the whole idea of staying on in London without you."

"She will."

"What makes you so certain?"

"You can always be certain with Bertha
One of her virtues is that she's absolutely pre
dictable. I can tell you verbatim what she'
going to say."

"I'd like to hear."

Claudia stopped to fish out a pebble from
her shoe. "Well, first of all she's going to ask
about the stove, because for the children it i
better not to eat hotel food even if it is good
And for us, it is better to go away for a littl
vacation by ourselves. And for her it is by al
means no holiday to sit with her hands in he
lap."

"You're leaving out the most importan
thing. Does she like Isabel?"

"Oh, very much. Before and after sh
turned out to be Lady Gresham."

Jerry laughed. Then he said, with a1
abrupt change of mood, "'I wonder if Davi
knows how rare it is to have everything a ma1
could want, packaged into one woman."

"He'd be crazy if he didn't. He says h
doesn't know what we ever did to deserv
her."

"I wasn't talking about Bertha," Jerry said
"Shall we start looking at the apartmen
before the sun goes down?"

Claudia nodded. It was easier to nod tha1

o reach for her voice above the sudden closing of her throat.

The doorman was calling cabs for guests already leaving for the theatre, when Jerry dropped her off at the hotel. She didn't ask him upstairs, for the two small rooms would have been a shambles, what with David dressing for the Woodburns, and the children undressing for bed. "I had no idea it was so late," she said, aghast.

"I didn't either. Tell David it was all my fault."

"But it wasn't. I was famished for a cup of tea, which is funny, because I never bother with it in the afternoon at home."

"We'll make an Englishwoman of you yet."

"Well, this is a fine time to show up!"

Claudia jumped. "David, I hate you, you scared me to death, coming up behind me like that!—And you're a good one to talk, you were supposed to be back at the hotel an hour ago!"

"I told you I was going to look at cars," he said virtuously.

"Did you find anything you liked?" Jerry asked with interest.

"The new models don't tempt me too much, but we're on the trail of one of the old twelve cylinder Rolls, with a special sports body, and very little mileage.—How was the apartment?"

"Perfect," said Claudia. "All we have to do now is break the news to Bertha."

"I'll call you in the morning to find out how she took it," said Jerry. "Good night, you two."

"Good night," said Claudia. "And thanks for everything, including tea."

"So that's what kept you so late," said David, as they waited for the lift. "You had tea."

"At Fortnum and Mason's. Jerry said it was part of my London education."

"We almost went there, too, but it looked crowded, so we stopped back at Annie's for a cocktail instead."

"So that's what kept *you* so late."

"I walked home.—Tell me about the apartment."

"Wait until we get upstairs and I won't have to describe it over again for Bertha's benefit.—What kind of 'flat' do the Dobsons live in?"

"Very nice. Comfortable, unpretentious

Like Jerry's. Maybe a little more so."

"More so how?"

He shrugged. "Two people instead of one."

"Pipes *and* flower vases."

"And one chair with an antimacassar that belonged to Pete's grandmother.—You'd better leave telling Bertha about our change of plans until the morning."

"I wouldn't dare put it off, she'll have too much to do."

"Then make it short, we can't keep the Woodburns waiting dinner until all hours."

It was on the tip of her tongue to retort that he should have thought of that before having cocktails with Ann Dobson, but he could have come back at her too easily. "It's not one of the things you can make short," she said instead. "Especially with Matthew around asking questions."

Fortunately, however, both children were settled in bed, with Bertha ruining her eyes trying to darn socks under a heavily shaded light so as not to disturb them. Claudia beckoned her from the doorway.

In one so nearly portly, Bertha's agility in orienting herself to new situations never failed to elicit a prayer of thankfulness in

Claudia. It was a pity, she thought now, that Jerry couldn't have been present to hear Bertha running true to form. Having accepted the general idea with whole-hearted approval, her concern centred on the kitchen. "Clean mattresses I do not have to worry about with someone like Lady Gresham, but how is the stove?"

"Well, I didn't stop to bake a cake in it," Claudia told her, "but it was immaculate, and it seemed to work fine."

"Does the heating work fine? That's more important," David put in from behind the wardrobe door where he was climbing out of his pants.

"Very fine, Jerry said to explain to you that the apartment has a separate unit from the house, so Bertha can have it as warm as she wants."

"The children are already getting used to not having it so warm," Bertha announced with a trace of pride. "But it is nice anyway to have plenty of heat, and to have two bedrooms is wonderful."

"With a lovely bathroom in between," Claudia threw in for good measure.

"*Gott sei dank*," Bertha murmured happily, inadvertently acknowledging that a bathroom across a public hall was proving a not unalloyed delight. Claudia got the sudden impact of everything having to be done in threes, which meant that the poor thing had no privacy and probably hadn't been able to take a bath or anything else until after the children were safely in bed and asleep. "Which reminds me, Bertha, that you'll have to have at least a couple of days to yourself before we leave. And no back-talk," she forestalled any argument.

"But that is foolish. What would I do?"

"Do Westminster Abbey," Claudia told her promptly. "Somebody in the family has to, and it certainly doesn't look as if we'll be able to squeeze it in."

David emerged into the open with a bathrobe slung over his shoulder as a sop to decency. "You do not 'squeeze in' Westminster Abbey," he informed her.

"Exactly," she conceded sunnily. "So we'll have to leave it until we get back to London. We'll take the children to the Zoo instead."

Bertha was all for it. "That I would like. I will go along, and it will be enough change for me."

"Bertha, you don't get the point," David

355

patiently pointed out. "If you go, we don't have to."

"Ach so. Then you do not have to, because I will surely not go out in the day time."

"Stubborn, stubborn, stubborn!" Claudia railed.

"But maybe some evening if you are home early," Bertha proceeded tranquilly, "I will go to visit Miss Bachman. She already invited me yesterday."

"Who's Miss Bachman?" David asked.

Bertha looked as if she could have bitten her tongue out, but as long as the cat was out of the bag, Claudia took the bull by the horns. "You have a short memory, my love. Miss Bachman is the assistant manager of this hotel. She gave us the hangers, the bathroom, the extra night table and the armchair. Remember?"

"Oh sure," said David affably. "I bet we owe them all to Bertha."

"Ach no," Bertha modestly decried.

"Ach yes," said David, "and see if you can wangle another towel or two," he added on his way to shave.

Claudia studied his departing back with satisfaction. "Mr. David has the nicest little pockets of infantilism," she remarked. "He's

356

in and out of them in no time flat."

Bertha nodded largely. "I do not understand what you said, but I know what you mean. Fritz was the same. I had sometimes to treat him like a child and then all at once he was the strong man again. I think maybe it is the best kind of man to be married to. Too much little boy in a husband is not good, and not enough is not so good either."

Claudia was in full accord with Bertha's sentiments, albeit it was a pretty tricky business to maintain the balance between being sickening and stuffy, which was what it boiled down to. The same probably applied to women as well, and if it did, David doubtless considered Mrs. Dobson a shining exponent of well-adjusted glands. Certainly, there wasn't a syllable of baby talk in her, and yet she had enough bounce to run around looking for second-hand cars. Perhaps Jerry was wrong, perhaps David didn't have everything he wanted packaged up in one woman, any more than Peter Dobson had found completion in his presumably perfect marriage. And yet it was disturbing to think that his wife had turned out to be David's dish of tea, being not only thoroughly conversant with politics and world affairs, but sharing his addiction to machinery and Montaigne as well. "I didn't know how good I had it with Linda," Claudia decided glumly.

"How soon can we move, Mrs. Naughton?"

She followed Bertha back to the apartment with effort. "Any time. It was repainted and cleaned while Lady Gresham was away. But I think you should see it first. After all, you're the one who's going to live in it."

"It is enough for me that you and Mr. Jerry like it so much."

"Still, I don't want you to be disappointed. It's not very fancy or anything. But then nothing in London is," she added with an air of authority.

She was judging, naturally, by their present surroundings, and David's saying that the Dobson's apartment was just like Jerry's, only more so, and above all, by the disarming simplicity of the dining-room in the House of Lords. It was a good thing that no one beside Bertha heard her hold forth so knowingly, for the hotel where the Woodburns were staying presented the ultimate in modern luxury. It was running over with liveried doormen, crystal chandeliers, and the proverbial soft carpeting that you sank into halfway up to your knees.

Claudia stopped short in the glittering lobby. "Well," she delivered herself elliptically.

"Don't tell me," said David, reluctant to believe the worst of her, "that you'd have wanted to stay in a place like this?"

"And may I ask why not?"

"But you might just as well be back in New York!"

"It would seem to have certain advantages," she vouchsafed merely.

"Such as what?" he took umbrage.

She stepped daintily into a gilded cage and they were wafted gently heavenward. "For one thing," she took her own sweet time in answering him, "I daresay that the Woodburns find no difficulty in accommodating their toothbrushes."

"Okay, okay," he said, which didn't sound like him, and showed how deeply disillusioned he was.

Attended by Mrs. Woodburn's personal maid, Claudia removed her wraps in a walnut-panelled boudoir that was as large as, if not larger than, the bedroom that Bertha was at this very moment sharing with Matthew

359

and Michael. Her wrath gathered against David's perverse devotion to the uncompromising London he had known in his youth. She was a fool not to have shot straight over here when she had the chance to, but again, how was she to have guessed that Linda was to be the lesser of two evils?"

David was waiting for her in the spacious foyer. "You didn't have to take all night."

"Don't you begin with me," she warned him.

"Now what did I do?"

"What didn't you do. Stop fighting, let's try to act as if we were reasonably happy together."

She managed a resolute smile as Linda met them at the door of the drawing-room, looking her best in a new dinner gown, or anyway, one that she hadn't worn on the boat. "We'd almost begun to think you'd forgotten!" Linda's voice vibrated all over the place. She gave David both her hands and extended her cheek towards Claudia, but it was more like she was kissing David and shaking hands with Claudia. "It's so wonderful to see you again. It seems so much longer than it really is."

"Yes, it does," said Claudia.

"I didn't know this was going to be a party," said David.

"It isn't," Linda placated him. "It's just the Blisses and the Nicholsons, and Bell of course, but Helen always sounds like a crowd, somehow." (Good girl, Linda, go to it with my blessing, David almost smiled!)

He scowled instead.

"I thought the Nicholsons got off at Cherbourg," he said.

Linda lowered her voice discreetly. "They did. They flew back to London this afternoon. That's why Aunt Emily asked them to dine with us. The less said about it the better," she broke off hastily, as Helen's voice hailed them from the far end of the long drawing-room. "What's the confab?" she called out, with an edge of suspicion. "Come on in you two, you've kept us waiting long enough, we're all starved!"

For once, David, who entertained the illusion that punctuality was exclusively a male virtue, had the decency not to put the blame on his wife. "I'm sorry we're late," he apologized civilly. "We had an unexpectedly busy day."

Mrs. Woodburn welcomed them graciously. "Of course you did. You have so little time to see so much before you leave for Switzerland. Linda said you were going to Westminster Abbey this morning."

"Yes, but we didn't get there," Claudia began.

"Our social young friends were probably monopolized by Lady Gresham," Helen Nicholson inserted nastily.

Claudia bit her lips to keep from telling her how nearly she had hit on the truth. "We went through Parliament," she said.

Bill Hendricks gave her a hug. "Baby, pay no attention to Helen. It's just sour grapes. She asked Lady Gresham to a cocktail party next Sunday, and got a turn-down."

"Oh shut up," Helen turned on him. "You can be bitchier than any woman I know." She eyed Claudia's sequin dress. "Waistlines are out," she said.

"Thanks," said Claudia.

"That's why Helen went to Paris," Mrs. Bliss volunteered with a warm pudgy wink. "She wanted to go to the showings and get a head start on her clothes."

Mr. Nicholson swallowed his drink, and poured himself another. "Let's not go into that," he said curtly.

"You're a big help," Helen muttered in a bitter aside to Mrs. Bliss.

"But that's what you told me, so I'm just repeating."

"Well, stop repeating," Linda made peace lightly. "All this bickering sounds as if we were right back on the boat. Let's turn over a new leaf and be nice to each other for a change."

Helen shrugged. "You needn't stick up for me. I admit it. I've had it. From a so-called genius with dirty ears and a dirtier tongue. I hope the little monster gets ten years."

"He won't, though," Mrs. Bliss opined sagely. "There'll just be a lot of that twelfth amendment business on television and the whole thing'll blow over."

"Fifth Amendment," Mr. Bliss corrected her.

"Dear, naturally I meant fifth, everybody knows I meant fifth, dear."

"Of course we did, dear," Bill said. "You were thinking of the commandments when you said twelfth."

"Bill, you're wicked," Mrs. Bliss chided.

He chucked her under her soft chins. "Oh come now, pet, it's all in the spirit of good, clean fun."

Mr. Woodburn took a breathing space from his duties as host, and sat down next to Claudia. She thought he looked tired, and was glad that David didn't have that skinned look of a new haircut. She wondered if Mrs. Woodburn noticed. "Are you sure you won't have something, my dear? A little sherry perhaps?"

"No thanks. I promised David to give up drinking."

He patted her hand, and smiled. "You and Emily. You know, you remind me of Emily when she was your age."

He was more sentient than she had thought him to be. Like David was sentient. She said, "I feel very complimented."

"She was a lovely thing. Still is, in my old eyes."

"You're not old."

"Seventy, my next birthday."

She was shocked. Seventy. She hadn't thought he was anywhere near that age. Why didn't he finally settle down in one of his many houses and relax?

"When do you and David leave for Switzerland?" he asked.

"We're not. We changed our plans. We'll be going to Paris next week instead."

Linda was standing near enough, talking to David, to overhear. "You never told me!" she reproached him.

"We just decided today," he said.

"But I think it's wonderful!—Did you hear, Aunt Emily?"

"I did indeed. And I hope they'll spend some time with us at Cap Ferrat."

"Greg will love having Matthew," Linda glowed, using the children as a smoke-screen, Claudia thought. "We're not taking Matthew and Michael," she said aloud.

Everyone was in on it by this time. "That's a twist. I'd have sworn you were the mother-hen type," Helen Nicholson said. "What are you doing with them, leaving them here in that crumb box of a hotel?"

"No. Bertha will housekeep for them. We found a little apartment this afternoon."

"Claudia, this is really exciting," Linda exclaimed. "No wonder you were so busy today."

"How'd you find an apartment so fast?" Helen Nicholson wanted to know.

"Through a friend of ours."

"Who?"

"Helen, you're nosy!" Mrs. Bliss expostulated.

"I have to be nosy. It's like pulling teeth to get anything out of them. What's the great secret, anyway?"

"No secret," Claudia answered hastily, not trusting the look of David's nostrils. "We heard of it through a friend of ours. Jerry Seymour."

"Gerald Seymour. I know him very well, if he's the same fellow," Mr. Bliss interjected. "I must look him up. I thought he was in Africa."

"He's the same fellow," Claudia said.

Mrs. Bliss looked pleased with herself. "Nice chap, clever chap."

Mrs. Nicholson's long finger performed its usual function of snaking the olive from the bottom of her glass. "Very clever," she confirmed. "He married a woman twice his age, and walked into a fortune three months later."

"That isn't true!" Claudia flared. She caught David's eye. He was right. What was the use of arguing with Helen? A few drinks always loosened the meanness in her tongue, and this evening, very likely because of having made such a fool of herself over Barry Conwell, she was more than usually vicious.

"Elizabeth Van Doren was six years older

han Jerry," Claudia resumed with control. 'He didn't marry her for her money, he was erribly in love with her."

"She was a poifectly beautiful woman, and very fine in every way," Mrs. Woodburn said. "I always admired her tremendously. And now suppose we go down for dinner? Henry and I have decided that the food in the hotel is as good as anywhere in London, and t's easier than dining in one of the big restaurants."

"Easier on your tax set-up too," Mrs. Nicholson added

"Wrong again, Helen." Mr. Woodburn smiled tolerantly. "Our stay abroad is purely pleasure this year."

"Well, ours is a business trip," she retorted. "Maybe you're rich enough, but by God, in our bracket, we just can't afford to go away for pleasure!"

Bill said, "My heart bleeds for you."

"What about all the new Paris clothes you always buy?" Mrs. Bliss wanted to know. 'You can't get away with deducting those, can you?"

"Part of it can be finagled if you have an accountant that knows his way around," Mrs. Nicholson said.

"You're talking too much," her husband told her shortly.

She tossed her head. "At least I'm honest about it!"

"That's one for the books!" Bill hooted.

"Oh the hell with it." Mrs. Nicholson subsided into a sodden martyrdom. "We might as well be living in Russia."

"Better smile when you say that," he advised.

Linda frowned at him. "Bill, will you please stop baiting her!"

"Me?" he protested innocently. "I haven't said a thing.—Come on Helen, old bean."—He put his arm around her. "Be my supper partner."

She pushed him away. "Go along with you, you've got two beans to your bow already. Safety in numbers, eh? You can't pull the wool over my eyes, you sheep in wolf's clothing, you!"

Linda switched sides. "That's really hitting below the belt, Helen."

"Oh pooh. It's all in the family, so why pretend? Anyway, he knows I love him dearly." Her voice blurred slightly. "Where are we eating?"

"We told you, Helen. Downstairs." Mrs.

Woodburn's patience was shredding. "Truly you oughtn't to be this way on two Martinis, with Henry especially careful that they were small ones."

"That's what I call hospitality," Mrs. Nicholson mumbled. "Damn lucky I had a snootful before I came."

"Please don't disgrace yourself at dinner," her husband said coldly. "It would behove you to remember that you happen to be a guest in this hotel, too."

"Let's remember that we all are," Mr. Woodburn said.

Mrs. Nicholson wagged a solemn finger at him. "All except Claudia and David. They don't live here, they have to be different and live in that old crumb box."

"So we do," said David, pleasantly.

"And the *prices* they have the nerve to charge! I know for a fact it's not cheap, because we have a couple of friends stop there from Ireland when they come to London. On my word, I saw beds stacked in the hall, and I didn't have too much to drink, either."

"Nobody sleeps in the beds," Claudia said, "until they get put into the rooms."

"Seriously, why do you really stay there?" Mrs. Bliss asked.

"We love it," said Claudia.

"It's a very English hotel, isn't it?" Linda contributed seriously. "It caters almost exclusively for the English, doesn't it, David?"

"Except for a few pretentious Americans like us," he agreed.

Mrs. Nicholson clapped him on the back. "You said it, old boy, I didn't!"

For a moment, Claudia was afraid he was going to return the clap, but he didn't. "I thought I'd save you the trouble of saying it," he said amiably.

Helen Nicholson didn't know when she was well off. "No trouble, my lad, it would have been a pleasure. False swank, I call it."

"We can all crowd into the elevator," Linda interceded, nervously.

"We'll wait for the next one," Claudia said.

It was too late for Linda to get out and wait with them. "You might as well give up, Linda," Mrs. Nicholson whispered noisily. "You're not going to get him. That little wife of his might look as if butter wouldn't melt in her mouth, but watch out for her!"

"What a horrible woman," Claudia shuddered as soon as the lift had dropped out of sight. "The whole evening is horrid. Why do nice people like the Woodburns put up with it?"

"Habit. Clan instinct."

"It could be. That's why they take themselves along with them, I suppose. They might just as well be back on the boat."

"Or in America. They live a picture-window existence on a different level."

"I'm glad we both like mullioned windows. I'm teasing you, I really wouldn't want to stay in this hotel. I even wish dinner were over. I feel uncomfortable. And sort of soiled."

"So do I."

"Linda's sweet, though," she qualified fairly. "And Mrs. Bliss is a good soul."

"Dumb as hell."

"Most good souls are. Wouldn't you hate to be a good soul?"

"Must you make conversation? You know me from the old country, remember?"

"You're grouchy."

"An evening like this is such a damn waste of time."

Ordinarily, she'd have asked him what he had in mind that was more exciting, but suddenly she wasn't as certain of the answer as she thought she was.

"I noticed," he said suddenly, "that you didn't mention Lady Gresham's name."

"I almost did, but it would have sounded like lording it over them if we said we'd had lunch with her. And also, it's none of their business that she's taking in paying guests."

He gave the nearest portion of her anatomy a pat as they stepped into the lift. It was a small pat, but it said, and answered, a lot of things. She squeezed his arm. "You're pretty nice yourself," she told him.

The dining-room was gala, with several tables arranged for large parties like their own. Claudia sat between Bill Hendricks and Mr. Nicholson and wished she were sitting next to David. She was struggling against a nightmare of sleepiness when Mrs. Bliss leaned across Bill and nudged her arm. "Look over there, at that couple just leaving," she said in a sibilant undertone.

Claudia looked, and recognized the unmistakable waddles of the bearded fat man and his fat wife.

"I don't imagine they're staying at the hotel," Mrs. Bliss said. "I imagine they just had dinner here, so many people do, if you know what I mean."

"We know what you mean." Bill gave a short laugh. "I don't suppose you have the slightest idea who they are?"

Mrs. Bliss bridled. "Why of course I do. It's those horrid people from the boat who came up from the main dining-room and sat next to us in the Café. I'd know his beard, and her shape anywhere."

"That beard and that shape," Bill informed her portentously, "happen to belong to none other than the Count and Countess Cozzoni."

"I don't believe it," Helen Nicholson announced flatly from the other side of the table. "Where'd you get that idea?"

Bill passed a hand over an honestly troubled brow. "For the life of me I can't recall at the moment who told me," he admitted, "but I know for a fact that that's who they are."

"The Count and Countess Cozzoni?" Mrs. Bliss looked ready to be knocked down with a feather. "Well, for goodness sake," she said.

10

CANDY'S voice over the telephone was like a fresh breeze blowing away the heavy aftermath of a stultifying evening. It was one of David's better inspirations to have suggested putting the call in while they undressed for bed. "John will be sending mail on to Switzerland if we don't let him know not to," he said.

"It's a nice excuse," Claudia exulted. "I've never talked across an ocean before." She tried to anchor the telephone to her ear while she squirmed out of the sequin skirt. "No waistlines indeed," she seethed. "There ought to be a law against changing everything from washing machines to clothes every year. It's enough to give the average housewife a neurosis."

"I can't hear a word you're saying," David mentioned mildly from the other side of the room.

"It's nothing important. I was just blowing off."

"You're getting a crick in your neck. Why

don't you hang up, and let the operator call back after she's got a circuit?"

"I don't want the bell to wake Bertha. The children would sleep through it, but she'd be up like a shot.—Be sure to watch your watch."

"What for?"

"Sometimes they forget to notify you when the three minutes are up. It's too bad we haven't an extension in the other room so that we could save time and both be on together."

"I don't want to be on together. You get through gabbling with Candy, and then allow me kindly a little peace and quiet to go over some office stuff with John."

"It'll cost a fortune."

"My end of the conversation will be deductible."

"Oh, nice. Couldn't what I say be deductible too? Like Helen Nicholson's Paris outfit?—Incidentally, how much money have we really got?"

"Why?"

"Helen asked me."

"It's none of her business."

"That didn't stop her. She kept harping back to our staying in this crumb-box. She said Hartley's estate alone was at least five million, and you were his only beneficiary. And an executor besides, so you didn't have to wait for the will to be probated. Or something like that."

"What did you tell her?"

"I told her that I hated anything that had anything to do with a will, and that anything beyond three zeros made no sense to me.—That's crazy, isn't it?"

"Yep," he agreed cheerfully, "but that's the way God made you."

"I mean, that it was crazy for Helen to say a thing like that. Hartley didn't leave us anywhere near that amount, did he?"

"Not after taxes; that takes a big chunk. But we'll manage to scrape along," he added dryly.

"It's too much, and too late."

He looked at her, arrested by the passion in her voice.

"I didn't mean it like it sounded," she faltered. "I meant that it seems so ironic. If we could only have given Bobby the pony he always wanted! But no matter how we scraped and figured our last summer on the farm, we couldn't swing it."

"We couldn't even swing the farm," said David.

"Mr. Woodburn was interested in why we'd sold it to Nancy Riddle. We were talking about it after dinner. It was the one bright spot in the whole dull evening. Not Nancy. Farming."

"I heard snatches of what you were saying, but I got stuck with Mrs. Bliss. I didn't realize that the Woodburns had a farm in Aux along with their villa."

"I didn't either. I said wasn't it an awful lot to run both places, just to have milk and fresh vegetables, but he said, no, farming was much easier in the South of France than in the middle of New England. I told him about our feed bills getting to be so terrific that we couldn't break even; and that it cost more to have the vet for one of the pigs than it did to have the doctor for the baby."

"The pig paid his way, we could sell him. But the baby was a luxury."

"So was the pony."

He took the receiver from her, and put it back in its cradle, and drew her to him. "Bobby had it good, darling," he said gently.

"I know," she said.

"You never stop thinking of him."

"Hardly ever."

"I know," he said.

"I wish that you believed that there was a hereafter."

He was silent. It was one of the few things that they couldn't see eye to eye about. He might have believed it secretly, against his will, but he wouldn't admit it.

The telephone started to ring. She reached for it swiftly. "I have your party on the line," Operator said.

"Claudia!"

"Candy!"

There were so many questions to ask, so many questions to answer. Candy couldn't get over their being so social all at once, and thought it was wonderful that they were going to take a vacation from the children. "Just that half hour on the boat and I was a wreck," said Candy.

"You make me feel a lot better about doing it.—Now tell me about the baby, and how's your mother-in-law, and have you been over to see what they've done on the house?"

David flopped into the arm-chair and yawned elaborately. "Jabber, jabber, jabber."

At last Candy turned the telephone over to John and Claudia talked to him, and then gave the telephone to David. She finished undressing. "Jabber, jabber, jabber," she said.

After he had hung up, she said in a small voice, "Between us, we talked almost twenty minutes, according to my watch."

"It was worth it," David said.

"The whole five million," she tossed in lavishly. "Only I wish I didn't know that the baby's cold before we left turned out to be the measles."

"It did? John didn't say anything about it." David seemed annoyed. "Why the devil did Candy have to mention it, there isn't a damn thing you can do at this distance, except stew about it."

"I don't think she intended to tell me, it just slipped out. Anyway, there are no complications, so I'm not really worried, but I gathered that Candy was pretty upset. She's not used to anybody she loves being sick. Don't you remember how hard she took it when she heard that we had to go to the mountains for a year?"

He smiled wryly. "Thanks for the editorial 'we'. Sure she took it hard. She's too dependent on us. She has to grow up, and learn to stand on her own feet."

"It's not easy. Sometimes I think I haven't learned yet."

"You've learned enough. I wouldn't be surprised if you were ready to graduate and get a diploma for your first thirty years."

"Thirty years." She stopped brushing her hair to stare into the mirror. "I don't even have to look close any more to see the grey hairs and the lines around my eyes."

"Poor old lady. Come to bed."

"Bertha will hear us if we talk in bed," she reminded him.

"Who wants to talk in bed," said David.

They got it over with the very next day, like a dose of castor oil. And then, with the suitcases packed, the perambulator folded, and the last-minute paraphernalia assembled in one ungainly bundle, Claudia lost her courage anyway. "I must have been out of my mind," she wailed. "Helen Nicholson was right, I am the mother-hen type. How can I march off and leave my children like this?"

"You're not marching off, they are. We're going to be playing right here in the hotel until next Monday."

"Don't be so bloody literal.—Why is bloody a bad word in England?"

"It used to be worse.—Look, what I'm trying to say—and get very little thanks for it—is that it's smart not to put off moving them over. It gives you plenty of time to see how it works out before we leave."

"That was the general theory, but it's springing it on Matthew pretty suddenly. He doesn't like any part of what's happening."

"He's afraid of missing a trick."

"I thought his attachment to Mrs. Tick-tack-toe would help."

"Do not be whimsical."

"It was in quotes. I can't imagine him calling her Lady Gresham, can you?"

"That's his problem. And hers.—Look here, I feel like a heel going out to the country to look at that car today. The salesman thought he could arrange it sometime over the weekend, but he just happened to track down the old geezer who owns it, and the appointment was made with the caretaker last night."

"You might as well get it out of your system, but it does seem an awfully long trip just to see one car."

"Not a car like this. You don't come on them very often. Ann certainly thinks it's worth going or she wouldn't be ducking out of the office to drive me there. It won't be a wasted trip in any event, there's a fine herd of Dexters in Cambridgeshire that I'd like to look at on the way."

"It sounds like fun," she said wistfully. "Especially the cows. They're those miniature ones, aren't they?"

"About as big as a small Angus. They don't need much pasture and they winter outdoors we might be smart to pick up some good breeding stock while we're here. But I wouldn't buy any without your seeing them," he assured her. "The car's different. If I think it's something you'd like, I'll drive it back, get it thoroughly overhauled, and we'll put it on the plane at Le Touquet and have ourselves a tour of France."

"That would be nice," she admitted, and added prudently, "how inexpensive is it?"

"The asking price is three thousand pounds."

"Ouch." She was remembering the first car they had had on the farm, an undistinguished relic of a sedan that managed to keep on running until they found a second-hand station wagon suitable for family use, and also for lugging bags of grain and two Great Danes.

"According to Annie," David continued, "it's one of the most beautiful bodies she ever saw."

"Annie ought to know," Claudia returned.

He was oblivious of any barb, intended or otherwise. "She should," he agreed. "She's one of the few women I've ever met with real car-sense."

"That's right, go off and leave me with an inferiority complex."

"You have horse-sense," he said. "That's even better."

"That's a bloody unromantic attribute in a woman."

"Never satisfied. And don't push your luck with 'bloody'." He gave her a hug and a kiss. "Good-bye, darling." At the door, he hesitated. "Look, if you think I'm wrong to pull out on you in the middle of moving, I'll not go."

"I told you there was nothing you could do; except exercise parental discipline at inopportune moments and complicate an already complicated day."

He accepted the accusation without demur. "I guess you're right." Then he said, seriously, "I'll tell you what. We won't look at the Dexters, we'll just look at the car."

"That's the silliest thing I ever heard. You talk as if I'd mind if you looked at cows without me."

"I could understand if you did. Cars aren't up your alley, but cows are."

"That's another dubious compliment. You'd better go before you get in any deeper. What time did you say you'd be home?"

"Not later than seven. That should give us time to stop for a bite of lunch on the road, before we give the car a good trial work-out."

"Only be careful. Please."

"Aren't I always?"

"No."

"Well, I will be. I promise." He kissed her again. "Good-bye, darling."

"Good-bye."

"*Darling*," he prompted.

"My pet," she compromised.

"Annie doesn't say 'my pet'."

"I didn't say she did." Claudia kept her voice level with difficulty. "You're very sensitive about her. And you needn't be. She's awfully nice, I liked her, and I feel very sorry her husband's divorcing her. I can't imagine why he should."

She hoped her claws didn't show, but if they did, he appeared not to notice them.

"Pete's lost his head," he said briefly. "The damnedest thing how a thing like that can happen to a first-rate guy."

She wondered if he knew that it was happening to him too. And then she wondered if it really was, or if she wasn't the one who was being over-sensitive. What was the matter with her? She had been the same way about Linda, and it had come to nothing. No sooner did David get within seeing distance of another woman, than she began to feel insecure. She didn't like the word, but it wasn't quite as humiliating as admitting that she was jealous. Which, of course, she wasn't. She had too much trust and confidence in David to be jealous. The fault lay within her, not him. There were no two ways about it, she just wasn't sure of herself. She kept building her virtues on other women's weaknesses. Far-fetched as it was the sea-sick pills and Mrs. Woodburn had been a case in point.

"Do not look so unhappy, Mrs. Naughton, you will not be far away from the children, even when you are in Paris."

Claudia smiled bravely, feeling like a hypocrite, since concern about the children had given place to a less worthy emotion. "I think it's a fine idea of yours to have an early lunch here, Bertha," she changed the subject. "Then they can take their afternoon nap in the apartment while you and I unpack and get settled."

It was wishful thinking. Even Michael showed no indications of quieting down for a nap. Lady Gresham had unearthed a hobby horse that had belonged to Christopher, and it was all they needed to make them more "ausgelassen" than they were. It was too short for Matthew, and too high for Michael, but pandemonium resulted nevertheless. "Pooh. You're too grown up for such a babyish toy," Claudia tried blandishments on her elder son. "Let's step out for a minute and look at the lovely little garden."

"There's no flowers, that ain't a garden."

"Not 'ain't'. And there will be flowers before long. And Matthew, please lower your voice, and try to behave halfway decently, or Lady Gresham won't want you to stay here."

"Who's Lady Gresham?" he demanded raucously.

"You know perfectly well who she is. And please remember that she's a very busy person and has other things to do than play tick-tack-toe with you."

"I always won, anyhow—I'm hungry."

"You are not hungry. You just had lunch."

"Isn't there anything to eat?"

"Bertha's going out to market as soon as she gets Michael off that hobby horse and unpacks."

A howl of indignation went up from Michael at that very instant. Bertha's lips were grim. "Mrs. Naughton, I had to give him a little slap so he should let go," she made a clean breast of her defection. "I am sorry."

"Are you? I'm delighted," said Claudia. "Give him another one and pop him into bed."

"I ain't going to bed!" Matthew averred loudly. "No sirree! Boy, this is a nifty place. Which room do you and Dad sleep in?"

"I explained to you, Matthew, that we are going to stay on at the hotel for a few days."

"Why?"

"Bertha has enough to do, cooking for you and Michael."

"She cooked for you and Dad home."

"Let's not argue it. You're just talking to hear yourself talk."

A sheepish smirk was sufficient admission. "I want a tomato."

Bertha paused, with Michael plastered to

her hip. "I will see if I can buy some." She was all in favour of tomatoes, albeit puzzled by Matthew's sudden yearning for them.

"He's pregnant," Claudia allayed her apprehension of a vitamin deficiency.

Matthew executed a dry skate around the room, duckfooted, and with chin thrust forward in a grotesquely unattractive fashion. "I'm pregnant, I'm pregnant!" he boasted.

"Do you know what pregnant means?" Claudia inquired coldly.

He was stumped. "I forget."

"It means 'naughty'," Claudia shut him up.

"That is good," Bertha murmured, relieved. "I would not want him to tell Lady Gresham he was pregnant."

"I doubt whether she would believe it," Claudia said. "Why don't you take him marketing with you? He's never going to settle down while he's so excited."

"That is a good idea. I will unpack when I come back. Even the bureau drawers are clean. Just a little dusting and I can put everything away."

"I'd do it for you while you're gone, but you're such a fuss-box, you'd only do it over again."

"I would," said Bertha. "I must know where everything is meinself."

"Come on!" Matthew tugged at her. "I wanna go."

"Want to," Claudia corrected him punctiliously. She hoped devoutly that Lady Gresham's tolerance of Matthew would not have worn off on dry land.

The crib looked like home to Michael after beds barricaded with chairs to keep him from falling out. He fell asleep instantly, aided and abetted by his thumb, and Bertha departed. The little flat was very quiet. Claudia wandered through the rooms, feeling aimless and unbelonging. Already the place bore the stamp of Bertha and the children, but there was nothing of hers or David's here. She imagined that a mother-in-law must feel a little like this, visiting her son's wife. You were welcome, but you didn't belong.

The telephone rang. She rushed to answer it, thinking surely it was David.

"How are things coming along?" Jerry wanted to know.

"Oh fine," she said.

"You sound tired."

"But I'm not!" (Her voice must have showed her disappointment.)

"Tell Bertha," said Jerry, "that I'll stop around for a formal visit tomorrow afternoon. Do you realize I haven't seen her or the children yet?"

"There was no room in the hotel, but now Bertha can really show off. She'll probably have a batch of home-made cookies to serve with tea. She was planning on sending some over to Lady Gresham already."

"Tell her to go right to it. Isabel can stand a little coddling.—Did David go off to see the car?"

"Yes. He wanted to stay and help, but he would have only been underfoot."

"Then you're well rid of him, and me. What are your plans for this evening?"

"David said he'd be back before seven, so we thought we'd have dinner at the hotel, and go to bed early for a change. Which means that you won't have to have us on your mind. Oh dear, there's someone knocking at the door. . ."

"Go ahead, I won't keep you. I'll call you in the morning. Good-bye for now."

"Good-bye, Jerry. And thanks again."

"What for?"

"For everything."

She hung up and hurried to the door that

gave on to a small landing with its flight of wooden stairs well guarded by a sturdy balustrade. "You can see that a child has lived here," Bertha had remarked appraisingly.

Lady Gresham was examining the rail. "Hello," she greeted Claudia. "I shall have to have this broken spindle mended at once. It's quite safe for the moment, but if Matthew's like Christopher, and I'm quite sure that he is, anything that's even slightly broken is fair game for destruction."

Claudia laughed. "I'm glad you have no illusions about him. Please do come in, won't you?"

"Just for a moment, if you're not too busy. I want to be sure that Bertha has everything she needs. I was going to stock in some provisions for her, but I thought she might prefer to find her own shops."

"She's doing just that, with Matthew. I wish you could have seen her face when she walked in here—all their faces—and you'd know how happy they're going to be."

"I hope so. They'll miss you at first, but I daresay by the time you leave for Paris, they will have got quite used to being on their own."

"I hope you will have got used to having them here. David and I both want you to promise to tell us if you don't think it's going to work out well. We can always change our plans again at a moment's notice."

"Stop worrying."

"You remind me of my mother," Claudia told her suddenly.

"You were very close to your mother."

"How did you know?"

"When one has had enough love in one's life, it's quite as obvious as the other way around. Possibly because we seem so wary of parental love in this day and age. I was fortunate that Barbara, my daughter, never shared the modern attitude of her friends, a large number of whom spend considerable time on the psychiatrist's couch." She smiled faintly. "The last tenants of the flat were friends of Barbara's. A most emancipated young couple."

Claudia remained silent, loath to trade upon the impulse that had prompted this quietly contained woman to have grown discursive. "Matthew is fortunate, too," she ended briefly.

"It's helpful to hear you say so. Because sometimes I'm not sure whether we're on the right track with him. He hasn't an easy time of it with us. David doesn't let him get away with a thing, and I try not to, either."

"He shows every evidence of being able to take it. And profitably. Also, he has a nice sense of humour for a youngster. So please don't feel that I shall be irked by having him at such close quarters."

"I have to warn you that Bertha can be a pest, too. She has a weakness for wanting to feed people up."

"Oh dear. Thank you for telling me."

"And she'll want to launder all your fancy lingerie. She's awfully good at it."

"But I haven't any fancy lingerie," Lady Gresham said in dismay. Claudia giggled. "Neither have I. That's why Bertha's so thwarted. I used to have at least one or two good sets though, that I could wear to the doctor's whenever I was expecting a baby. And always a couple of fussy nightgowns that I saved for the hospital."

Lady Gresham studied her thoughtfully. "Do you know, my impression of you on the boat was rather confusing."

"I don't wonder," said Claudia.

"I think you'd like Barbara. When you return to the States I wish you'd look her up.

And Douglas, her husband, is rather David's sort, I think."

"We'd love to," Claudia said. "Knowing them will be one of the nicest mementoes of our trip."

She felt that she was being terribly graceful about it, but it was the truth. She meant it.

Lady Gresham stayed a little longer, but the baby didn't wake up, and there was no sign of Bertha and Matthew. After she had gone, Claudia telephoned the hotel to find out if there were any messages. "Yes, Mrs. Naughton Mrs. Harwell telephoned and would you please to return the call. No other messages."

She felt foolishly disappointed. Not that she had really thought he'd try to reach her at the hotel, he knew she intended to spend the afternoon helping Bertha get organized, but still, he should have called her at the apartment. He had asked her for the number and she had written it down for him very plainly, on the flap of the envelope from John's letter. She looked at her watch. It was four o'clock. Perhaps he was waiting until after he had seen the car, but it wouldn't have hurt him to telephone from wherever they had stopped for lunch. There wasn't any actual reason for him to do so, of course, since there was no great problem involved in taking a taxi to Kensington and unpacking a few suitcases. She had told him that herself. Just the same, she'd expected him to telephone. He always did, at home. Sometimes twice a day from the office. Even when there was nothing to telephone about. "I'm spoiled," she decided. The Dobsons probably weren't the telephoning kind—not at this point of their relationship they weren't—and it would have been a little out of place for David to make a thing of saying hello to his wife only a couple of hours after he'd said good-bye.

She walked to the window and looked down into the garden which was well fenced in. Lady Gresham had told her that Christopher used to play out by himself with his mother keeping an eye on him watching from upstairs. But Bertha had said firmly, "That I will not do." Claudia hadn't persuaded her. It was all to the good that she bent backwards when it came to the children's safety. Christopher was probably a little gentleman, but Matthew wasn't above climbing up over the fence, and wandering off by himself. The episode on the boat had been ample proof of his entirely dishonourable intentions.

While she was looking out of the window, he came around the edge of the building at a run, his arms encircling a large paper bag which he dropped. Bertha puffed along after him, her arms full of marketing, too. Claudia hurried down to help pick everything up. It was quite a mess. "*Dumbkopf*," she said. She shivered. The weather had changed abruptly. A cold rainy wind was blowing up. "It's going to snow, boy," Matthew announced with a swagger, as if he were in sole command of the elements.

"Ach, it feels nice and warm inside," Bertha rejoiced. "Warmer than the hotel. And such lovely shops."

"We got tomatoes!"

"They were not so very nice," Bertha admitted. "But beautiful fruit. And some Swiss chocolate for hot cocoa."

"I'd like to board here," said Claudia. "Lady Gresham came to see you, but she couldn't stay. She said if you needed anything to let her know. Now what can I do to help?"

"Nothing," said Bertha hastily.

"It is better I put away everything mein-self," Claudia anticipated her.

Matthew stopped in the middle of a tug of

war with his overcoat. "How did you know Bertha was going to say that?"

"How could I not know."

"Mamma teases.—Ach, do not tear the sleeve, Matthew please.—How about a cup of nice hot coffee, Mrs. Naughton? I found the same kind we have at home."

"What's the sense of getting used to good coffee," she refused longingly.

"Then wait only until I look at my baby, and I will fix you a cup of tea."

"Your baby is sleeping and I don't need any tea."

"I want hot chocolate!" Matthew shouted. "With a marshmallow!"

"We have no harshmelleys," said Bertha, who had never quite mastered the word. "Tomorrow I will try to buy some."

"He can live without them," said Claudia. "Matthew, listen to me. Bertha has a great deal to do, cooking and cleaning and taking care of you children, and I want you to promise me not to be demanding."

"What's demanding?"

"Asking for harshmelleys.—Don't throw your coat on the floor, hang it up!"

"Where?"

Again Claudia felt like an outsider. "Where

do you want him to hang it, Bertha?"

"I do not know all the closets yet. Just leave it on a chair.—First I put my marketing away. The ice box is not big, but it is big enough."

"The man in the butcher store called the ice box a Fridge," Matthew volunteered. "Why?"

"'Y' is the Fourth of July."

He looked blank. She gave him a hug. "I'll see you tomorrow, question box."

"Fridge, midge, squidge, bidge!" he chanted, and began his silly dry-skating around the room.

"He feels good," Bertha commented contentedly.

Claudia knocked on wood. It was raining outdoors, but the sun was shining in Bertha's small new heaven.

Matthew skated into the kitchen for his tomato and hardly knew when she left. She had difficulty in finding a taxi, so she walked up the wide avenue, bending against the misty sleet that bit at her face. This was a lonely time of the afternoon, with the lights shining through the fog. David wouldn't be home for another two hours, at least. He'd be damp, and probably chilled. She'd have a hot bath ready for him, and if Linda thought that she could beguile them to the ballet, or even to the theatre, she was mistaken. With the children gone, they could have dinner sent up to the other room—Miss Bachman had suggested moving the beds out, and although Claudia told her that it was a shame to go to all that trouble for just a few days, Miss Bachman insisted that it was no trouble at all. "Then you will have a sitting-room with an open fireplace."

"Three cheers for Miss Bachman," Claudia thought.

A taxi passed, but she didn't hail it. She wanted to become acquainted with the neighbourhood where Bertha and the children would be living. And for once, she could window-shop and investigate antique stores without David putting on a face about it. She passed only one antique store, however, and it was locked up tight, which was silly. She knocked and waited. Knocked again, and walked on. She came to a large department store, and drifted in. She looked at cashmere sweaters for Candy, but they seemed a little baggy. She drifted out again. A little farther up the street, she stopped in front of a speciality shop, with a black chiffon nightgown and a chiffon *négligé* to match in the window. It wasn't something she had expected to see in the neighbourhood of Peter Pan and the Victoria and Albert Museum, but so much to the good. She'd never owned a black nightgown, but tonight was a fine time to begin, with dinner in front of a crackling fire, and the memory of Ann Dobson slightly jaundiced by smudges of cargrease. You couldn't investigate the insides of a car without getting at least a little sticky.

Luckily, David had given her another package of pound notes, which was more than enough to cover the purchase of the chiffon ensemble. It was a shame not to wait until she got to Paris, but the saleslady assured her that this was a "little import", and it wasn't very expensive anyway. It shouldn't have been. The hems were machine made. But David wasn't the type to know the difference. The general effect was quite nice, even over her tweed skirt, and without anything at all underneath except herself, the effect could easily be quite intriguing.

The saleslady, who was painfully skinny, was obviously relieved to make the sale and to remove the thing from the window. "I don't own the shop," she made clear with a tightening of her lips. "I only work here."

"I'll buy that little purse-size perfume too," Claudia decided. She knew what kind it was without smelling it, because Julia had once given her a huge bottle of it, and it had lasted all through the farm. She hadn't used much perfume on the farm, or the year in the mountains either. She'd planned to buy a lot of it for gifts, in Paris, where it was half the price. In the meantime, a dram of it would do nicely for tonight. The black chiffon wouldn't have been complete without perfume.

What with one thing and another (she bought a knife for David, curled back into an old English coin), it was six o'clock when she finally got back to the hotel. Mr. Lindt was behind the desk. She returned his cordial smile, with her eyes glued to the white messages in the box. "I hope you will find everything to your satisfaction," he said. "We moved a desk into the sitting-room, and a small cabinet with ample glassware," he added delicately.

"Oh thank you," said Claudia.

"I trust the new flat will work out well," he continued. "I do not, myself, approve of hotel living for children, unless, of course, there is no alternative. Your key—" he dropped the key into her outstretched hand, "and two telephone messages."

"Oh thank you," Claudia said again, and felt the most ridiculous let-down because one of the messages wasn't from David. Mrs. Harwell—3.28.—Mrs. Harwell, 5.46, and as if that weren't rubbing it in enough, duplicate messages were stuck in the door upstairs. She had learned, in her short but intensive stay at the hotel, that sometimes you didn't get your messages at all, but when you did get them, you certainly got them. "I'd better let David call Linda back when he comes home," she thought. Linda would probably be encouraged by the fact that he had gone off by himself, not knowing of course, that he hadn't gone off by himself at all.

She was glad that the children's room had been changed around; it helped to keep her from missing them. Also, it was almost spacious with the three beds out, and a long narrow sofa flat against the wall. They could at last ask Jerry up for tea or a drink, now that they had glassware. Mrs. Dobson, also. And Linda and Bill Hendricks and the Woodburns. No need to have Helen Nicholson, as they had refused her invitation to cocktails on the excuse that they would have probably left London. As for the Blisses, Claudia didn't care whether she ever saw them again or not. David was right. Mrs. Bliss was dumb as hell. "I'm a good one to talk," Claudia reflected, as she let the hot water into the tub. She hadn't even caught the slip about the fifth amendment.

She noticed that there were lots of towels in the bathroom, thanks to Bertha's influence, and treated herself to using more than she needed. She wished, however, that there were a longer mirror, so that she could see herself from top to bottom and in one fell swoop, in the black chiffon nightgown. She contented herself by looking at herself in sections, which was rather seductive, as a matter of fact. She slipped on the *négligé*. You couldn't exactly see through, but you almost could, which was even more effective. She used the perfume lavishly—both ears, and quite far down. She looked at her watch. She called the desk to ask the time. Six thirty-four. Her watch hadn't stopped after all. Anyway, David would be home any minute, now. She put the knife she had bought him on the chiffonier, and discovered his key-ring. Also the envelope flap with the telephone number that she had written out for him. So that's why he hadn't called! It made her feel a lot better. Except that it wasn't like David to let the key to his briefcase be around, with passports and money, and everything else in it. Either he must have been in one of his "little boy" moods with his mind on the new car, or he hadn't been in a little boy mood at all, with his mind on Mrs. Dobson.

At seven o'clock she put more perfume on. She'd better not go overboard on it, though, because very often you couldn't smell yourself, and too much perfume could turn around and go in the opposite direction. With David, anyway, "Pfui!" he'd say, and the whole purpose of it would come to nothing.

At quarter past seven, she picked up Margaret Remington's latest novel. It wasn't to be published until the end of the month, but Jerry had an advance copy and had lent it to her. "I can't give it to you, because it's autographed," he'd explained dourly. "*To darling J—with the love of Maggie*", Miss Remington had scrawled in huge sprawling letters all over the title page. "Silly damn thing, autographing books," Jerry had commented. "It means you can't give them away if you want to. This isn't Maggie's best," he'd added. "She's writing herself out too fast."

Emphatically, Claudia shared his opinion. The opening chapter, at any rate, seemed forced; she kept sliding off the involved sentences, and esoteric references. She gave up on it, and telephoned Bertha. She had intended to wait until David came home so that he could talk to the children, but if she waited any longer they would be in bed and asleep.

Matthew answered. It always made her furious when a child's pipey voice answered the telephone. It was an abhorrent custom. You couldn't help feeling a little silly when you tried to explain to a four or five-year-old who you were. It had been taboo for even Bobby to answer the phone.

"Hello, who is it!" Matthew's voice almost broke her eardrum.

"None of your darn business," she told him with asperity. "Put Bertha on. At once."

"I can't! She's giving Michael a bath. I had my bath. We ate supper in the kitchen, and Bertha found a blackboard and some chalk in a closet. Can I use it?"

"May I.—You might ask Lady Gresham when you see her."

"Who's Lady Gresham?"

"Matthew, I'll bat you one."

He laughed uproariously. "That's a crazy name!"

"Not as crazy as Mrs. Tick-tack-toe. I would advise you calling her properly, like a gentleman."

"Lady Gresham!" he shouted, making it sound like he looked when he skated around the room duck-footed.

"Stick to Mrs. Tick-tack-toe," she said tersely. "Go tell Bertha I'm on the wire. If she's still busy with the baby—Matthew! Are you there? Matthew, come back, I'm still talking to you!"

He must have got side-tracked on his way to tell Bertha, because it seemed like an eternity before she heard Bertha's doubtful voice say, "Is anybody there?"

"Of course anybody's there," Claudia retorted irritably. "I was just about to hang up!"

"Ach, I did not hear the telephone ring, I saw only that the receiver was off the hook. Matthew forgot to tell me—"

"Matthew and his father both," Claudia muttered to herself. "How is everything?" she asked aloud.

"Beautiful!" Bertha assured her, and went into satisfying, but intimate detail. "And we have plenty of good hot water, and everything could not be better, so do not worry.—Did Mr. David buy the car?"

"He's not quite home yet?"

"Ach, so late! And you are all alone?"

"I should hope so."

"I meant that it is not so nice with the children not there."

"It will be," Claudia said. "We're going to have supper by the fire."

"That is what I wanted to ask you, did Miss Bachman fix the room nice?"

"Very. I might have known you were behind it.—Bertha, I have to ring off, I hear Mr. David at the door!"

"That is good." Bertha's voice sounded relieved.

"He'll probably be wet and tired, so he won't call back to talk to the children until the morning, so don't keep them up."

"Then I will put them right to bed, and after I finish unpacking, I can maybe bake some cookies to try the stove out."

"Enjoy yourself!" Claudia hung up and skated to the door, like Matthew. "Was I ever glad to see anyone!" she began, and almost threw her arms around the porter.

"Oh—" She stepped back into the room, abashed.

"I'm sorry to disturb you, Mrs. Naughton." The porter too backed discreetly away. "Mrs. Harwell telephoned while you were talking on the line and left word for you to return her call as soon as possible."

"Thank you," said Claudia. "And oh, would you please have a dinner menu sent up?"

"Certainly, Mrs. Naughton. I'll have the waiter come immediately."

"No, not the waiter. Just the menu."

"Yes, Madame." "Madame", all at once. It must have been the diaphanous effect of the black chiffon. "I hope I wasn't standing in the light," she thought in dismay.

She called Linda. Linda evidently didn't know when she was licked, poor thing.

Linda's voice answered at once. "Claudia—"

"Yes, Linda. I'm sorry I didn't call you before, I just got in a little while ago, I was with the children all afternoon."

"I imagined you would be." Linda's voice sounded as if she had a cold. "I know you've had a busy day, I rather hated to call you, but

I knew you and David would want to know."

"Know what, Linda? You sound awfully choked up. What's the matter? Is anything wrong?"

"Uncle Henry died at noon today."

Claudia couldn't speak. Shock dried her throat, and made her lips feel wooden. "I can't believe it," she whispered.

"None of us can." Linda's voice broke. "He seemed so well last night. Though Aunt Emily said she was a little worried about him, she said she didn't like the way he looked."

"I thought he seemed tired. There was just something about him, I can't explain—" Claudia offered diffidently. They had talked together so briefly, and yet he had said so much. He seemed to have gone back into the years. "You remind me of Emily when she was your age. She was a lovely thing—" Yes, he had seemed tired. Claudia remembered wondering why he didn't settle down in one of his many houses . . .

"He was looking forward to the next few months," Linda went on brokenly. "He loved the combination of sea and farm—Aunt Emily says that that's where he'd want to be, so we're leaving for the South of France, just as we'd planned. Only sooner." She stopped to gain control of herself. "I'm ashamed of being so emotional, but I don't see how Aunt Emily can bear it. She's so quiet, so strong. She said she'd known for a long while about Uncle Henry's heart, but she hadn't told anyone. He didn't want to be treated like an invalid."

So much that Claudia hadn't understood became suddenly clear—the slow, leisurely walk of the Woodburns around the dance floor, the way they held hands on deck in the moonlight before going to bed, even the little deception about the seasick pills. "She was a lovely thing when she was young—Wonderful little sailor . . ." How little one could judge another human being. To the very last, Mrs. Woodburn had managed never to let him down. Claudia felt humble. She had been aware, but awareness without understanding was an arid waste, a perception of the mind, without the education of the heart.

She must have asked whether there was anything that they could do—because Linda was saying, "Nothing. Bill's attended to everything, he's been wonderful. But there'll be a very small service before we leave, so if you and David would come, I know Aunt Emily would like it."

"Oh we will," said Claudia. "We'd want to be there."

The tears came after she had put the receiver back on the hook. She laid her head down on the ugly little hotel desk and wept. It was strange, to be weeping, so deeply for someone who was almost a stranger to her, someone she had known for only the space of an ocean voyage. It had not been given to her to weep so freely, so mercifully, when death had taken her mother, or Bobby or Hartley and Julia. It was as if sorrow had become an intimate part of her through the years, opening her eyes to vision, and her ears to hearing, and her heart to feeling.

A light swishing sound caused her to look up. The porter had slid the menu beneath the door. She had forgotten about ordering dinner. She switched on the desk lamp, and peered down at her watch. It was a few minutes past eight, and David wasn't home yet.

11

SHE tried to use a little of the horse sense with which David had so unromantically credited her, telling herself that a single bottleneck in traffic could have held him up for an hour or more, provided English roads were anything like the parkways around New York. In New York, there weren't as many bicycles ambling along, either, to appear like phantoms out of the dark, often without sufficient lights on the back mud-wings to give proper warning. Surely, at any moment, he was bound to thump on the door, contrite and worried for having worried her.

She picked up the menu from the floor, undecided whether or not to order something while the kitchens were still open. She decided against it. She couldn't bear the thought of food, although when she had asked for the menu, she had been ready and able, if not willing, to eat even jugged hare. Breakfast had been hurried that morning, and lunch sketchy, but the news about Mr. Woodburn robbed her of appetite, and had left her instead with a sick feeling in the pit of her stomach. Even had David been here with her, a cosy dinner in front of the fireplace would have been a pretence. He, too, had grown to have a genuine affection for the Woodburns.

The sitting-room was cold. She added a shovel of coal to the fire, and lowered the half-open window. The street lights spattered dimly through a milky fog, giving her an eerie sense of being isolated and completely helpless. If David didn't come soon, what should she do? She had no way of knowing where he was, or what had happened. Traffic couldn't have delayed him all this time, or if it had, he would have managed to get to a telephone. She had remarked on the telephone booths space at intervals along the road from Southampton, and he had told her that driving in England was easier than in America, for not only could you call for help in case of a breakdown, but the automobile club scouts kept cruising around on motor-cycles with an eye out for trouble.

At ten o'clock she could feel her detachment and calm, falsely borrowed from the larger comparison of Mr. Woodburn's death, sweep at her sanity in a flood of rising panic.

413

If only Bertha were here to offer some wise advice! A fine example she was of standing on her own two feet, when her legs were trembling so that she had to sit down to think clearly. Never mind trying to develop her character, it was time for action of some kind. There were only two people she could turn to—Jerry or Mr. Dobson. Mr. Dobson was probably the one she ought to call without further delay, but some nebulous impression of their quick meeting in Jerry's flat made her hesitate. She remembered him to be all of a colour, sandy, and a little bloodless, as if his juices were beginning to dry up, affecting even his voice which had a rather toneless and tenor quality. And yet he couldn't have been a pallid person, or his image would not have rebuilt itself so clearly in her mind; she could not negate the sense that in spite of his mono-tone exterior, he possessed a certain in-exorableness that was not without magnetic force. She could understand Ann having fallen in love with him, yet finding her marriage wanting in fullness and warmth. Where David's contempts were patrician and entirely human, Peter Dobson's standards might be so unbending as to be edged with cruelty. It was not easy for such a man to reconcile his own defections with his intellectual concept of integrity. "It could backfire, and I don't want to make him mad at David, or put Ann in an embarrassing spot," Claudia summed up her reservations in the broad terms of instinct. She decided to call Jerry instead, and looked up his number in a small leather address book that David had left on the dressing table with his keys. Her eyes filled. The little pile of his forgotten belongings added to her loneliness for him. She had longed for the assurance of his closeness ever since she had heard about Mr. Woodburn, needing desperately to dispel the vicarious taste of widowhood with the strength of his arms around her, and the touch of his lips on her own. At moments like this, it was right and natural for people who loved each other to draw close in thankfulness and a renewed awareness of being together.

Jerry's number didn't answer. The hotel operator said, "I could try a bit later, Madame," and then, at that instant, the receiver at the other end lifted, and Jerry's Bertha (Claudia couldn't think whether her name was Martha or Matilda) panted out a breathless "Hello."

"I have your line now, Madame."

"Oh thank you!" Claudia breathed. "Hello, is Mr. Jerry home, Matilda?" (It was Matilda.)

"Oh, Mrs. Dobson! I'm sorry I kept you waiting, I was in the bathroom when I heard the bell."

"This isn't Mrs. Dobson, Matilda, it's Mrs. Naughton."

"Oh, I beg pardon, you sounded like her voice, and that's a fact. No, Mr. Jerry isn't here. He had a bite of supper at the Club tonight."

"Oh. Could I reach him there?"

"I expect so, if he hasn't left. I could give you the number. Or if you'd rather, I could call him instead."

Claudia blessed the New England streak of propriety in Matilda's English soul. It was better not to keep the line to the room tied up in case David were trying to telephone. "Oh, I wish you would, Matilda. I'm at the hotel."

"Yes, ma'am. I'll tell him. That is, if he's there. If not, wouldn't know where I could reach him."

"Thank you."

God had been good to have let Matilda hear the telephone ringing while she was in the bathtub; now if only He'd see to it that Jerry was still at the club. "Of if You'd please,

416

please, let David walk in the door," she made a blanket bargain, "I wouldn't have to bother You with a lot of little favours."

Apparently God was in a mood to grant the smaller petitions. As quickly as she could have prayed for, the telephone rang and Jerry said at once, "I'm glad Matilda caught me, I was just leaving the club. Claudia, what's wrong?"

She mustn't be a baby, David wouldn't like it. "How did you know anything was wrong?" she asked, as naturally as she could.

Matilda said you seemed upset. Is it one of the children?"

"It's David." Her voice went shaky. "He hasn't come home yet."

"Oh." Jerry sounded relieved. "I thought it was something really serious."

"But he said he'd surely be back before seven."

"It's a beastly night, they've probably been detained on the road."

"I thought of that. I've thought of everything."

"Where was he when you last heard from him?"

"I haven't, that's just it. Not since he left this morning."

"Oh?" Jerry's second "Oh" seemed less certain. "Look here, does he usually telephone?"

"Every hour on the hour. That's why I'm so worried. I put off calling you as long as I dared."

"You shouldn't have," he said. "I'll be over directly?"

"But I told you that this was one evening that you needn't have us on your mind."— She tried for a laugh. "How soon will you be here?"

"The next face you will see will be mine," he answered in kind.

"I'd rather see David's, if you don't mind."

"We'll get busy on it. In the meantime, I have a strong feeling that there's nothing to be alarmed about, actually."

She felt as she often felt when David allayed her fears. At such moments she became like a child, and believed him. He hadn't lied to her, ever. He had told her, at the very beginning, that her mother was going to die. "You have to accept it, darling. You have to learn to make friends with pain." She had never forgotten those words. They had helped her through many difficult spaces in her life. But they didn't help her now.

This was different. This wasn't the final, still and awful pain that Mrs. Woodburn was living through at this very moment. This was the fierce agony of uncertainty. It could not last for ever, but at the end of it, then what? How could she live out the next hours of not knowing? She had thought—and wrongly—that she had lived through enough, and that from now on, she had earned one long holiday of happiness. It was the old bargaining idea, again, but there weren't any bargains in life. Maybe you thought that you had had more than your share of grief, until you picked up a newspaper, or listened to the radio. Mine disasters, train wrecks, kidnappings, drownings. God didn't play favourites. You took what you had to take, and according to your stamina and pride, you took it as decently as you could, remembering that anything could happen to anyone without any warning. It had happened that way with Bobby. One moment he had been so alive, and the next moment, a truck, lumbering out of nowhere, had destroyed all that could die of him.

Helen Nicholson had been telling Barry Conwell about it one day on the boat, and they'd both quickly stopped talking as

Claudia had passed their chairs. Then she'd heard Barry drawl out some disparaging remark about soap opera. It was his favourite literary aspersion. What he couldn't understand, what he had never experienced, he chose to damn as "soap-opera". Why was it, she wondered, that some people sailed through life as if their minds were a passport to oblivion? It was like the taxes that everybody was always complaining about, the more you possessed, the more you had to pay. Maybe it was better to be an intellectual bankrupt, like Barry Conwell, in which case you didn't have to like your mother, love your wife, or bother with children. You could simply by-pass your heart, and make a career out of being a cynic. Jerry might have ended up like that if he hadn't married Elizabeth. . . .

How long would it take him to get here? She began to pace the floor, her nails brutal against the palms of her hands, as if the clenching of her fists could hold back the wild flood of her imaginings. Were there as many automobile fatalities in England as in America? There she was, back again to the newspapers. You couldn't pick up a single edition without reading about some hideous accident, and often it made no difference

420

whether you were experienced at the wheel like David, you could be the victim of someone else's carelessness. Or suppose they were in the old car that they had gone out to see? The brakes might not have held, or the tyres might have been worn. And if they were in Ann's car, was there any assurance that she was the expert driver that David thought she was? She bit her lips against the hysteria that was rising fast within her. She kept seeing Mr. Woodburn, last night, and tonight. Why were there so many widows in the world? At least Elizabeth had been spared a second widowhood. Perhaps the only way that a woman could escape the fate of her sex was to do what Elizabeth had done, marry a man younger than herself, and then the chances were apt to even out a little more.

A light tap sounded on the door, followed by the turning of the key in the latch. It was only the night-maid, the voluble one with the pushed-in nose and pushed-out teeth, who boasted that she'd worked in America. "Mercy, excuse *me*, I thought you was out for the evening, I could come back after if you like."

"No, it's all right."

She swished in with an armful of towels

which she plumped down on the chest of drawers while she uncovered the beds. "My," she tittered admiringly, "you look real dressy. That wouldn't be a night-gown by any chance?"

"Underneath," said Claudia wearily.

"What they won't think of next! It won't get dirty around the hem, that's one good thing. When you walk around, I mean. Though I'd say it was too nice for just plain sleeping."

Claudia couldn't wait for her to leave. Why had she been stupid enough to let her come in in the first place? Was she so pampered at this point that she couldn't open her own beds? "There isn't anything to do in the other room," she said. "Nobody's been in it all day, the children aren't here."

"They already told me outside. Must be real lonesome for you. Well, I'll just put some extra towels in the bathroom, and tidy it up a bit."

Jerry stood at the partly opened door. "May I come in?"

She ran to him. "I thought you'd never get here!"

"I came as fast as I could."

"It seemed forever."

"David hasn't called yet?" She shook her head numbly. His arms went around her as naturally and simply as the first day of their meeting at Albany. She said, "Your coat's wet."

"It's raining."

"David will be sopped—"

"Serve him right. Dear, you're trembling."

"I can't help it. What will we do?"

"There's not very much that we can do, unless he told you exactly where they were going?"

"He didn't know. He just mentioned Cambridgeshire."

"That covers a sizeable area. I'll call Pete Dobson in case he's heard anything.—Unless you've already called him?"

"I wanted to, but I didn't."

He gave her a swift look of commendation. "It wasn't self control," she explained honestly, "I didn't see what good it would do. If Ann had been able to phone home, David certainly would have."

"True," said Jerry. He took off his coat and looked around for a place to put it. "We'll go in the other room," said Claudia. "At least there's a sofa to sit down on."

He laid his coat across the sofa, but he

didn't sit down. "Look here," he said, "you're quite right in what you say, but it won't do any harm to call Pete, anyway. Ann might have been a little more explicit as to their whereabouts." He picked up the telephone from the desk, and gave the Dobsons' number. "No answer," he said at length. "Have you a directory? I have a fair idea where I can reach him."

Claudia found the directory under one of the night tables in the bedroom. Jerry riffled the pages, and moved his finger down a column of names. "Here we are," he said, a little grimly.

It seemed as if there mustn't be any answer at that number either, and then there was a click at the other end, and very faintly, Claudia heard the threading of a woman's voice.

"Mr. Dobson, please."

There was a sharp silence, as if the woman were slightly nonplussed at the assumption that Mr. Dobson was there.

"Please tell him," Jerry continued in a tone that brooked no denial, "that Gerald Seymour wishes to speak to him. It's urgent."

From the one-sided conversation that ensued, Mr. Dobson was disgruntled at the intrusion on his privacy, but Jerry made short shrift of an apology. Briefly, he explained the purpose of his call, but apparently Mr. Dobson, who knew nothing of his wife's whereabouts, was slow to alarm. On the contrary, Claudia gathered that he considered the whole affair in the light of petty retaliation. Jerry's nostrils dilated in a manner reminiscent of David. "That's a pretty damned sick reaction, Pete, but I won't go into it at the moment. The important thing is for you to get back to the flat in case any messages come in."

Mr. Dobson chose to be obtuse at this point, and Jerry, much against his will, had to spell it out for him. "The car is licensed in your name, Pete, and Ann's driving licence would be the only traceable identification.— No, I emphatically hope not. However, let's play it safe. Good-bye."

Claudia could scarcely speak over the pounding of her heart. "You think there's been an accident, and the police might have been trying to reach Mr. Dobson."

"Nonsense. I was simply covering every possible angle to put your fears at rest."

She said, "Mr. Dobson isn't worried, is he?"

"Not a bit. That ought to cheer you up."

"It doesn't. He's trying to make himself believe that—"

"That what—" he prompted gently.

"That this isn't any accident to start with," she said with difficulty.

Jerry was silent. After a moment, he said, "Pete's not himself. He ought to have his head bashed in, he knows Ann too well to think a thing like that."

"He can't help it," said Claudia tonelessly. "It's the only way he can justify his own transgressions."

Jerry looked at her, arrested. "This sort of thing is so alien to anything you've ever touched, how would you know?"

"Because it's so easy to build your own strength on the weaknesses of others. And I suppose infidelity isn't much different than seasick pills or babytalk. I'm making sense," she assured him hastily, "but only to myself."

"Then that's quite sufficient," he said, and put his hands on her shoulders. "Claudia, you're not giving credence to anything Pete might say? Or try to make himself believe?"

"How could I?" she asked him simply.

"You couldn't." He smiled. "Any particular reason why you're clutching that bundle of towels?"

"Oh. No." She laughed shakily. "I picked them up when I got the telephone book. The maid dumped them on the chest and left in a hurry. I don't think she approved of your being here."

"I do recall a certain emanation as I came in. However," he added, "much as I dislike to compromise you, I'm not leaving until David gets here. That is, unless you want me to."

"I don't know what I'd do if you weren't here." She turned away so that he couldn't see the trembling of her lips, and carried the towels to the bathroom. She caught a glimpse of her face in the mirror above the basin, and it was a stranger's face, white and drawn. Lipstick and powder invited her from the glass shelf, but it made no difference now how she looked. It seemed another lifetime that she had been primping before this very mirror and dabbing perfume behind her ears.

When she returned to the sitting-room, Jerry was putting the last of the coal on the fire. "I expect it's too late to call down for more."

"What time is it now?"

"It's not actually late," he corrected himself, "it's just late for coal.—Come over here in front of the blaze where it's warm. Not too near, It's much too pretty a *négligé* to burn up, especially with you in it."

"I bought it this afternoon to surprise David. And it would have surprised him too, it's not my style exactly."

"Not exactly," Jerry conceded gravely, "but I think he'll like it after the first shock wears off."

"You seem so sure that—" her voice broke. "Oh Jerry, I'm frightened. Do you think Mr. Dobson has got back to his apartment yet?"

"He damn well better have. I'll call and see."

"It might look as if you're checking up on him."

"I am. Besides I'm not certain that I told him where he could reach me."

"I'm not either. Anyway, it's an excuse to phone."

She sat nervously on the edge of the sofa while he waited for the connection. Mr. Dobson had returned. "I forgot to tell you that I'm staying here at the hotel with Mrs. Naughton until we get some word," Jerry said tactfully. He hung up and turned back to

Claudia. "No news is good news. Odd, how clichés become profoundly significant, isn't it?—Oh come now." He gave her his handkerchief.

"I'm always borrowing your handkerchief," she gulped. "The last time it was for ice-cream."

"Did the spot ever come off your suit?"

"Not for me, it didn't. It's at the cleaners."

He lit a cigarette and sought to keep up a semblance of normalcy in their conversation. "All went well with Bertha and the children this afternoon?"

"They seemed to love the apartment—I'm glad they're not here tonight. Bertha's as much of a worrier as I am, and Matthew's got to the age when he sort of senses things in the air, the way Bobby always did.—Divorces must be awful for children."

"Yes."

"It's lucky the Dobsons haven't any. And you can't say that it mightn't have happened if they did have, because it doesn't seem to make much difference these days. Marriage bonds just don't seem to hold the way they used to."

"Made of plastic, or one of these new synthetic materials that drip-dry," Jerry suggested. "That wasn't very witty, was it?"

Claudia managed a wan smile. "Not very. But you're doing your best to try to keep my mind off.—What time is it now?"

"About ten minutes later than when you asked me before.—Tell me, did you have a pleasant dinner party with the Woodburns last night?"

The tears came in a torrent, and grief, vicarious and overpowering, finally had its way with her.

"Darling—" Jerry was beside her, his arms close and protective. "Please, dear, don't. David's all right, nothing very serious has happened. I feel certain of it."

"It's Mr. Woodburn—" she sobbed. "He died, and it brings everything back."

Jerry said, and he sounded like David in his tenderness and compassion, "You poor kid." He cradled her head against his shoulder, and she cried and cried until there weren't any tears left in her.

The telephone rang once. Jerry left her to answer it in the other room, and mercy dulled her feeling, and left her suspended in a vacuum of numbness. "It was only Pete," he reported to her, "wanting to know if we'd heard anything. He said, 'No news is good news'."

"If he's that down to rockbottom, he must be more upset than he thought he was going to be."

"Your astuteness never fails to astonish me," Jerry said, half seriously. "It's an ill wind, and all the rest of it. Do you think you could get a little sleep?"

"I couldn't. But I have no right to ask you to go without sleep."

"You're not asking me, silly girl. Do you actually think I'd leave you here alone?"

"Jerry, is there no possible place you could phone?" she implored him. "Hospitals—or—police-stations—"

"Pete would have heard, dear."

"I keep forgetting."

He banked some pillows against the sofa. "Put your feet up and rest. I'll bring a cover from the bed, it's very cold in here, your hands are icy."

"I wish you'd lie down too, and get some rest."

"I often sit up and read most of the night," he assured her cheerfully.

"Your hands are as cold as mine, though."

"Warm hearts, you know. We could really

go places on clichés tonight, couldn't we?"

"It's not tonight any longer. We're half into tomorrow."

He brought the cover. "You smell very pretty," he said, as he tucked it over her shoulders. "I think I'll see if I can rustle up some coal in that empty room across the hall. I'd rather not bother the porter at this hour."

"It doesn't matter. I guess my reputation's pretty much ruined, anyway. No sooner do I get rid of my children, and my husband's away, then I have a gentleman caller spend the night."

"In black chiffon, no less. Do you know, this is all very reminiscent of our first dinner together in the little red cottage I rented down the road from the farm?"

She smiled in spite of herself. "David would never admit it, but he was really jealous when he came over and found me there. It was the first time he'd ever had to be away overnight.—The only time, even in all these years. Except for the war. And now."

The telephone cut through the air. Jerry reached it before she could get to her feet. "David!" he all but shouted.—"Yes, she's all right. Hold on a moment, you can tell her yourself—"

She was trembling so, she could hardly talk. "You don't sound very all right," David told her.

"You don't either."

"It was pretty awful not being able to get to a telephone. I'm glad Jerry was with you. Darling, I can't hold up the booth, Ann wants to call Pete, and there's a line of people waiting to use the phone. There's no use our starting home now, the fog's ahead of us. We'll spend what's left of the night at some little inn around here. I hate to think what you've been through, darling. I'll be home as soon as I can."

She hung up, her knees liquid with the immense relief that flooded her. "They were lost in the fog."

"I was afraid so. I got a weather report before I left the club."

"Why didn't you tell me?"

"I didn't want to. A lot of accidents happen in an English fog, but evidently it was too dense for them to try to get through it."

Claudia wet her parched lips. "Can it really be as bad as that? That you just have to sit in the car and wait until it lifts?"

"Believe me, it can. It's an incredible experience. I was on my way to Amsterdam about this time last year—the boats depart from Harwich to the Hook of Holland—and all of a sudden the damn thing came down like a thick curtain. I found myself going around in circles and ending up in somebody's garage or back yard. I finally gave up,—or in, rather. There wasn't the ghost of a chance of catching the boat."

"I'm getting a very strange reaction," Claudia said slowly and clearly, "of wanting to wring David's neck. Why did he have to go off like a half-baked school boy looking for a second-hand car in the first place! And that goes for your friend Annie, too!"

Jerry grinned. "That's not as strange as it is healthy, and I heartily endorse your sentiments."

"I'm not fooling."

"I can see that you're not."

"I could really bust."

"Don't. Take a sleeping pill instead."

"I haven't got any new ones, but I still have a couple of the ones that Hartley gave me of his, when we were staying with them in New York."

"Good. Better let me see them, though."

He recognized the little yellow capsules. "Take one to start with. If you wake up, and

David's not home yet, take another."

He filled a glass with water from the bathroom, and brought it to her. "Swallow it down and pop into bed."

"Don't be so bossy. I have to wash my teeth first.—No I don't, I washed them before dinner and I didn't have any dinner. And practically no lunch, and hardly any breakfast."

"My heart aches for you," he teased. "But every cloud has a silver lining. The pill will work like a charm on an empty stomach."

"Oh Jerry, I might be mad at David, but I'm so happy and thankful," she said tremulously.

"So am I. Now into bed with you." He picked her up in his arms and carried her into the other room.

12

IT was against her principles to fall asleep before David was safely back, but the sedative really did work like a charm, as Jerry had predicted. She didn't hear him go out, and she didn't hear David come in. When she opened her eyes it was morning, and she knew that he was home because the wardrobe was ajar, and his tweed coat was suspended on a hanger from the top of the door, which meant that it was too damp to hang away. She leapt out of bed. The feeling of the soggy cloth confirmed her apprehensions. He'd be lucky if he hadn't caught his death of cold.

The water was running out of the bath, and he was standing before the basin, with a towel around his middle, cleaning his razor. The bathroom was pleasantly steamy, and redolent of the spicy lotion that he used after shaving. It was more comfortable, perhaps, to have a bathroom to yourself, but it was cosier to share one with a husband, especially if you could afford the luxury of double washstands and medicine cabinets, which David planned to install in the little hip roof house. She remembered, when they were first married, how he'd mistaken a tube of cold cream for toothpaste, and how she'd forestalled his murderous intent by furiously accusing him of using up her good cosmetics.

A sound escaped her, half-laughter, half sob, merging past and present. He saw her then. He put down the razor, and pulled her to him. And suddenly, against all reason, restraint came between them, and they were like strangers with each other. "I was glad you were sleeping when I came in," he said, a little lamely.

"Jerry made me take a pill."

"That was good. You must have been frantic until I telephoned."

"I was. I felt helpless for the little while Matthew was lost on the boat, but this was a thousand times worse."

"Your men-folk give you a lot of grief."

She wanted to say that it was worth it, but somehow, the words wouldn't come. "Did you buy the car?" she asked inanely.

"Never even looked at it. That blasted salesman gave us the wrong directions to begin with, and we were miles out of our way when the fog came down. It wasn't bad at first, we managed to crawl along, but then it got so dense that all we could do was stop dead at the side of the road. Or what we hoped was the side of the road. Some poor devil has a ruined flower patch. Unless you've actually been caught in a bad fog," he thought to explain, "it's hard to believe that you literally can't see ten inches beyond the windshield. It's as if a thick curtain had dropped in front of you."

"That's what Jerry said."

"You can bet it was a comfort for me to know he was here with you. How long did he stay?"

"Most of the night, I imagine. I didn't hear him go.—If you're finished shaving, I'll take a shower to clear my head."

"I'm finished." He stepped aside, and seemed to notice her black nightgown for the first time. "Say, what did you do, go into mourning for me, already?"

"Don't be funny," she bit back her irritation. "I'm sorry you don't like it."

"I didn't say I didn't like it. You can see through it like nobody's business."

"That's the general idea behind it. And stop looking like you want to ask me if I went around in front of Jerry like this. I didn't. It has a *négligé* that goes over it."

"It better." He gave her a kiss, which, for her taste, was a little brotherly. "How about ordering breakfast? We didn't have any dinner last night."

"Neither did I," she informed him tersely. She couldn't understand what had got into her to make her act this way. Ordinarily, she would have been very upset to think that he had gone without food for so long. "Why should I keep on being mad about nothing?" she thought. She decided to be only grateful that he had been sitting in a fog instead of lying mangled in a wreck. "Order lots of breakfast for both of us," she said, trying for gaiety, "and incidentally, you didn't tell me if you were surprised at our having a sitting-room."

"I didn't tell you a lot of things," he said.

"I don't think I like the sound of that. It could mean almost anything. Name one."

"I love you," he said promptly.

"Oh. Well, that'll do for a start."

She had every intention of turning back the clock to last night's fire, pyjamas included, but when she joined him in the bedroom a little later, he was already in his trousers,

439

putting on a fresh shirt. A belated concern took precedence over her smarting pride. "I thought you'd want to go to bed and try to get a little sleep at least?" she remonstrated.

"What for?"

"What for!" She could literally feel her nose snap out of joint. "You didn't stay at whatever inn you stayed at long enough to get much rest," she managed in a level voice.

"We didn't bother with an inn. We thought we'd better keep driving as long as the fog was lifting. It was slow going, though."

"Then you certainly must be exhausted."

"Surprisingly, I'm not. We had a couple of hours sleep in the car while we were stuck."

"More than I had," she muttered under her breath. Aloud she said, "You must have froze just sitting there for hours."

"On and off," he admitted. "Those English heaters aren't too hot, if you know what I mean, but luckily Ann had a fur robe in the car."

"It sounds chummy," she vouchsafed coldly.

"It was. It had to be, if we wanted to keep warm. Ann was a good sport about it though."

"That was big of her, considering that it was her brilliant idea in the first place to go gallivanting off to look at somebody's old second-hand car."

He left his tie dangling to put a conciliatory arm around her. "Look, I don't blame you for being scratchy," he offered with great magnanimity.

"Thank you." She removed his arm. "In other words, I'm being catty."

"That wasn't in my mind, but now that you mention it, you are, somewhat. About Ann, I mean. She couldn't have felt worse about the whole thing. She said you'd never forgive her if I caught pneumonia."

"That's putting it mildly."

"Anyway she unearthed an old sweater of Pete's in the trunk of the car, and made me put it on, if that makes you feel any better."

"It makes me feel bully."

"Oh come on, now."

She wasn't to be cajoled, not at this point. "My one satisfaction is, that it must have killed you, knowing how beneath your manly pride it is to wear something warm."

"I hear breakfast coming," he was pleased to change the subject. "I ordered sausages for you, how's that?"

Fury locked her jaws. Orchids for his girl-friend and sausages for his wife. She picked up the chiffon *négligé* from the bed and slipped it over her gown as the clatter of china sounded outside the door. "That's right," David commended her, "you looked pretty diaphanous standing there. Or should I say pretty and diaphanous."

"Anything you say after what you've said can only make matters worse.—Oh good morning," she broke off to smile graciously at the waiter. "Will you set up the table in the other room, please?"

"Certainly, Madame."

"Which reminds me. It's awfully damn quiet without those brats around here," David mentioned.

"It's nice of you to miss them. And it was particularly nice of you to call the apartment after lunch."

"Hell, I left the number here with my keys and stuff," he told her contritely.

"So I noticed."

"I tried to get it from Information, and couldn't.—How are they, and how did they like the place?"

She clapped her hand across her mouth in dismay. "I should have phoned them as soon as I woke up, I'm going to do it this minute."

"Eat your breakfast first. They're all right. No news is good news."

She winced.

"What's the matter?"

"I never want to hear those words again."

He cleared off the top of the chest by stowing most of the things into his pockets. He glanced at the two telephone messages and tossed them into the wastebasket. "Linda's certainly persistent," he remarked. "Don't tell me it's another dinner party." He turned quickly. "Now what's the matter? He stared at her. "Claudia, you're crying!"

"I—I don't know how I could forget—it must still be that sleeping pill," she faltered.

"Darling," he said gently, "don't be so hard on yourself. You had a bad night. And I had a bad night. Let's both of us try to forget everything about it, except that it's all over and done with."

A part of her knew, with shame, that she fell far short of his stature, and that she was unready to say that everything was all over and done with, but now was not the time to try to probe the unfinished business in her soul. She yielded to his lips and the fitting, familiar pressure of his body. "Oh, David, I needed you—" she whispered.

"I needed you too," he said, quietly, "so very much."

To her seeing eyes, he looked deeply tired, all at once, with a depletion that was not entirely the weariness of his physical being. He was right. It hadn't been an easy night for either of them. She took the clean handkerchief that he had just put into his pocket, and wiped her eyes. "What we need is some hot coffee," she said.

She would tell him about Mr. Woodburn after breakfast.

He was deeply shocked, and, for a wonder, refrained from his usual dissertations on the Hereafter. Except when it came to animals, particularly dogs, he was apt to be quite cold-blooded about the simple act of dying, which, he insisted, carried with it no especial sanctity. The mere transition from life to death did not make a saint out of a scoundrel, or turn a coward into a hero.

Henry Woodburn, however, was someone to be truly mourned, a kind and gentle man, who would continue to so live in the memory of those who honoured and loved him, and in them, and them alone, the miracle was wrought. Even David had to admit that the Blisses and the Nicholsons, gathered once again in their tight little circle in the hotel drawing-room, seemed to have achieved a kind of spiritual projection of themselves. They wore a new dignity of awareness, muted with a fearful humility in the vast presence of the ultimate. But Mrs. Woodburn remained unchanged, composed and separate in her quiet acquiescence. Claudia touched her lips to the soft pale cheek, more in homage than in pity. Mrs. Woodburn smiled and pressed her hand firmly. "Linda tells me that you moved the children to their little apartment yesterday."

"Yes," said Claudia. "We just left them. They love it, they don't even miss us." She turned to Linda, whose face was white and ravaged with grief. "Bertha says could she have Greg, there's plenty of room."

"That's dear of her, but Aunt Emily's maid took him with her to the villa. They left yesterday, she and Jacques will have everything in readiness for us by tomorrow."

"Greg needs his childhood more than most little boys," said Mrs. Woodburn. "It was better for him not to be here."

445

"He began stuttering badly again," Linda explained. "Which wouldn't have been too good for Matthew," she added frankly.

Claudia said, "Not any worse than Greg catching ketch-up on spinach."

Helen Nicholson shuddered. "That sounds utterly revolting."

"It is," Claudia assured her.

Helen's rather forced laughter ended in a startling wheeze. Mr. Nicholson produced a small atomizer from his pocket, and gave it to her. "Better use it, dear," he said in an undertone.

"Oh thanks, I didn't know you'd brought it along." She inhaled the spray briefly, and put it in her bag. "Thanks," she said again.

"In all the years I've known Helen, I never knew she suffered from asthma until today," Mrs. Bliss mentioned, with a hint of respect in her voice.

"It's a poifectly horrid sensation," Mrs. Woodburn sympathized. "Henry had it quite severely the first few years we were married, but after that, I don't think I remember him being troubled with it at all. It was one of the reasons we started having a boat."

"With me, it's mental," Helen stated with unwonted candour. "I had an awful attack in

Paris a couple of days ago. I guess this is the left-overs."

"Where's Bill Hendricks?" Claudia asked Mrs. Bliss under cover of Helen's asthma.

"Attending to everything for the morning. Emily wants just a simple little service for Henry's friends and business associates before we board the plane."

"Are you going with them?"

"Of course. The Nicholsons too. We'll have to come right back, but Bill's changed his London plans, and he'll stay on with them for a while. He's been simply wonderful, I want to tell you."

"He certainly has," Mrs. Nicholson stopped her wheezing long enough to interject. "Well, it just proves that you can't tell who your friends are until a tragedy like this happens."

"You're quite right, Helen, except that you mustn't pull me down by calling this a tragedy," Mrs. Woodburn paused briefly at Mrs. Nicholson's side on her way to answer the telephone. "Henry and I had forty years together and we made the most of every one of them. I have no wasted spaces to look back on and regret. And if I'm lonely, I love him enough not to begrudge his going first. It would have been very hard on him to be the one to stay."

Helen's eyes followed Mrs. Woodburn's staunch progress to the hall. "That one's got what it takes," she said elliptically.

"You mean she's had what it takes," Mr. Nicholson amended. "She and Henry had a fine marriage, and I don't imagine it was all a bed of roses, either. It never is."

Mrs. Bliss's chins trembled with emotion. "I'm like Helen. I just couldn't be that brave or philosophical."

"Frankly, I'd rather see her not so brave," Mr. Bliss gave forth. "This isn't normal, she's bound to crack up a little after the first shock wears off."

David spoke for the first time. "I doubt it," he said quietly.

"So do I," said Claudia.

Linda came back into the room with a tall vase of red roses and a handful of telegrams. "Oh, aren't they lovely," Mrs. Bliss brightened. "Who sent them, anyone we know?"

"The girls in Uncle Henry's London office."

"Very sweet of them. I must say I like the personal touch instead of a wreath. Helen too. That's why we decided to send a blanket of violets together.—Who are the wires from?"

"Such nosiness," Helen observed, without malice.

"At a time like this, we're all one family," Mrs. Bliss said.

Linda split an envelope and glanced at the lengthy message. "This one's a cable from Nancy Riddle. She read about it in today's *Times*."

"You'll be getting thousands," Mrs. Bliss offered sagely. "Keep them all in one place, and Helen and I can help answer them later on.—Wasn't Nancy Riddle coming over, by the way?"

"I think so." Linda opened the cable again. "Yes, she says she'll be seeing us in a few weeks.—Nancy's a client of yours, isn't she, David?"

"Under protest," David admitted wryly. "She bought our farm, and wanted Palladium columns on a salt-box house."

Linda smiled. "That sounds like Nancy, but she's a good soul under all her blundering.—Where's Aunt Emily?"

"I believe she answered the phone," said David.

"Oh dear, I was on the other wire with Bill, and didn't hear it ring. She oughtn't to put herself through the strain of talking to people."

"I'm very glad I did," Mrs. Woodburn said, from the doorway. "It was Cora Vanderlip. She wanted to come over for a few moments this evening."

"Well, that woman!" Mrs. Bliss expostulated, drawing her chins in. "Now really, I must say."

Helen gave one of her broad winks. "This certainly makes a liar out of you, my girl. You told me she slashed her wrists, and an ambulance met her at the boat to take her to the hospital."

"That's what I was told," Mrs. Bliss insisted indignantly.

"Well, you've been cheated," Helen retorted good-naturedly. "Anyway, Emily, I hope you told Cora off."

Mrs. Woodburn took a moment to rearrange the roses. The scent of them suddenly drowned Claudia in memories. The flowers had poured in with Hartley and Julia, and with Bobby, too. It was true, you didn't know how many friends you had until tragedy struck. And with them, it had indeed been tragedy—not the natural ending of long, full years, but a perverse snuffing-out at the crest of life. Her heart became a living, aching thing in her breast. A heart was never the same once grief had entered it, you always felt it inside of you vigilant and responsive.

Mrs. Woodburn was saying, "How fragrant they are. The girls in his office knew that Henry's favourite flower was red roses. It's nice of them to have remembered. And it's nice of Cora to want to come this evening, it must be an effort for her if she's been ill. I told her that Henry would appreciate it. He was very fond of Cora's mother, you know. We both were."

"Emily, you're a saint," Helen Nicholson blurted out.

"We're none of us saints," Mrs. Woodburn returned. "Linda, would you ring for tea, dear?—Or would you rather have a cocktail, Helen?"

"Tea, please," Helen said.

Claudia caught David's eye, and they both rose. "We must be going," she said.

Mrs. Woodburn did not try to detain them. "Henry had grown very fond of you two," she said, "and I'm sure he'll understand if you don't come tomorrow, it brings back so much. He'd rather that you came to see us later on, he said he wanted to show you our farm in Provence."

Claudia nodded over the lump of tears welling up in her throat. "We'll come," David answered for her. "Later on, and tomorrow as well. Claudia doesn't like to run away from things."

"Don't be so stoic," Helen Nicholson advised. "What's it going to get you? Good God, when I think what you've been through this past year." She brooded on it thoughtfully. "Funny, isn't it, they say death always comes in threes."

"Helen, *please*!" Mrs. Bliss clutched blindly at Mr. Bliss. "That's a perfectly dreadful thing to say. What with poor Linda's husband, it leaves one of us still to *go*!"

"I can count," said Helen.

Mrs. Woodburn smiled faintly. "Don't worry about it. If there's any truth in what Helen says—and I doubt it—I shall be happy to be the candidate, if the Lord so wills."

"What idiotic talk," Linda said, unnerved. "If Bill were here, he'd shut you all up."

"Bill!" Mrs. Bliss echoed on a small shriek of relief. "That's wonderful, I forgot about

Bill's wife, that makes the three!"

"Saved by a hair's breadth," Mr. Nicholson said with an attempt to be jocular about it. "Emily, I think I'll have a whisky instead of tea, if you don't mind."

"So will I," said Mr. Bliss.

They walked the short distance between the two hotels. The mist was damp against their faces, but it felt cool and welcome after the warm, flower-scented room. "This must be the end of the fog that you were in last night," Claudia said. "I hope it won't get any worse, on account of the children."

"It's lifting," said David. "The weather doesn't seem to bother them anyway, they look fine."

"They really do, I think it's all right if I don't worry about them, don't you?"

"I think it would be a great step forward."

She was silent for a moment. Then she said, "David, I already took my great step forward for today."

"Tell me about it."

"When we get home. You see, it's a little complicated because there are little steps inside the big step. Could we have dinner sent up to the room? In front of the fire?"

"Where else," he said.

He was extravagant and ordered caviar, as if in celebration, but when the waiter called for the table, he was dismayed that they had eaten hardly anything at all. "Everything was delicious but we weren't very hungry," Claudia told him.

David got up to find his pipe, and on the way back to the sofa, put out the lamps so that only the darting flames of the fire lit the room. He sat down beside her. "Do you mind if I smoke?"

"Now isn't that silly?" she asked tremulously. "Have I ever? And if I did, wouldn't you?"

"I guess it was only a way of saying that I love you, and I'd do anything in the world— even not smoke—to make you happy."

"I feel the same about you, David. I suppose that's why I didn't wear the black *négligé* tonight. You didn't like it."

"It made you look so pale."

"I was pale inside of me. Like Mrs. Woodburn was pale. Only there was a kind of magnificence underneath her paleness, and there was nothing underneath mine except fear. That was the big step forward that I took. I learned acceptance today."

He took her hand and carried it to his lips, and she felt, as she felt when Jerry had made the same gesture, that it was more than a kiss. She said, "The little steps are easier to talk about, particularly with your calling Jerry of your own accord to thank him for staying with me last night."

"That was my private step," said David quietly.

"If it was, it helped me with mine. I'll never be tempted to undignify your trust by having to explain anything to you, ever. And you were right about Ann," she went on with difficulty. "You said she was a good sport. She was more than that, coming to see me this morning the way she did. I was glad you went downstairs to buy cigarettes and left us alone. She said that Pete was half out of his mind by the time she got in, so she knew what I must have been through."

"I think Pete took a step in the right direction, too," David said.

"David—"

"What dear?"

"All of this leads up to what I want to say. And it's this. No matter what happened—or didn't happen—I accept it, the way Mrs. Woodburn accepted—and understood about

455

Cora Vanderlip's mother. If two people are blessed enough to have a lot of years together, they can't all be the same kind of years. We've only had the first dozen, and look how full of sickness, and war and grief they've been, but we had so much health and love and happiness sandwiched in between that we were able to take the rest of it, and ought to be able to take whatever lies ahead of us, too. I guess that's why Mrs. Woodburn was the only one in that room today that wasn't crying. Or scared. They were crying for themselves, and scared of all the years they'd wasted in ugliness. Or restlessness. Or just plain being rich and spending money.—I didn't mean to make such a long speech, I never do, so don't hold it against me. There's only one more thing I want to say. On the boat, I told you that Mrs. Woodburn and I were a lot alike underneath. I flattered myself."

This time David kissed her lips. "Let me be the judge of that," he said huskily.

13

CLAUDIA dreaded saying good-bye to Bertha and the children. She had visions of Matthew clinging to her at the last minute, Bertha developing delayed qualms at the responsibility of being left alone with them, and the baby acting up in sheer contagion. Not a bit of it. She found Bertha making yeast cake, Michael taking his afternoon nap, and Matthew, having recently discovered the questionable embellishment of sopping his hair with water, laboriously combing it sideways into a crooked parting before the bathroom mirror.

"What are you doing with your hair and why don't you try a little on your face?" David suggested.

"I'm wetting it to make it stay. I have to look nice. I'm going to a birthday party," he replied with immense importance, and no concern whatsoever regarding their imminent departure.

"You don't know anybody to have a birthday," she remarked.

"Ach, I will tell you all about it," Bertha said. "We met such a nice little boy and girl in Kensington Gardens yesterday—"

"She is not a girl, they're twins!" Matthew took umbrage, "and they're both seven years old today."

"Seven or seventy, you're not going over to a strange house," Claudia said firmly. Bertha was jumping to conclusions. She might know her Central Park children from head to toe, but in England even the babies spoke with an English accent and sounded polite.

"They live only in the apartment house on the corner," Bertha offered hopefully. "It is no distance at all, he can even go by himself."

"Proximity is not the immediate problem," Claudia explained. "If you only met them yesterday for the first time, you can't know anything about them."

Matthew read the handwriting on the wall. The comb dropped from his hand, and water dripped into his anguished eyes. "I have to go!" he croaked hoarsely. "Bertha said I could go!"

Bertha calmed him down. "Be quiet, kindchen. Mrs. Naughton," she said, "you are right. If Lady Gresham did not say that it was such a lovely family, I also would have said he could not go."

"Does Lady Gresham know who they are?" David asked.

"Oh, surely. I asked her, and the father is one of the doctors' names that she wrote down on a pad for me with the butcher and the grocer. He took out Christopher's tonsils before he went to America."

"Well, Bertha you damn fool, why didn't you say so!" Claudia exclaimed. "You can go, Matthew."

"Yippee!" Matthew shouted, making a roundabout bee-line for his coat.

She caught him on the run. "Aren't you going to kiss us good-bye?"

"Good-bye," he said, "I'm late."

"I did Bertha a grievous injustice," she admitted on the way to London Airport. "Those twins are a wonderful package-deal, group spirit and medical supervision combined."

"You're two of a kind," David said dourly. "I bet you twenty cents she gets Matthew a free look at his tonsils.—Say, what the hell was the meaning of that thoroughly obnoxious and imbecile duck-footing around the room with his neck out?"

"He was skating," Claudia said.

It was incredible. It seemed as if they were hardly up in the air before they came down again, and everybody was talking French, including David, and the beautiful roll of his "r's" impressed her greatly. This trip was certainly bringing out unsuspected talents in him, but unfortunately it wasn't bringing out a thing in her that was a refreshment to their marriage. She couldn't even wear a black nightgown with any outstanding effect. And as for her French, the only words she could think of all of a sudden, were German ones, bits and pieces of expressions that she had picked up from Bertha. "Instead of 'Merci beaucoup, Monsieur,' I keep wanting to say 'Danke schoen, gnadige Herr'," she told David in agitation. "What'll I do about it?"

"Just don't," he advised succinctly. "Sit here on this bench and keep your mouth shut while I get through the Customs. I won't be long."

"Don't you want any help?"

"Not from you, my love."

The Customs took more time than they should have, and when David reappeared, he had lost a little of the bloom off his undying affection for France. His ill-humour didn't last long, however. His eyes embraced the Paris streets like a lover, but Claudia tried to see everything at once. "What are all those little buildings with feet underneath?" she asked curiously. "We keep passing them on every corner, almost?"

"Nothing of any interest to you," David said. "But tomorrow we'll take a long walk through the Tuilleries and along the Left Bank."

"Tomorrow I'm going to buy me some clothes," Claudia informed him silently.

Jerry was waiting for them in the hotel lobby. "I hope you'll like it here," he said; "it's not considered one of the great luxury places any longer; but I've never stayed anywhere else. To me this has always been the most beautiful part of Paris."

David nodded. "Who could ask for more? The Madeleine at one end, the Chamber of Deputies at the other, and sheer magnificence in between."

"I don't know about that, but I couldn't ask for more of a hotel either," Claudia said. "I think this is most luxurious." From the bustling lounge, lined with lighted showcases full of bags and perfumes and jewellery, she could see vistas of reception rooms, and a graciously elegant dining-room, into which a jugged hare would never dare show its face. She was charmed with their suite, too. It wasn't large, but the drawing-room was full of Louis Quinze furniture, and there was a tall vase of airy white lilacs with a card bearing the compliments of the management. Disappointingly, they had no real lilac smell, but the bathroom was simply huge, with an immense marble basin, and a tub big enough to satisfy even David, with his long legs. "I agree with Claudia," he said. "I think this is the height of luxury." With becoming reticence, neither of them remarked on the resplendent double bed of polished brass with its satin quilt billowing up beneath a white lace spread.

Jerry, pleased because they were pleased, drew back a damask drapery from one of the heavy casement windows. "You haven't seen anything yet."

David stepped out on to a small balcony. "This is Paris," he said with eloquence.

"I thought the Place de la Concorde only looked this way in pictures," Claudia exclaimed.

Jerry smiled. "I felt the same kind of

astonishment when I saw Pisa for the first time. I turned to my father and said, 'Good Lord, Dad, it actually *does* lean.'—By the way, I hope you two are planning to spend a little time in Italy while you're here."

"I hope so too," said David, "but you're a better man than I am if you can sell the idea to my wife. I'll be lucky if she doesn't want to head back to London before the week's over."

"Claudia, you'll break Annie's heart if you do," Jerry warned her. "She called me from Villefranche this morning to say that she expected us next Wednesday. Which still gives us six full days of Paris."

"She'll be busy enough trying to sell the place without bothering with house guests," Claudia demurred.

"She decided not to sell. She had an offer to lease it to an Australian couple over the summer, and she accepted it. They won't take possession until the tenth of March, however, so she said to tell you that you were welcome to the place until then. We both have to be back in London by the first, at the latest."

"That's awfully nice of her," Claudia said, "but if we did go down, which I doubt, we'd have to stay with the Woodburns. They invited us on the boat. Especially now, we ought to. Mrs. Woodburn will be pretty lonely, I imagine."

David fixed her with a steely eye. "Tell all your reasons, Cheat."

"Mrs. Woodburn asked us with the children," she confessed. "But we don't have to decide anything now, do we? Say, if that Ormulu clock is as right as it is beautiful, no wonder I'm starving, it's half past seven already!"

"Calm down," said David, "you're not as hungry as you think, we're an hour later than London. How about Laparouse, Jerry? Is it as good as it used to be?"

"I haven't been there recently. Anyway, you're dining with me this evening. I think Claudia ought to go to Maxim's her first night in Paris. I've made a reservation for nine-thirty, so I'll leave you to unpack and relax for a bit."

"I should have thought of Maxim's," David said, after Jerry had departed for his own room down the hall. "You'll enjoy it more than some little Left Bank restaurant."

Claudia shrugged. "I wouldn't say so. To tell the truth, I was sort of looking forward to eating in that lovely dining-room downstairs."

"Nobody but old ladies with elderly companions eat at their hotels in Paris."

"You make it sound like not fishing with worms."

"It is, more or less."

"But I thought there was no such thing as bad French food."

"There isn't. But if there were, hotels would have it. Which closet do you want?"

"We could both fit into one, they're so big.—I hate the idea of having to have clothes made to order, I should have asked Ann where to go for ready-made things. She steered me awfully well on this suit, don't you think?"

"Your non-sequiters are outdoing themselves—I'm leaving you the closet with the sliding drawers."

"I love sliding drawers. We're having them, aren't we?"

"I presume," he said, "that you're referring to our dressing-alcove at home."

"Now what else," she asked reasonably, "could I possibly be referring to, as you so elegantly put it.—Did you see that chocolate-coloured poodle in the lobby?"

"No poodles," he replied firmly.

"They are a little dressy," she conceded,

465

"but they do have character. This one snapped at me when I talked to her."

"It was a he.

"What sharp eyes you have, Grandma.—Move, please."

He moved out of her way and then dropped an armful of shirts to drag her back. "You don't drink tap-water in France," he adjured her sternly.

"Why not?"

"Because you don't."

"That's silly. Go in and feel how nice and cold it is."

"Don't argue. I'll ring for a bottle of Perrier. Or would you rather have Evian?"

"What's the difference?"

"One bubbles."

"Which one?"

"Perrier, of course."

"Why 'of course'? Does the other one taste like a laxative?"

He emitted an ominous sound, like air going out of a tyre.

"I'll stick to plain water out of a plain faucet," she decided. "I can't be running to a bottle every minute."

"You'll be running to something else if you don't." He had already pressed one of the many little buttons on the night-table, and before she could get back to the bathroom, the waiter appeared, looking as pretty as the groom on top of a wedding-cake. "Monsieur-Dame," he invited their pleasure with a charming little bow.

She was intrigued at the expression, which she had never heard before. How un-British it all was! And how fluently David was explaining that they would like a small bottle of Perrier and also a small bottle of Evian so that Madame could have her preference. And a bowl of ice, if you pleased.—She was surprised and gratified that she could understand everything he said, though she couldn't have rattled off whole French sentences like that even if she read them off a piece of paper. "No wonder women fall in love with you," she said adoringly.

It was little short of dishonesty for him to have accepted her homage with such complacence, for at dinner that night, she discovered that he wasn't so wonderful, after all. Jerry's French was so really French, that she couldn't understand a word of it.

Secretly, she suspected that the Louvre was going to turn out to be another Westminster

Abbey, because David was all set to go there the first thing in the morning, when a roll of blueprints arrived by special airmail. He opened them eagerly, and spread them across the desk.

"The Kip Memorial?" she inquired with a pretended smile.

"Yes. John incorporated the ideas I had on the boat, and they look pretty good at a quick glance. They'll need some working over, of course. I ought to get them back to him as soon as I can."

"Are you or are you not supposed to be on vacation?" she unveiled her disapproval.

"Once these plans are off my mind, I can relax in earnest."

She knew what he was leading up to, but she didn't bat an eyelash. "If you intend to take me to see La Saint Chapelle after the Louvre, we'd better get started," she remarked pointedly.

He looked uncomfortable. "Darling, I'm afraid we'll have to put off the Louvre for today—"

She waited stolidly, without comment.

"I'll try to be through by lunch," he finished lamely. "Even if I'm not, I'll take a break and we'll go out for a bite."

"It sounds wildly exciting, our first day in Paris."

"I know. It's a damn shame. Too bad Jerry's in a huddle with his publisher until noon." He cleared his throat. "Do you think you could manage to go around a little by yourself?"

Her face was a blank. "I wouldn't have the vaguest notion how to get to the Louvre," she said.

"Forget the Louvre. I meant couldn't you do a little shopping or something?"

"Oh." She considered it. "Shopping is such an immoral waste of time, when we only have six days in Paris, unquote, but I might as well be thoroughbred about it."

He got to his feet. "Get out of here before I bat you one!" he bellowed. "Hey, come back, here's some money!"

He unlocked his briefcase, and gave her a thick pile of notes, separated into smaller piles with rubber bands. "My, they're real pretty," she said.

"Quit clowning and listen to me." Painstakingly, he showed her which was which, from the delicate little fifty franc notes to the larger notes with the lovely pastel pictures on them. "There are," he explained, "roughly four hundred francs to the dollar."

"That's very cheap," she marvelled. "Much cheaper than London, where a whole pound is nowhere near that much."

"France is not cheaper than England," he disillusioned her tersely. "Now pay attention: if something costs fifteen hundred francs, how much does it cost in American money?"

Her brain addled.

"Come on, it's easy," he encouraged her.

She stood her ground stubbornly. "For me, it's difficult."

"Use your fingers. I haven't got all day."

"Don't agitate me."

"Hurry up."

"Four dollars," she hazarded. "Roughly."

"To be exact, it's three-seventy-five."

"And you don't call that cheap!" she exclaimed. "Why, in London, fifteen hundred shillings would cost a bloody fortune!"

His silence thickened on the air. He removed the pile of notes from her hand, and returned them to the briefcase. He opened his wallet and gave her the taxi fare. "Disregard all previous instruction," he said in a dead voice. "Send anything you buy to the hotel. They'll pay for it."

"Now that's much more sensible!" She kissed him with great gusto. "Good-bye darling, enjoy your blueprints. I'll be home when I get back."

He followed her to the door. "Remember. No German." Misgiving obsessed him. He caught up with her at the elevator. "Wait a minute, do you know where you're going?"

"Who, me?"

"Yes, you, you crazy idiot!"

"Oh," she said nonchalantly. "I thought I'd just wander."

"They'll come and get you with a net," he prophesied darkly. "Now listen to me: Go out the side entrance. That's the rue Boissey D'Anglais. Turn right, and you'll come to the rue du Faubourg Saint Honoré—"

"You're mixing me up with all those names," she whimpered. "Why can't I just keep walking until I come to a shop, and then I'll look in the window, and if I like what I see in the window, I'll go into the shop and buy it. It's perfectly simple. Don't be such a *worrier*!"

The massive gold-and-velvet elevator laboured upwards. She almost said. "Guten Morgen" to the dapper little old man who pulled back the door, but she caught herself in the nick of time. "Bonsoir!" she chirped.

She wasn't sure whether it was the elevator, or David, who groaned.

She found that his directions were pretty good. She went out the side entrance of the hotel, walked to the corner, and practically bumped her nose against a shop window that held all the dreams she never knew she had. It wasn't a tremendous shop, as shops go, and yet there was nothing that they didn't seem to have, whether it was made of leather, silk, wool or gold. A long counter near the entrance door held a drift of heavenly scarves, and stacks of beautiful gloves, accessible and irresistible. "Combien—"

The lean young woman in charge of the department anticipated the question. "Twelve hundred franc, Mademoiselle." "Mademoiselle." It made her feel young. Why didn't David call her "Mademoiselle" to the waiters instead of "Madame!" Oh well, on second thought, maybe it was better to stick to "Madame."

"We have other qualitay and colour, of course, Mademoiselle. I prefer thees glove, for example, eet ees a leetle bit more long, and has the charming cuff."

"You talk English!"

"Oh, not so very, but I am learn."

"You talk a lot better English than I talk French," Claudia assured her. "What price is the pair with the cuffs?"

"Twenty-five hundred franc, Mademoiselle."

"Oh. How much is that in dollars?"

"I will ask—"

"No, never mind," said Claudia hastily. "I can reckon it out." She didn't use her fingers, and she hoped she wasn't moving her lips. It was quite simple, at that. If the first pair was twelve hundred, it would be three dollars. Twelve from twenty-five was half as much. Or rather twice as much. And that would be roughly six dollars; probably less. And where could you buy an imported pair of gloves in New York with fancy cuffs at that price? You couldn't.

"I'll take two pairs," she said. "One black and one tan."

The girl measured the width of a glove across Claudia's closed fist. "Perrfect."

"Then give me one size larger in the black, and one size smaller in the tan. And I'd like two scarfs. A pair of gloves and a scarf should make a nice present, shouldn't it?"

"Oh mais oui, Mademoiselle!—For a young girl, or perhaps an older personne?"

Candy could still pass for a young girl, but Elsie Robinson looked pretty matronly. She chose a lovely blue and gold stripe for Candy's taffy-coloured hair, and a soft green print for Elsie, who sort of varied her colour. "Could you wrap them small, please, so that they don't take up much packing-space?"

"Always, Mademoiselle. We have the charming flat box. And they will arrive at your hotel almost immediately."

"Thank you," said Claudia.

"Merci bien, Mademoiselle."

She congratulated herself for having completed her first French purchases so quickly and easily. What next? Handbags wouldn't take up much room, either. Bertha's old black bag was coming apart, she could certainly use a new one. And Candy was mad about alligator. Real alligator was terribly expensive in New York, and with the tax added, they were astronomical. Apparently there weren't any taxes here—at least for Americans—which was a saving it itself.

After she had bought the two bags, and a silky pin-seal leather wallet for John, she decided that she might as well finish up all her gift shopping and get it over with. She found some lovely things on the floor above, and on an impulse, chose a cashmere shawl for Candy's mother-in-law for a mere few thousand francs. And she ought to get something for Lady Gresham to show her gratitude. But Lady Gresham was such a simple person, she wouldn't want anything in gold, or silver; and she didn't seem very interested in things to wear. One couldn't go wrong on a hand-bag, though, and never had she seen anything quite so lusciously beautiful as the bag she had picked out for Candy. There had been another one, also in alligator, and just as handsome, though perhaps not quite as youthful in its shape. It would be perfect for Lady Gresham. The saleswoman had assured her, in surprisingly good English, that a bag of equal quality and style could not be had in the States for under a hundred and fifty dollars, and Claudia knew for a fact that it was true. Here, the price was well under a third of that. Two alligators times forty-thousand francs would be only eighty, plus no tax, and Bertha's black leather was only twenty, plus no tax again.

The saleswoman welcomed her reappearance effusively, and applauded her decision to buy both alligators. "Mais oui, Mademoiselle. A separate box, naturally. And to be delivered to the hotel with the other two bags. Approximately at noon."

"Oh. And one more thing, could you tell me where the perfume counter is?"

"I regret it is the one department we do not carry. But directly next door, Mademoiselle, is a very good shop for perfume. Ask for Madame Gronsky, and say to her that Mademoiselle Dupont has recommended you. She will see that you are well pleased."

"Oh thank you," Claudia said.

"Avec plaisir, Mademoiselle."

She passed by the shop, and had to walk back again to find it. Somehow she hadn't expected a perfume shop in Paris to be such a business-like cubicle, with innumerable boxes of powder, creams and bath oils stacked in shelves along the walls like the shoe store where her mother used to buy her patent-leather-bottoms-and-white-tops, when she was a little girl. A small bell attached to the door heralded her entrance, and at the sound, a stout woman, dressed in musty black, emerged from the shadowy rear of the shop.

Claudia cleared her throat. "Mademoiselle Dupont dit que je—"

"What can I do for you, Miss?" the woman interrupted crisply.

"I was told to ask for Madame Gronsky," Claudia held doggedly to her course of action.

"I am Madame Gronsky." The woman's mirthless smile of even white teeth implied that Mademoiselle Dupont was of no consequence whatsoever, in fact it was expedient to ignore her existence completely. "Have you a special perfume in mind?" she came directly to the point.

Claudia hesitated. "Now that I see so many different kinds, I don't know."

Madame Gronsky moved towards a surgical-looking tray of atomizers that stood on the counter, selected one, and directed a misty spray towards the lapel of Claudia's coat. "Something very new, and hard to get in your States. You will be very smart to take some back with you," she remarked unemotionally.

It occurred to Claudia that she had not mentioned to Madame Gronsky either her nationality or her intentions, but the gratuitous sample of perfume beguiled her instantly and completely. She sniffed. "It's lovely," she said, hoping it would last through lunch.

Madame Gronsky was a woman of action. She immediately chose a second atomizer and sprayed the other lapel of Claudia's jacket. Claudia directed her nose in the opposite direction, and looked thoughtful. "I think," she said doubtfully, "that it smells just a little like vanilla."

"It is the musk," Madame Gronsky expounded. "Now that I have studied you, I can tell you that you should definitely not wear the heavy perfumes." She held up a simple square bottle. "This is your type, this is for you."

"Only if somebody gave me a present of it," Claudia qualified. "It's supposed to be the most expensive perfume in the world."

"Costly it is," Madame Gronsky acknowledged, quite unruffled. "Such a bottle you will pay ninety dollars for in the States."

"Ouch," said Claudia. It wasn't a big bottle either, you could swallow it down in a single gulp.

"But of course, over here," Madame Gronsky ignored the interruption, "it is for nothing."

"What's for nothing?" Claudia couldn't resist finding out.

Madame Gronsky shrugged her lumpy

478

shoulders. "Half," she said dramatically.

Claudia tried to register jubilance and failed. "Half is twice as little, I realize that, but it's still a lot. I'd like something cheaper, please."

"By all means then, take a smaller size." Madame Gronsky's voice grew plushy in her wish to co-operate. "Myself, I prefer it, it does not evaporate before you have the chance to use it up. Or if you wish, I can give you the little purse size for—" she checked herself—"for almost nothing."

"I hate to ask you, but what's 'almost nothing'?"

"Ach—" (she began to sound like Bertha), "a few dollars, perhaps. I can make you a good price, if you wish to buy for gifts and to put away for yourself for a long time. I have ladies come in who buy for years ahead."

"Will it keep that long?"

"Keep that long! It will keep forever if it is fresh stock.—Meurice!" she broke off to call out into the dark hinterland of the shop.

"Oui?" A partly-old man in a sagging coat materialized from the shadows, dusting bits of packing straw from his trousers.

"Meurice, when did this shipment arrive?" she demanded severely.

"Immediately this morning," he said, and vanished.

"So." Madame Gronsky opened the bottle, picked up Claudia's right hand, and drew the glass stopper across it. "With this perfume I do not spritz everybody," she confided.

Claudia lifted her hand to her nose. "Oh that *is* lovely!"

"And when you use the cream and the face powder, the whole effect becomes like a garden of delicate flowers." Madame Gronsky peered, her black eyes knowledge-able and appraising. "You have a beautiful skin, my dear, you take good care of it, like all American women."

"I just wash it with soap and water," Claudia murmured.

"Soap. On soap I can give you a wonderful buy if you take enough of it."

"But I don't need any, I only want a little perfume. I haven't room to pack very much."

"It is always so. But I will make such a small package that you can carry it on one finger by a string. Take your time, I have other perfumes before you decide." She selected three separate atomizers from the tray. Claudia needed no prompting. She extended her left hand, and sniffed. Then she sniffed her old right hand for comparison. "I think I like the first one better." She wavered. "I'm not sure, though, maybe that was the one that smelled like vanilla."

"Let it stand for a little and come back to it," Madame Gronsky advised. "Now this one has body but it is not heavy. Let me see. The shoulder is too near the lapel, it confuses. Come, give me your elbow."

Claudia gave Madame Gronsky her elbow. "That's quite nice," she allowed.

"It is a perfume that is very much in vogue. In the States, it is twenty-nine dollars an ounce, and I can sell it to you for only sixteen dollars an ounce. And, if you pay in American money, I can take off another fifteen per cent."

"Oh I'd much rather pay in American money!" Claudia said eagerly. "Then I know exactly what I'm spending." Her eyes returned to a slim crystal bottle, shaped with the purity of a Greek vase, and filled with a delicate amber liquid. She had noticed it before, but she knew it was high up in the costly bracket because it had always been one of Julia's favourites, and it was also widely advertised in New York—SEND HER YOUR LOVE WITH LOVE. She wondered whether

Love, also, was half price in Paris, with fifteen per cent off for dollars. She wondered what it smelled like—whether it was musky, or sweet, or spicy. Well, why not have a little spritz of it? She still had an elbow left.

She hurried back to the hotel. The streets looked oddly deserted, with taxis racing off without passengers, and all the shops closed down with heavy gates across the entrances. On the stroke of noon, she had yet to learn, Paris went to lunch.

David was still immersed in his blueprints when she rushed in. "Hello, darling." He looked up abstractedly. "Are you back already?"

"That's a fine greeting, aren't you going to kiss me?"

Reluctantly he put aside his drawing pencil. "All right. Come on. Kiss."

He pulled her down to him, only to thrust her from him. "Pfui!" he cried, affronted.

She was delighted. "Oh good, then I do smell, and I was afraid I didn't. My nostrils must have got used to it, because I couldn't smell a thing, coming home.—David, sniff at me in sections, and see which you like best. My left lapel is the most expensive—ninety dollars a bottle in New York, forty-five here, and if I pay in American money, fifteen per cent off that. Of course I didn't buy the ninety dollar size, I didn't buy the big sizes of anything, but even so I spent sixty-four dollars, but it'll last for the rest of my life—What do you think?" she broke off anxiously.

"I think you stink," he said.

"Don't be silly, of course I do, I'd be a fool if I didn't! And I bet if I wanted to I could get spritzed all over Paris for nothing, only I already bought everything in this one shop, so it wouldn't be honest.—Though maybe I'm too quixotic," she added thoughtfully.

"You're not quixotic, you're plain dumb!" David snorted. "The place is obviously a clip-joint. When will you learn that it's false economy not to go to the best shops?"

"That's ridiculous, why spend more if I can get a discount? I said the money would be at the desk, that is, if I didn't go back after lunch and change a little of what I ordered. I bought both hands in small sizes for presents, but what do you think about my left lapel and my right elbow? Do you like them well enough for two medium bottles each, or shall

I change to one apiece, and buy three bottles of my left elbow instead?"

He backed away from her. "Buy ten bottles of all your elbows, only don't make me smell you again!"

While he was writing out a traveller's cheque for the perfumes, the porter delivered her other purchases. He looked like something out of a musical comedy as he staggered in under a pyramid of boxes, all uniformly and handsomely wrapped. David put his pen down. "What are those?" he demanded.

"More presents."

He found his voice. "You certainly managed to pick out the most exclusive shop in Paris," he said slowly.

She was both surprised and gratified. "Blind luck," she confessed. "For all I knew it could have been another clip-joint.—Is that the bill? I lost trace, I told you it's hard to reckon in thousands and you didn't believe me. How much does it come to?"

He looked at the slip of paper for quite a long while, and then folded it carefully and put it in his pocket.

"Oh, about six hundred and fifty dollars," he said, with an airy flick of his cigarette.

"Oh don't be silly, tell me."

"To be explicit, six hundred and fifty-nine dollars."

She shrugged. "Go ahead, be an idiot, see if I care.—You don't have to pay for it, anyway," she added. "The desk paid already, which is awfully nice and convenient, incidentally. I'm glad you suggested it. Thanks."

"It is I who must thank you, my dear."

She looked at him, concerned for the first time. "David are you angry with me for spending all that money for perfume? If you are, I don't blame you, I went absolutely berserk."

He started to say something and didn't. Instead, he took her in his arms, and gave a wonderful growl against her ear. "Do I look angry, you little fool—"

The telephone rang. It rang until he answered it.

"Who was it?" she asked lazily.

"Jerry. I forgot to tell you that he's taking us to a little bistro on the Left Bank where we can get oursins."

"What's oursins?"

"You'll see when you get there. Hurry up

and get dressed, he's waiting downstairs for us."

Jerry always rented a car in Paris, which he drove himself. You didn't actually drive across the Place de la Concorde, he prepared them, you merely closed your eyes, stepped on the gas, and prayed you'd get there. Claudia gripped the seat until her knuckles were white. "I don't see how anybody keeps their fenders on," she gasped.

The little bistro looked like somebody's kitchen, which it probably was. It had wooden tables and red checked cloths, and in a way, Claudia liked it better than Maxims. She was starved, which might have contributed.

Like a trusting fool, she ordered oursins, too, but they turned out to be the French equivalent of jugged hare, as far as she was concerned. They looked like little wet snails swimming around in big fur coats. "Merci beacoup but no," she said.

"You don't know what's good," David told her.

"Try one," Jerry coaxed.

She shook her head and buttoned her lips. Jerry grinned. "You look like Michael," he said.

After lunch, he said he had an appointment, but he hadn't. He said it, because he was reluctant to intrude too much upon their privacy. "You two take the car and go off by yourselves," he suggested.

"We're by ourselves when we're with you," said Claudia.

He seemed quite moved. "I'd like to believe that."

"You can," said David.

Jerry had to fly back to London two days later for a conference with an American editor. "This won't interfere with our trip south," he promised them when he said good-bye. "I'm just staying overnight."

"But I haven't made up my mind to go yet," Claudia protested. "Nobody can make me believe it's right to walk off and foist your children on strangers."

David put on his best crucified look. "So Bertha's a stranger, after twelve years."

"I was thinking of Lady Gresham. She's probably regretting it like crazy already."

Jerry however, brought back a first-hand report, that allayed all her worries. "Isabel regrets nothing," he first made clear. "She's feeling a bit stuffed now and again, but she thinks she'll get used to it. And she was charmed with the beautiful alligator bag, and will write to tell you so.—Item number two: The children couldn't be in better form . . ."

"That's ambiguous," Claudia caught him up.

He modified the statement: "They're bursting with health and spirits, is that better?"

"It's more accurate."

"How's Bertha holding together at the seams?" David inquired. "We might be wanting to use her again after we get home."

"Bertha's not only holding together, she's blossoming out," Jerry said with a reminiscent smile. "She says she expects to have company dropping in quite often for after-supper kaffee-klatches. It appears that a Miss Beckman—"

"Bachman . . ." Claudia said.

"—has quite a large circle of assorted relatives, who enjoy not only our Bertha's society, but her home-made yeast-cake. She says she hopes you don't mind."

"Mind? I think it's wonderful, she's never had much fun in her life."

"She's having it now," said Jerry. "She loves everything and everybody. Even the

English. So what do I tell Annie? I said I'd let her know whether or not to expect us."

Claudia turned to David. "You'd really like to go, wouldn't you?"

"Very much."

"Then I'd like to, too," she said.

On the last Sunday, she declared an end to culture, and got Jerry to take her to the Flea Market while David, in deep contentment, meandered toward his old haunts and special loves.

"He's been to La Saint Chapelle twice already," she said, as Jerry threaded his way through a not so beautiful section of Paris, "and what do you want to bet that he's standing staring up at that steeple this very minute. He says it's the most pure Gothic flèche in the world."

"Never begrudge a man dedication to his work," Jerry advised.

"I don't. But just the same, I want to go to the Flea Market whether David says it's a waste of time or not. He says it's nothing but a lot of awful junk."

"It *is* a lot of awful junk," she admitted after an hour of tramping, "but I'm not going to give him the satisfaction of telling him so."

She ended up buying a tiny white figure with a dark crack across the base for five hundred francs, solely as a memento. "I'll keep it to show to my grandchildren," she said.

"What did you buy?" David asked her at once, and with nothing nice in his smile.

"I think it's quite beautiful," she stuck up in advance for the little figure.

He looked at it. His lips straightened, and he didn't say a word, to her surprise. He took it to the window and held it up against the light, after which he examined it under a lamp. Then he said, in a funny voice, "This happens to be a piece of Mennecy, you little ignoramus."

It rang a bell in her mind. "Isn't that the porcelain that Julia and Hartley had a collection of, and gave to a museum, and Bluff broke a piece of it wagging his tail?"

A heavy silence was sufficient answer.

"And I'm an ignoramus?" she bridled.

He wrapped the little figure very carefully in a wad of cotton. "I suppose I'll never hear the end of this," he said, enveloped in gloom.

"You never will," she assured him, sweetly.

She couldn't have wished for a more perfect finish to their week in Paris.

14

THEY started off at dawn the next morning, their luggage piled up on the rear seat of Jerry's small hired car. It meant that the three of them had to cram into the front seat, which was more sociable than one of them having to sit alone in the back. Claudia made herself as small as possible, leaning up against David to give Jerry room to drive in comfort. When David took the wheel after lunch, she did the same for him. It was pleasant for everyone.

They spent the night at a good hotel in Lyons, with David and Jerry reluctantly agreeing on the wisdom of sacrificing atmosphere to comfort. "It's a crime that we have to race through like this," said David regretfully.

"It is," said Jerry. "I wish we had the time to go by way of the Loire and the Château country."

"I've seen just enough to make me want to come back and see everything we've missed," Claudia said.

"I'll hold you to that," David told her.

Before they fell asleep, she said, "David, I hate to stay at peoples' houses, and have to be polite in the morning, and answer questions whether the bed was comfortable, and 'please just leave it and don't bother to make it up' . . . especially at Ann's where she doesn't have any help."

He didn't say anything.

"David, are you listening. There must be lots of hotels around there."

"I'm listening. And there are, I suppose. Why don't we wait and see what happens after we get there?"

"Of course, but I just thought I'd alert you, so that if I gave you the high-sign, you'd know what I meant."

"I know what you mean," he said, quietly.

She wished she had had the courage to have come right out with what was really in her mind—aside, of course, from their not being congenital house-guests, which was true. Apparently David wasn't quite sure how it would work out either—the four of them under one roof for a week. Their relationship to Jerry was as easy and happy as it had always been, but neither of them had seen Ann since the morning after the fog. David

492

had said, "Wait and see what happens." Nothing was going to happen, she hoped, except that they might all feel strained and uncomfortable. She was glad that she had left the Mrs. Woodburn as a loop-hole, in case a hotel looked too obvious.

Again they started out at crack of dawn so that they could arrive at Villefranche before dark. With her first glimpse of the Corniche, with the sea on one side and the hills on the other, and purple bougainvillaea ranging along the scattered rows of little pink villas, Claudia lost her tongue with the sheer, unbelievable beauty of it. She understood why Matthew under emotional impact, frequently relied upon the single expletive of "Boy!" to express everything he felt.

There was bougainvillaea climbing over Ann's little villa, too, and from the bed-room window, they could see the blue endlessness of the Mediterranean. It was such a tiny little house that it was evident why Ann had moved into a book-lined cubicle that Pete had used as a study, and why Jerry was sleeping on a couch in the living-room. "This makes it easier for us to leave in the morning," Claudia lowered her voice discreetly as they washed up in the one small but adequate bathroom. "It's ridiculous for us to impose this way. Jerry's so fastidious, I wonder why he lets himself in for it, because even if we weren't here, he'd be sleeping on the sofa."

In the morning, she could see why he didn't mind a few inconveniences. They weren't important, all at once. She said at breakfast, "David and I think we ought to go to a hotel, but we really don't want to."

"Then why are you?" said Ann. She hadn't asked them how they slept, and she fully expected Claudia to make her bed and help with the dishes.

"Because we're putting you out of your room, which is unnecessary. I'd loathe having to move out of my room, for anyone else to sleep in."

"I loathe it," Ann said, "and I wouldn't do it if I didn't want to. If you'd be happier in a hotel, I can't stop you, but I wish you'd stay."

"So do I," said Jerry. "And it's an odd thing, you know. By all standards, this should be grubby living, but it isn't. Perhaps there's too much sky, and sea, and fragrance—or perhaps it's because Ann isn't a grubby person, herself. Pete's a clutterer, she lets him have his way in the apartment, but not

494

here. She insists on exercising her monastic tendencies. In addition, she's a capable but not fanatical housekeeper, and better food you'll never have, and without any fanfare either."

"That's good," said David, in tacit acknowledgement that they wouldn't be happier in a hotel. "Women who make a big noise about cooking with herbs and wine get on my nerves."

"That's why I don't cook with herbs and wine," said Claudia placidly.

Ann laughed. "Well, I do, but I promise not to give you a blow by blow account of what you're eating. Do you want to try out my *coq au vin* this evening, or would you prefer to go to Nice or Cannes? There are several good restaurants at either place."

"By all means *coq au vin*," Jerry answered for them, "but not this evening, and not Cannes or Nice either. Let's dine at the Casino in Monte Carlo. I can't wait to see Claudia play roulette for the first time."

If Claudia had been a person who clapped her hands, she would have clapped them. "And I'll treat you to dinner with the money I win!" she promised largely.

"Bless her generous little dumb heart,"

said Ann. "The last time I went with Pete, we tried out a new system and didn't eat for a week."

"Oh, that won't happen to Claudia," David said. "She'll have her own infallible system. She'll place her bets on the children's birthdays, and on the day we bought the farm, and on the day I got back from New Guinea . . ."

"And win," Jerry injected dourly.

"And win," said David.

The days flew past their jealous counting of the hours. The quick laughter, the rich silences, could not be nourished by constraint, or the lingering uncertainty of distrust. It was a little like their relationship with John and Candy, except that Jerry and Ann were older in their living, protecting, rather than having to be protected. Claudia admitted to Ann, "It's all I can do to worry a little now and again."

"Set aside a regular time each day so you don't forget," Ann advised her solemnly.

She spoke to the children and Bertha every evening, as a sheer hostage to happiness. "Fine," Bertha always said. "Fine, fine." On the last call, she varied it. "Ausgesichen," she said, which David got mixed up with "aus-gelassen".

"'Ausgesichen' is better," Claudia explained, much pleased. "It means something like 'out of this world'."

David telephoned John just once, to check on whether the corrected plans had arrived, and then he said, "Well, everything seems fine—fine—fine at home, too, so I guess I can forget the office from here on."

"High time," said Claudia.

The only thing that bothered her was that they hadn't let Mrs. Woodburn know that they were in the South of France. "Ann and Jerry won't go visiting, and we'd be wasting a whole day going over by ourselves. What should we do?"

"I'll leave it to your conscience," David got out of it neatly. "Of course if we're flying to Italy, we can stop over in Monte Carlo for a day or two, and run over to see them."

It was an underhand trick. She was full of conflict. He knew Italy was too far from London for her peace of mind, but he also knew how she felt about Monte Carlo. They'd planned to go back after that first memorable night, but they'd never got around to it, there were so many other things to do in so short a time.

Her conflict was resolved by a call from Linda on their last evening. Linda had telephoned to Paris, and the hotel had given her their forwarding address. She wasn't calling to chide them, as Claudia immediately surmised; on the contrary, Linda was overjoyed to discover that they were already on the Riviera. "Now there's no excuse for you not to come to our wedding. Bill wants David to be best man, and I want you to be matron of honour. Aunt Emily says to tell you that she'd love to have the children, too, but the Nicholsons and the Blisses will be staying for a few days, and Nancy Riddle will be here, so there won't be room."

"I wouldn't dream of it anyway," said Claudia. "The children are very well off where they are.—Linda, it's wonderful news, I'm so glad for you, but really not too surprised."

"You're not?" said Linda a little wistfully. "I thought you would be. But everyone seems to feel that same way, as if it were a foregone conclusion."

"Anyone could see that Bill was in love with you," Claudia explained, a little lamely.

"I feel so sorry for them," she told the others, as she rejoined them on the terrace for after-dinner coffee.

"Why?" Jerry asked, puzzled. "Knowing who both of them are, I suspect it will be heralded as a very glamorous romance, and the social event of the season to boot."

Claudia shook her head. "Linda says it's to be a very small, quiet wedding on account of Mr. Woodburn's death—I think that's why it happened. Bill was so wonderful all during that time. But they're not really romantic about each other.—I think Linda could easily have become romantic over David," she added simply.

"Who could blame her," said Ann, just as simply.

"What are you two females trying to do, make me feel like a jackass!" David flailed out at them. "Let's be serious about this, Claudia—"

"I was serious," she murmured.

"So was I," said Ann.

"Oh, cut it out," he mumbled, as embarrassed as a schoolboy. "What I'm trying to say is, that I don't see how we can get out of going to the wedding."

499

"Neither do I, without hurting them," said Jerry.

"I don't think they should try to get out of it," Ann spoke up. "A social wedding on the Riviera is part of their education abroad."

"It'll be Americans, mostly," said Claudia.

Ann grinned. "That's what I mean."

"Then what's the point? I'd much rather drive back to London with you and Jerry,—wouldn't you, David?"

"If you're dead set against Italy, I certainly would."

"I'm set against Italy, and I think we've got to go to Linda's wedding," she settled it.

David appealed to Jerry. "You see what I'm up against?"

"Any time you get tired of her," said Jerry, "let me know."

Nobody said anything after that. Claudia wondered whether they were all thinking the same thing—thinking what a wonderful week it had been, strange, and a little dangerous, and filled with so much to remember always.

"Who's going to help me clear the dishes?" Ann finally broke the silence.

"Claudia will do my share," said David, "while I put a call in to John. I'll have to let him know our change of plans."

"Yell out to me when you're through," Claudia said, "I want to talk to Candy."

"The lines are down in Connecticut," he reported a short while later. "It may be days, they're having a record blizzard. I'll get a letter off to him, and mail it right away."

"Save the bottom of the page for me," Claudia said. "I'll add a postscript."

She added a postscript to the postscript. "P.S.," she wrote, "we're going to stay at Monte Carlo for a few days before we go to the Woodburns, which is the only thing that atones for saying good-bye to Ann and Jerry. I'd rather play roulette than eat, so you can imagine. David says the only thing that will cure me is to lose my shirt. He lost his, but I won thirty-thousand francs the very first time I ever played in my life,—mostly on your birthday, twenty-eight came up twice in succession and by mistake, I left a lot of chips on it from my last play. I'm glad you were born, or did I ever tell you that before?—I used the money to buy a dress, which I never got around to doing in Paris. Ann took me to a lovely little shop in Cannes, and I got a beautiful dinner gown ready made which I can certainly use at 'Plaisance',—that's the name of the Woodburn estate. David's glaring at me, I'd better stop before he kills me. Much love and kiss the baby for me . . ."

"Thanks for ruining my letter," he said, coldly.

"Don't be so crabby, how can a little postscript ruin a letter."

"That's a postscript?"

"Certainly. I didn't use an extra page, I went around the sides and top.—Where are we going to mail it?"

"In Nice. It'll go faster from there. We're all driving over. It's a beautiful night and the moon is full."

It was the most beautiful night of all. It was hard to believe that there could be a blizzard in Connecticut.

She wished that they had never gone back to Monte Carlo. She won again, and David won too—not very much, but a little—and yet the magic and the excitement had vanished. "I'm almost bored," Claudia admitted. "Do you think it's because we miss Ann and Jerry?"

"We miss them, but I don't think that's the reason."

"What is, then?"

"We go through our phases fast, I guess."

"That sounds so fickle. And it isn't really

true. We never got tired of the farm. Or changed our minds about wanting to buy the little hip-roof house; we can't wait to get back to it."

"That's different," David said. "The real things aren't phases."

"You cheer me up," she said. "I was afraid we were being terribly—insular. Unadventuresome."

David considered it. "We might be, just a touch," he said. "Still, we managed pretty well when we picked up stakes and moved to a little shack on top of a mountain for a year."

"That was important. So was New Guinea important. Monte Carlo just isn't, I suppose."

"Let's get the hell out," said David. "Mrs. Woodburn won't mind if we come a day earlier."

Mrs. Woodburn was delighted, and so were Linda and Bill. Linda looked pale, and Bill was more subdued than he had been on the boat, and Mrs. Woodburn seemed somehow smaller, and quite frail. She was a dynamo of energy and competence, however, for even a quiet wedding crowded the days with excitement, and things to be done. "Perhaps she'll just wear herself out and drift gently off,"

Claudia thought compassionately. Perhaps Mrs. Woodburn had the same thought. She said, "I don't think I shall leave here ever again. I feel very close to Henry, especially when I'm in the garden. Linda and Bill are going back to America for their honeymoon; they'll close up the house in Newport, and ultimately it will be sold, along with the farm at Aix. But not Plaisance. Even Greg loves it here. And thrives. His stuttering is better, don't you think so?"

"I do," said Claudia. "Much better."

"That speaks well for Bill," said Linda softly.

Bill patted her hand. "I admire the little chap, we'll get on in great shape. But don't give me too much credit, this place is a heaven for children."

"It's a heaven for anyone," said Claudia. "Sea, and hills and almost always the sun."

"Like Aunt Emily, I'm beginning to think I never want to live anywhere else," said Linda, "and so does Bill. We were almost tempted to settle on Aix, but Bill isn't a farmer.—You'd be interested in the place, David. As an architect, I mean. Uncle Henry built the cottage about ten years ago, but the old Roman foundation is still intact."

"I'd like to see it," said David. "It's a part of a world that's always fascinated me. It can't be too far from Arles, is it?"

"No, Arles's an easy drive from the farm," Mrs. Woodburn told him. "It's a part of a world that fascinated Henry, too. He often spoke of restoring the old foundation, and spending more time at the farm."

Claudia said, "He was awfully proud of it, he wanted to show it off to us."

"Why don't we drive over with them?" Bill suggested to Linda.

"When?" she asked him dubiously.

"Oh, we'll find time."

It was easier said than done. On the morning that the Nicholsons and the Blisses were to arrive from Paris, Linda said, "David, this is the ideal moment for you and Claudia to take one of the cars and drive to Aix by yourselves. You hate female cackle and there's going to be a lot of it until they've seen every single person, with a detailed account of who sent which and all the rest of it."

"I can well imagine," David returned wryly. "Your offer is gratefully accepted."

"She's not being entirely altruistic," Bill warned. "There's a huge load of dairy stuff and fresh vegetables for you to bring back from the farm. Jacques' helping to set up the pavilion and can't go for them."

"I'm still grateful," David told him.

"So am I," said Claudia. "I'll take any excuse just to drive along the Corniche."

"You can taste the air," David exulted, as they sped off in a small English roadster with the top down.

Claudia sighed. "Doesn't it make you feel guilty to think of Bertha and the children freezing in London?"

"It would if they were but they're not. Jerry told you last night over the phone that the weather was beautiful."

"Well, then, doesn't it make you feel guilty to think of Candy and John knee-deep in snow?"

"Do you have an overwhelming urge to feel guilty?"

"Not so much guilty, I suppose, as sorry. So much beauty going to waste. More people ought to realize that it's here to use. And enjoy."

"'More people' happen to have to work for a living," David replied succinctly.

"You don't have to, any more, David." For an instant, she was horrified, afraid she had said it, instead of thinking it. "Do they ever have fog here?" she asked hastily.

"No, but we'll be getting into the mistral country."

"I wonder if you'd mind a French wind as much as a New England one."

He gave her a quick look, and then turned his eyes back to the wheel. "I can't figure out what's in your head, but I know damn well you'd mind the social climate—a lot of phony expatriates and half-wits like the Nicholsons and the Blisses."

"You're just a snob," she accused him. "Like Lady Gresham."

"I could do worse," he said shortly.

She leaned forward. "This isn't the same kind of magnificence as the Corniche, but it's just as thrilling in a different way, isn't it?"

"Aix," said David, as if he owned the place, "is supposed to have the most beautiful main street in the world. We'll be passing through it in a little while."

"Somehow, in spite of Mrs. Woodburn's explicit directions, he missed the road, and they reached the farm from another direction.

"This is it," he said.

Neither of them spoke very much on the way

home. David said only, with a dry twist of his lips, "I hope Mrs. Woodburn isn't expecting these vegetables for dinner."

Claudia said, "Pierre made me think of Fritz, when he took us to see the new calf. The French and the German of it didn't seem to matter, all at once. The soil must be a great leveller. Like sickness and death."

David didn't say anything, but of course he told Mrs. Woodburn what he thought of the farm, and as usual, Helen Nicholson didn't mind her own business. "If you're so crazy in love with it, why don't you buy the damn place? God knows you can afford it, even if you only live there three months a year."

"You don't buy a farm just to visit three months a year," Mrs. Woodburn told her. "Henry always felt a little immoral about it. I think it was his secret dream to retire and live there for good, one of these days."

Helen shrugged. "Well, Claudia and David can live there for good. David doesn't have to work any more, he can be a gentleman farmer. What's to prevent him?"

"It's certainly a healthy life," Mrs. Bliss offered. "I hear there's so much influenza and pneumonia in New York now, it's just terrible."

Long after they were in bed that evening, Claudia sent a small voice into the dark. "David? Are you asleep?"

"If I was, I'm not any more."

"You weren't, because I heard you looking at the ceiling."

"Is there a law against looking at the ceiling?"

"They weren't so wrong, you know."

"That Helen Nicholson is the noisiest woman that ever lived."

"At least she had the courage to come out with what was in her mind. We didn't. I suppose we're not very adventuresome after all."

"I have no right to be adventuresome," David said tersely. "I have a profession. A partner. An obligation."

"David, I know how you feel," she began hesitantly, "but the best thing that ever happened to you—professionally, I mean—was when Roger Killian retired and went to live in California for his health."

"So it's my damned lungs you're thinking of!" he flung at her furiously. "I might have known it."

Her anger flared to meet his fury. "Why are you such an ostrich! Facts are facts and you can't get away from them. It's a wonderful life and a wonderful climate for me, and the children, *and* you. As for John—well, it isn't a misfortune for a man who's under thirty to head his own firm."

It was hard to tell whether he was asleep or smouldering. Then he said, rather oddly, "What about the house? Just walk out and leave it with the library half-finished, the barns half built?"

"You can't be tied to possessions all your life." She gave an hysterical little giggle. "Nancy Riddle will be here tomorrow, we can always sell it to Nancy." Her voice broke. "Candy. Candy would be devastated."

"Candy doesn't worry me," said David. "It's the best thing that could happen to her. She might be heartbroken for a while, but it's high time she grew up and stopped being dependent on us; and our living a couple of miles away from her isn't going to help her to learn to stand on her own two feet."

"You're right," Claudia acknowledged meekly. "Besides, they can visit us every winter." She stopped herself. She was talking as if they'd already decided to buy the place. She wondered if David noticed. He was saying something. "Speak up," she said, "I can't hear you."

"I said, "How do we break the news to Bertha?"

"Bertha doesn't care where she lives any longer. She has no family left."

"That's true," said David soberly.

They stayed for an extra day after the wedding in order to see the farm again. "Let Pierre take you around," Mrs. Woodburn advised. "Get the feeling of the place. You might find that it isn't where you'd be happy after all. Though I hope not. I've grown very fond of you two."

Impulsively, David bent to kiss her soft cheek. "We've grown to feel the same way about you," he said.

It was another beautiful morning. They drove along the High Corniche, spellbound with the grandeur of the sea below. They passed Ann's little villa purposely, and slowed down to see what it looked like with the new tenants in it. "Nothing is changed, but it looks different," said Claudia. "Something happens to a house when the person who loves it goes out of it. I'm glad she's coming back to it. It's nice to know that we'll have friends here."

"I imagine we'll be seeing quite a bit of Jerry, too," said David.

"I imagine," said Claudia.

They wandered around with Pierre until noon, and then left for an hour or so, to have lunch at Arles. David could scarcely tear himself away. He went back, and back again, to pause and worship before the little Maison Carré. "What a world to live in," he said, half to himself, and Claudia knew, before they returned to the farm for the second time that day, that they would want to buy it.

They could talk of little else on the way back to Cap Ferrat. "That litter of new pups," Claudia mooned. "We'll keep every one of them, can't we?"

"There were eleven, if I counted correctly."

"No matter.—What kind are they?"

"Chiens sans Race," said David. "And next to a good Dane, there's nothing like a good mutt."

The sun was leaving the heavens when they turned off the Corniche, and took the road down to the sea. "I don't think I'll ever forget what a wonderful day it's been," said Claudia.

"Let's not," David said. "Days like this are hard to come by."

As they drove past the gates that marked the imposing entrance of "Plaisance", Mrs. Woodburn's maid, Marie, came from the cutting garden with her arms full of flowers and stopped them. She said that Mrs. Woodburn had said to tell them that Jacques had taken her to the airport to meet Mrs. Riddle's plane, and dinner would be at half-past eight.

"Good," said Claudia.

"What's good about it?" David commented, starting up the motor again. "I can live very nicely without Nancy. I was hoping she'd keep missing her planes until we left."

"I meant that it's good that Mrs. Woodburn won't be alone after we go back to London."

"She told me she didn't mind being alone."

"Linda minds.—Don't let me out. I'll drive on to the garage with you and wait while you put the car away."

"A pleasure, Madame."

"Call me 'Mademoiselle' just for the novelty."

He called her "Mademoiselle", with trimmings, and then in the middle of it, he saw a taxi drive up. "Holy smoke," he said after a moment, "that looks like Nancy."

It could be no other. She still wore the same old outlandish hat with a bunch of forget-me-nots in the middle like a doctor's light, and the same old baggy suit spanned her broad middle, and hung to an unflattering length against her thin legs. She didn't see them. She was counting out the fare meticulously, presenting a final fifty franc note with a small flourish. "And that's for you," she told the man. He stared at her. "Pour *vous*," she enunciated clearly. "Cette fifty franc pour vous."

The man dumped a large suitcase of ancient vintage to the ground, spat, climbed back into the car, slammed the door and steamed off in a disgusted scatter of gravel. "Well!" Nancy exclaimed indignantly to no one. "Those French!"

"Hello, Nancy, what are you doing here, Mrs. Woodburn's on her way to Nice to meet you!"

"Oh dear, I caught the plane ahead! Well, that's too bad." She recognized David belatedly and her jaw dropped. "Well, what the hell are you doing here!" she retorted. "Why aren't you home tending store! Be careful of that suitcase," she broke off to warn a house-boy, "the strap's broken.—*Comprenez?*—He doesn't. You tell him for me, David. I'm too exhausted to cope with these monkeys. What a trip. Every time I fly, I swear I won't. Ten hours late taking off from New York, and then they didn't have the same room I always have at the hotel in Paris, so *that* was an aggravation. How was the wedding? And how's Emily, bearing up? It was awful about poor Henry, I was shocked."

"We all were," Claudia murmured.

Nancy eyed her. "You look good. You both do. But I must say it's a fine time for you two to be taking a vacation with John in the hospital."

"John in the hospital!" David echoed. "What in God's name are you talking about?"

"Oh, Nancy must be mistaken," Claudia quieted him down. "Or being funny."

Nancy gave her a withering look. "I should try to be funny about a thing like that? And don't tell me I'm mistaken either." A little network of thread-like veins beneath her skin suffused into a solid pink. "Maybe I put my

515

foot in it. Maybe you weren't supposed to know."

"Know what!" David shouted. "For God's sake, come out with it!"

Nancy bit her lips. "You've put me in a spot. I can't tell you very much. I telephoned the office just before I left to ask John to draw up some plans for a swimming pool, and start work on it before I get back, because the doctor says I need the exercise, to have it in by summer—"

"Go on," said David tensely.

"Well, the secretary told me that John was home sick, and you were in Europe, so naturally I asked when John would be back in the office and she said not for a while, he was operated on for an appendix."

"Oh David, it can come on out of the blue, and it isn't much these days," Claudia breathed her relief, "I had one, too!"

"Sure it's not much these days," Nancy agreed in her cracked elderly voice. "That's what I figured. I said, 'Well, I can talk to him in the hospital,' I said. 'He ought to be back at work in a couple of weeks at most.' But the girl sort of beat about the bush and hinted that she wouldn't count on his being back for quite a while, he had complications."

"What kind of complications?" David asked whitely.

"She said she didn't know, but I finally got it out of her. Seems he shot a lung embolism after he was almost all well. And that's not pretty. I'm surprised his wife didn't let you know."

"Candy *would* have let us know, I'm sure there's some mistake!" Claudia cried. "Excuse me—" She started after David, who was already up the veranda steps and into the house. Nancy caught her arm. "Wait a minute," she said in an odd voice, "maybe there is some mistake, maybe the secretary had a standing order to make up some excuse no matter what, to keep me out of the office, and I was pretty insistent. Oh, I don't kid myself, I know I've been a nuisance with my terraces and pillars and everything, and they've only taken me on because I bought your farm and David didn't like to see it spoiled.—But a swimming pool wouldn't spoil it," she added, rather pathetically, "now would it?"

"Of course not. And the secretary wouldn't make up such a dreadful thing as an embolism—"

"Listen. It's quite common after an

517

operation, and it's not so dreadful any more, tell David, with this new drug they have—it thins out the blood, and you're out of danger right away if you live."

"I'll tell him," said Claudia, feeling a sudden pity for this tragic misfit that was Nancy.

She found David tearing open a letter from Candy that must have arrived after they had left for Aix that morning. He read it quickly and tossed it aside. "She wrote it three days ago. Not a thing in it. Just about the blizzard, and the lines being down, but everything was all right, not to worry.—Start packing while I try to put a call through."

The tears streamed down Claudia's cheeks. "All of a sudden," she said, "Candy seems to have grown up."

Mrs. Woodburn stood at the door. "Nancy just told me," she said quietly. "I'd like to say that it's probably foolish for you to fly all the way back to New York when it mightn't be necessary, but I can understand that you'd want to. There's a plane from Nice to Paris leaving in fifty minutes, Marie will help you pack and Jacques will drive you to the airport."

"Oh, thank you!" Claudia said.

David hung up the receiver. "No circuits to America."

"Try to get Bertha—"

"You haven't time," Mrs. Woodburn said. "You can phone them from Le Bourget, you'll have an hour's wait." She turned to go, abruptly. "I shall miss both of you very much. And I'll be thinking of John and Candy. And praying."

David said, "Pray hard, will you? And thank Nancy for us. Tell her we're grateful."

"Tell her," Claudia added, "that David's gone back to 'tend store', and he'll draw up the plans for her swimming pool right away."

David opened his brief case for the passports. "That's a hell of a thing to promise," he said.

Candy said that for as long as she lived, she would never forget how she felt when she walked out of John's room and saw them standing in the hospital corridor. "I'd been wanting so desperately to telephone you to come home that I thought maybe I'd done it without knowing it—in my sleep or something."

Candy hadn't had much sleep, thought Claudia. She didn't look like a little girl any longer; it was as if she had moved into her face to stay. Suffering had lined it with a new depth and significance, and door-to-door salesmen would never again mistake her for her own daughter. Claudia remembered how it had used to happen to her too, even after Bobby and Matthew were born . . . And then suddenly, no matter how young you kept on looking, no one could ever again mistake you for anything but a woman.

She put her arms around Candy. "You should have called us," she said gently. "It was David's place to be here. John will get well faster if he isn't worried about what's going on at the office."

"Or at the house," Candy said. "It's bothered him that no one has been over to supervise the workmen for a couple of weeks. I think that's why the doctor let David go in the room. John hasn't seen anyone the last few days, not even his mother. But he doesn't want me out of his sight," she added. "He says I'm quiet, and it makes me feel so— proud."

"It should," said Claudia. "It even makes me proud."

"But I haven't been quiet inside. Every morning I've been afraid to walk down this hall to his door." The tears came in a rush. "I haven't cried since that awful moment when he was sitting up in a chair by the window, ready to go home the next day, and then suddenly, without any warning, the pain seemed to come like a knife through his chest—and now, isn't it silly, he's out of danger and I'm bawling like a baby."

"I'll join you," said Claudia.

It was too early for anyone to see them making fools of themselves. From the eternal wicker waiting-room at the end of the long corridor, Claudia saw masses of flowers, banished for the night, still banked outside the doors, awaiting the indifferent ministrations of the nurses. Nurses weren't what they used to be, she reflected, they used to love fussing over the long boxes of flowers. Now it was like frozen foods, or dried soups. They came pre-arranged in handsome moss-filled containers, and all a nurse had to do was to add a little water.

"David's been in with John almost ten minutes," Candy said nervously.

"Give them a little longer and then go in and yank him out," Claudia advised.

It wasn't necessary. A moment later, David was coming towards them. He looked a little shaken. "He's had a rough time of it," he told Candy, "but I bet you twenty cents that in another two weeks you'll forget it ever happened."

Candy shook her head. "The doctor says it'll be at least a month before he feels like himself again."

"Don't kick," said David. "I was out of commission for a year."

"Which is exactly why John kept insisting that you needed this vacation, and now look what's happened to it. Will it take long to get things in shape at the office so you can go back?"

"He has to draw up the plans for Nancy Riddle's swimming-pool first," said Claudia firmly.

"Nancy Riddle," David rejected the assignment with equal firmness, "needs a swimming pool like we need a farm in France." Startled, his eyes met Claudia's, as if the words were spoken before he realized that he had meant to say them, or that they were even in his thoughts to say. They stared at each other until, after a moment, they found acknowledgement in laughter.

Candy smiled for the first time. "I haven't the least idea what you're laughing at," she said, "but it sounds wonderful to hear you, and you're both as silly as ever."

"I hope you'll never know," said Claudia, "how silly we could have been."

It was too late for David to go to the office, and anyway Claudia said she wouldn't hear of it after sitting up all night in a plane. Fortunately, they had made connections from Nice to Paris without mishap, and there had been time to talk to Bertha and to call Jerry besides. He had been shocked to hear about John. "Of course you must go," he said. "Don't give a thought to the children, stay as long as you feel necessary."

"We'll have to telephone to let him know that John's over the worst of it," David said, as they left the hospital, "but there's no telling how long we'll be here. I talked to the doctor a few minutes and he said that the next few days would tell the story."

"Mrs. Payne thinks Candy should have insisted on a New York hospital for the appendix operation."

"Candy's had her hands full," David replied obliquely. "She used her head. John's better off up here, it's a good hospital, and he had a competent surgeon. An embolism is a completely unforeseen complication."—He looked at his watch. "Let's have a bite of lunch somewhere in the village, and drive over to the house."

"Whose house?"

"Whose house do you think?"

"Oh," she said. "I thought maybe you thought we ought to stop in and see the baby and John's mother."

"We'll do that afterwards," said David. "I'd like to catch the workmen before they leave."

In mutual accord, they ordered a hot dog and a cup of coffee. "It tastes like America, it tastes wonderful," said Claudia.

"As long as John's off the critical list, let's have another," said David.

"Let's," said Claudia. "This time with relish *and* mustard."

Once out of the village—which, like all suburban villages, was building up into a small city,—the snow lay piled in high white drifts on either side of the country road. "Oh how beautiful!" Claudia exclaimed. "It looks just like Switzerland!"

"And how would you know?" he asked her ironically.

She shrugged. "You don't have to see everything with your eyes."

"According to that same unique theory, I daresay you've been to Westminster Abbey, too."

"Quite.—Oh, look, nothing's changed, we're passing Elsie Robinson's house!"

"Did you expect it to move away while you were gone?"

"The garage is empty, so she must be out marketing, or having her hair done. Isn't it a blessing I got all my presents bought in Paris?"

"A blessing," he agreed. "I can tell Candy's been using John's car, it drives like a truck."

"You haven't changed either. In your book, all women are congenital idiots at a wheel."

"Not all. Ann wasn't."

It was perfectly obvious that he said it to make her mad, and she wondered why it didn't. Perhaps it was because they were turning off into their little private road that led past the river, and she could catch a glimpse of the hip-roofed house beyond the snow-laden branches of the towering pines. The house looked larger, more beautiful, but strangely unviolated by its new additions.

"David, you're a good architect," she breathed.

The mockery had left his eyes and the taunting had vanished from his voice. "I'm glad you think so," he said.

Now she could see the untidy rows of cars lined up in the half-finished driveway. "We have company," she said. "Exciting company."

"I see the plumber's here, that's one good thing. John said the radiators were in, and the furnace ought to be working by now."

It was. The hall was as warm as toast, and the new plaster was dry enough for painting, and the honey-coloured panelling in the library looked exactly as she had dreamed it would look that first night on the boat.

"They're farther along than I expected they'd be," said David, deeply gratified. "They've done a lot in seven weeks."

"Is it seven weeks already?" she asked incredulously.

"Seven weeks yesterday, and that's a long enough vacation for anyone," he said.

He had the sheepish look of Matthew, waiting to be reprimanded for boldly stepping out of line. She knew that she ought to tell him that he was wrong, but in her heart, she knew that he was right. She knew that she ought to remind him that they had to go back for the children, but suddenly it seemed so unnecessary to take that long trip for no good reason. Bertha was perfectly capable of packing up, and Ann and Jerry would see that they got safely on the plane. Or boat. "I'd rather they came by boat," Claudia decided there and then, "with Mertie and Hawkins to look after them." She could see them, trooping down the gang-plank, Michael no longer submitting to the indignity of Bertha's arms, and Matthew acting and looking quite the English school-boy in the new suit that Lady Gresham had supervised the buying of, and with the suspicion of British accent that Jerry had prepared her for, over the telephone only a few days ago. She had kept this last bit of information discreetly to herself against the ironic moment when David was bound to discover that his elder son was still a pain in the neck.

"Seven weeks can be a life-time," she answered David's question belatedly. "Let's go out to the garage and see if we can get the old station-wagon to start so that I can drive you to the train in the morning."

"It'll probably need a new battery," said David.

It didn't. It was as surprised as they were to find itself going. "There's nothing like one of these fine old English cars," Claudia murmured.

"Nothing," David agreed.

Later, they walked out to the barns and gazed up at the new silos, and then wandered along the river, lying like a dark velvet ribbon between the snow-covered banks. They stood quietly, absorbing the strange and lovely beauty of winter's end.

"This is our world," said David.

THE END

GUIDE
TO THE COLOUR CODING
OF
ULVERSCROFT BOOKS

Many of our readers have written to us expressing their appreciation for the way in which our colour coding has assisted them in selecting the Ulverscroft books of their choice. To remind everyone of our colour coding— this is as follows:

BLACK COVERS
Mysteries

★

BLUE COVERS
Romances

★

RED COVERS
Adventure Suspense and General Fiction

★

ORANGE COVERS
Westerns

★

GREEN COVERS
Non-Fiction

ROMANCE TITLES
in the
Ulverscroft Large Print Series

FICTION TITLES
in the
Ulverscroft Large Print Series

2M

3098